It's do or die.

"We can't let the media get this," Kay said to Sergeant Savalas in front of the rest of the task force. "Not yet. I don't know about anyone else in this room, but I'm not willing to write Micky off. Until I see her body for myself, I'm going to assume she's alive."

"I'm sorry, Detective." Savalas's voice tightened. "But these aren't your decisions to make. A statement to the media might generate tips. We have a missing cop and—"

"And we're going to have a *dead* cop," Kay muttered.

Finn knew her anger wasn't about her sergeant or about politics. This was about finding a missing cop. One of their own. And he had seen Kay's determination first-hand too many times to think that anything, or anyone, was going to stand in her way.

Praise for the electrifying thrillers of
Illona Haus

BLUE MERCY

"A wickedly well-done page-turner. . . . Here's to seeing more Kay Delaney tales in the future!"

—Jeffery Deaver, *New York Times* bestselling author of *The Sleeping Doll*

"A taut, tense thriller. Illona Haus is an impressive new voice in crime fiction. A riveting debut!"

—Ed McBain

"Chilling. . . . The author's impressive ability to get inside the heads of multiple characters . . . and her refusal to shy away from morbid detail, will keep readers enthralled."

—*Publishers Weekly*

"Chock-full of suspense. Kay Delaney is a haunting character who fights the demons inside her to ensure that justice is served. . . . Gripping."

—*Round Table Reviews*

"In the tradition of Michael Connelly and others, Illona Haus has given us an excellent story and another voice to listen for in this genre."

—Tom Mayes, ILoveaMysteryNewsletter.com

BLUE VALOR

BLUE JUSTICE

ILLONA HAUS

POCKET STAR BOOKS
New York London Toronto Sydney

Pocket Star Books
A Division of Simon & Schuster, Inc.
1230 Avenue of the Americas
New York, NY 10020

This book is a work of fiction. Names, characters, places, and incidents either are products of the author's imagination or are used fictitiously. Any resemblance to actual events or locales or persons, living or dead, is entirely coincidental.

First Pocket Star Books paperback edition October 2007

POCKET STAR BOOKS and colophon are registered trademarks of Simon & Schuster, Inc.

For information about special discounts for bulk purchases, please contact Simon & Schuster Special Sales at 1-800-456-6798 or business@simonandschuster.com

Cover design by Jae Song; photograph of barn by Gregory Morris

Manufactured in the United States of America

10 9 8 7 6 5 4 3 2 1

ISBN-13: 978-0-7434-5810-8
ISBN-10:   0-7434-5810-9

This one's for Mary Ripple,
whose dark and twisted mind rivals my own.

And in memory of Gin Ellis.
You are deeply missed by many, and continue to inspire.

Acknowledgments

Writing is a solitary business, but it cannot be done alone. I owe a huge debt of thanks to those who have supported me over the years with their encouragement and their wisdom. Researching and experiencing the world about which I write is a major and constantly evolving component of my novels, and I am indebted to numerous individuals for their patience and expertise in fielding my many dubious, deviant, and often gruesome questions.

These are the major players behind this story:

Vickie L. Wash, Assistant State's Attorney (retired) for Baltimore City

Dr. Mary G. Ripple, Deputy Chief Medical Examiner, OCME, State of Maryland

Det. Robert F. Cherry Jr., BPD Homicide

Rosalind Bowman, Baltimore City Police Laboratory Section

Dr. Joyce Ohm, postdoctoral fellow, Oncology Department, Johns Hopkins University

Sgt. Jason Grabill, Fort Detrick Police, Maryland

Det. Sgt. Gary Childs, Baltimore County Homicide

John L. French, Crime Scene Supervisor, BPD

Sgt. (retired) Lou Castle, Culver City PD, K9 trainer/instructor

As always, special thanks go to:

Det. Sgt. (retired) Steve "Sparky" Lehmann, BPD Homicide, without whom my fictional world would never have breathed life;

and to Bob Cox, who braved the heat and the
washboard to show me the darker corners of
the Catoctin Mountains.

Also, many thanks go to my proofreaders, Janet Dixon, Patricia Cooper, and Pat Brown, and to Chris Brett-Perring for his encouraging nods throughout the brainstorming process.

And last, but certainly not least, I would like to thank my many readers for their enthusiasm, their hunger for more, and for their patience.

PROLOGUE

DARYL EUGENE WARDELL wasn't a smart man. Never claimed to be. After all, genius had never alighted on the branches of the Wardell family tree. Like him, his daddy never finished high school. And neither had his mother, who—according to Daryl senior—ran off when junior was barely out of diapers, taking up whoring to pay for her drug habit. But it was his brother who'd been the dumbest dumb-ass of the brainless lot, dead at age twelve after adopting the unexplained, overnight notion that he was Superman and could stop a speeding train along the Conemaugh & Blacklick Railroad just west of Wildcat Run.

Yes, the Wardell lineage was like a dip in the shallow end of a sun-bleached, kiddie-sized gene pool.

And so, Daryl Eugene Wardell lived by his strengths. His third-grade teacher had noted in his report card that young Daryl had a "keen sense for problem solving" and seemed more "mechanically inclined." Of course, his daddy—with his limited literacy—interpreted the notation literally and assumed Ms. Agnew was suggesting junior become a mechanic. From that day forward, Daryl carried a wrench in the back pocket of his jeans, proud in the knowledge that he would follow in his daddy's footsteps.

But genius and mechanical inclination aside, Daryl Eugene Wardell knew it didn't take brains to recognize a good specimen when he saw one.

From behind the wheel of his 1965 Ford F-100, Daryl watched her negotiate the trash-littered sidewalk of Govans. He studied her form: the slope of her shoulders under the spaghetti straps of the hot-pink halter top, the roundness of her hips and rump under the latex mini-skirt, and her long, lean calves made even longer by the three-inch pumps she wobbled on.

She didn't look at home in the shoes. Or maybe she was just too pissed off to walk straight.

He'd first spotted her back on Edmondson where the rest of the hookers plied their trade to a thinning stream of late-night johns in the 2:00 a.m. heat. She'd stumbled out of a gray Cavalier idling at the curb, hurled a few choice words at the john, then slammed the car door and strutted off in those heels.

It was when she turned up the side street that Daryl recognized his opportunity.

He followed with the truck, saw the quick flame from a lighter when she lit up. A nasty habit. Cigarette smoke wafted through the open window of the pickup, and somewhere down the block he heard a corner dealer yelling out his wares: "Yellow-tops. Yellows. Got yellow-tops here," as if he were selling fruit at some farmers' market instead of crack cocaine.

The dealer's call reminded Daryl of his junkie mother, but he pushed the hatred deeper. Focused on his mission.

He trailed her at a distance, past a burned-out store and deserted row houses, past a small clutch of jugglers heading down to the Edmondson corners to sell their dime bags of rock, until a block and a half in she finally glanced over her shoulder.

She eyed the truck. Shook her head. Then waved a dismissive hand at him as the end of her cigarette flared.

Daryl moved the truck up alongside her, his good Bridgestones rubbing the curb. Her small breasts jiggled with each step as she maintained her determined pace. When she finally glared at him through the open passenger window, her anger excited him.

"You still working?" he asked her over the truck's idle.

"In your dreams, asshole."

His laugh erupted before he could stop it.

"You think that's funny, dickhead?"

But he didn't answer, only laughed again as he gunned the 352 V-8 under the hood and left her there in the canyon of dark row houses.

In your dreams. He wondered if she'd think it was funny when he explained to her later the reason he'd laughed. Wondered if she'd believe him when he told her she *had* been in his dreams.

It wasn't that Daryl Eugene Wardell entertained notions of psychic powers or ESP, and he didn't believe in omens either. But sometimes . . . when he really needed them, answers came to him in his dreams.

Last night he'd had such a dream.

And the answer his dream had presented to him was now perfectly framed in the Ford's rearview mirror.

Daryl Eugene Wardell's smile faded. Sweat snaked down his back under his damp shirt as he watched her grow smaller in the mirror and finally disappear when he took a left two blocks up.

Circling back onto Harlem, he parked the pickup just past the mouth of a cluttered back alley, the hood bathed in the sodium glare of a streetlamp. He left the headlights on, grabbed his rope, and got out of the cab, then jogged across Govans. From one block down he could just make out the staccato of her heels striking the concrete.

He nudged back the beak of his cap and clenched the rope tighter. Pressing himself flat against the rough

Formstone of the corner row house, he closed his eyes. Rehearsed the moves in his mind.

The clacking of her heels grew louder.

Anticipation bristled every hair, and a prickling heat climbed up between his shoulder blades and the back of his neck. Unbidden, the memory of his last girl seeped into his brain. The sweet smell of the shed. The feel of her pinned beneath him. The rhythmic slapping of his thighs against her rump. Her flesh between his teeth and her muffled squeals. And finally . . . finally, the taste of her blood, glorious and hot, filling his mouth when he exploded inside her.

And tonight a new one. New tastes. New opportunities.

Nestling his head back onto the paint-chipped windowsill, he felt his heart rate surge as adrenaline spilled into his bloodstream. His senses heightened.

She was so close. He imagined he could almost smell her now: her perfume, and beneath that her sweat. He could sense the warmth of her flesh, hear her blood coursing through her veins. And when she emerged at last around the corner of the row house, he wondered how she couldn't hear his own predator's heart hammering in his chest.

She stopped, her gaze swinging left to the pickup's blazing headlights. He saw tension tighten the muscles along her bare back, then heard her mutter, "Fucking asshole."

Daryl knew she couldn't see inside the truck through the streetlamp's glare across the windshield, knew she couldn't tell if he sat behind the wheel or not.

She flicked her cigarette toward the gutter. It tumbled through the air, sparks flying from its tip when it hit the asphalt and rolled away. Every detail crackling in his brain, registering in slow motion as the hunt unfolded.

And when she finally turned, his heart roared in his ears.

A thin gasp of surprise barely escaped her lips when he stepped away from the house and took out her legs in one well-aimed kick. She went down like a sack of feed, one arm pinwheeling uselessly behind her.

She hit the sidewalk hard, the air coming out of her in a rush. Stunned. And he was on top of her. His training kicking in.

She was winded. Couldn't scream. He threw her over, face into the concrete, his knee driving into the small of her back, pinning her as his hands expertly worked the rope.

The street was empty, but he had to be fast. Headlights whipped by a block west.

Daryl Eugene Wardell smiled as she struggled beneath him, her feeble desperation arousing him. And when she threatened to scream, he clamped one hand over her mouth.

His first error.

He swallowed his own scream when her teeth sank into the flesh of his hand, and the sharp, crushing pain coursed up his arm. With his good hand he grabbed her hair and slammed her forehead into the concrete. Once. Twice. And on the third blow his hand came free of her jaws at last.

She was still then. Knocked out, he guessed. He leaned in close, smelled her fear oozing from every pore, and he couldn't help himself.

He slid his tongue along the back of her neck, greedy for the elixir of that fear. One taste. Tide him over.

Daryl Eugene Wardell realized his second error too late.

The pain blinded him before he'd even registered her tactic, her head snapping back, her skull connecting solidly with the softer bone and cartilage of his face. Searing, fucking pain like a knife driving into his forehead. Stars exploding behind his eyes.

This time he did scream.

His blood flowed, and he felt her squirm away. He expected to open his eyes and see her in full flight down the sidewalk.

But this one was full of surprises.

Kneeling on the gritty concrete, his bloodied nose cradled in one hand, he looked up. And she was there. Her mouth covered in his blood, and undiluted rage in her eyes as she glared down at him.

And then Daryl knew: this one was different.

"You low-life piece of shit!" she said. "You have no *fucking* clue who you're dealing with, do you, motherfucker?"

He tried to see past the bloodred blur of the pain, tried to collect the scattered thoughts that stumbled through his brain. So scattered that Daryl Eugene Wardell didn't immediately realize how lucky he was that she wore those three-inch pumps. Only later would he thank his maker for them, because when she raised her foot, determined to strike out at him, she teetered on one stiletto heel. It took little effort to bring her down then. Snatching her kick in midair, he clamped onto her small ankle and yanked hard.

This time when the whore came down, she stayed down.

1

"I HATE MIDNIGHT SHIFT." Kay Delaney squinted against the blaze of morning sun off the rear window of a delivery van cruising in the westbound lane ahead of them. Working midnights for the past week, Kay felt as if she'd just spent a month underground, barely snatching glimpses of the sun between the office and her home, the curtains of her bedroom drawn tight each day so she could catch a few hours of sleep. And this morning, nursing a headache that had started sometime around 3 a.m., Kay wanted nothing more than to be home in that dark bedroom.

"Where did they say this was?" she asked Bobby.

"Govans." At the wheel of the unmarked, Detective Bobby Curran studied the street signs along Edmondson. The former Bostonian wasn't a rookie anymore, having ridden with Kay for the past year and a half in a loose partnership that had never quite been made official since her sergeant's retirement. This morning he looked as tired as Kay felt, his tailored suit a little rumpled and his shirt creased. Behind his mirrored Oakley shades, Kay easily imagined the fatigue in his eyes. Still, the kid had stamina.

"And why's Vice calling this one in?" he asked.

"They didn't say."

"Well, whatever it is, I sure as hell hope *this* one's dead," Bobby said. "I'm tired of running out to every OD and shooting. I want a victim. A *dead* one."

It had been a frustrating week for Bobby. Kay had caught the first homicide of their midnight shift back on Monday: a drug shooting in the gang war that had turned east Baltimore into a war zone over the past month. But working secondary wasn't Bobby's game. He wanted his own case to sink his teeth into. For three nights now he'd responded to every call, with Kay in tow, and last night's marathon had left Bobby particularly irritable. Four overdoses, two questionable deaths, and three shootings in just six hours. They'd been to Shock Trauma three times, only to find in each case that their victim had survived. *"Almost too bad they patch 'em up so good,"* Bobby had said the last time they'd walked through the Medical Center's sliding doors. *"Spend all that energy fixin' them up only to have them go out and put a bullet in someone else. Save us a whole lotta bother if these gangbangers would just do it right the first time."*

"There's Govans." Kay pointed to the side street, and when Bobby took the right, they could already see the two radio cars and a couple of unmarked. No EMS, no Mobile Crime Lab, no police tape.

"Doesn't look like any crime scene to me." Bobby parked the Lumina at the curb, reached for his Grande latte, and tipped the Starbucks cup toward the two unmarked units. "I thought Kojak went home."

Past the two District unis and their radio cars, Sergeant Teodora Savalas stood at the hood of an electric blue Mustang along with Lieutenant Kennedy and Detective Jack Macklin from Vice. No one called Teodora Savalas "Kojak" to her face, but Kay guessed her new sergeant was well aware of the nickname whispered around the CIB offices. Kay also guessed that the ballbusting feminist probably liked it.

Barely two years after passing her sergeant's exam, Savalas had been the surprise appointment to Homicide when Ed Gunderson's heart attack and subsequent retirement had left a sudden vacancy. With no Homicide experience and only a few short years as an investigator with Narcotics, Savalas had a long road to prove herself to her squad. Some felt Savalas didn't belong in the Criminal Investigations Bureau, that she was the token female sergeant and part-Hispanic to boot, answering two minority quotas in a single appointment. Others saw Savalas as merely Captain Gorman's pawn, set up to fail and thus prove his unspoken, chauvinistic conviction that women didn't belong in the higher ranks within the department. Still others rumored it was a quota in Deputy Commissioner Powell's bed that Savalas had met to secure the post. But Kay felt otherwise. From what few glimpses she'd seen of Teodora Savalas behind the badge, Kojak was there to make a point. To herself. To her colleagues. To the world.

"So where's my body?" Bobby asked as they left the Lumina and crossed toward Kojak.

In the shadow of the narrow street the morning was already heating up, and the stink from the trash in the neighboring alleyway was beyond ripe.

Savalas looked drawn, her black suit making her dark complexion seem as pale as the white shirt she wore under the creaseless jacket. Savalas had lost weight since coming to Homicide, Kay noted. Her expensive suits sagged on her lean frame, and in her black hair, tied into a tight ponytail, there were a few more traces of gray. The price you paid to prove a point, Kay thought.

Savalas broke away from the men.

"What's going on, Sarge?" Kay didn't like the feeling

she was getting as she sensed the tension between Lieutenant Kennedy and Macklin behind Savalas.

"We've got a . . . situation." There was a gravity in Savalas's face that Kay couldn't remember having seen in her eight months of working under the woman. She cleared her throat, worked furiously on a breath mint before tucking it into the side of her mouth. "Do you know Detective Luttrell?"

Kay nodded. "Yeah. Micky. She works Vice with Macklin."

"She's MIA."

"What do you mean?"

"Her husband's still downtown. Showed up an hour ago because Luttrell didn't come home after last night's shift."

Behind Savalas, Jack Macklin pushed away from the Mustang. "That's *bullshit,* Lieutenant, and you know it!"

Savalas nodded back to the Vice cop as he started to pace. "Macklin and Luttrell worked a prostitution sting last night. Washington Boulevard and Patapsco. Macklin says they had a couple rough collars so they ended shift early. Micky apparently wanted to walk home, so he dropped her off down the block."

"Micky lives here?" Kay scanned the empty side street. Boarded-up doors, busted windows, graffiti and trash. A losing battle against the tide of drugs and violence.

"She and her husband have a house on Harlem. Couple blocks up."

Jack Macklin made eye contact now. He seemed twitchy, Kay thought. She knew the Vice detective only in passing, but thought she recognized the weight of guilt that pulled at his features. He was a tall, athletic man. Blond and beautiful. A playboy and a heartbreaker, she'd thought the few times their paths had crossed in the CIB offices. But this morning Jack Macklin didn't look as if he'd be capable of breaking any hearts. Worry had chewed him up and spit him out all before breakfast.

"If we've got a missing cop," Savalas explained, "like anything else police-related, it gets bumped up. Homicide's running this show. Look, Kay, I know you got that Ashland Boys shooting from Monday night, but I need you to back-burner it for now. I . . . I need your help on this one." And Kay guessed it wasn't easy for Savalas to ask, that this was probably as close as the sergeant would ever come to admitting she was out of her league.

"Come on." Savalas gestured to the Mustang. "I'll let Macklin fill you in."

Jack Macklin looked rough. The black Harley T-shirt tucked into his jeans was wrinkled and he needed a shave. "Micky didn't just take off, Lieutenant," he was saying to Kennedy. "Goddamn it!"

"Hey, Mack."

He turned when Kay approached, and in the anxious flash of his blue eyes she could tell he was desperate for an ally.

"Catch me up, Mack." Leaning one hip against the fender of the Mustang she guessed was his, Kay spoke calmly, hoping to bring the Vice detective down a notch.

"Something bad's happened to her, Kay."

"What time did you drop Micky off?"

"Just after two this morning. We'd already made a whack of collars and had the arrest teams up to their asses in Central Booking by one a.m. Micky wanted to get home, so we figured on doing the runsheets and reports in the morning."

"Sergeant Savalas said you guys had some rough collars?"

"Yeah. Yeah. Couple of johns got pissed off, one took us on a short chase with Micky still in the car. That's when she said she'd had enough. She was fine though. More fed up than spooked, you know? So I said I'd drive her home."

"But you dropped her down on Edmondson instead?"

"Christ, if I had it to do over—"

"Why *didn't* you take her all the way to her door, Mack?"

"She said she needed air. I argued with her, but she wanted to walk." Mack gestured angrily up Govans, then raked his fingers through his hair, digging at his scalp with his nails. "It's only a couple blocks, dammit!"

Tension rippled off Macklin. She felt it in the mere connection of her hand to his elbow when she reached for him then. "Listen to me, Mack. You need to calm down. I need you clearheaded, okay?"

His eyes looked vacant.

"Okay?" she asked again.

"Two goddamn blocks, Kay."

"We'll find her."

But Macklin shook his head. "Something bad's happened, Kay."

Behind her, Lieutenant Kennedy cleared his throat. "We don't know that, Detective. There's no sign of foul play." Kennedy smelled of cheap cigar smoke. "And until we do, I'm not letting this turn into a three-ring circus. The Department doesn't need the embarrassment, and I'm sure neither does Detective Luttrell. So let's not make this into a red ball until we know for sure she ain't shacked up somewhere or hungover at a girlfriend's house, or a boyfriend for that matter—"

"What the fuck are you talking about?" Mack turned on Kennedy. "Micky's my partner. I think I know her well enough to say she hasn't gone off on some bender. Trust me. You wanna *bet* I'm wishing she's getting laid right now by some bronzed Adonis or got herself shit-faced down at J-Ray's last night. That way I can person-ally beat the living shit out of her for pulling a stunt like this!"

"Mack." Kay positioned herself between the Vice detective and his lieutenant. "What *do* you think hap-pened?" she asked.

"I think Micky got picked up," Mack said, finally pull-ing his glare off Kennedy. "There's hookers all over this area that time of night, 'specially down on Edmondson. They were still working when I let Micky out. Who's to say some asshole didn't follow her?"

"Did she have her gun?"

"Not on her," he said, then answered Kay's admonish-ing stare with "Look, we've done these stings dozens of times. She never packed. Said the guys could always tell. She had her shield though."

Kay wondered how long Jack Macklin had been on the force. Four years? Maybe five? It was the young cops who harbored the crazy notion that a shield could somehow protect them, that it granted them respect on the streets.

"All right. This is my case?" she asked Savalas, and waited for her sergeant's nod. "Then this is what I want. I want hospitals called."

"Already done," Kennedy said.

"I want the ME's office notified." Kay hated to suggest it. "We need to be sure there haven't been any Jane Does wheeled in from one of the counties. I want uniforms down here. A class from the Academy if we have to, and a K9 unit if we don't come up with something in the next hour. I want every inch from here to Micky's house swept. If she *did* get snatched, she could have been dragged into any one of these alleys or abandoned houses."

"What about a canvass?" Bobby asked.

Kay scanned the vacant buildings, some boarded up, others crumbling and used as a neighborhood dump. "Wherever there are residents, I want them questioned."

Next to her, Savalas clutched a police radio in one hand, her fine-boned knuckles white around its rubber grip. "I'll make some calls," she told Kay.

"And while we're waiting for more manpower," Kay said to Bobby and Mack, "I want to retrace Micky's steps. Both sides of the street."

Kay removed her jacket as she crossed to the Lumina.

Bobby was right behind her. "What are you thinking, Kay?"

"I'm trying not to," she said, tossing her jacket in the backseat. "I don't want to think the worst here, but . . . Tell me, wasn't Luttrell pregnant not too long ago?"

"Yeah, I think she came off a maternity leave in the spring."

"That's what I thought."

"Why?"

"Well, I guess I'm having trouble imagining a mother with a newborn waiting at home going off on some bender as Kennedy suggests, or shacking up with someone. Come on." With Savalas and Kennedy behind them radioing for more uniforms, Kay led Bobby and Mack up the cracked concrete of Govans. Step by step. Ducking briefly into the first tight alleyway, searching past mounds of trash, discarded appliances, an old mattress and box spring. No sign of Micky. And on the other side, a maze of low, rusted chain-link fences that had once defined shallow backyards.

Side by side, spread across the now closed-off street, they worked their way up to Harlem. As they did, Kay noted Mack's tension and tried to keep her own fears at bay as the image of Luttrell's fresh, young face refused to leave her mind.

It was almost fifteen minutes later that they finally hit Harlem.

"Micky's house is down this way." Mack directed them east just as Kay saw the first dark smears in the gutter on the west side of the street.

She'd almost missed it. Brown streaks stained the littered sidewalk. Light directional spatter. Whole drops of blood. Then drag marks.

She was aware of Bobby crossing the street to join her. "What is it, Kay?"

Kay stared at the dried blood. Prayed it wasn't Micky Luttrell's and said, "I think we've got a crime scene."

2

DETECTIVE DANNY FINNERTY sympathized with Andy Luttrell. The man had sat for almost two hours in the Vice offices down the hall from Homicide, no doubt forgotten in the back interview room during the shift change. When he'd emerged during Vice's roll call and gone in search of a washroom, he'd found Finn instead.

"I gotta get home," he'd explained, after telling Finn why he'd come to HQ. "My neighbor's watching the baby, and she's gotta get to work."

Sergeant Spurlock had agreed to let Finn drive Micky Luttrell's distraught husband home just after nine, and now, in the passenger seat of the unmarked, Luttrell seemed lost in his worry. As the man's knee bounced and he rubbed the plastic head of his car key with his thumb, Finn wondered if the man's imagination was screening nightmare scenarios of what might have happened to his wife.

"I can get your car out of the parking garage if you want," Finn offered. "Have someone drive it over." Luttrell had already explained how he and his wife shared one vehicle, and that she'd taken it last night to go to work.

Andy Luttrell nodded then and worked at removing the key from his chain, his hands shaking as his fingers fumbled with the tight split ring.

"This'll all get sorted out," Finn told him, doubting Luttrell took any comfort in the words. "We'll find her."

But when Finn steered the Impala onto Harlem Avenue, it wasn't looking good.

"What's all that?" Luttrell sat straighter in his seat. Past the windshield, Harlem was barricaded with a radio car, and a uniform directed cars south to Edmondson. What concerned Finn more was the presence of the Mobile Crime Lab's van.

"Look, Andy, why don't I drop you at your house and I'll check this out. Let you know if—"

"No. This is about Micky. I need to see."

There was no arguing with him. With a cop for a wife, Luttrell knew this kind of police presence could only mean something big.

Finn parked the Impala just outside the barricade of radio units. "You should stay here, Andy." But Luttrell was already out the door, the officers letting him past when they saw Finn's shield.

"Andy," Finn called after the man, but there was no stopping him. "Andy!"

"I want to see my wife. Micky. Micky!"

And then there was Kay. Finn didn't spot her until she stepped from behind the Crime Lab's van, calmly intercepting Luttrell.

She caught his arm. "Mr. Luttrell?"

He nodded slowly, mumbled, "Andy," and searched past her shoulder to where the crime scene technicians worked.

"Andy, I'm Detective Delaney. You shouldn't be here."

"I want to see my wife. If something's happened to her—"

"Micky isn't here."

"Then why's the street blocked off? Why's the Crime Lab here?" He started to push past her, and this time Finn helped Kay keep Luttrell back.

"Sorry," Finn mumbled to Kay, and he wished it didn't suddenly feel so good to see her.

"It's all right," she said. "Listen, Andy—"

"What have you found?" Luttrell pointed across the street to where the Crime Lab technicians had set up yellow plastic placards marking evidence being photographed, while brown paper evidence bags sat along the curb like a collection of lunches. "Where's my wife?"

"I already told you, Micky's not here." Kay forcibly turned Luttrell from the scene then. "We haven't found her. We're still searching. I can fill you in on everything when I know more. I promise."

"But what did you find? The lab wouldn't be down here unless—"

"We're just processing what we've got. I'll come by the house just as soon as we wrap up here, all right?"

She waited for Andy Luttrell's slow nod, then started to escort him off the crime scene. But at the hood of the nearest Western District radio car, Luttrell stopped suddenly. Finn followed his gaze. On the other side of Harlem, hovering over one of the Crime Lab technicians, Jack Macklin had caught Luttrell's stare. The Vice detective held it for a moment, then turned his back. Finn wasn't sure how to interpret the silent exchange between the two men.

"I'll be by soon," Kay promised again, and urged Luttrell.

Together they watched him walk back down the block to his house, until Finn was too aware of Kay at his side. He tried to remember the last time he'd really spoken to her. Not just the clumsy greetings if they passed in the corridors of the CIB offices when their shifts overlapped. But actually talked.

It had been Gunderson's retirement party late last fall at The Admiral down in Fells Point. He'd gone out to the terrace, spotted her at the railing, and almost left. But he'd been drawn to her, just like the first time they'd met on the eighth-floor terrace at Headquarters five years ago.

Kay had asked him how he was. And he'd lied. Finn suspected she lied as well when she told him things were great. They'd laughed, but it was awkward. He'd wanted to ask so many things. He'd wanted to tell her the truth. But the silence had taken over, and then her date had joined them. Some metrosexual from New York. A flaming narcissist, with his highlighted hair gelled into perfection, wearing some pretentious designer suit. Kyle was an artist, Kay had mentioned quickly, almost nervously. And as Finn had watched them walk back inside, arm in arm, he kept thinking that they just didn't look right together.

Finn wondered now if Kay was still seeing the meat-head, then pushed the thought out of his mind.

"So what's going on?" he asked her now, turning onto the crime scene, needing to put some distance between them.

"So far we haven't found a body," she said, following.

"Is that blood?" On the opposite sidewalk a crime scene technician took samples.

Kay nodded. "Most of it's here." She indicated the curb west of Govans, the stains appearing more startling as they approached. "But there's blood on the other side too, like maybe he jumped her when she turned the corner." Kay walked Finn back along the trail of placarded bloodstains, across Govans, to the source. "We've got some medium-velocity spatter here at what looks like the initial contact. And a fair bit of it."

The blood was drying in the morning sun, some of it in clearly defined drops, some sprayed back across the concrete. One small pool actually ridged up from the sidewalk, having coagulated against the gritty concrete sometime in the early-morning hours.

"This kind of spatter usually indicates a struggle. Or beating," Kay went on. "Then these."

Finn followed her back again.

"See here?" She pointed out the dozen or so drops, some small, some as large as a dime. "This is forward spatter. These elongated drops indicate the direction of travel this way. She was either walking or being carried."

"Not running?"

"No. The trajectory of the drops and the low satellite spatter indicate a slower rate of travel."

"What'd you do, take a course?" But Kay didn't catch his smile.

"Actually, Bobby and I had that beating in Guilford

two months ago. Had a blood-spatter analyst up from Quantico. Learned more about spatter than I ever wanted to know." She stepped around one section of stained sidewalk where a technician used fingerprint tape to lift a sample from one dried blood smear. "There's some contact bleeding here," Kay went on, "like maybe he set her down, then these swipe patterns, probably from dragging her through her own blood. And then, nothing."

"So, he stuffed her into a vehicle?"

Kay nodded solemnly. "Most likely. There's no more blood past this point, and we've searched these immediate houses and the alley."

"Do we even know yet if this is Micky Luttrell's blood?" Finn asked.

Kay shook her head, but still the image of the young detective flashed into Finn's mind. He remembered the morning he'd first met Micky Luttrell a year and a half ago, still in uniform, hugging herself from the cold as they stood over an excised human heart dumped outside a private high school. A pretty girl with an innocent face and quick, blue eyes. He'd entered a letter of commendation into her personnel jacket for her preservation of the crime scene as the responding officer, and he remembered her eager smile when she'd come up to the offices several weeks later to thank him.

Finn didn't want to believe the blood was hers. "And we're sure this wasn't just some street fight?"

Kay shook her head, then gestured toward the largest of the evidence bags next to the MCL's van. As she led him to it and fished a pair of fresh latex gloves from her suit jacket, Finn finally allowed himself a full stare.

Kay looked good. Too good. She'd let her hair grow out a bit, but the blunt cut was still short, black, and gleaming in the sun as it framed her face. She looked a little pale, and Finn chalked it up to her and Bobby's working midnights all week. Still, if he had to, he'd say she looked better than he'd ever seen her. Confident, strong, at peace, even though he could see the implication of this morning's scene tugging at her features and her cool, gray eyes as she opened the bag.

"We found this just here in the gutter." She lifted a short denim jacket from the bag and held it up for him to see.

"It's hers?"

"Yeah. Macklin confirmed it. And her shield was in the pocket."

"What else?" Finn asked as Kay returned the jacket to the evidence bag. "Any witnesses?" He scanned the decaying stretch of Harlem Avenue. The block behind him where the Luttrells lived struggled at the edge of a wide strip of forgotten row homes. Bright red graffitied warnings decorated the heavy plywood used to secure the doors and windows of ruined houses—DEATH BEFORE DISHONOR and GANG BANG IS REAL—and the once white marble stoops were grimy and banked with litter.

Kay shook her head. "Nothing so far. Uniforms are still banging on doors down Govans, checking empty houses. I want to hit the streets tonight, down on Edmondson, talk to some of the ladies while they're working. Maybe someone saw Micky."

"There's gotta be *something* to go on."

"Well, there's this." She opened another evidence bag. "Bobby found it up against the stoop of that corner house." Kay withdrew a ball cap. It was frayed, the bill lopsided and the camo pattern faded and stained. "There's blood on it." She showed him the spots. "And since there was no other blood found by the stoop, it's my guess Micky's attacker lost it in a struggle. Looks like it came off forcibly. We found hairs." She pointed to the back snap-closure, torn open. "Three of them. About eight inches. Blond. Roots intact."

"Her abductor's?"

"We can only hope."

"What's with the patch?" Finn looked closer at the threadbare embroidered patch sewn to the crown of the cap. The words MORGAN HUNT AND FISH CLUB formed a three-quarter circle around an image of two crossed long-rifles, and at the bottom of the insignia were the initials MCM.

Not wearing his own gloves, Finn took hold of Kay's wrist and had her bring the hat closer. "What is that MCM? Roman numerals?" he asked.

"Nineteen hundred?"

"We need to find out about this hunt club. Not much else to go on, huh?"

Kay returned the filthy hat to the bag, then nodded back to where she'd calculated the initial attack had oc-curred. "I'm hoping that some of that blood back there is her attacker's. There's a lot of it, and the way it's spat-tered . . . it can't all be hers. I've asked the techs to run it back at the lab, see if we've got two different blood types. My suspicion, and my hope, is that Micky put up one hell of a fight before he took her."

Again, unbidden, the image of Micky Luttrell's pretty face came into Finn's mind. She was just a girl.

"Christ, Kay. So we've got a cop abduction?" Finn wondered if she felt sick to her stomach as well.

Her nod was slow coming. And then: "Unless we find a body, that's what it's looking like."

3

THE LOT OF THE MCDONALD'S along U.S. Route 40 was barely half-full, the drive-through lineup a trickle of cars. In the cab of his pickup, parked in the most southern corner of the lot, Daryl Eugene Wardell watched the flow of westbound traffic and the eighteen-wheelers thundering past.

On the bench seat next to him, the Double Quarter Pounder with cheese was growing soggy in its box, the fries turning limp in their own steam. But now that he'd ordered the Value Meal, he wasn't sure he was hungry.

Oddly enough, he'd slept soundly last night. But when the sun had pierced through the curtains and into his brain, bringing with it consciousness and the pain from last night's ordeal, Daryl had dragged himself from the sweat-dampened sheets to wash down several Advil with warm juice.

Still, the headache throbbed behind his eyes, stemming from the bridge of his nose. Last night he'd worried the bitch had broken it. Faint bruising had started under his left eye, along with some minor swelling around the fresh scab.

The girl at the drive-through window had stared at him when he'd paid for his food, then smiled nervously while he'd imagined smashing his fist through her face, ramming her designer braces down into her throat.

Daryl angled the rearview mirror to inspect the angry scab. The hooker had got him good last night. Definitely more fight in her than any of the others.

The scream of air brakes startled Daryl and set his heart squirming in his chest. The sound always had that effect. He watched, eyes narrowed against the morning sun, as a big rig pulled off the Pike. His hand went to the keys in the Ford's ignition, ready to leave if the trucker turned his rig toward the McDonald's. But the semi continued west on the service road.

Too many memories. If he were well-to-do, he'd probably have had therapy to sort out those memories from that influential time in his life. Then again, Daryl would never have been able to tell a shrink, or anyone, what he'd done to that fag trucker almost twenty-two years ago.

At seventeen, finally growing enough hair on his balls to run away from his daddy, Daryl had hitched his way south. Elroy was his name, the trucker who'd picked him up just past the Virginia state line, but Daryl would always remember him as "that fag trucker."

That fag trucker, with his groping hands. After twenty minutes of barreling south through the dark, he'd propositioned young Daryl with a smirk. *"Git us a motel room, you and me?"* And even at seventeen Daryl knew when he was out of his league, when it was in his best interest to play along. But even as that fag trucker fondled Daryl's crotch through his jeans, Daryl swore it would be the last time any man would touch him, ever again.

A half hour later, in a motel room with shag carpeting and a vibrating bed, Daryl Eugene Wardell had brandished his gutting knife and carved a neat swath across the throat of that fag trucker. Never knew a man could bleed that much, or that it would take him so long to die. And the whole time, Daryl had smiled.

He was still smiling after that fag trucker was dead and he castrated the son of a bitch. He wore the fag trucker's leather gloves when he did it, because the thought of actually touching the chicken hawk's privates almost made him throw up. And when he was done, he jammed that hacked-off cock into the fag trucker's mouth, calmly washed up in the bathroom, cleaned out the pervert's wallet, and walked off into the night.

Now, Daryl pushed the memory aside, but not before taking a sense of power from it. The smell of the cheeseburger and fries was strong in the Ford's cab. Still, Daryl could smell traces of her.

He eyed the bloodstained rope in the passenger-side footwell and remembered the whore's small, mewling sounds as he'd driven last night. He also remembered how pissed off he'd been when he realized he'd lost his hat. Must have come off when she'd fought with him. Her fault. And as he'd driven, he'd punched her a few times in the ribs for the loss of the cap.

Still, the mission had been satisfactory. No real hitches. And the objective had been met. Nothing to be but proud.

And as he at last opened his Value Meal and plunged into the cooling cheeseburger, Daryl Eugene Wardell felt great promise in the day.

4

THE SECOND FLOOR of the Luttrells' narrow row house was cramped and hot. An AC unit sat idle in one window of the bedroom overlooking Harlem Avenue, and Kay wondered if Andy had forgotten to switch it on or if the Luttrells were trying to conserve on their BG&E bills.

She and Finn had rooted through the upstairs for twenty minutes now, concentrating on the bathroom and the master bedroom. They worked in the watery light, the lace curtains drawn against the midday sun that baked the cracked asphalt outside, searching for anything that seemed out of the ordinary. Kay hated her intrusion, ferreting through Micky Luttrell's belongings, her dresser drawers, and her nightstand. But it was a necessary evil. Working Homicide almost nine years now, Kay had learned that victims of violence maintained few secrets after their parting. Bad enough their body was cut open, prodded, and examined on a cold, stainless-steel slab at the medical examiner's office downtown in front of a flock of interns, but then their entire personal life—belongings, secrets, relationships—was laid out and scrutinized.

In death, nothing was private.

Kay checked herself mentally. Micky Luttrell wasn't dead. She had to believe that.

Still, they had to go through Micky's belongings, just as Bobby was going through her locker back at Headquarters. They needed to get a sense of her life, search for anything that might give them a clue as to why she'd been so violently snatched off the street thirteen hours ago. But so far, Kay and Finn were batting zero.

Across the room, Finn stood over a corner desk with an old-model PC. As he leafed through bills and paperwork, Kay wondered how he was.

An hour ago, when Savalas had returned to the scene, she'd pulled Finn aside. "I talked to your sergeant, and he's agreed to give you to me for this while Scooby covers your cases," she'd said, referring to his partner, Wayne Scobee. "We need our most experienced detectives on this. I understand you and Kay were partnered before, right?"

Finn had nodded, and Kay doubted Savalas knew there was a reason they'd requested to work on different squads.

"Good. So I'll leave you two to it," Savalas had said,

and ever since Kay had considered the potential awkwardness of working side by side with Finn again.

Yes, they *had* been partners in the past. Much more than that, until Kay had turned down Finn's marriage proposal, then balked at the idea of moving in with him a year and a half ago. She'd never once blamed Finn for going back to his ex-wife.

As Kay watched him at Micky Luttrell's desk, she wondered how he and Angie were doing. She'd sensed Finn's lie eight months ago at Gunderson's retirement bash when he'd said he was great.

Even now, she couldn't put her finger on it, but something seemed different. He looked good though, his six-foot frame lean and his shoulders well-defined beneath the crisp cotton shirt. He still kept his sleek black hair long enough to be pulled back into a short, neat ponytail, and with his tan features Finn always looked more like a Colombian mafioso instead of the Black Irish murder cop that he was, born and raised in Baltimore.

Remarried life appeared to suit Finn.

"You two just about through?" Andy Luttrell stood in the doorway. He was young, too young, Kay kept thinking, and in the thin light those youthful features seemed to sag. His dun-colored curls didn't sit right on his head, sticking up as though he'd been caught in a sudden gale. Kay guessed he hadn't showered because of the baby's colic that he'd said had started just last week.

"Yeah, we're done here," Kay said.

Andy pointed to the two evidence bags in Kay's hand. "What's that?"

She held them up. "Samples." She wished he hadn't seen them. Hairs from Micky's brush in one, and her toothbrush in the other. "Is this Micky's?" Kay asked about the toothbrush she'd found on what was clearly Micky's side of the bathroom vanity.

Andy nodded. "You're gonna compare her DNA to the blood you found, right?"

"Yes."

"Hm." Andy chewed on the inside of his cheek. He looked shaky.

They'd already filled him in on everything they'd found even though Finn had questioned the wisdom of giving Andy Luttrell all the details. But Kay had been determined. "If it was you missing, and this was Angie I was going to talk to," she'd said when they'd stood on the Luttrell stoop a half hour ago, "she'd want to know everything, wouldn't she?"

So Finn had conceded. Andy Luttrell had taken it all in rather well, considering. The details of the blood, the jacket, Micky's shield. But now, seeing Kay with the samples that would be used to confirm his wife's blood, Luttrell appeared suddenly struck with the reality of the situation.

"Andy, what about family?" Kay asked. "Is there someone who can come and be with you?"

"My family's all in Georgia."

"And Micky's?"

He shook his head, and as Kay joined him in the doorway, she saw the beads of perspiration along his forehead. He leaned back against the doorjamb, and Kay guessed Andy Luttrell was barely holding it together.

"Micky's got no family," he said finally. "She grew up in foster homes. Never knew her dad, and she was only two when her mom killed herself. Then, when she was twelve, her adoptive parents were murdered during a break-and-enter. Micky says that's when she decided she wanted to

be a cop. Even with the shit she sees every day, she loves it.
If she's got any family besides me and Emma, it's the Department. Come on"—he gestured to the stairs—"it's hot
up here. I got some iced tea downstairs."

They followed him into the coolness of the kitchen,
where Andy poured them tea.

"Maybe we could get someone to help you out here,"
Kay said. "With the baby and all."

Andy shook his head. "I'll be fine. I don't have . . .
I'm not working." He seemed embarrassed. "Got laid
off. That's why Micky went back to work, pulling in
overtime with Vice and these damn sting operations. Just
when we were thinking we had enough to move out of
this shithole neighborhood."

He'd poured himself some tea but it sat untouched.
"Only reason we bought this house was because it qualified under HUD's Officer Next Door Program. We got it
at half the asking price."

Kay had often considered buying for that very reason:
the U.S. Department of Housing and Urban Development offered great incentives to officers to buy within the
city, with huge breaks on properties situated at the edge
of crime.

"But the violence just keeps coming on down the
street, block by block. You can see it every month, getting
closer. First the graffiti. Then the hookers and the junkies.
The crack houses and the dealers. They talk about 'white
flight,' but now it's even 'black flight.' No one can live in
this."

The baby monitor crackled to life just then and the
baby's restlessness carried from the upstairs nursery. Even
as Andy excused himself, Kay could hear the infant
cranking up to a wail.

In Andy's absence, Kay scanned the narrow kitchen. The Luttrells had clearly tried their best with random renovations, but the sad truth of it was, the old Formstone row house would probably never see the full reno it begged for and would end up just like the rest of the properties down by Govans, boarded up and mothballed with the faint hope of an upturn in the neighborhood's fortunes sometime in the future.

The crying from upstairs eased, and when Andy joined them again, he bounced Emma in his arms, soothing her with the gentle movement. A pacifier moved feverishly in the baby's mouth, and her round face was red, her blue eyes wide, as she took in the two strangers in her kitchen. Kay felt an unexpected pang, a wrenching sensation deep inside her, when she gazed at the infant.

"We gotta get out of this neighborhood," Andy said, sitting with his daughter and jostling her calmly. He nodded to the front window where more lace curtains blurred the view beyond. "We can't have our daughter growing up here. All this crime. Can you believe we got eight churches within three square blocks of here? *Eight*. And there's candlelight vigils on the street every other week, and rallies to stop the violence. Like it does any good."

The infant spat out her pacifier and began to squirm. Andy cooed to her, then expertly popped the rubber nipple back into her mouth before she could start screaming.

"That's what this is probably about, you know? Micky missing. It's the dealers down the street."

"They know Micky's a cop?"

"Course they do. Fucking dealers. If you ask me, they should just put a damn fence around them all and let them finish each other off. Let the junkies OD, let the dealers shoot each other, the hookers—"

"Andy." Kay stopped his rant. "Were there ever any incidents?"

"You mean with Micky? Course. She'd gone out there and kicked the kids off the corners, the prostitutes back down to Edmondson. And when the dealers started migrating up this way, she had words with them too."

"So you think her disappearance could be connected?" Kay asked.

"What else could it be?"

Kay shrugged. She didn't want to be the one to suggest that Micky could have been picked up by some sexual predator targeting hookers.

"We're going to find her, Andy. Sergeant Savalas is putting together a task force right now. State and county police have all been notified, and we have every available resource at our disposal for this one. I promise, we'll find Micky," she said, and hated making the promise.

But Andy Luttrell needed it. He closed his eyes, nodded quietly, then placed a kiss on his infant daughter's downy head.

"Listen, Andy—" Kay pulled out one of the wooden chairs at the table and sat across from him, the sweet smell of talc and milk strong from the baby. "I have to ask, how are things . . . between you and Micky?"

A sigh. He knew why she was asking, and she hoped he'd forgive her.

"What do *you* think? I'm jobless. Micky's working too many hours. We live in a neighborhood of prostitutes and dealers. And we've got a newborn. Things are tough. Are you asking if we fought? Hell, yeah. You gonna ask me for a fucking alibi next, Detective?"

"Come on, Andy," Finn said now. "You know we have to ask."

"I have a colicky baby. I was home, Detectives. All night. Micky had the car, remember? So how the hell am I supposed to have done something to my own wife, huh?"

"I'm sorry, Andy," Kay said, and meant it.

He shook his head, his eyes going to the baby in his arms as though seeking solace in the bright, glassy eyes gazing up at him. "Look, I know the way this works. You gotta grill the husband. But I'm telling . . . no, I'm begging you, don't waste your time looking at me as a suspect, okay, Detective Delaney? Just find my wife. Find Emma's mother."

5

FINN COULD FEEL KAY'S FRUSTRATION. For two hours now they'd beaten the strip of steaming asphalt along Edmondson—Kay, Bobby, and Finn—speaking with the hookers, who flaunted their bare midriffs and exposed thighs in the late-night heat to a steady flow of customers, regardless of the presence of three Homicide cops.

Taking a break on the white marble stoop of an abandoned corner row house, Kay ran one hand through her short hair. In the other she held a copy of the photo of Micky they'd gotten from Andy Luttrell. Kay looked drained, and when she met Finn's stare, she gave him a quick smile. He wished that smile didn't have such an effect on him.

It had been a long day for everyone working the case.

After leaving the Luttrell house midafternoon, the baby screaming in the background, Kay had gone home. She'd seemed upset, and Finn guessed that seeing Andy's despair had simply been too much. When she rejoined them at Headquarters a couple of hours later, her hair was still damp from a shower and she wore a fresh suit.

Savalas had already set up the boardroom and gathered them all together: Finn, Kay, Bobby, and Purnell and Mitchell, two other detectives from Kay's squad. The six of them sitting around the main table, all looking a little shell-shocked that one of their own was missing. Savalas had offered a breakdown of what action had already been taken on the case, but it was minimal.

It was Kay who'd suggested—based on Andy Luttrell's suspicion of the dealers in the area—that they should bring in the Western District. "We need a profile of the sector," Kay had advised. "Find out who the major players are, what kinds of retaliations there have been down there, who's getting busted and who's getting squeezed by the District. We should talk to Redrum as well." Kay had directed her last comment to Bobby, who'd worked in the DEA-affiliated task force for a couple of years before Homicide, investigating gang and drug violence throughout the city and using the federal clout to gain harder sentences.

With no other direction, Savalas had agreed, and by 7:00 p.m. three sergeants from the Western and two of Bobby's former fellow deputized Redrum detectives walked them through a who's who in the crime wave befalling Edmondson and Harlem avenues. But in the end Finn had agreed with Kay: even a dumb-ass dealer would know better than to draw attention to his neighborhood by messing with a cop.

Kay had seemed at a loss, but Finn sensed she had her own theories brewing. Theories she wouldn't voice until she was ready.

"You should go home," Finn told her now, joining her on the marble stoop.

"I know."

"You get anything?"

"Not much." She shoved her thumb at a long-legged hooker in fishnet stockings. "Barbie over there thinks she saw her. Says she thought Micky was one of Puddy's—pimp who runs his girls down around Mulberry. *And* she saw the same red pickup Bobby's witness spotted turning up Govans after Micky."

"Anyone else see the truck or the driver?"

Kay shook her head.

The night was heavy with heat.

Silence fell between them as they watched the girls. In the blue-green glow of the old mercury-vapor lamps they looked sallow, almost bloodless. Like walking cadavers, Finn thought.

"You think she's alive?" he asked then.

Kay shrugged. "I don't know. But if I let myself think otherwise, then there's no hope, is there?"

A distant siren wailed somewhere to the east of them, then a second, and a couple blocks down the bass of a car stereo vibrated through the night's humidity.

"You doing okay?" he asked, watching with her as a young girl slid out of the passenger side of a john's ride only thirty feet down the block.

"Sure," Kay said, but he didn't believe her.

The hooker stood at the curb, righting the strap of her halter top and straightening her tight skirt. Finn didn't want to imagine what the girl had just put herself through behind the sedan's tinted windows to earn the few bills she tucked into her bra now.

When she turned, her young gaze settled on Finn and Kay. Finn waved her over.

Her name was Velvet, or so she said as she braced the heel of one red pump on the bottom step and jutted out her hip. Her navel was pierced and the tip of a tattoo peeked out from under the short top. She couldn't have been more than eighteen or nineteen. His daughter's age.

"Never seen her before in my life," Velvet said, and tried to hand Micky's photo back.

But Finn pushed it at her again. "Take another look."

"Hey, man, I can look at it all night if you pay me, but it ain't gonna change things. I never seen her."

"Did you see a red pickup truck?"

"Last night? Fuck yeah."

"Did it have mud on it?" Finn asked, based on the description another hooker had given them.

"Mud. And shit too, probably. Why? Did that creep do something to someone?"

"You talked to him?" Kay came off the stoop.

"Only as many words as it took to get through to the slimeball that I wasn't interested."

"He was a customer then?"

"Not one of mine. No way. Any girl got into that truck with him, they're just asking for trouble. And last night, it wasn't gonna be me. You gonna tell me that asswipe hurt one of these girls down here?"

"We don't know that yet. So what can you tell us about him?"

Velvet scanned the street and Finn wasn't sure if she hoped to spot another trick or if she somehow expected the red pickup truck to suddenly appear. "He looked normal, I guess, only not," she said at last.

"What do you mean?"

"I didn't get a good look at him, but he had weird eyes."

"How so?"

"Sorta cold, I guess."

"What else?"

Velvet shrugged. "Scraggly hair, and a creepy smile. And his skin . . ." She shuddered.

"What about his skin?"

"Just his arms, I guess, from what I could see. His skin was all . . . I dunno, bumpy or something."

"And that's why you turned him down?"

"Yeah. That and he smelled bad."

"Bad, like what?"

"Pigs."

"You're sure?"

"Hey, I grew up in Iowa, okay? I know the smell of pig shit. And I'm telling you, just like I told that creep, I ain't gettin' in no truck with no pig farmer."

"So do you think you'd recognize him again if you saw him?" Finn asked.

"Fuck yeah. No, wait, you're not going to ask me to pick him out of a lineup are you? Cuz I really don't need that shit right now with—"

"No, Velvet. But we would like you to come downtown tomorrow morning. Look through a few photos?"

"What's in it for me?"

When Velvet turned her eyes onto him, Finn saw that the whites were bloodshot, the pupils too large.

"Looks like you're high enough for tonight, Velvet. But maybe I can arrange for some kind of compensation."

Finn handed her his card. "You call me in the morning and I'll set up a ride for you."

Velvet fingered the card, then tucked it into the waist-band of her miniskirt.

"And if you *don't* call," Finn added, "I'll be back here tomorrow night. And the next. I'm sure we can drum up a few charges, take you downtown. Then you'll have *lots* of time to look through some books."

"Yeah, yeah, yeah. I get it. I'll call." As she strutted off, Finn hoped Velvet wouldn't lose his card.

"That's it." Kay massaged the back of her neck with one hand. "I've gotta get out of here." She waved Bobby over. "You okay to head back with Finn? I need the car."

"No problem. How'd you two make out?"

Finn filled Bobby in on Velvet's description.

"Sounds like the same guy who propositioned my girl," Bobby said. "Says she'll never forget his face. I've got her coming downtown tomorrow to look through some mugs."

"Maybe we'll finally have something to work with," Kay said, then nodded across the street. "Goddamn it. What the hell's *she* doing here?"

Finn followed Kay's gaze to where Jane Gallagher and her cameraman stood on the opposite corner. WBAL's chief investigative reporter had already cornered Velvet, and the prostitute was tucking a folded-up bill inside her bra.

"Gallagher's *paying* for leads now?" Kay said, about to storm across the street.

"I'll take care of it." Finn caught her hand. He knew all too well that when it came to Kay and the reporter who'd relentlessly hammered at the Department's and Kay's "incompetence" for the death of Kay's partner Joe Spencer four years ago, there was little love lost.

"Last thing we need is our only lead going out to the media. Goddamn Savalas for letting this go to the press already," Kay said. "I *told* her it would get out of hand."

But Savalas hadn't seemed to understand, or care. This afternoon, in the boardroom, Finn had watched the tension between Kay and her new sergeant hit its peak when Savalas mentioned the press.

"We can't let the media get this," Kay had said to Savalas in front of the rest of the preliminary task force. "Not yet. I don't know about anyone else in this room, but I'm not willing to write Micky off. Until I see her body for myself, I'm going to assume she's alive. And giving anything to the media at this point could cost her her life."

Savalas had appeared confused, her thinly plucked eyebrows knitting over the bridge of her streamlined nose.

"Micky's attacker didn't find her shield," Kay had explained, then decided she needed to spell it out. "If Micky's alive and this guy finds out he's got a cop instead of just some crack whore, don't you think he's more likely to kill her on the spot?"

"I'm sorry, Detective." Savalas's voice tightened all of a sudden, and her words became stuttered. "But these aren't your decisions to make." And it was then that Finn realized just how much of a puppet Teodora "Kojak" Savalas was for the brass.

"Lieutenant Kennedy and Captain Gorman have both agreed that this situation needs to be widespread," Savalas had continued. "That a statement to the media might generate tips. We have a missing cop and—"

"And we're going to have a *dead* cop," Kay had muttered as she stood, gathering her notebook and pen, "because this is gonna turn into the mother of all red-ball cluster fucks."

"Goddamn Savalas," Kay said again now, and Finn knew her anger wasn't about her sergeant or about politics. *This* was about finding a missing cop. One of their own.

Finn had seen Kay's determination firsthand too many times to think that anything, or anyone—including Savalas, including Jane Gallagher—was going to stand in her way of finding Micky Luttrell.

6

Monday, July 30

MICKY LUTTRELL WAS ALIVE.

Any other possibility was simply too hard for Kay to swallow, especially after spending more time with Andy Luttrell last night.

She'd left Finn and Bobby to deal with Jane Gallagher on Edmondson sometime after 11:00 p.m. and had driven the two blocks up to the Luttrell house. The lights had been on, and when Andy had opened the door, it was clear he'd been crying, his eyes bloodshot, his face puffy. Kay had sat with him for a while as the baby slept upstairs, listening to Andy's stories of how he'd met Micky five years ago after she'd graduated from the Academy. He talked about her commitment to the job, how he'd wondered if anything—even their new daughter—could ever compete with the passion Micky had for her detective's shield. The more he talked, the more Kay realized how similar she and Micky Luttrell were, and the connection she'd already felt with the young detective deepened.

At the door, Kay had tried to reassure Andy, then hugged him, and he'd almost broken down.

She'd gone home after that, the evidence racing through her head: the blood, the hat, the red pickup truck. And when she *had* finally found sleep, Kay dreamed of pigs.

By 6:00 a.m. she was out of her apartment, a large coffee from the Cross Street Dunkin' Donuts cradled in the center console as she steered the Lumina west along Edmondson then up to Harlem Avenue, where she stared at the blood that still stained the sidewalk.

Kay would have loved that the blood had never been there. She would have loved to find out that Micky had simply walked off, taken a break from it all, the pressure of everything reaching a boiling point: the job, the new baby, the bills, the neighborhood.

But after last night's talk with Andy, Kay thought she knew Micky Luttrell better than that. Micky wouldn't have just walked away. In her mind Kay saw Emma Luttrell's wide blue eyes. No way would Micky have left her daughter.

What kind of mother walked away from her new baby?

Kay stared at her reflection in the mirror of the women's washroom down the hall from the Homicide offices. In the unforgiving glare of the fluorescent bulbs, Kay wished she wore makeup. Just enough to add a little color to her almost sallow complexion, a little lightening of the hollowness that marked her eyes this morning.

Cupping cold water in her hands, Kay splashed her face several times. The punishing bite of the paper towels against her skin almost felt good.

What kind of mother? she thought again.

"You in here, Kay?" In the mirror she watched Finn step around the barrier and lean against the corner of the first stall. "You okay?"

"I wish you'd stop asking me that." She finished drying her hands.

"I will when you stop looking like that." He pointed to her reflection.

"I'm fine." She turned to face him. "Just a rough week."

He nodded thoughtfully. "How are you doing with the Ashland Avenue case?" he asked, referring to the retaliation murder she'd caught Monday night. The twenty-third casualty in the bloodbath that had ravaged east Baltimore in the past month. Only this time the victim was Big Mo—formerly known as Little Mo Mo, before he'd gained a hundred pounds during a two-year stint in the State Pen—the head of the Ashland Boys gang that was responsible for distributing kilogram quantities of cocaine and marijuana around Ashland Avenue.

For now, it seemed, the war had cooled off, but Kay knew it was merely the quiet before yet another storm. The Ashland Boys were lying low, adjusting to the sudden shift of power while they determined if the hit had come from The Doggos, a rival gang, or from within their own ranks. And once they did, Kay suspected east Baltimore would see the mother of all street-justice showdowns.

As for Big Mo's homicide—number 145 on the board—it was likely a dead-end case, in spite of at least a dozen witnesses to the gang leader's drive-by execution. Residents of the Ashland neighborhood had learned the rules of the street through hard lessons. They knew to keep their mouths shut. Kay, however, hoped she'd found the one exception to the rule.

"I hear Savalas asked you to back-burner the investigation," Finn added.

Kay tossed the paper towels in the trash. "Well, I can't. I have a witness I still need to get a statement from. That is, *if* those thugs up on Bond Street haven't killed him already."

"Someone's willing to talk?" Finn sounded surprised.

She held up her crossed fingers.

Linus Mooney was just another weaselly addict looking for his daily fix along that desperate strip of Ashland Avenue. But in the two times she'd talked to him, Kay had seen something in the young man that had given her hope in finally having a witness in the case. Linus was remorseful about his addiction, and he wanted out, he'd told her—out of drugs, out of the neighborhood, out of the city. Kay half-believed him, so she'd been shuffling through bureaucratic channels and begging favors before her witness became the twenty-fourth victim in the east Baltimore war.

"Let me know if I can help," Finn said, and she knew he meant it.

"Thanks."

"Listen, those girls are finished. I'm just going to run them home." The two hookers from last night had been in the Homicide offices for the past two hours going through dozens of digital arrest photos under Finn's supervision.

"Did they come up with anything?" Kay asked.

"Nothing from the mugs, but they've done composites."

"Get anything decent?"

"Don't know yet. I think the guy's still finishing. I'll catch up with you later?"

"Yeah." Kay felt an awkwardness between them as he

ushered her through the door first, and as they headed in opposite directions, she was sure Finn had turned to look back at her.

In the empty boardroom, the whiteboards were too bare. Kay stared at the notes in black marker she'd made based on the hookers' information: the muddy red pickup truck, the driver's "bumpy" skin, his long hair, and the smell of pigs. No tag number on the vehicle, no bumper stickers or decals. Nothing identifying.

Still, they'd put out an immediate statewide BOLO this morning, advising all district, county, and state police to "be on the lookout" for the red pickup. It wasn't going to be a fun day for anyone driving a red truck, Kay thought. The meager information had also been entered into the NCIC, the national database operated by the FBI to alert all police jurisdictions nationwide of various wanted persons, guns, and vehicles.

Savalas had informed them this morning that the Warrant Apprehension Task Force was also at their disposal, providing whatever manpower was needed to assist with surveillance, leads, banging down doors. If only they had doors to bang down.

They were doing everything they could.

And it wasn't enough.

"What's going on, Kay?"

Kay turned from the boards as Jack Macklin entered the boardroom. Micky's partner looked like hell, wearing the same black T-shirt and faded jeans she'd seen him wearing yesterday morning.

"You shouldn't be here, Mack," she said, seeing his eyes go to the displayed photos of the bloodied sidewalk.

She ushered him out of the boardroom, to the floor-to-ceiling windows of Homicide that overlooked the concrete sweep of the Jones Falls Expressway arcing north out of the heart of the city.

"You should go home, Mack. Shower. Sleep."

"I can't. I *need* to be involved."

"You know you can't—"

"She's my partner, Kay!" Macklin's voice rose over the din and the unit's TV playing in the corner of the eighth-floor offices. He lowered his voice. "I *have* to be included. Micky's out there and—"

"And we're doing everything we can."

"I've got six years on the job, for God's sake. Two of those Vice. I can help."

"You're too close, Mack."

He chewed at the inside of his cheek before turning his anxiety to a hangnail on his thumb. "This is killing me, Kay. You have no idea what this is like."

"Actually . . . I do. I lost a partner too." She tried to block the images that came with less frequency now, but still came. Joe Spencer charging around the corner of that south Baltimore row house. The flare from the muzzle of her duty weapon. The way Spence seemed suspended for a moment before he collapsed, so quietly, onto that filthy corner of yard. And the way his eyes never left hers as the blood pumped out of him.

"Then at least tell me where the investigation's at," Macklin pleaded. "Tell me you've got *something* to go on."

Kay debated, then put herself in Jack Macklin's shoes. She'd be frantic too. And as she described the red pickup and offered Mack a vague description of the driver, Kay hoped he'd take comfort in knowing that they at least had some direction.

"My advice, though, is you stay away from this investigation." But she knew he wouldn't. With Mack's Vice connections to the street he'd be asking questions, pushing buttons. Kay knew because that was exactly what she'd be doing.

It was her turn to lower her voice. "But listen, if you *do* hear something on the streets, from these pimps, the girls, you know . . ."

Mack nodded, absorbing what she was suggesting.

"You come to me, right?"

Another nod.

"If you talk to anyone else on this task force, I guarantee they'll have your sergeant put you on leave. Now go home, Mack. Clean yourself up. Get some sleep."

"You'll keep me posted?" he asked, his eyes pleading.

Kay nodded. "I'll do what I can."

And as she watched him follow the nearest chute of cubicle baffles and disappear around the far corner of the Homicide floor, Kay doubted Mack would go home.

About to return to the boardroom, Kay stopped when she caught the image of Jane Gallagher on the TV. Her heart dropped. The chief investigative reporter had the lead story for WBAL's news at noon. Her face filled the screen, then the image split to offer a photo of Micky Luttrell: a six-year-old photo taken when she'd graduated from the Academy, smiling, cap in hand. With the noise of the eighth floor, Kay snatched only fragments of the report: *". . . a man driving a red pickup truck . . . down here on Edmondson Avenue . . ."* A night image of the street filled the screen, and Kay guessed Jane's photographer had shot it last night before Finn had gotten to them. *". . . witnesses in the vicinity of the abduction Saturday night . . . pig farmer . . . person of interest. Back to you . . ."*

Kay didn't reach the TV in time. The Channel 11 reporter's face was gone before she could hit the volume button, and the anchor moved on to the next story.

"Goddamn it!" Kay stormed across the floor.

Savalas's door was closed. Kay didn't wait for a response from her knock. She threw the door open and found Savalas calmly sitting at Gunderson's old desk. It had been Savalas's first order of business, rearranging her predecessor's office, claiming it as her own with plants and framed photos and certificates from various special programs she had attended. Kay never trusted anyone with a desk as neat and void of work as Savalas's.

"Jane's gone live with the pig-farmer angle." Kay couldn't bite down on the anger. "I *warned* you it would get out of hand the second you went to the press."

"I'm not sure I know what you're talking about, Detective."

"The pickup truck. The pig shit. Channel 11's got our only lead running as their top story. Or didn't you know?"

"In fact, I didn't."

The blankness on Savalas's face made Kay wonder if the sergeant was really that incompetent, *that* inexperienced that she couldn't even comprehend the potential damage Gallagher's report could create.

"You do realize, however," Savalas went on, "that we don't exactly have the luxury of approving everything the media puts out there."

"No, but Jane Gallagher would never have been shadowing us down on Edmondson last night if it hadn't been for you releasing Micky's identity. Did you even stop to think what this guy might do to Micky once he finds out she's a cop? Not to mention when he hears we've got witnesses *and* a physical description of him and his vehicle? Christ!"

Savalas's face remained calm, and Kay disliked her even more for that.

"If the son of a bitch kills Micky because of this leak, it's on you, Sergeant. You!"

"Listen, Detective, I understand you have a history with the press, and with Jane Gallagher specifically."

It shouldn't have surprised Kay that Savalas had educated herself on her squad and her detectives' histories, but the fact that she was airing it out now like a load of dirty laundry . . .

"This personal hatred of yours aside," Savalas went on, "there are times when it can benefit an investigation to have some media coverage. Besides, going to the press was not *my* decision, Detective. Both the captain and Lieutenant Kennedy—"

"It *was* your decision. It's your goddamn task force. *You're* the sergeant of this squad."

"And as this squad's sergeant I have to take orders as well. If the brass comes down on me to get this out to the media—"

"The brass? If the *brass* comes down on you?" Kay couldn't stop herself. "Or do you mean Deputy Commissioner Powell coming down on you?"

This time there was a reaction on Savalas's face, one that showed Kay the sergeant hadn't missed the double entendre of her accusation. And as Savalas held her stare, her mouth tight and her eyes unblinking, Kay wondered if Kojak had known about the rumor of her sleeping her way into her current post or if this was the first she'd heard of it.

Savalas stood, her chair wheeling back and striking the

wall. When she lifted a hand to tuck a stray lock of hair that had fallen away from the ponytail, Kay could see it was shaking.

"Detective Delaney—" Savalas struggled to keep her voice even.

Kay braced herself.

"Have you met Detective Ryan? He's with Robbery."

Kay followed Savalas's gesture just as the young detective stood from the chair behind the now open door.

"Detective Ryan is trained on the E-FIT program," Savalas went on.

Gone were the days of civilian artists, contracted by the department, sitting down with pad and pencil in a small room with a witness. Now it could all stay in-house, with the UK-developed Electronic Facial Identification Technique program being taught to selected detectives from various units. Artistic talent was obsolete when a few clicks of a mouse could produce a computer-generated likeness in a fraction of the time.

Savalas handed Kay the printout.

The eyes that stared back at her looked peculiar, at odds with the other features. But then the essence of the E-FIT program was to produce a picture based on ten comprehensive databases within the facial-composite software, so various parts didn't always mesh in the finished product.

Besides the narrow, vacant eyes, the nose was long, and the mouth angry, the lips thin and tight with the corners cutting downward. The hairline was lost under the beak of a cap, but what hair could be seen was "scraggly," just as Velvet had described.

"What about the other girl's composite?"

Savalas seemed to hesitate, then handed Kay the second portrait.

Kay took in the round features, the full lips, and the wide eyes. "You're kidding me, right?"

When she turned to the Robbery detective, he shrugged meekly.

"Jesus Christ." Kay tossed the drawings back onto Savalas's desk. "They don't even look like distant cousins!"

"It's what the witnesses' individual memories came up with," Ryan tried to explain.

"Then their memories are crap." Kay turned to Savalas, gesturing at the composites. "We got nothing here."

"They're the only visual reference we have of our possible suspect." Savalas handed the printouts back to Kay. "Get it out there."

"Which one? Or are we saying we had *two* pig farmers sniffing around for hookers that night?"

Kay didn't know what to do with the anger now. She felt the room closing in as she held her sergeant's stare. Felt Savalas's impending censure already crawling under her skin.

"Kay, line three," someone shouted from the main floor.

Savalas pushed her phone toward her, the light flashing, and Kay tried to swallow her rage. Grappling with the receiver, she jabbed at the blinking light.

"Delaney." And her eyes never left Savalas, the silent war continuing.

"Kay, it's Gunderson. I just caught the news on this missing cop. You working it?"

"As a matter of fact, yes."

"Good. Then you need to talk to me. Now."

7

AS KAY STEERED WEST onto Pimlico just north of the city line and followed the directions Ed Gunderson had given her, she counted back the number of months it had been since she'd last seen her former sergeant. His retirement party at The Admiral in November.

Eight months ago, and she hadn't made any effort to see or even call the man who had not only been her sergeant for eight years, but who had been her greatest advocate. When she'd been laid up in the hospital after Eales's beating, half-dead and wishing the other half would die too because it had been *her* gun that had killed Joe Spencer, it was Gunderson who still believed in her while everyone else blamed her. It was Gunderson who'd visited every day, and who had refused to let her turn in her shield.

Eight months.

Less than a half mile west of the sprawl of Robert E. Lee Park, Kay steered through the neighborhood of Twinridge. Ed Gunderson's cottage-style house sat on a narrow strip of property that backed onto older trees. The house looked as if it needed work. The lawn too. Bare patches had baked dry in the unforgiving July sun and the grass was withered and yellow.

He'd owned the house for decades, raising both his boys, now grown and long gone. One was a pilot with Southwest, and the other a high school teacher who'd moved to Oregon to be with his wife, Gunderson had told Kay once, and she'd noted the disappointment in his voice that neither of his boys had followed in their father's footsteps.

Kay couldn't remember how long Sarge had been alone. As long as she'd known him anyway. His wife had died of breast cancer years ago. Gunderson had rarely mentioned her and he'd never remarried.

Parking behind Gunderson's Lincoln, Kay stepped out of the air-conditioned police car and into the wall of heat that had settled over Baltimore. Beyond the stand of trees at the back, she heard the traffic whip along I-83 as she took the walkway to the gate. A four-foot chain-link fence circled the narrow yard, and as she reached over to unlatch the gate, Kay wondered if Sarge had a dog.

She rapped on the door of the closed-in porch and heard one low gruff. Through the door's window she could see the brindled-and-white bulldog haul itself up from the front doormat. The dog looked ancient, squinting up, its round eyes blinking from its compressed, wrinkled face, and its short ears half-pricked. When it barked again, its upper lip caught on a protruding canine.

Past the dog and through the open front door, Kay spotted Gunderson coming through the kitchen. He waved her in, pushing the huge bulldog aside, as the covered screen door squealed on its hinges. Kay smelled dog and fried bacon.

"How ya doin'?" he asked her.

"Good." It was strange seeing him like this, dressed in old khakis and a white T-shirt, standing in his socks. She turned her gaze onto the dog and started to reach for it.

"Don't bother," he said, stopping her. "Dog stinks. Cap, g'wan." Gunderson gestured at the dog, but Cap merely sat back on his haunches with a wheeze. Looking into the round, jowly face, Kay considered the theory of owners looking like their pets. Cap came close.

"You riding solo?" he asked her then.

"For now."

"Kojak doesn't know you're talking to me, does she?"

Kay shook her head. Savalas was having a hard enough time filling Gunderson's shoes. Last thing Kay needed was Savalas riding her ass for speaking to her former sergeant about a case.

"Good."

"So how are you, Sarge?"

"Never better."

But in the dim light of the closed-in porch, Kay reserved her judgment on Gunderson's appearance. The mild heart attack he'd suffered last year had altered him. He'd lost weight, and as he ushered her inside, she could see Gunderson's color wasn't so good.

The cool, bright kitchen would have been classified retro if it hadn't actually all been original. Kay nodded at the set of clubs in the corner under the coatrack. "You getting in much golf?" she asked, noting the dust on the Naugahyde club covers.

"A bit."

"Maybe I should go out with you sometime? For golf, I mean." She wasn't sure why she'd suggested it. Pity? Concern? Except for occasional visits to the driving range, she'd only ever golfed a half dozen times in her life, and she wasn't good.

In the look he gave her, Sarge seemed to have sensed the impulse behind her suggestion, and Kay regretted asking.

"You'd never keep up," he joked finally.

And she laughed. "You're probably right."

"You want something to drink?"

"No. I'm fine."

"Good. Follow me." He crossed the kitchen to the

open cellar door. Overhead, a hundred-watt bulb flooded the worn wooden stairs with light. Gunderson had to duck, his six-foot-plus frame too tall for the riser of the stairs overhead, as he descended into the basement.

Behind her, the bulldog's nails tapped out a rhythm against the linoleum, then stopped. At the bottom of the stairwell Kay looked up to see Cap lying at the top, jowls draped over the transom.

"Probably should have moved this shit upstairs years ago," he told her. "Kathryn never liked 'the job' in the house. Had me banished to the basement before the boys were even out of diapers. Guess I just kinda got used to it down here."

The shag carpeting was old, with a path worn almost to its backing leading from the stairs to the far corner. The furnishings were sparse: a plaid-upholstered sofa and a threadbare La-Z-Boy, a couple floor lamps, and a desk with a computer. Along the far wall, Gunderson had built in floor-to-ceiling shelving, two-by-four studs and heavy-duty plywood. But instead of power tools or fishing tackle, firearms, or anything else one would expect a retired cop to collect, the shelves were crammed with file boxes. Dozens of them.

"What's all this?" Kay scanned their labels, the dates spanning ten, fifteen years.

"You got a bottom-drawer case, Kay?" Gunderson asked. "That case that never gets solved? The one that sticks in your side like a thorn from the day you walked onto the crime scene?"

She was still taking in the sheer volume of it all as she shook her head.

"Course you don't," he said. "You're probably still maintaining that ninety-five percent clearance rate, huh?"

She caught his smile. "Well, this is my bottom-drawer case," he said, gesturing at the boxes.

"All of this is one case?" Kay asked.

"*I* think so. And I think it's connected to your missing cop."

8

FINN HAD BEEN SITTING in the Impala for forty minutes now across from J-Ray's Tavern at Herkimer and Carey streets. He'd parked in the shade of the two-story Formstones that lined the dead-end street, with the windows down, the heat washing over him.

It had been five years since Finn had been down here. Washington Village it was called now that the neighborhood had been gentrified. But any good born-and-raised "Baltimoron" still referred to the area as Pigtown, even though decades had passed since any livestock had been run from the B&O Railroad through Cross and Ostend streets, bound for the slaughterhouses and meatpacking plants in south Baltimore.

J-Ray's Tavern was the only reason Finn had ever come down here. The cop bar was frequented by the Southern and Western districts as well as Homicide, and Finn guessed that his old tabs alone had probably financed the owner's new Land Rover parked in the rear alley sporting the vanity plates J RAY.

Finn stared at the bar's heavy wooden door across the street and wondered how much longer he'd have to wait. At the curb ahead of him sat Jack Macklin's metallic blue Mustang. It was Scooby who'd tipped Finn off about the Vice detective's early-afternoon binge, having grabbed a quick lunch with the boys an hour ago, and Finn figured it was the best place to talk to Macklin. Cop to cop.

Something in the tension he'd seen flare between Macklin and Andy Luttrell yesterday morning at the crime scene hadn't felt right. Coupled with the Vice detective's binge this afternoon, Finn knew something was up. He'd been a drinker himself, years ago, when he'd first met Kay, before she'd convinced him he had a problem. And Finn knew firsthand: nothing turned a man to the bottle faster than guilt.

Just when Finn imagined he might have to go into J-Ray's himself, Jack Macklin stepped onto the sidewalk. The Vice cop lifted a hand to block the sun, and his head seemed to wobble.

Finn got out of the car.

"What're you doing here, Finnerty?" Macklin asked, the soles of his gator-skin Western boots scuffing the hot asphalt as he crossed Herkimer.

"Rough day, huh, Mack?" Finn asked, ignoring his question.

"Hell, yeah."

"Listen, I'm sorry about Micky. Just want you to know, we're doing everything we can."

"Right." Macklin's skepticism seemed exaggerated by his alcohol level.

"Had a few more questions about the other night though," Finn said. "Just trying to sort some of the details."

Macklin didn't look anywhere *near* in the mood, but he let out a breath stinking of booze and said, "Shoot."

"Just wondering about your sting that night. You and Micky . . . Kay says you guys had a couple rough collars?"

"Yeah, it was a shithole night."

"Anyone harass or threaten Micky when they found out she was a cop?"

Macklin laughed. "Uh, yeah. That's what these slime-balls do when the shield comes out."

"And did you arrest them all?"

"No. Sometimes they wise up too soon and you can't catch 'em with their pants down, so to speak. So best you can do is scare 'em a bit."

"Could one of them have followed you after you all wrapped up? Maybe tailed you up to Edmondson?"

Macklin closed his eyes against the glare of the sun. When he opened them again, he seemed genuinely confused. "Christ, you don't think . . ."

Finn shrugged. "Just asking if it's a possibility."

Macklin shook his head. "No. No. I mean, I'd've seen someone tailing us."

"What about Edmondson? Where you dropped Micky off, did you see a red pickup truck?"

Again Macklin shook his head. "I wasn't in cop mode anymore, you know? Wasn't paying attention."

Finn wondered how Jack Macklin, or *any* cop, could just turn it off like that. The only place *he'd* ever been able to switch from cop mode was when he had the sails of *The Blue Angel* unfurled and the spinnaker full of wind, out on the bay, cutting through the waves and feeling the salt spray on his face. But with both feet firmly planted on land, the job was with him.

"So why *didn't* you guys go back to the office? I mean, there's paperwork, the twenty-four-hour reports, incident reports."

Finn could tell that between his questions and the heat, Jack Macklin was turning real sour real fast. Macklin jangled his car keys in one hand, then looked up the street as if maybe he expected to see radio cars parked there.

"Tell me, Finnerty," he said at last, "why's this feeling like the third fucking degree all of a sudden?"

"I don't know, Mack. It shouldn't. Unless you're hiding something." Finn smiled because he knew it would get under the Vice detective's skin. And that's exactly where Finn wanted to be.

"Yeah, right." Mack reached for the door of his Mustang.

"Are you?" Finn called after him.

"Am I what? Hiding something?"

Finn shrugged, remained calm, as Macklin came at him.

"Right, Finnerty. You're abso-fuckin'-lutely right." He stopped within two feet of Finn and brought his hand down on the Mustang's spoiler. "I got my partner right here in my goddamn trunk. You want my keys so you can check for yourself?" He thrust them toward Finn.

Macklin's inebriated offer was tempting. An invited search. Who knows what he might find in the detective's trunk?

But Macklin quickly withdrew the keys. "What *are* you doing here anyway, Finnerty? This ain't exactly your watering hole anymore, is it? Or do they got one of them AA meetings around the corner?"

It was a low blow, and while Finn wondered how Jack Macklin had even known of his drinking problem from five years ago, Macklin went on.

"You feeling the urge for the bottle again, Finnerty? You off to a meeting with the rest of them pansies to drown your sorrows in fucking *words*?"

Macklin had had enough. He unlocked his car and swung the driver's door open too hard. It bounced back and caught him in the hip. Macklin staggered, and Finn debated the wisdom of letting him go.

But he didn't have to debate long.

Tom Fahey from Vice stepped out of J-Ray's just then. "Hey, Mack." He jogged across the street. "Come on. I'll drive."

"I can drive my own damn car, Tommy."

"Course you can, but I wanna see what this baby's got under the hood." Tommy gave Macklin an attaboy slap on the back and took his keys. "Get in, Mack."

Macklin's eyes never left Finn's, the muscle along his jaw working overtime as he ground his teeth, before finally giving in.

When Macklin circled the rear of his muscle car, Finn leaned in just enough to block him.

"Just so you know, Mack," he whispered, "I don't trust you. I don't trust anything about you."

"You think *I* did something to Micky? Jesus Christ, she's my fucking partner!"

And Mack pushed by him at last. "Fuck you, Finnerty," Macklin yelled as he got into the passenger seat and Tommy started the engine. "Fuck you!"

9

KAY HAD HELPED GUNDERSON carry two of the boxes from the basement up into the bright kitchen. At the table, he took out the top file. Across the front of the red pressboard cover he'd printed JANE DOE in black marker. The folder was beaten, the pages stained and dog-eared.

"When I heard Gallagher's report on the news," he

said, "interviewing those hookers down on Edmondson, I knew."

"Knew what?"

He tossed the case folder onto the table in front of her. "My guy's still out there. Snatching up hookers."

She opened the file to the first page, a list of the contents: investigative notes, incident reports, evidence documentation, and autopsy protocol. The complete, photocopied file.

"This case is twelve years old," Kay said.

Gunderson nodded. "My first homicide. Go on. Read the file."

She started, but he wasn't silent for long. "This guy your hookers saw, he have long hair?"

Kay nodded.

"We found some long hairs snagged in my Jane Doe's bracelet," Gunderson explained. "Never did find a suspect to go along with them though."

Kay was about to launch into the first pages of the incident report, then stopped. "Wait a second, Sarge. Some of the dates on the boxes down there"—she shoved her thumb toward the open cellar door—"those cases are fifteen years old. You're suggesting this guy has been operating all this time?"

He nodded, the look on his face making her feel that he was just waiting for her to catch up. "The Green River Killer gave King County a twenty-one-year run."

"So you've been looking for this guy all these years? In all those cases downstairs?"

"Twelve years. Starting with that one." Gunderson pointed at the file in front of her. "Go on," he repeated. "Read it."

And she did.

The Jane Doe, estimated between eighteen and

twenty-five years of age, had been found off Washington Boulevard on a narrow service road just south of Carroll Park. She had had no identification on her, no tattoos or scars, nor had there been any hits on her prints. There had been considerable effort on Sarge's part to connect the Jane Doe to missing-person cases around the time of her death, but no match had ever been made.

"Harse ruled it a vehicular homicide?" Kay asked, reading the ME's report.

Gunderson nodded, then reached across to flip to the first four-by-six color photos, making Kay wish she'd skipped breakfast.

"Her legs weren't fractured," Gunderson pointed out. "And there were no bumper injuries like you'd see if she'd been mowed down. But then it's pretty clear she wasn't standing when he ran her over."

He pointed to a close-up of the Jane Doe's legs. A coarse, natural-fiber rope had been knotted tightly around both ankles.

"He hog-tied her." Gunderson showed Kay the next photo, the cord traveling up the back of the victim's legs, past her pantied buttocks, and still attached to one wrist. The other arm, Kay noted, was missing.

And as though reading her mind, Gunderson flipped the page to show her the photos of the Jane Doe's missing appendage. "We found her right arm in the ditch about fifteen feet down the road. At first I thought he'd tried to hack her up, but Harse determined it was actually severed from the force of the tire grinding through it when he ran her over."

He flipped another page.

"Jesus." Kay's eyes settled on the visual documentation of the carnage.

There were tire marks on her thighs, and stretch-mark-like tears in her skin from the sheer weight of the vehicle rolling over her. Another tread pattern was clear on her bare pelvis below her short top.

Kay tried to make sense of what she saw, the full picture coming slowly. And then: "He ran her over twice?"

"That's what I always figured. I think he had her in his truck and was driving when—"

"Truck?" Kay interrupted him.

Gunderson nodded. "Lab analyzed the pattern of the tread marks. Narrowed it down to brand and size and determined they had to be on a truck or an SUV. The way I figure it, he's driving, the ropes come loose, and she starts fighting back. We found skid marks a couple hundred feet back. Probably the truck swerving. She decides to bail. Hits the center of the road. And then we have these braking marks."

More photos.

"Best estimation, she fell here, he braked here." Gunderson had flipped back to a wider pan of the whole crime scene and pointed to the black skid marks at the far right. The Jane Doe lay a third of the way back.

"He stops, throws the truck in reverse, and backs up over her. ME noted this round contusion on her forehead." The black-and-white photo taken at the medical examiner's office showed a ruler scale next to the large, circular dent above her left eye. "Said it could have been the ball of a trailer hitch. I figure, with the rope still on her, she was trying to get up, probably sitting in the road when he hit her with the rear of the truck. Hopefully that's what killed her. Hard to tell though with everything being so mangled and him driving over her head."

As Kay stared at the photos before her, she wondered whether it was anger or thrill that had fueled the man behind the wheel that night twelve years ago.

"And after he backed over her"—Gunderson flipped more pages, his familiarity with their sequence illustrating his long obsession with the case—"he threw it in gear and ran her over again. That's when she got snagged and he hauled her for a good thirty feet before she dislodged."

Then came the relentless close-ups of the Jane Doe. Burns from the pavement glared against the white skin, smeared with blood and road grit. Deep lacerations marked her face and legs and remaining arm, while close-ups of the roadway showed a long, grisly trail of blood and skin and remnants of clothing.

Kay turned the pages herself now, feeling hollow inside.

Photos displayed the results of the grinding action of tires moving from the surface of the road, up and over the body, stripping the skin and fat from the underlying tissue. Tires that had been accelerating, Kay realized, *not braking*.

"We found grease on her," he said, "from the undercarriage of the vehicle. And something else. Something that makes me think this is the same guy who attacked this cop Luttrell."

"What?"

"Manure. Embedded in her skin. Probably sloughed off the tires as they went over her. I pushed the Lab for more testing and they said it was hog shit because of the high ammonia or nitrogen levels."

Kay wasn't sure what to feel. The implication of the cases actually connecting, actually committed by the same perp, overwhelmed her.

"Back then," Gunderson went on, "there were still a couple of slaughterhouses operating in that area. With the pig shit, I always figured this guy must have worked for one of them. The way he had her tied up, it was obvious he was taking her someplace. And where we found her was only a block away from a place killing hogs and lambs."

"It's a stretch," Kay said, already formulating the words it would take to convince Savalas of the possible tie between the two cases.

"Course it's a stretch. But that's not what your gut's telling you, is it?" Gunderson smiled but looked serious at the same time. Dead serious.

"So what about all those other boxes downstairs?" Kay asked. "They're all homicides?"

"Most. Some are still missing."

"How many cases are we talking about?" she asked, but didn't really want to know.

"A few dozen. But those are only the ones that caught my eye over the years. The ones that got me wondering. Do you have any idea how many prostitutes go missing every year in this city? And who knows how many others that *aren't* reported? Sure, some crawl away and overdose, some just up and get the hell outta Dodge. But I don't think we can even guesstimate how many truly go missing, and how many end up as Jane Does every year."

"And you're thinking this guy has been operating for the past twelve years?"

"Probably longer," Gunderson answered. "It shouldn't surprise you this could be the same guy, Kay, that he's been doing this for years. Hell, he's not the only one preying on these women. What *should* be surprising, though, is that the dumbfuck hasn't got caught yet."

10

DARYL EUGENE WARDELL didn't make a habit of watching the news. Sometimes he supposed he should. But he'd learned a long time ago that no one really missed a whore. The media didn't care. The police didn't care. What was one more whore off the streets?

In fact, the way Daryl saw things, the cops should be thanking him. Along with city officials. Hell, even the mayor. After all, wasn't he doing them all a favor by cleaning up the streets?

Now, as Daryl swirled the last of his Natty Bo in the bottom of its bottle, he paid only half a mind to the TV mounted behind the bar. From his usual corner booth, his back to the wall and a clear view of the door, Daryl had the best vantage point while his beer warmed in its bottle. His gaze shifted from the TV to Haley, the bar's owner, as she wiped glasses.

Haley was fat and homely. It regularly amazed Daryl that anyone would want to confess their personal problems to a cow like that. Blubbering drunken bastards, crying in their beer, like anyone gave a shit.

When she looked up suddenly, the bar owner caught his stare. Daryl calmly shifted his focus onto the TV again, but he wasn't seeing the commercials flash across the screen. He was seeing fat Haley's ugly, round face in his mind. He was imagining her scream in his head as he visualized his hands around her wide, soft throat, her eyes bulging out of her head and her lips going purple. He found it curious that, in all the years he'd been coming to her bar, he never fantasized about raping her the way he did with most women.

Haley the heifer he only imagined killing. In so many different ways.

This afternoon's fantasy involved his meat saw. And Haley's screams.

This particular fantasy had sparked months ago, as he'd sat in the cab of his truck, parked outside, waiting for her to close. Revolted by her girth, Daryl had found himself strangely intrigued by it as well. He'd wanted to see her out from behind the bar. To see how she moved with those enormous thighs rocking against each other as she waddled from the bar's door to her Buick, the old car sagging on its chassis as she heaved her mass in behind the wheel.

He hadn't thought she'd seen him that night, sitting in the dark. But two days later when he walked into the bar, she'd waved him over and swore to him that if she ever found him sitting in her parking lot again after hours, she'd not only call the cops, but he'd never be served another drink at the Haley's Comet.

Now Daryl tossed back the last of his beer and was about to take the fantasy one step further in his mind when his whore's face flashed across the television screen. Daryl's heart raced.

He almost didn't recognize her in the cop's uniform. But it was her. And then he felt the bar tilt and everything blurred, as if there were only him and the TV and the whore's photo.

A cop? *How in hell . . .*

Daryl tried to hear the reporter's words, but the bar was too noisy and there was a buzzing in his head, like a whole nest of hornets was suddenly loose inside his skull.

A cop.

It made sense though. The way she'd fought him.

The way she'd stood her ground instead of running.

A goddamn, fucking pig.

The cops would dig deeper, hunt harder for one of their own.

What if they found him? What if he'd left something behind?

And then Daryl started to sweat.

The hat. His goddamn hat.

His mind was wild now. Frantic. He had to get home.

As Daryl left his corner booth, his legs shaky and his armpits wet, the buzzing grew louder. He barely heard Haley as he passed the bar for the door.

"Hey, Red," she called after him. "That's on your tab, and I want it paid up by the end of the week, you hear?"

He didn't look at the fat cow, only waved a hand in her direction and kept walking. Through the doors and into the hot, evening air.

A fucking cop.

How was he supposed to have known she was a cop?

And what the hell was he supposed to do now?

In the sanctuary of the cab of his F-100, Daryl was still shaking. And as his rear tires smoked out of the parking lot, Daryl Eugene Wardell knew he'd have to decide, before he got home, whether he could afford to keep her now.

11

AFTER LEAVING GUNDERSON'S HOUSE with two of the boxes from his basement in the trunk of her police car, Kay had driven back to HQ for an update. Bobby and Finn had spent the afternoon with District uniforms, randomly sweeping neighborhoods with the E-FIT composites of their suspect, but had garnered no new witnesses or leads.

Together they'd debated whether to interview more prostitutes, and Bobby agreed to draft the aid of several Southwestern uniforms to talk to more girls in other sectors of the District in case their suspect had more than one hunting ground.

Kay hadn't filled Finn or Bobby in on her visit with Gunderson, nor had she stayed long in the boardroom, preferring to avoid Savalas until she had something to prove a connection between Micky's abduction and Gunderson's Jane Doe.

And now Kay hoped she'd found that proof.

She'd spent an hour up in north Baltimore, in the nondescript, concrete warehouse used by the Department as a repository for evidence, walking through the maze of metal shelves jammed to the rafters with cataloged boxes. Evidence from closed or inactive cases was routinely moved from the basement of Police Headquarters, along with whatever hadn't been destroyed in the flood during Hurricane Isabel.

It was there, in a dust-covered box cataloged as H-95-192—Gunderson's Jane Doe—that Kay had found the hairs: several long, blond strands folded carefully into a snap-cap plastic vial.

Kay felt the vial in her jacket pocket now as she swung open the steel door that led from the police parking garage to the elevators. Manuel Costilla at the Crime Lab upstairs was waiting for her, and Kay tried not to let her hopes rise. After all, as much as she hoped Gunderson's theory of someone hunting prostitutes in Baltimore City for the past twelve years was wrong, a connection *could* exponentially increase the base of evidence, along with their chances of finding Micky.

Kay stabbed the button for the elevator just as her cell went off.

It was Bobby. "You know Savalas has been trying to get ahold of you?" he asked.

"Yeah." Kay hadn't felt good about ignoring the sergeant's calls all afternoon while she rode out her hunch.

"Where the hell are you?"

"On my way to the Lab. You?"

"I'm down at the Eastern District. Visiting your friend Linus Mooney."

"What?"

"Fucking idiot got himself arrested."

"On what?"

"Possession. I think he staged it though," Bobby said. "Got himself the crazy notion we'll protect him if he's inside."

"Son of a bitch. We'll protect him when he decides to testify. Besides, did you tell that dumb-ass that both the Doggos *and* the Ashland Boys have members on the inside? Christ, they're probably even *more* likely to get him in prison than on the damn street."

"That's why I pushed Savalas to have his dumb-ass segregated for now. By the way, she's having Munroe do the interview."

"Linus isn't going to talk to him. He won't even talk to *you.*"

"That's what I told her."

"Fine. Let her waste Munroe's time. In the meantime, tell Linus to keep his mouth shut until I come see him tomorrow. And he better be ready to talk or he'll be in general population by the end of the week."

The elevator arrived as Kay snapped her cell phone

shut. She stepped inside and jabbed hard at the tenth-floor button.

But Kay didn't get past the eighth. When the doors slid open at the floor of the Homicide offices, Savalas was standing in the corridor, her soft briefcase slung over one shoulder. The sergeant's eyes widened and she caught the doors with one slim hand before they could close again.

"I've been calling you," she said.

"Sorry. My cell was off," Kay lied.

"Where are you going?"

"Lab."

"I'll save you the trip. The results are in my office. Come on." Savalas turned before Kay could argue, and as she followed Savalas into Homicide and past the first bank of industrial-gray, modular cubicles, Kay felt the sergeant's tension in her slipstream.

"Close the door," Savalas ordered as she circled her meticulous desk. She didn't sit. Behind her, dusk settled over the city, the last of the light catching the gold-gilded upper dome of City Hall.

Savalas handed Kay the Lab report.

"The blood on the sidewalk matched the samples you took from the Luttrell house," the sergeant said, even as Kay scanned the results. "And, as you suspected, there was a second source."

Kay flipped to the report's second page.

"They lifted samples off the sweatband of the cap," Savalas went on, "and it matched the second source of blood."

"So the cap definitely belongs to our perp."

Savalas nodded. "It might be all we've got to go on right now."

"Where are we at with the cap's logo?" Kay asked. "Did Purnell and Mitchell get anywhere with it?"

"Not yet."

"We need to know where this hunt and fish club is. Talk to members." Kay handed back the report. "So when is this profile being run through CODIS?" she asked, referring to the FBI's Combined DNA Index System program. The database linked local, state, and federal labs in an exchange and comparison program of DNA profiles to connect crimes to each other and, hopefully, to convicted offenders. But it was time-consuming, and each lab nationwide had only predesignated days in which to submit their inquiries at the national level, which often meant waiting more than a week for results.

Micky Luttrell didn't have a week. Kay was sure of it.

"It's already in the system," Savalas said, and Kay wondered what kinds of strings the sergeant had pulled to push the sample up the queue. "We may have something preliminary as soon as tomorrow. Even if they get a hit, the official match-procedure will take days. Confirmation of identity, issuance of letters, warrant, and retesting of the identified individual. But the prelim will give us probable cause to at least move on this guy."

"Thanks," Kay said, "for getting the CODIS entry bumped." And she meant it.

"Despite what you might be thinking, Detective, I *do* want to find Micky Luttrell. Alive."

Kay nodded. "I never thought . . ."

Savalas's stare was fixed, her face illegible, and for the first time Kay wondered what had happened in the woman's past that made her into such a hard woman.

"Listen, about what I said earlier, in front of Detective Ryan—"

Savalas held up one hand and with the other shouldered her leather briefcase. "That's not something I'm willing to discuss at this time, Detective. Now, if you'll excuse me, I have to be somewhere." She moved past Kay, opening the door to the sound of bleating phones and laughter from farther back in the clusters of cubicles. "I've asked everyone to convene by eight a.m. tomorrow. I'm pulling in Nolan and Corbett to give us a hand, and I want everyone briefed and ready to move on any hit we might get with this DNA."

Savalas ushered Kay out of the office and started for the elevators again. Then stopped and turned. "Oh, and, Detective? Leave your cell phone on, will you? I consider this a high-priority case," she said, as though implying Kay didn't.

Kay tried not to let the jab bother her as she watched Savalas follow the line of cubicle baffles. Withdrawing the evidence vial from her pocket, Kay tapped the plastic-encased hairs against the back of her hand, waiting for Savalas to disappear around the corner before she headed for the stairs.

And as she jogged up the two flights to the labs on the tenth floor where she hoped Manuel Costilla was still waiting for her, Kay knew she needed to share her hunch. Needed to share it with someone who trusted her gut as much as she did. Someone who'd seen—firsthand—how her intuition paid off.

She needed Finn.

12

FINN MET HER out in the graveled parking lot of the marina on the east side of Hanover Street where the Vietnam Veterans Memorial Bridge spanned the Middle

Branch. The crowded basin, nestled in the shadow of the Locke Insulator Plant, had been the berth for Finn's forty-three-foot Slocum cutter and his home for the six years he'd been separated from his wife, Angie, maintaining the sailboat as his residence even while he'd dated Kay off and on until he went back to ex-wife last year.

After leaving the Lab, Kay had called Finn, wired on the results from the hair analysis. Finn's suggestion to meet on *The Blue Angel* shouldn't have surprised Kay. After all, meeting at the house he shared with his ex-wife and daughter would be awkward, as would meeting at Kay's. He hadn't been to her apartment since he'd cleared out his things fifteen months ago and left the key on her desk back at HQ. Kay remembered the day too well: the numb feeling she'd had when she'd found the key, the drive home through the pounding rain, and the immense emptiness she'd felt from the moment she'd walked through the door.

She had cried that evening, alone in her dark apartment. When she was done, Kay had sworn she wouldn't cry for Finn again. And she hadn't. At least, not for another four months, when she'd lost that last precious piece of him.

"What the hell is all this?" Finn balanced the two boxes from the Lumina's trunk.

"Dead and missing prostitutes," she told him as she grabbed the takeout she'd picked up from Chiapparelli's in Little Italy.

Finn led the way down the east pier, past gutted fiberglass shells and several speedboats in various stages of refurbishment. Riggings slapped quietly along their masts and water lapped against the hollow hulls. The memories flooded back.

But there was no room for personal feelings or past hurts. She was here for Micky Luttrell. One hundred percent.

Still, it wasn't easy. Taking the companionway steps down into *The Blue Angel*'s teak-appointed galley, Kay was struck by the familiar intimacy of the boat. As though she'd been here only yesterday, sharing the tight space with Finn, sailing out on the bay or just relaxing after work.

She'd expected the boat to feel empty, deserted, with Finn back in Hunting Ridge with Angie and his daughter. But it felt as if he'd never left. As if *they'd* never left. A couple of jackets hung on the hooks by the steps, and there was fruit on the narrow galley counter. As Finn cracked open two sodas, Kay let her gaze sweep the place.

"Did you hear we had a couple tips come in?" Finn asked then, his discomfort mirroring hers as he stood in the middle of the galley.

"When?"

"This afternoon. Because of Jane's segment earlier today." He took a long swig from his soda. "Of course, they didn't pan out, but at least there's a chance we might get something because of this media release."

It was Kay's turn to shake her head. "Right, and how good are tips if he's already killed Micky, huh?"

"Kay—"

"Am I the only one thinking he'll kill her when he finds out who she really is?"

"I'm not disagreeing with you. But you have to admit, it's a tough call saying which strategy is the better one. Not getting the news out there means we don't generate tips. Sure, it could buy Micky a few days, if he hasn't already killed her, but what good is buying her more time if we're not getting tips?"

Kay held up her hand. "I'm not getting into this with you, Finn."

"Fine." He gestured to the boxes. "So let's talk about dead hookers then."

She had told Finn little over the phone, and now, as she opened the take-out containers of pasta, Kay filled him in on Gunderson's Jane Doe and the results of the hairs.

Up on the tenth floor of Headquarters, Manuel Costilla had been confused when Kay had pushed for him to run the comparison right then and there.

"High priority," she'd explained as she followed Costilla into the lab.

"Since when are the dead in a rush?" Costilla had mumbled, then looked at the label on the plastic vial. "Especially on a twelve-year-old case?"

"When that twelve-year-old case could be part of this missing-cop red ball."

"All right," he'd said, pulling up a tall stool to one of the side work areas and opening the vial.

It wasn't the first time the quick-talking, hyperactive lab technician had done her a favor. Last year, in his enthusiasm, Costilla had analyzed dog hairs found on a crime scene and scientifically proved her killer owned a pit bull. And as the analyst mounted one of the long, blond hairs onto a slide, Kay had remembered that pit bull and the round she'd been forced to fire into its skull. Not one of her fonder memories of her job.

Using a comparison microscope on the twelve-year-old hair and one taken from the cap found on Harlem Avenue Sunday morning, Costilla had started his analysis, hemmed and hawed, before finally inviting Kay to look for herself.

"When you do the side-by-side examination like this,"

he explained, "you're looking at a variety of characteristics. Color, diameter, length. Then cortical characteristics, root and tip morphology . . ."

He'd rambled as Kay studied the two samples in the dual fields.

". . . cuticle features. Thickness, size, and pigment distribution."

"I'm not sure what I'm supposed to be looking for," Kay had said, "but these look the same to me."

"They are. And . . . they aren't. They do share a lot of characteristics, but there *are* some discrepancies between the two samples."

"So you're saying they're *not* from the same person?"

"It's not that easy, Kay. These two hairs *could* have originated from the same source, but the level of certainty is never absolute. We need to take into consideration how aging and environmental influences can affect a comparison like this and—"

"Are they or aren't they from the same guy?" Kay had finally asked, her surging adrenaline sparking impatience.

"I'd say yes. *But* for the high level of certainty you'd need in court, you have to do DNA."

Now, as Kay watched Finn tuck into his gnocchi slathered in Chiapparelli's special tomato sauce, she explained, "The DNA match on those hairs will take at least forty-eight hours. And that's *with* a high-priority push."

"But otherwise Costilla's saying it's the same guy?"

Kay nodded as she opened her own take-out container.

"So this long-haired mope has been killing prostitutes for the past twelve years?"

"Maybe longer." Kay pointed at the boxes. "Gunderson's got cases going back twenty years."

"Does Kojak know about this connection?"

"Not yet." Taking a mouthful of manicotti, Kay realized how hungry she was. "I wanted to go through Gunderson's boxes first. See if we come up with any other cases."

Finn opened the nearest box. "So what are we looking for?"

"Any similarities. Witness statements that mention a pickup truck or this guy with the long hair. A guy who tries to tie them up. Anything to do with pigs or manure. Also"—she slid over a photo of Gunderson's Jane Doe showing what was left of her face—"any of them that look like her. The physical similarities to Micky could be more than coincidence. He might target this particular type or look. Small build, tiny frame, dark hair."

Finn shoved his dinner aside and pulled out the first file.

There was no order to the cases Gunderson had squirreled away. He'd admitted as much this afternoon when he'd carried the boxes to her car, then explained that the files he was handing over were the cases that he felt had the most in common with his Jane Doe's.

Some were homicides. Some undetermineds. Others remained missing persons. One prostitute after the next. Found in motel rooms, back alleys, abandoned cars, or simply dumped on the side of the road like trash.

Kay searched the highlights of the investigative notes of each case, looking for any links. She read Gunderson's notes scrawled on the backs of the photocopied pages, in the margins, or on sticky notes flagging what he felt were possible ties between the individual cases: vague reports of a man in a pickup but with short hair, a man with long hair but in a late-model sedan, a guy who smelled like manure but drove a panel van, another man who even claimed to be a butcher. Case after case until the girls' faces started to blur, the details almost impossible to differentiate from one another.

"So, you still seeing that artist from New York?" Finn asked as he opened another soda. "Kyle Taithleach, right?"

When she looked across to him, Finn wouldn't meet her eyes.

"No," Kay said, and was certain she hadn't offered her date's surname when she'd introduced him at Gunderson's retirement party. She wondered how long after meeting Kyle Finn had looked him up. Probably Googled the successful painter, then run a complete background check. She wasn't sure whether to be amused, flattered, or pissed off.

She'd met Kyle at the Meyerhoff last fall, during one of her symphony dates with Vicki DiGrazzio, the assistant state's attorney and good friend. Kyle had introduced himself during intermission, charming and suave, and after the performance he'd extended Kay an invitation to his show-opening the following week in the city.

The torrid fling had lasted only a couple months. In fact, Gunderson's retirement bash had been their last date. Kay had gotten a call from a witness around midnight just as Kyle had been sliding the short black dress off her hips in her bedroom, and that had been the last she'd seen of him. He hadn't waited for her to come home, but had driven back to New York that night. And the relationship—if it could be called that—simply faded. Kay always imagined that Kyle had met someone more in-line with his lifestyle, someone who didn't work wild shifts or get call-outs in the middle of sex.

Truth was, she never really missed Kyle, which had spoken volumes about the true worth of the relationship.

"Here's another witness report of a guy in a panel van

with some kind of butcher-shop sign on the side," Finn said. "You think it's connected?"

Kay checked her watch, startled to discover it was almost 1:00 a.m. "If it's not, then we're looking at a hell of a lot of coincidences."

"You think Gunderson might be onto something with his slaughterhouse theory?"

Kay nodded.

"Are there even any slaughterhouses still operating in the city? I thought all the meatpacking plants moved out years ago."

"I think we need to find out," Kay said, not liking the images that scrambled through her exhausted brain. "And I think we need to start talking to butchers."

13

THE PIGS WERE RESTLESS.

It had probably been one of them squealing that had startled Micky from her sleep. If she could call it sleep on her makeshift bed in the corner of the dirt-floor pen. She'd been dreaming of Emma again. Hearing her infant daughter's cries, a high-pitched keening from down a dark hallway, making her breasts ache.

Micky lifted her head from the musty blanket she'd balled up as a pillow and listened. The pigs grunted in their sleep in the next pen.

Then Micky listened beyond that. Something else. Not the pigs.

Panic threatened to paralyze her. Her eyes wide, taking in what little light crept through the slatted-board exterior, she scanned for any movement within the dark shed. Was he here? Watching her?

Twice now she'd woken to find him standing on the other side of the steel partition staring at her.

No. She was alone.

Just the pigs.

She hated those pigs. Their stink. Their shit.

Shivering, more from hunger pangs and the low-simmering fear that cramped her insides, Micky clutched the thin, moth-eaten blanket tight over her bare shoulders. She wasn't cold. At night the shed retained a lot of the heat from the relentless sun, but no matter how high the temperatures, the scratchy, threadbare blanket had become a shield of sorts and she refused to take it off.

He'd stripped off her clothes that first night. Completely. Hadn't even left her panties on. She didn't remember him doing it though. Only remembered waking naked, vulnerable, in a fetal position on the dirt floor of the pen with the shackle on her ankle.

The heavy, iron shackle. Micky had no idea where he could have gotten such an archaic device, but the hinged fetter with its crude steel lock looked newly forged, the iron gleaming. She'd already tested its strength and knew the only way out was with the shackle still around her ankle. Unless she could somehow snag the key hanging on the post across the aisle. She was certain the large, medieval-looking key belonged to the shackle's lock and that he'd hung it deliberately in sight but out of reach to taunt her.

She'd spent whole hours staring at that key, looped over the rusted spike, could almost see it through the pitch-dark now.

Curled up in the nest she'd made for herself of straw

and the old blankets she'd found in the enclosure, Micky winced as she tucked her legs tighter into her body, the locked shackle biting into her flesh. The iron edges hadn't been filed properly and her skin was chaffed and weeping.

She kept the flies off it with the blanket. Keeping them off her scalp, however, hadn't been so easy. The injury she'd sustained to the back of her head when he'd taken her down two nights ago on Harlem Avenue had bled profusely, and the dried blood attracted the flies. When she was awake, she could keep them off, but when she'd collapse, exhausted from working at the large eyebolt sunk deep into the foundation beam where the shackle's chain was attached, she'd wake to feel the flies crawling over the crusted wound.

She worried about infection. Worried about the maggots that could start hatching if the flies laid their eggs.

Two days. And now her third night, and *still* she had no idea what he wanted from her. He hadn't touched her. At least, not that she remembered.

Her memory was scattered from Saturday night. She remembered the sting operation and her argument with Mack. She remembered walking up Govans, and then she'd been blindsided.

After that, there was the drive. The city lights flitting past when she'd regained consciousness briefly, the eerie glow of the dashlights illuminating his face and the wildness in his eyes when he'd looked over at her. And then him pounding on her again, punching her in the ribs and head until she'd passed out a second time.

She'd woken just before daybreak, screaming until her throat was raw and dry, but he hadn't come. Not for hours. And when he did, he hadn't looked at her as he'd unceremoniously dropped a plastic bucket into her pen, ignoring the questions and curses she yelled at him.

There'd been a bottle of water in the bucket. He'd given her one this morning as well. Warm and stale. But she'd refused the bucket of scraps: bread crusts, apple cores, a browned banana, two stale doughnuts with red jelly leaking out. The flies had buzzed around the bucket all day until he'd come back and fed the untouched contents to the pigs. Again, saying nothing to her.

There'd been no scraps today, and Micky had already sworn to herself that no matter what was in the next bucket he offered, she'd eat. She had to maintain her strength. She knew her blood sugar was low. Her muscles were shaky, and her pulse felt thready as her heart tripped over itself inside her chest.

So she would eat. For Emma.

And she would fight. The first chance she got. She'd beat the son of a bitch senseless.

Because she *would* see her daughter again.

And because they were looking for her. Macklin. Her fellow Vice detectives. Probably Homicide was working the case too. As Micky tried to find sleep on her make-shift bed, she wondered who would be heading the investigation. She wondered if they knew her, if they cared about her beyond her being a fellow officer.

Curling up even tighter, Micky tried to comfort herself with the reassurance that they were coming for her. She ran the thought through her mind, over and over, as she hugged herself and rocked. And she pretended it was Andy's arms around her now.

But somewhere between wake and sleep, in that lull before dropping off, the door of the shed flew open. The boards slammed against the concrete barrier the same instant the lights blazed on. Two bare, hundred-watt bulbs hanging from dusty cords burned into her eyes.

Micky squinted as she drew herself up. She clasped the blanket tighter around her.

The pigs started up now, roused by his entrance, deep snorting and throaty squeals.

But he was coming for her. Bypassing the pigs' pen, following the narrow aisle. And he was moving fast.

He ducked past a set of hanging scales, then kicked a bucket out of his path, the tin clattering as it bounced down the passageway. At the gate he stopped.

He teetered there for a moment, bracing himself against the steel railing. His white shirt was stained and the buttons misaligned. As his bleary eyes held hers, Micky wondered if he'd been drinking.

"What do you want?" she dared to ask him, her heart in her throat. "Just tell me what you want."

He didn't budge.

The low ceiling made him appear even bigger, and with the light behind him now, she couldn't make out his expression.

"Say something," she demanded.

But he didn't. Instead, with a sort of grace, he lifted one leg high over the barrier. Then the other.

Micky swallowed her cry.

This was it. He was going to kill her.

She was sure of it.

He must have finally discovered she was a cop. And now he was going to kill her.

No!

You have to fight, Luttrell. For Emma.

But she was frozen. Her fingers numb, her legs like rubber.

And he was fast.

Before she'd even managed to scrabble off the make-shift bed, he was on her. With one violent yank of the chain attached to her ankle, he took her down.

Instantly dazed, Micky felt the wind rush out of her. Tasted her own blood on her lip.

"Just tell me . . . what you want," she said again, in be-tween gulps for air. "I'll do . . . whatever . . ."

But he wasn't listening.

He drove her into the floor of the pen, his knee crush-ing the small of her back, as he forced her face into the dirt and brittle straw. She felt him grapple with the blan-ket, and when he swore, Micky realized it was the first time she'd heard him speak.

And then she felt him. Groping beneath the blan-ket, calluses rough against her bare thighs, her buttocks. Micky gasped, her sharp intake of breath sounding more like a whimper. She hated the show of weakness.

"Fucking asshole!" She tried to buck him off, but he was strong. Too strong. And the more she struggled the harder he pushed her into the dirt until she could hardly breathe.

"What the fuck do you want from me? You wanna rape me, you fucker? You want a piece—"

But Micky's words were lost in her cry then. Part shock, part pain, as his thick, work-roughened fingers rammed inside her. The wide knuckles tore against her dry labia and vaginal opening as he thrust his raping fin-gers even deeper inside her, then groped around as if he was searching for something.

Her eyes watered and she bit back her cry.

And then, without a word and just as quickly, he with-drew.

She thought she heard him wipe his hand on his pants, then leave the enclosure and stomp back down the aisle in his work boots. But Micky didn't look.

Only once she heard the snap of the light switch and the slam of the door did she dare move. In the pitch blackness, she crawled across the dirt floor, the chain dragging behind her, groping for the straw bed.

And as the pigs in the next pen shifted and grunted in the dark, Micky drew her knees tight against her chest and rocked herself. She swallowed back her tears, refusing to cry. Because crying was weakness. And for Emma she would be strong.

14

Tuesday, July 31

"MICKY LUTTRELL HAS BEEN MISSING well over forty-eight hours." Standing in front of the boardroom's main whiteboard, Savalas addressed the task force she'd assembled: Kay, Finn, and Bobby, Purnell and Mitchell, as well as John Nolan and Ricky Corbett, all from Savalas's squad.

"As per our statewide BOLO," Savalas went on, "we've got the districts, counties, and state police pulling over red pickup trucks. Nothing so far."

Finn guessed he wasn't the only one in the room who noticed the sergeant's anxiety as she punched holes in the lip of her styrofoam cup with her thumbnail. She looked small this morning. Beaten almost. The stress of the case already beginning to take its toll. Her normally dark complexion was pale, and with her hair drawn into a severe ponytail, the puffiness around her eyes seemed even more pronounced. Finn knew the brass had to be riding her ass hard with the Luttrell case.

"We've got just about every resource we could want at our disposal," she went on. "All we need is a direction to point them in. In the meantime, Captain Gorman has pulled our squad out of the rotation, meaning we won't be catching any new homicides until Micky Luttrell is found. I want everyone on this."

Finn didn't need to look across the table to Kay to sense the quiet disapproval bristling from her. Last night on the boat she'd spoken freely about her concerns of having Savalas at the helm of the task force, rightfully worrying that the sergeant would too quickly cash in on the resources offered to her and turn the entire case into a class-A cluster fuck that could cost Micky her life.

Finn knew Kay had already connected emotionally with Micky. He'd watched it start at the Luttrell house on Sunday as they'd gone through Micky's belongings. He'd seen it in the way Kay looked at the Luttrells' infant daughter. And then last night, on the boat, in the intensity with which she'd poured over the files from Gunderson's boxes.

If anyone was going to find Micky, it was Kay.

Yes, Finn understood her intensity. He admired it. Respected it. And he missed it.

She sat forward in her chair now, brushing a hand through her hair and sweeping the blunt cut behind one ear as she opened the case file in front of her.

Finn let his gaze linger.

"Kay, can you brief us on the status of the evidence?" Savalas asked then.

Kay cleared her throat. "We won't have the official reports for at least a week, but we do have confirmation from the Lab that the DNA found on the cap from Harlem Avenue matches the second blood source. So, we're assuming *this* is our perp's." She stood then, color photocopies of the faded ball cap in hand.

She gave one of them to Bobby beside her and slid the rest across the table. "What have we got on this Morgan Hunt and Fish Club?" Kay asked Bobby.

"I've got feelers out."

"We need more than feelers. I want a location. Members' names. Someone knows our guy," Kay said. "We've also got the perp's DNA profile running through CODIS. If we get a hit, we'll have direction. In the meantime . . ." Kay reached for a file folder and withdrew a computer-generated list. Handed out copies.

Finn recognized the first half dozen names from Gunderson's collected case files. Names, case numbers, dates, location of their abduction, and dump sites where applicable.

Kay mustn't have slept at all last night.

"This is a list of cases involving missing or murdered prostitutes," she started, but Savalas stopped her.

"These date back fifteen years, Detective," she said, list in hand.

"Twenty actually, yes. And a lot of them have similarities to Micky's abduction. Especially this Jane Doe." Kay sent Gunderson's copy of the vehicular homicide file sliding across the boardroom table.

Savalas caught the file, but Kay didn't wait for her to peruse it.

"We need a current status on all these cases," Kay continued, regarding her list. "Whether they're closed.

Whether a suspect was found, questioned, arrested, whatever. We need lists of the evidence, witnesses with current addresses so we can reinterview. And there are more cases. Dozens, probably hundreds, of missing prostitutes."

As Kay filled in the team on Gunderson's Jane Doe, Finn thought of the other box still on his galley table. Last night, at 2:00 a.m., he'd suggested she leave it so he could continue working through the files, and now he wondered if she'd expected him to itemize each case as she'd obviously done with the other box.

"I'm not sure this is the direction we need to be going right now, Detective," Savalas interrupted at last, her back rigid and her fine jaw clenched.

"I'm afraid it is." Kay's voice was sharp but calm. "I had the Lab run a comparison on hairs found on the Jane Doe and the hairs from our suspect's cap." She met Savalas's eyes squarely then. "They match."

She held up one of the photos illustrating the violent demise of the Jane Doe. "*This* is somehow related to Micky's disappearance. And I want to know how." She tacked the photo up onto the display board alongside those taken the morning of Micky Luttrell's disappearance.

"Through a number of these prostitute cases there is one common thread," she said. "And that is the possible link of a slaughterhouse. Whether it's witness accounts of the smell of pigs or a butcher's van or a description that could match our suspect in this case, these *are* connected."

"So, what, you think this guy's a butcher?" Bobby asked.

"Not necessarily a butcher," Kay said. "Maybe a slaughterer. With this pig manure angle in the Jane Doe case and with witnesses along Edmondson remembering the smell of pigs on this guy, we're looking at someone who's dealing with *live* animals, not just dead ones.

This isn't someone working in a meatpacking plant or a butcher shop."

"So someone who actually does the killing?"

Kay nodded. "I've already checked with the city's licensing office, and there's only one slaughterhouse still operating inside city limits. Krajishnik's on Ostend. It's been operating for decades and was certainly in operation when Gunderson's Jane Doe was found only two blocks away. As far as I can tell, and unless someone is keeping pigs as pets, Krajishnik's slaughterhouse is the only place within the city limits where we should be finding pig shit."

15

KRAJISHNIK & SONS sat at the end of Ostend Street in south Baltimore, in the heart of Pigtown, surrounded by a high, wooden fence boasting large NO TRESPASSING signs.

When Kay and Finn pulled up to the windowless structure there was no red pickup truck.

"You'd think there'd be some kind of ordinance against killing animals in the city," Finn said as they left the car. He pointed north, past the railway tracks. "Shopping center right there. A school one block over. Houses on the other side of the fence. It just seems so barbaric."

Kay agreed.

Through the front doors of Krajishnik's, Kay and Finn found themselves in a wide, cool vestibule. To their right was a walk-in freezer door, and to their left a glass entrance for customers. Straight ahead a windowed door—smeared with brown fingerprints—looked into the butchering area.

The dense, miasmic odor of blood and viscera permeated the place. Not too dissimilar from the basement of the medical examiner's office downtown, Kay thought, only here, there was the underlying rankness of animal waste.

Finn was right behind her as Kay entered the "store" area. At a Formica-covered counter, she rang a service bell next to an old-fashioned register. Past it, through a long, open serving window, men in stained aprons and white hairnets worked at several stainless-steel stations. One of them made eye contact and shouted, "Jewel! Customer!" just before a band saw revved up.

There was the high-pitched scream of the blade as it ripped through a large slab of meat, and then the odor of burning bone.

"Jewel" came through the swinging door. She was a large, plain-looking girl with masculine features and a thin-lipped smile. "Help you?"

"I'm Detective Delaney. This is Detective Finnerty." Kay opened the folder on the counter and spread out the two E-FIT-generated composites. "I need to know if either of these men look familiar."

The girl shook her head. "I don't think so."

"Are you sure?" Finn asked from behind Kay. "It might have been a while ago. Ten . . . fifteen years ago."

Still she shook her head, and Kay guessed that Jewel had probably been only five years old when the Jane Doe's mangled body had been found several blocks away.

"Can we talk to Mr. Krajishnik?"

"He's in the back. C'mon."

They met her in the vestibule, and she ushered them into the bright cutting area.

Kay had never seen so much meat. Racks of ribs,

Whole sides of pigs and what she guessed were lamb carcasses hanging from large hooks.

The concrete floor felt slippery, no doubt slick with the transfer of fat from under the employees' shoes. Five men worked in the cutting area, manning saws and wielding knives, slicing easily through the marbled slabs of meat, tossing trim into buckets and filleting meat off bone with frightening skill. All far removed from the neatly wrapped trays in the Metro Food where Kay shopped.

Jewel stopped at a double-wide set of swinging doors and opened it far enough to lean into the next room. "Dad. Couple of detectives here," she shouted. "They're looking for some guy."

When Jewel stepped back, she held the door open for them.

Neither the butchering area nor Kay's vivid imagination had prepared her for the slaughtering chamber. The narrow, windowless room was rank with the smell of death, blood, bile, and feces, the air warm with the presence of so much blood.

Kay's eyes adjusted to the damp murkiness. Looming in front of her, with heavy chains secured around each hock, two massive steers hung from a heavy steel railing that ran the length of the room. The closest animal had been completely decapitated, while the other—no doubt in the same condition—had been lowered shoulder-deep into a large steel barrel.

The barrel hadn't caught all the blood. Not nearly.

In the dimness Kay spotted Mr. Krajishnik in the far corner. A tall, rawboned man, he glanced up. "Best stay there," he said, and finished hosing a powerful stream of water across the blood-washed floor, flushing it all into a wide gutter.

He tossed the hose aside, and the soles of his high rubber boots skated across the greasy surface as he joined them. "So who're you after?" Krajishnik looked to be in his late fifties. He had a handsome face with an easy smile that seemed out of place in the gore surrounding them.

Kay withdrew one of the composites and held it up for Krajishnik. "We need to know if you recognize this individual."

Krajishnik looked at it long and hard, and the longer he looked the higher Kay's hopes soared.

But then Krajishnik shook his head. "Sorry."

"What about this one?" Kay handed him the second composite. "An employee maybe? Past or present?"

"You looking for *two* guys?" he said, obviously—like Kay—seeing no similarity between the two composites.

"Do either of them seem familiar in any way?"

Krajishnik shook his head again. "Sorry. I don't hire on that many workers. My boys all work full-time for me, and then I got maybe a half dozen who do contract."

"What about suppliers?" Finn asked. "Guys who bring in the livestock?"

"I don't think so. It's the long hair," Krajishnik said, shoving a thumb in the direction of the composites Kay returned to the folder. "Don't see many hippies these days."

And just as Kay wondered if Krajishnik had spotted Finn's small ponytail, the man's eyes flitted to Finn, clearly realizing his faux pas just then.

He shrugged it off. "So what're these guys wanted for?"

"We're not at liberty to say." Kay held up the photo of the cap. "What about this? Do you recognize the patch?"

"Sorry."

"Do any of your employees drive a red pickup?" Finn asked.

Krajishnik thought for a moment as he took up a knife, then expertly ran the blade along the sharpening steel hanging from his waist in a repetitive and expert motion. "Nope. Sure does look like you two are barking up the wrong tree."

He moved back to the steer over the barrel and reached for a dangling hand-switch. With a button he started a hydraulic hoist, and the steer over the bucket came up. The head was still on, but a wide, gruesome swath had been cut through its thick throat, exposing muscle, sinew, and arteries.

"What about *past* employees, Mr. Krajishnik?" Kay asked, wanting out of the slaughtering chamber.

"You're asking a lot of my memory, Detective. You got copies of those pictures?" he asked, pointing to the file with his knife.

"Yes."

"Why don't you leave them," he suggested, starting to work at the steer's mutilated neck. "Maybe something'll come to me. In the meantime, I can have my daughter send you a list of employees. Will that work for you?"

"Absolutely. But we'll need the list to include the past fifteen years."

"No problem."

"Thank you, Mr. Krajishnik." And she was out the door before Finn.

Kay couldn't get out of the slaughterhouse fast enough. Leaving the composites and her card with Jewel, she welcomed the heat of the day as the humidity settled on her chilled skin.

"Where next?" Finn asked.

Kay shook her head. "There aren't any other slaughterhouses in the city."

"Then we broaden the field. Include the counties."

"Farms too," she said, realizing the enormity of what she was suggesting even as she said it. "Any place we'd find pigs."

She looked at her watch. Micky Luttrell had been missing fifty-nine hours.

"We need a goddamn break," she said, throwing open the passenger door of the Impala.

Finn started up the police car and cranked the AC. "Why don't we grab some lunch," he said. "I'll bet you haven't had breakfast."

"I'm not hungry."

"Come on, a big juicy tofu burger. On me."

She caught his smile and realized then how much she'd missed it over the past year. She wanted to tell him that, but she wouldn't.

When Finn steered out of Krajishnik's lot, Kay's cell phone went off at her hip.

It was Savalas. She sounded a little surprised that Kay had answered so quickly.

"Lab just called," her sergeant told her, and even over the static of the connection Kay could hear Kojak's anxiousness. "We got a hit. On CODIS. Two of them."

16

"YES, WE GOT TWO HITS. But not on any known perps." The chief DNA analyst in the Crime Lab on the tenth floor of Headquarters had met Kay and Finn at the front counter with a file in her hand. Alexandra Domokos, with her soft green eyes and a glowing smile, was too attractive for the cold, sterile setting of the lab and the perpetually crisp lab coat, Finn had often thought.

"When you run comparisons through CODIS," Domokos explained, "the database checks against not only known felon profiles, but also against evidence from past crime scenes. So what we *got* was two hits on profiles from old cases. And you're lucky to have those."

"What do you mean?"

"Do you remember a couple years back when ABC News and the police department joined forces, splitting the cost of fifty DNA tests in unsolved rape cases?"

Finn shook his head even though he vaguely remembered the stunt.

"It was all to show what could be done if police departments actually had the budget to process every rape kit for DNA. That effort by ABC alone got five cases solved and one innocent man exonerated," Domokos said. "And now there's the two your profile got hits on. They were part of that original fifty."

"Wait, the hits came from rape cases?" Kay asked. "Not homicides? So the victims are still alive?"

"They certainly were when your guy left them." She handed over the file and Kay opened it immediately, scanning the printouts. "One attack occurred nine years ago, the other seven. Those are your victims' names, date of birth, state arrest record where applicable. I dread to think how many other women this guy may have raped. Right now there are over five thousand unsolved cases with intact, biological evidence like rape kits, all of them backlogged and collecting dust on departmental shelves awaiting DNA analysis. The ABC venture pulled only fifty of those.

"Fifty cases out of five thousand," Domokos repeated.

"I don't know about you, Detectives, but I don't like the math. Either this guy's a prolific serial rapist or it's pure coincidence that his two assaults made it into that fifty-case pool."

Finn could feel Kay's energy as she closed the file, thanked Domokos, and turned out of the Lab. She even opted for the stairs, as though the elevator couldn't get them down to the eighth-floor offices fast enough.

Five minutes later, in the cubicle she now shared with Bobby, Kay was at the computer bringing up the Department's online systems, linking to the MVA, Department of Corrections, and finally accessing Auto Track, a database of information compiled from public records. Her fingers flew across the keyboard.

It felt strange standing in the cubicle he'd once shared with Kay. Involuntarily, Finn scanned her work area, searching for evidence of the life she was now living. He looked to the photos she had tacked to the baffle of her cubicle.

The first was a photo Finn knew she'd had for years. One of her and Joe Spencer with the fully geared Quick Response Team in the background. Kay looked a little washed-out, wearing her black Kevlar vest over a white T-shirt, Joe's arm flung over her small shoulders. Kay's first arrest in Homicide.

Next to it was a photo of Kay's dad, back in Maine, a skein of fishing net over one shoulder as he stood on the deck of his boat. Finn had taken the photo himself of Frank Delaney when he and Kay had visited two years ago. Finn wondered how the old man was doing. He and Frank Delaney had hit it off. Maybe too well for Kay's taste.

Of course, what Finn remembered most about that visit was the long drive home, the dead-quiet stretches of

I-95, Kay silent in the passenger seat, and he not knowing what he could possibly say to take everything back.

He'd gone about the marriage proposal all wrong. Overcome by the sudden sense of tradition, Finn had made his biggest mistake in his relationship with Kay by asking her dad first. Since then, Finn had often wondered if Kay might have said yes if he'd handled the whole proposal differently.

And finally, in the row of photos, was a shot taken at the BPD annual awards ceremony where Kay and Finn had both received Bronze Stars for ending the vicious spree of an insatiable killer. A killer who'd almost added Kay to his list one night three years ago in the basement of a funeral home. The shot was of Finn and Kay, with Gunderson standing between them.

Finn stared at Kay's image, sexy in her formfitting, short dress, and wondered if she kept the photo because of Gunderson. Or because of him.

And as Finn scanned the rest of her desk, he was surprised at his relief when he found no evidence of Kyle Taithleach.

He'd kicked himself for giving in to his jealousy and asking Kay about the New York painter last night. *And* he'd kicked himself for not telling Kay the truth.

When she'd left the boat at 2 a.m., suggesting she let him get home to Angie, Finn hadn't corrected Kay. Letting her believe the marriage was still intact.

A lie by omission, but still a lie.

Three months had passed since he'd left Angie. For the second time.

It had been his ex-wife who'd pushed for the reunion last year, and in the wake of nearly losing Maeve, his only surviving child, to a killer who had taken the life of her best friend, Finn had been overcome with the need for a sense of home. A sense of belonging.

And by then Kay had made it amply clear that he wasn't going to find that with her. First the marriage proposal, and then she'd turned down the idea of them buying a house together.

All things considered, it had been a remarkably easy breakup, with Kay simply stating she understood. Sometimes Finn had admired her for that, for her maturity and insight in recognizing her inability to meet his needs the way he thought Angie could. But other times Finn resented her for not even fighting, for not wanting to at least try.

As for him and Angie, it hadn't been long before they'd slipped into their old habits. The familiar walls had started to come up as the long hours of Homicide took their toll. And by the time Ang confronted him, wanting to work on the issues, Finn already had too much on his plate. New battles he wasn't willing to share with Angie.

Or with Kay.

Another lie by omission.

"I'm not finding anything on this first victim," Kay said then. "A couple possession charges after the rape, but then nothing. And Auto Track can't find her after her last release. It's like she fell off the face of the earth."

"Or under it," Finn suggested. "She could be buried in a ditch or rotting in some vacant row house, dead of an overdose. Wouldn't be the first prostitute who just up and disappeared."

"She never had a solicitation charge."

"What?"

Kay shook her head, staring at the screen. "She wasn't a prostitute. And neither was this other victim, Stacey

Blyth. She's got no criminal record. In fact . . ." Kay punched at the keyboard, waited for the screen to refresh. "Stacey Blyth, age twenty-four, appears alive and well and is currently a student at Johns Hopkins."

17

STACEY BLYTH LIVED in a bright, one-bedroom apartment on the 2600 block of North Charles Street, three blocks down from the Hopkins campus. When she answered her door, Kay barely recognized the girl from the photos in her case file, photos taken at Mercy Hospital the night of her attack, her face battered and swollen.

Blyth was a pretty girl with a fit figure and short, brown hair. Gray streaks were already visible and the lines in her face made her look older than her twenty-four years. Kay wondered if it was genetic or if the attack seven years ago had prematurely aged the girl.

Finn had agreed to let Kay handle the interview alone. Rape victims were far more likely to open up to women and were often skittish around strange men.

Blyth was no exception.

Now, as Kay perched on the edge of the white sofa, she made small talk with the girl, about school, her roommate, her studies. On the coffee table between them sat a half dozen heavy textbooks: *Molecular and Computational Biophysics, Biochemistry, Thermodynamics, Molecular Genetics.*

Kay liked Stacey Blyth. Wearing a pair of gray flannel boxers and an oversize T-shirt, Stacey cradled a mug in her hands. With her legs drawn up beneath her in a deep armchair, the girl appeared to relax by degrees.

"I don't have classes Tuesdays," she told Kay.

Unlike her roommate. Becka was a tall, slender woman with dark, almost exotic, features who'd excused herself shortly after their introduction to prepare for class.

"So what happened?" Stacey asked, the tightness in her voice betraying her otherwise relaxed composure. "Did you get the guy?"

"Not exactly," Kay told her.

"Did he rape someone else?"

"Probably. You definitely weren't his only victim."

"You said you're Homicide?" Blyth asked then. "So he killed someone then?"

"We're not certain." Kay silently weighed her options. Giving Blyth too much information about Micky Luttrell's attack would breach the confidentiality Kay preferred to maintain on the case. But not enough and Blyth would be unable to sympathize and might opt to give Kay nothing.

"Well," Blyth stated then, "if you get the guy, I'm telling you right now, I'm not testifying. I already told that to that TV producer when he came around here a couple years ago, talking about how they'd pulled my rape kit for testing." When she glanced up at Kay then, Blyth looked torn. "It's not that I don't want to help, but you gotta understand, I've spent the past seven years trying to forget that night. I'm not going to sit in a courtroom and have to relive it all over again . . . have to look at him."

When Blyth's roommate walked into the living room then, a leather bookbag over one shoulder, there was concern in her face as she moved to Blyth. She settled one slim hand on Blyth's shoulder, and Kay realized in the gesture that the girls were more than roommates.

"You sure you don't want me to stay?" Becka asked her.

Blyth shook her head. "I'll be fine."

Blyth's partner leaned in then, pressed a quick kiss to her lips. "My cell's on, babe."

Blyth nodded but remained silent as her partner slipped into her runners in the foyer, and Kay couldn't help thinking about Finn's daughter, wondering whether Maeve had told her father yet that she was gay. Kay had found out herself just last year, during her and Finn's investigation into several serial murders that included Maeve's friend. But Julia Harris had been more than a friend of Maeve's, Kay had discovered during one visit to the girl's hospital bed, and as far as Kay could tell, Maeve had kept the full extent of her grief to herself.

Not until Becka had closed the door behind her and the dead bolt slid home did Blyth finally meet Kay's eyes.

"I was gay before that son of a bitch raped me," she said, her voice flat and matter-of-fact.

Kay nodded.

"All that son of a bitch did was make me not trust men."

"Tell me about the attack," Kay asked, hoping that in her partner's absence Blyth would open up more on the subject. "I know it's not easy but—"

Blyth shook her head.

And Kay knew she'd have to tell her.

"Listen, Stacey, this isn't something that'll be released to the media, but we know, through DNA, that the man who raped you . . . he attacked an undercover police officer Saturday night."

"The woman on the news?"

Kay nodded, hoping she'd struck a soft spot. "Micky Luttrell is your age, Stacey. She has a husband who loves her. And she has a newborn daughter."

Blyth listened.

"I won't lie to you," Kay went on, "if this goes to trial, your testimony would definitely help, and the State's Attorney's Office will push for it. But right now, I don't care whether you testify or not. My primary concern is for Detective Luttrell's life."

"So you think she's still alive?"

"I'm counting on it. And anything you can tell me about your attacker could help me find her."

The girl's knuckles were white around her ceramic mug.

"I need your help, Stacey," Kay urged, then let the silence fill the apartment. Hoping, praying, that the girl would feel obliged to fill it. And when Stacey Blyth finally looked up, she wiped a tear from her cheek.

Her voice was thin. A little shaky. "I saw him on the corner. From the bus stop. I was waiting for the number eight. I was the only person there."

She clenched her jaw several more times, the memory clearly distressing her. "He looked like he was just out walking, you know?"

"He didn't have a vehicle?" Kay had expected another report of the red pickup or a butcher's van.

"No. No car. And I remember he checked his watch once and kept looking back over his shoulder, so I figured he was waiting for the bus too. When he got close though, I just didn't get a good feeling about him."

"So you got a good look at him?"

Blyth shook her head. "Even if the lighting had been better, I was trying to avoid eye contact with the guy."

Kay opened the file folder she'd brought and handed the two E-FIT composites to the girl.

Blyth shook her head, handed them back. "It was a long time ago."

"What *do* you remember about him?" Kay asked.

"Just that there was this *feel* about him, you know?" Blyth bit her lip, and when she looked to the mantel of the fake brick fireplace, Kay saw she stared at a framed photo of her and Becka, as though to take strength from it.

"When he reached the bus stop, he kept walking," Blyth continued. "And I remember being relieved. That's when he grabbed me."

She shook her head. "I don't remember how he got me into the alley, but I know I fought him. And I screamed. But no one came. I remember thinking how weird that was, you know? How *no* one heard me?"

Kay nodded.

"Once we were in the alley though, he threatened me. Told me if I screamed again, he'd kill me."

"Did he have a weapon?"

"He told me he had a knife."

"But you didn't see it?"

"I was seventeen, Detective. He said he had a knife and I believed him. He threatened to cut my throat and gut me right there in that alley."

The image of the slaughtered steer over the barrel with its throat slashed wide-open at Krajishnik's this morning flashed in Kay's mind. "He used that word? 'Gut'?"

Blyth nodded. "Gut me 'like an animal,' he said. And then, when he started pulling at my clothes, at my pants, I just kept thinking that it wasn't really happening, you know? I mean, you read about this kind of thing. You see it on TV. But it doesn't actually happen. Not to you."

Kay nodded again, silent.

"He had me alongside a Dumpster. And there were trash cans. He pushed me into them, face-first, and if I tried to turn, he'd threaten me more."

The toll of reliving the memories was visible in the young girl's strained features. "Once he got my pants down, I think I knew I wasn't getting out of it. I remember hearing the bus drive by. It didn't even slow down because there wasn't anyone at the stop, but I screamed anyway, and he smashed my face into the trash can. I was bleeding and crying. And I kept thinking that I had to stay alive. That I had to just give in."

Blyth's voice grew softer. Kay knew what was coming, and she fought the urge to take the girl's hand, to tell her she could stop. But she needed her to remember. Needed her to relive that savage night.

"He had my shirt, was almost choking me with it. And he had ahold of my hair too. Then . . . he used his teeth too."

Kay remembered a photo in the file she'd scanned on the drive over with Finn, taken at Mercy, of the bite marks along Blyth's shoulder.

"And . . . and when he came inside of me, he smashed my face into the trash can. Three, maybe four times. I think I blacked out. But when I came to, he was still on top of me. I could hardly breathe."

Blyth swallowed hard, fighting back the tears. "And that's when he raped me the second time. Anally." Her voice was so soft Kay wasn't sure she'd heard right. "He raped me anally. I don't think he came that time, and maybe that's what pissed him off. The last thing I remember, besides the pain, was him dragging me back and smashing my face into the side of the Dumpster." Her fingers went to her temple, tracing the mar of pale skin, and Kay knew—as with her own scars—that the memories would pulse behind that scar for the rest of Blyth's life.

"Next thing I remember was the medics," Blyth said finally.

"Is there anything else about him that you recall?" Kay asked. "Even the smallest detail. His hair. His eyes. Voice. Build."

"Whatever's in the reports from seven years ago. My memory won't be any better now than back then."

And Kay knew Blyth was right.

"There is something else though. I'm not sure it'll help." Blyth hesitated. "It's not in the reports."

"Go on." And Kay could tell by the agitation in the young girl's face that the hardest memory was yet to come.

"It was his skin. On his arms, the skin was all . . ."

"Bumpy?" Kay offered, remembering the hooker's description of the man in the red pickup.

"Yeah. Like he had all these warts or little tumors or something under his skin. I'll never forget how his skin looked, even in the little bit of light that came into the alley."

Stacey Blyth started to stand, as though to end the interview.

Kay stopped her. "I don't understand," she said, visualizing the rape in her mind again, playing it out as Blyth had described. "You said he had you turned, your back to him the whole time."

A flash of tension crossed Blyth's face. She nodded, but barely.

"And he had you pinned?"

Another nod.

"Then how could you have . . . ?"

Stacey Blyth bit her lip. Looked away.

"Stacey? How is it you saw his arms?"

When the girl finally spoke, her voice was broken. "I wasn't turned around the whole time. I mean, not exactly."

"Tell me."

She didn't wipe the tears that came now even as she clenched her jaw. "I never told the other detective, the woman from Rape. I was seventeen."

"You were embarrassed?"

Blyth nodded slowly.

"What else did he do to you, Stacey?"

She shook her head.

"What did he do?"

"After he raped me . . . the second time, he turned me around. Forced me to my knees."

Again, Kay wanted to stop her, wanted to take away the girl's memories right then. But she knew nothing could accomplish that.

"He forced me to my knees and stuck his cock in my face." Seven years of anger finally came out in Stacey Blyth's words now. "He pushed it into my face and told me to 'clean it off.' And . . . he didn't mean with my hands. The son of a bitch raped me again, on my knees, seventeen years old, like twice wasn't enough."

18

THE DOE WAS STILL ALIVE.

As Daryl Eugene Wardell approached the entangled animal, it froze, hoping to escape detection. It was a small doe. Skinny. Regarding it from thirty feet away, Daryl wondered if it was sick.

Its flanks heaved for air, and one wide eye locked onto

him. Daryl felt the animal's panic rising beneath the fear-paralyzed muscles.

All around him the forest crackled with the relentless drone of cicadas high in the maples and basswood. The dense odor of rotting vegetation compounded the heaviness in the air, and the afternoon humidity beaded sweat along his skin. Mosquitoes hovered at his face and head, their high-pitched buzzing like screams in his ears.

When Daryl swatted at one, the doe finally sprang.

But the razor wires instantly snapped her back.

Flighty, unpredictable animals. And stupid as shit, Daryl thought as he watched its destructive struggles. Legs flailing, head thrashing. The taut wires buried deeper and deeper into the animal's flesh. In a shaft of sunlight, Daryl saw fresh blood begin to flow down the doe's neck and haunch, brilliant red against its tawny hide.

Deer were always ruining his snares. Last year he'd spread coyote-urine powder around the traps to repel them, and it had helped, but he hadn't been as diligent about it this year.

Daryl swatted at more mosquitoes as he pushed through the laurel and knee-high ferns. The doe's thin legs were a flurry now, and Daryl wished he'd brought his twelve-gauge. Deer could do some serious damage with those flying hooves.

The doe's eyes were wild, nostrils flared, its mouth gaping for air as the wire across its throat drew even tighter. Daryl wondered how long it would take for the wire to cut all the way through. He contemplated just watching, basking in the doe's slow death. But the mosquitoes were relentless.

From his belt, Daryl drew out his Buck knife. The

weight of the four-inch blade with its gutting hook had always felt good in his hand.

It took three tries before he managed to snag the doe's flailing head, his left hand wrapping across the top of her bony muzzle. And with one determined sweep of the knife, the honed blade sliced cleanly through the animal's throat. Blood splashed the trunk of a tree and spilled across the foliage underfoot.

And Daryl watched closely. The slow fade of life. The exhilarating arrival of death.

Still holding the doe's head, he studied his own reflection in the animal's wide, black eye as she died, his silhouette fish-eyed against the backdrop of the deep woods and the smattering of sky that filtered through the dense canopy overhead. Not until the life was finally gone did he drop the doe's limp body to the forest floor.

There was the familiar twitching in his groin then. Deep and primal. One bloodied hand went to the crotch of his stained jeans, shifting the partial erection into a more comfortable position.

And then, raising the knife over his head, Daryl roared. The deer's life force circled him, its energy filling the small clearing and finally moving through him. He yelled again, his bellow reverberating through the deep woods.

It took work to untangle the dead animal, squatting in the blood-soaked leaves until his shirt was wet with sweat and blood, and the snare was completely destroyed. Standing at last, Daryl sized up the doe. The big chest freezer he kept running in the basement was full. The meat was useless to him. Still, he couldn't just leave it lying out here. In this heat it would be only a couple days before the carcass was bloated and rotting, the stench easily carried on the slightest breeze.

No. He'd have to get her to the pit.

Shimmying the animal up against the tree, he managed to drape it over his shoulders. His body still ached from the struggle he'd had with his girl Saturday night. And it wasn't like he was getting any younger, he thought to himself as he started off in the opposite direction of the house. Two more days he'd turn thirty-nine. He'd have to have himself his own little celebration.

Out in the shed.

And an involuntary smile came to his lips.

The thorned barberry bushes tore at his clothes as he navigated the rough slope down to the pit. There wasn't any visible path. He knew better than that. Knew not to take the same route twice. Never create a mark on the forest floor. A trail only led others back to you.

A couple dozen yards from the pit, Daryl was surprised it didn't smell more. The old, abandoned well was a deep, dark hole straight down into the black earth. Roots had penetrated the stone walls, and years ago he'd lowered a pruner and a flashlight down into the shaft and cleared out what he could.

Still, it was plenty deep and the web of roots wasn't thick enough to prevent any rotting bits from slipping through into the farther depths.

Kicking aside the slatted cover, the stench of decay wafted out and the buzzing of flies filled the air. It had been over a year since he'd had to toss a whole girl down there. But there'd been the stillborn piglets from this spring, plus the remains of another previously snared deer.

Daryl dropped the doe, resting briefly before he heaved it over the bricked-up lip of the well. He watched it drop into the dark, a tangle of bloodied legs, and wondered if he had any lime left back at the house.

Heading up the slope to the house, Daryl's thoughts went to his girl. His erection still pressed against the zipper of his jeans. Last night when he'd checked, her menstruating had stopped. She was ready.

Sweating and covered in the doe's blood, he stepped into the clearing, leaving the forest and the mosquitoes behind. He looked past the house and the maze of rusted parts-vehicles to the shed. And massaging his growing hard-on, Daryl decided it was time.

19

KAY NEEDED A SMOKE. The craving only deepened with the lingering odor of cigarettes in the department's Impala that Finn and Scooby shared.

"You got any cigarettes?" she asked, checking the glove box.

Behind the wheel, Finn shook his head and merged into the southbound traffic of Saint Paul. Sunlight splintered off buildings and cars, glass and chrome, making it feel even hotter.

The need rose. Four years ago she'd kicked the habit. Cold turkey. Lying in a hospital bed for two weeks after the beatdown she'd suffered at the hands of Bernard Eales had made quitting a no-brainer. But still, at times, when the stress and frustration ate at her, Kay regretted quitting. This was one of those times.

Stacey Blyth's description of the rape had made Kay grateful she worked Homicide. After all, in murder cases she never had to hear the victims' pain in their own words, or see the emotional toll that violence exerted.

On murder scenes, the victims were already dead. Their pain over. It was only their body on the ground, another piece to the puzzle, evidence that would help Kay bring their killer to justice.

She'd tried to distance herself from Blyth's emotional account of the vicious assault, but internalizing the girl's suffering had been inevitable, and Kay had been affected more deeply than she'd been prepared for.

As Finn pulled alongside the curb outside a corner convenience store, Kay was still remembering how Blyth's hand had trembled in hers during their parting handshake.

"I'll be right back," Finn said, and Kay watched him circle the hood of the car and disappear inside the store.

Angling the AC vents, Kay let the chilled air blast her. She thought of Micky Luttrell, imagined the young cop in the hands of the man who had brutally assaulted Blyth.

Or had he already killed Micky?

When Finn returned, he tossed a pack of Camels into her lap, waited as she tore off the cellophane, then lit her up. Kay savored the smoke rolling to the back of her throat and curling down into her lungs, her nerves easing by degrees.

"How is it?" Finn asked, lighting one for himself.

"Tastes like shit. But it's good." She cracked the window. Took another few puffs. "Of course, now I'd really like a drink too."

He shared a quick smile. "She really got to you, didn't she? Blyth?"

Kay nodded.

"So are we looking at the same guy?"

Another deep draw on her cigarette. "Yeah, but the

MO's completely different," Kay said. "He raped her right there. No attempt to abduct her like he did Gunderson's Jane Doe."

"Maybe he found that taking them was too much trouble."

Kay couldn't live with Finn's theory though. Because that would mean he'd dragged Micky off, raped her, as he had Blyth, then dumped her body someplace.

"This is just so different from the Jane Doe," Kay said. And cigarette in hand, she described to Finn the seven-year-old rape.

"If the MO's so different, maybe the Lab screwed up," he suggested when she was done.

"No. It's the same guy. Blyth described the bumps on his skin."

Silence and smoke filled the interior of the Impala.

"How's this guy been working so long and not gotten caught?" Kay asked finally.

Finn shrugged. "He's careful. Knows what he's doing."

Kay shook her head. "He's sloppy, Finn. Dragging this girl into an alley less than fifty feet from a bus stop. That's just stupid."

"Or very bold. Either way, he's gotta trip up sooner or later."

"It needs to be sooner. For Micky's sake." Kay stared at the cigarette balanced in her fingers—as if it belonged there—torn between regretting the recidivism and wondering why she'd ever quit in the first place, when her cell vibrated at her hip.

Bobby's tension came through clear over the digital connection: "Savalas is after your head."

"Why?"

"Cuz you're not here. And Linus Mooney is."

Kay checked her watch. "Shit." She'd forgotten about her witness in the east Baltimore gang shooting.

"I got him out on a writ like you wanted," Bobby said. "He's down here for his statement. And sure as hell he ain't talking to me."

"Shit," she said again. "I'll be right there, Bobby." Kay crushed the butt into the ashtray as she nodded for Finn to pull into traffic. "Tell him ten more minutes. And he better be ready to talk."

20

SHE'D KNOWN IT WAS COMING.

It was only a matter of time. She'd imagined it happening, visualized how she would fight him, how she would never let the son of a bitch violate her.

But in the end, she'd barely stood a chance.

Micky shivered in spite of the sweat that dampened her skin beneath the musty wool. Knees drawn to her chest, she rocked herself. She sucked at her bottom lip and spat out blood, while her tears stung the abrasions across her cheeks.

Her gaze went to the empty water bottle lying in the dirt. She should have used some of the water to rinse the dirt from the deep scrapes, but instead, she'd used every last drop of it in a feeble and desperate attempt to wash him off her.

His smell.

His touch.

And his cum.

Micky closed her eyes and worked at blocking the images. But she knew they'd be with her forever.

Fortunately, it hadn't taken him long to get off. At least, not that she remembered. A lot of the attack was a blur of pain. Several times she thought she would black out. Wished she could.

Trembling, Micky touched her shoulder. Her fingertips fluttered over the painful lesions, and she felt the small, hot bumps that denoted each tooth mark.

He'd taken her from behind, like a fucking animal, forced her down across the straw bales near the corner of the pen she'd used to relieve herself for the past three days. The coarse stalks had ripped into her skin as he'd pinned her down, until he finally forced himself inside her with one hard, dry thrust that locked a scream in her throat.

He'd twisted her hair in one fist, and if she tried to struggle, if she so much as swore at him, he'd smash her face into the jagged straw. Over and over. Until her whole face was burning.

Micky hated herself.

Hated herself for letting it happen.

She'd had a plan. Its conception had come last night, as she'd lain awake. And in the first light of day, she'd traced a line in the dirt floor with her toe. A wide semicircle marking the outer limits of her reach, as far as the shackle and chain would allow.

Outside the circle, the pig-man was untouchable.

All so carefully strategized. Choreographed in her mind: him coming into the pen, stepping inside the line. He wouldn't stand a chance, she'd decided by noon, impatient and disappointed that he hadn't yet made his appearance. She'd imagined her fingers burying into his eye sockets. Imagined his screams when she'd ram the heel of her palm up and into his nose, breaking the soft cartilage, and driving it deep into the brain that nestled beneath that evil skull.

She'd been *so* ready.

And then . . .

Then she'd heard him out in the woods. Howling like a wild animal. And when she'd seen him through the slats of the shed, angling toward the shed, she'd known it was time.

But nothing had prepared her for the sight of him when he reached her pen. Clothes covered in blood. Even across his ugly face were blood smears, like warrior paint.

The vision had shocked her. Robbed her of the determination she'd spent all day building, and when she'd attacked, it was out of fear. And it was premature. He hadn't been inside the circle, and before she'd ever reached the end of her chain, he'd smiled, stepped calmly back, and shook his head as he made a tsk, tsk, tsk sound.

The miscalculation had not only blown her chances, but it had cost her her balance. Her own velocity had worked against her, the chain snapped taut, and she'd come down hard.

He'd moved fast, snatching up the chain and dragging her across the pen.

At some point, in the midst of his brutal thrusts deep inside her, Micky had surrendered. He would have killed her if she didn't. And when he'd come inside her, her body had gone limp, as if it weren't hers. As if it were only a shell he was violating.

She lay on the dirt floor, listening to him leave the shed, slamming the door behind him, and then she'd heard him out in the yard. Another curdling howl that sapped the last of her strength.

But she needed to be strong, Micky thought now.

She'd been strong all her life. Through all kinds of adversity.

Her mind went back to that turning point in her life. That one moment when she knew, beyond a doubt, that she was a survivor. The night a man named Giles Baldwin had broken into their home and slaughtered her adoptive parents in their bed while she had huddled in the crawl-space attic above her bedroom, listening to their screams echo up through the vents. She was a fighter, yes, but a survivor, number one. Somehow, at twelve years old, Micky had known that Baldwin would have killed her too, that there was nothing she could have done to help the Andersons. It was that night, and many others after it, that Micky had sworn she would survive.

This was no different.

On the other side of the partition, the pigs rutted in the muck and manure-soaked straw. So far, they'd left her alone, almost ignoring her presence in the corner pen. Six of them, she'd counted. They had the run of the shed, as well as the outdoor pen surrounding it, from what little she could see through the slats.

As Micky stood now, her legs shaky and her insides feeling bruised, she braced herself against the wall of the shed. She tried to ignore the pigs, but their deep guttural noises were different somehow. Insistent.

And when the largest of the pigs heaved himself up onto the partition, Micky gasped. He was enormous, almost taller than her, with his cloven feet buttressing his immense weight against the top bar. The flat, fleshy disk of his snout angled and snorted as he sniffed the air. Smelling her, Micky thought, while his beady black eyes fixed on her.

She screamed as she snatched up the fly-infested bucket

of scraps and hurled it at the boar. There was the satisfying clunk of the bucket meeting its mark, then his piercing squeal as he disappeared behind the partition again.

Micky wiped at her tears, angry now. Yes. She needed that anger, she thought. Needed to harness it. It had gone hand in hand with survival in her past.

Clutching the blanket tightly around her, Micky hobbled across the pen. And once more, with one toe, she redrew the line in the dirt floor.

Next time she'd be ready.

Next time she was going to kill him.

21

IN THE DIM COOLNESS of the Luttrells' kitchen, Finn watched Andy's futile struggles with his colicky daughter. He bounced her gently as he paced the narrow kitchen, desperate to soothe her crying. Finn couldn't help wondering how much of Andy's own anxiety fed the infant's agitation.

"Kay told me I shouldn't talk to them." Andy nodded to the street where two television satellite vans were a blur beyond the drawn lace curtains.

"Good advice," Finn said. The task force had already discussed the possibility of Luttrell appealing through the media for his wife's return, but even Savalas had agreed that too much media attention could force Micky's abductor's hand. Of course, that was assuming Micky Luttrell was still alive.

"Are you getting any sleep?" Finn asked.

Luttrell waited for a pause between the baby's cries. "Would *you* be able to?"

Finn shook his head and tried to imagine. If it was Kay missing, no, he wouldn't sleep. Couldn't. Every moment, every breath, would be about finding her.

The thought had barely passed through his brain when Finn realized the incongruity of the parallel he'd drawn. When challenged to put himself in Andy Luttrell's shoes, it was Kay he'd automatically thought of, not Angie. Not the woman he'd married, the mother of his children.

Kay.

When he'd pulled up to the back of Headquarters a half hour ago to drop her off, she'd seemed wound. He'd guessed part of it was the cigarette. She'd tossed the pack of Camels to him, unwilling to keep the temptation with her, and he'd wished her luck on her witness interview. But Finn had known her thoughts were with Micky, not the Ashland gang murder from last Monday night.

Kay hadn't spoken yet of the images that were forming in her mind about the man who'd taken Micky Luttrell three nights ago, but Finn knew they were taking root, especially after her interview with Stacey Blyth. He'd seen Kay on cases in the past. Obsessed. Fixated. Determined to grasp the psychology of the murderers she hunted, to comprehend their motives and instincts. And it was Kay's ability to get inside the heads of the men she sought that gave her an edge over any other partner Finn had worked with in his eighteen years on the force.

"You have no idea how hard it is to just sit here," Andy said over the wails of the baby, "while Micky's out there somewhere. I just feel so damn useless."

"You're taking care of your child, Andy."

The baby's face was red, her cries intensifying as Andy Luttrell's frustration rose.

Finn gestured to Andy for the infant. The baby was hot,

but not feverish, the terry-cloth jumper slightly damp.

"Have you tried rubbing her back?" Finn asked.

Andy shook his head, his face sagging with relief to have handed the baby over.

Emma Luttrell's wide blue eyes locked onto Finn's, and her crying eased simply on account of the change of scenery. Supporting her bobbing head, he turned her over, laying her across his lap, then gently rubbed her small, hot back.

"I had two of my own," he told Andy, remembering the long nights of Maeve's colic. Toby had been easy, but Maeve . . .

"Had?" Andy asked.

Finn nodded. "I lost my son."

"I'm sorry."

"It's all right." Finn hated apologies. So many *I'm sorrys*. Even eight years ago they'd sounded empty. Just like all those *It wasn't your faults* he'd heard too. Hollow, meaningless sentiment from people who couldn't remotely understand what it was like to live every day knowing that if he'd turned the wheel right instead of left and taken the hit from the eighteen-wheeler on *his* side of the Nissan his son might be alive today.

In his lap, the baby calmed. Her exhausted cries tapering into a pacified cooing.

"And the other?" Andy asked. "You said two."

"My daughter." Finn continued to rub Emma Luttrell's back, trying to remember Maeve this small. "Eighteen going on thirty," he said, handing the baby back to Andy.

He stood from the table then, making moves to leave, as Andy laid the infant in a bassinet.

"So you guys really don't think this has anything to do with the dealers down the block?" Andy asked.

"No. We've had the Western District brief us on their latest activity down here, and they've brought in several of the major players for questioning. We'll keep ourselves open to the possibility, but it's not looking like this is street-related. Like I said, though, we've got leads. We've got DNA." Finn had kept the details vague when he'd updated Andy upon his arrival. "We'll find her."

Andy nodded as he followed Finn to the foyer.

"Listen," Luttrell said at the door. "I know you say you've got this DNA evidence and all, but . . ."

When Andy's exhausted eyes met his, Finn could see his uncertainty. "What is it, Andy?"

"It's just, I think you need to be looking at Jack Macklin. I . . . I don't trust him."

"Did Micky ever say anything about him?"

"No, she wouldn't have. But from the day I met him . . . I just don't trust him."

"I've already talked to Macklin," Finn told him, remembering the Vice cop's hostility outside J-Ray's yesterday.

"Yeah?" Andy didn't seem reassured. "Well, for Micky's sake, don't let up on the son of a bitch."

22

"I'M NOT CUTTING THAT WEASEL a deal." Vicki Di-Grazzio nodded through the one-way window to where Linus Mooney's thin frame rocked in a Steelcase chair, his tangerine-orange Department of Corrections jumpsuit the only splash of color in the gray interview room. Unable to feed his heroin addiction for twenty-four hours, he chewed ravenously at his cuticles. He had the shakes, and Kay knew they'd only get worse, with forty-eight hours generally marking the peak of withdrawal.

"What are you talking about, Vicki?" Kay asked. "He's our only witness in the Big Mo shooting."

The assistant state's attorney's subtle perfume filled the narrow observation room. So did her impatience. For the past fifteen minutes she'd listened through the intercom as Kay worked at Mooney in the interview room, and Kay could tell by the look on her friend's face that none of it had convinced her.

"He's unreliable, Kay. If you tape his statement now, while he's jonesing for a fix, he is *not* going to sound credible. Just look at him. He's ready to jump out the first window you offer him."

"And when this case finally goes to trial," Kay said, "he'll be clean. Vicki, the kid *wants* to get clean. *Wants* a new start."

"Yeah, well, he *might* be clean by the time he gets in front of a jury. Or he *might* be dead. And then all I've got is a tenuous statement that even the greenest public defender can make into Swiss cheese. Besides, who knows if he's even telling the truth, Kay?"

"He is. The guy's an addict, not a liar."

"Right. And junkies never lie to get their next fix?"

"It's not a fix he's after, Vick. It's a goddamn chance."

But Kay knew better.

Following Vicki's gaze through the one-way window, she watched Linus's bony legs bouncing, his knees almost knocking together under the table as the muscles spasmed and cramped from the withdrawal. They didn't call it "kicking the habit" for nothing. And the chances of Linus actually getting clean and staying clean were slim to none.

Probably even more than Vicki, Kay had dealt with her share of junkies and from her experience, Linus Mooney was as close to a lost cause as they came. His face was hollow-cheeked, his whole frame gaunt. What the guys on the job called a skel—a long-term user whose body has wasted to little more than a skeleton. The backs of his emaciated arms had scabs from fits of heroin-induced scratching. And down the insides of his arms, the track marks were red and ulcerated.

Still, Kay needed his testimony, needed to keep him clean at least long enough for that. And afterward? Who knew? Linus Mooney could still surprise her by turning his life around, but Kay wasn't holding on to any hope for that. Finn had warned her too many times in the past that she couldn't save them all, and in Linus Mooney's case, Finn's warning seemed justified.

"Vicki, come on. I *need* this guy's statement for my case. Besides, he's in on a two-bit possession charge. Any decent lawyer's gonna get him off," she suggested, even though she knew Linus would never be able to afford one. "But *with* the charge we've got leverage."

Vicki's eyes stayed on Linus through the window, the silence stretching thinner, until finally: "Fine. I'll look into dropping the charge. It won't be till late tomorrow though. He'll have to go back to the Pen for now."

"Thanks, Vick."

She shook her head as she shouldered her briefcase. "Do you have any idea the asses I'll have to kiss to get him into rehab? Even then he'll have to wait for a bed to open up."

"I understand."

"And I want to hear his taped statement in the morning. If it's no good, the offer disappears."

After walking Vicki out, Kay stopped in the lunch-room to pour Linus a coffee. Back in the interview room, the junkie was as jumpy as ever. His pupils were dilated and his eyes looked glassy. He rubbed at the tears forming in the corners and wiped his nose with the back of his hand, both symptoms of withdrawal.

"So you gonna put me in witness protection?" he asked, blowing on the hot coffee.

Kay shook her head. "Baltimore doesn't have anything like that, Linus." For any kind of real witness protection, she'd have to go to the Feds, and cooperation was un-likely. Not to mention that it would take time. Time that Linus didn't have. "The State's Attorney's Office is offer-ing you witness assistance."

"And what'll that do for me?"

"It'll get you out of the neighborhood, and into an inpatient treatment facility."

The junkie nodded furiously and pointed one shaky finger at her. "Yeah. Yeah, that's what I want. A treatment facility."

For the next fifteen minutes Kay went over the deal, and as the tape recorder whirred quietly on the table, Linus Mooney gave his verbal account of the shooting of Big Mo Monday night on Ashland, naming their sus-pect—Deandre "Casper" Thompson—and describing in detail the drive-by he'd witnessed from a side alley across the street.

"One more night," Kay told Linus when they'd wrapped up and stood in the hallway waiting for one of the four elevators. "I'll get the paperwork from the State's Attorney's Office tomorrow and come get you out, all right?"

Linus nodded, rubbing one wrist inside the handcuffs. A technicality, but she'd put them on as loosely as she could.

"Might be a couple days for a bed to open up in one of the facilities," she said. "I'm not taking you back to the neighborhood. You got someplace you can go until then?"

"Yeah. Yeah." He thought for a moment. "I got an aunt up in Hampden."

"Good."

The elevator arrived and Kay ushered Linus inside, then came up short when she realized the car wasn't empty.

"I'm going down," Savalas informed Kay, waving her and Linus in, then stabbing at the buttons so the doors would close.

Linus settled into the back corner and Kay was aware of his gaze on the sergeant.

"I was just upstairs in Major Beals's office," Savalas said as the elevator started down. "The testing results came in today."

The muscles along Kay's shoulders instantly knotted. She'd lost count of the number of times Savalas had recommended Kay write the sergeant's exam. Almost from the day she'd come onto the unit and taken over Gunderson's squad, she'd been on Kay to "set an example for other women in the department." Even going so far as to hand Kay the exam application.

Savalas cleared her throat. "Your name wasn't on it."

"I know."

"You didn't pass?"

"I didn't make it down there." Truth was, though, Kay *had* gone down to the Academy on Guilford that afternoon two weeks ago. But as other sergeant hopefuls filed past her, choosing their tablet-arm chairs in the hot, stale classroom, Kay had felt just a little weak in the knees.

She'd studied. Knew she'd ace the exam.

Trouble was, she didn't know that she *wanted* to. Passing the exam would mean leaving Homicide. It would mean a transfer out of the CIB to command within one of the Districts, to begin working her way up, proving herself as she had when she'd been assigned her first investigative position in Sex Offense years ago.

And standing outside of that classroom, Kay decided then that although pushing papers behind a sergeant's desk might be Kojak's calling, it wasn't hers.

Savalas nodded, but said nothing, even when the doors opened on the garage level. And as Kay led Linus in the opposite direction to the unmarked steel door to the parking garage, she doubted there was little hope left for any level of a truce. She didn't care.

Not until they stepped out into the dankness of the garage, the smell of exhaust, old grease, and cigarette smoke surrounding them, did Linus finally break the silence. "Who was that?"

"The woman in the elevator?"

"Yeah."

"Sergeant Savalas."

"No shit. She's a sergeant?"

Kay nodded, spotting the Central District radio car idling down by the garage entrance, waiting to take Linus back.

"You don't like her much, huh?"

Kay wondered if it was that obvious and started to lead Linus down the ramp.

"I'm guessing that's a no," Linus said, then stopped. He lowered his voice. "You know, if you want, I could give you something on that sergeant of yours."

"What's that supposed to mean?"

Linus shrugged. "Anything you want it to. But, hey, if you're not interested—"

"Interested in what, exactly?"

"Dirt. On your sergeant."

"You're full of shit, Linus. You don't even know her." Kay prodded him down the ramp, but again he stopped.

This time when he lowered his voice, it carried a lucidness she'd not yet heard from the junkie. "But I *do* know her. From a long time ago. Before this shit got so bad." He lifted his cuffed hands and nodded to his forearms where his homemade addict's tattoo of a spider's web no longer served to hide his track marks. "I know her from when she was just a street cop, not some high-'n'-mighty sergeant. And I know about something she did."

Kay shook her head, wondering if she'd underestimated the junkie's desperation. "Jesus, Linus. The assistant state's attorney already cut you a deal. It's not getting any sweeter than what you just signed upstairs."

"Well, maybe this thing I got on your sergeant, maybe it's just between you and me, know what I mean?"

"I don't have anything to offer." She gestured down the ramp at the radio car.

"Not now. But maybe down the road I need a favor. Or maybe not. Maybe I'll tell you this just because I hate bad cops. To me, a bad cop's worse than any of them Doggos and Ashland Boys, cuz a bad cop, they be abusing the powers we the people give 'em."

Not Teodora Savalas, Kay thought. The woman determined to set an example for all female officers. Linus Mooney had to be grasping.

"You don't think I seen what I seen?" the junkie challenged.

"What I *think,* Linus, is that you've gotten everything you're going to get out of us. And I need to get back upstairs."

"Cold blood," he said then. "Shot a man in cold blood, she did."

A hot, tingling sensation worked its way from between Kay's shoulder blades and up her neck, her scalp feeling suddenly hot. The conviction in Linus Mooney's glassy eyes looked far too genuine. "I don't believe you."

"Hollywood," Linus said at last, matter-of-factly. "You can look it up. Jimmy Hollywood. Shot in the face. Right after she blew his dick off."

23

THE NUMBERS WERE MIND-BOGGLING.

Finn had managed to get through only half of the box Kay had left on the boat, the photocopied cases collected by Ed Gunderson over the years. As the pizza grew cold in its carton, Finn had documented the pertinent dates, names, and locations. And while he did, he tried to make sense of Andy Luttrell's intense dislike of Jack Macklin, as well as his own suspicions of the Vice cop.

But the DNA didn't lie. Micky's abductor was the same man who'd raped seventeen-year-old Blyth and who had violently mowed down a woman with his truck twelve years ago. So how could Jack Macklin be involved?

"What time's your mom expecting you home?" Finn asked, not looking up from his notes.

Maeve had called at seven, asking if he'd eaten, as if suddenly she were his mother instead of his teenage daughter. And when she'd arrived with a pizza, Finn had guessed right that her mother was working late again.

His renewed relationship with his daughter was probably the only good thing that had come of his brief reunion with his ex-wife. Spending her early teen years withdrawing from her father after her brother's death and then the separation, Maeve had, thankfully, outgrown her sullenness over the past year even if her dark sobriety still remained.

"Mom didn't say," she answered eventually, from the other end of the short galley table where she'd been reading a paperback novel for the past hour.

"You working tomorrow?"

"Not till eleven. Listen, Dad, there's something I should probably tell you." Only then did Finn realize she had set aside the novel in exchange for one of the case files. On the table in front of her the file lay open to an array of crime scene photos of yet another murdered hooker.

Finn reached across and snatched up the file. "You shouldn't be looking at these."

"Why not? It's reality, isn't it?"

"Not *your* reality."

"Well, maybe one day it will be."

"What?"

She took a breath, as though to bolster herself. "Fine. I'll just say it: I'm not going to college in the fall."

His nod was slow coming as he absorbed the information.

"I'm telling you first cuz Mom will probably freak out."

"So what, then? You want to take some time to travel? Work a little?"

Maeve had raved all summer about her job at the racquet club in Catonsville. For five years she'd taken tennis lessons there, and this summer she'd finally begun giving them.

"What about UM?" Finn asked. "Will they let you defer their acceptance?"

Maeve shook her head.

"Your mom and I could talk to the dean."

"No, Dad. I'm not going at all." Her dark eyes settled on his. He'd always admired his daughter's strength, her unmovable conviction. But when that determination was turned onto him, it always had a way of putting him on edge.

"What do you want to do then? Tennis?"

"No. This." She waved her hand at the box of case files, then grabbed another one. On the table in front of her she planted her hands firmly on the folder so her father couldn't take it away.

"What do mean 'this'?"

"Police work."

Finn was shaking his head even before he left the table. "You don't know what you're talking about, Maeve."

"It's what I've always wanted to do."

"You've *never* shown any interest in my work—"

"Of course I did. You just wouldn't ever talk about it. That's why you and Mom always had such a disconnect."

"A disconnect? What are you, Dr. Phil all of a sudden? Giving me relationship advice?"

"Little too late for that, I'd say."

"You don't want to be a cop, Maeve. Trust me." But when he met her dark-eyed glare, he recognized her mind had been set long ago. "Do you have any idea what the job is like? The toll it takes on you?"

"Um, yeah, Dad." He hated the lilt of teenage contempt in her voice.

"For God's sake, Maeve, you're only eighteen."

"Yeah, and so were you when you went into the cadet program."

Finn turned to the dishes and the now cold pizza. Over the quiet running of dishwater he heard Maeve turning the pages of the case file.

"Put the file away, Maeve."

But she didn't. "Is it because I'm a girl you don't want me being a cop?"

"No. It's because this is Baltimore." Second only to Detroit as the most dangerous city of its size, and where a cop's shield often meant fuck-all on the streets.

How was it that he could still so clearly remember every detail of Maeve's first day of school, her lunch box in hand, her long hair in braids, her beaming smile directed at a father who could do no wrong.

But when Finn looked across the boat's low-ceilinged galley, his daughter's braids were gone. The thick black hair she'd inherited from him was chopped short and styled into a haphazard mess of fashionably gelled spikes. A diamond stud glistened along the side of her nose, and there were too many small silver hoops in her ear. And as he watched her pore over the crime scene photos, Finn realized it wasn't just the braids and her youth that were gone. Maeve's innocence had also been lost. The death of her best friend last year had altered her forever.

"Did you see this one, Dad?" she asked without looking up. "Sounds like your case."

Finn crossed to the table and scanned the investigative notes, and when Maeve turned the page to a crude sketch, recognition made him cold. He snapped open his cell phone and Kay's number was ringing before he'd finished reading the notations beneath the sketch.

"Delaney."

"Kay. It's Finn. We got another one."

"Another what?"

"Another living victim."

24

DARYL EUGENE WARDELL was an angry drunk.

Dangerous was the word his ex-girlfriend Norma Rae Broyles had once used, then showed him the bruises to prove it.

It had only happened twice though. Daryl never knew why she'd gone so apeshit over the incident. Then again, Norma Rae had never been that stable to begin with. They'd dated barely two months when she informed him she was moving in. Didn't ask. Just told him over breakfast, and by the afternoon her cousin Billy had arrived with his truck full of her stuff.

Of course, she'd done nothing but complain after that. The house wasn't good enough. She hated the pigs. Daryl never thanked her for meals, the sex was too rough, he didn't "appreciate" her. Even the truck wasn't good enough for Norma Rae. Said she felt like a hick riding in it. So Daryl had bought her an old Escort and started fixing it up, cannibalizing parts from his junkyard of relics.

He'd never finished the car though. Never even got the thing running before Norma Rae walked out on him.

Moving through the clutter of his small, dim kitchen, Daryl grabbed another beer from the fridge, took it with him out to the porch. He settled back into his chair, cracked open the Milwaukee, and listened to the sounds of the deep woods around him as he remembered Norma Rae's departure so many years ago.

He hadn't believed her accusations until she'd shown him the bite marks along her shoulders. But they weren't the reason Norma Rae left. No. It was the threats she said he'd made the night before, in a drunken rage, telling her he'd kill her, then cut her up and feed her to the pigs so there'd be nothing left of her.

She must have been making plans to leave all along though, Daryl had realized that morning, because only an hour later Billy pulled up in his truck to get all her shit out of the house. Daryl never tried to stop her. Just watched. And when she'd looked at him that last time from the porch, he was sure she was hoping he'd ask her to stay . . . when all the while he was wishing he'd just killed her when he'd had the chance.

He'd never heard from Norma Rae Broyles again. And the faded Escort still sat in the far corner of the dirt yard, like an old sore.

Truth was, though, he never missed Norma Rae. He *did* miss the sex, but when all was said and done, the hookers were easier.

In one hand he crushed the empty beer can now and hurled it into the old wooden crate on the porch. It was better this way. With his girl in the shed he could take her as much as he wanted, day or night. He *needed* to. After all, it wasn't just for pleasure. The process was only just beginning.

When Daryl stood, a little bleary from the beer, he studied the vague outline of the shed in the darkness and imagined her inside. He felt the need rise, only slightly dulled by his buzz.

Daryl took the bowed wooden steps then, and as he did he started stripping. There was no moon, but he didn't need light to navigate the clearing. Around him the night was alive with the sounds of frogs and crickets, and insects fluttered across his exposed skin.

And by the time he reached the shed, Daryl Eugene Wardell was stark naked and ravenous.

25

Wednesday, August 1

KAY PUNCHED THE ACCELERATOR and the 4Runner surged into the left lane, flying past a flatbed truck with Virginia tags and mud flaps sporting the Playboy logo.

She was making good time.

She'd left the city limits a half hour ago under a blazing morning sun that sent mirages shimmering across the black ribbon of I-70. Unwilling to waste time explaining to Savalas, Kay had taken her own vehicle this morning, stopping only for gas and two large coffees. She opened the second foam cup now and watched for the signs for Frederick.

She thought about Micky.

They were headed into their fourth day. More than anything now, after the confirmed connection to Stacey Blyth's rape and the twelve-year-old Jane Doe homicide, Kay was sure the young cop had fallen victim to a sexual predator.

And with each new case they could link to their perp, the greater the chances of actually finding him. Of finding Micky Luttrell.

As Kay drove, her mind went back to the Luttrell house, the cool light of the kitchen, the strange quiet in the house, and the sweet smell of the baby.

Kay had been glad it was Finn who'd gone to update Andy Luttrell yesterday. She couldn't have handled seeing the baby again. She'd been far more affected by the infant than she'd ever anticipated, and even now, as she gauged the westbound traffic, Kay realized her hand had unconsciously settled on her belly.

She needed to bring Micky home.

And with the case Finn had brought her last night, there was the first real glimmer of hope

He'd called after ten and she'd had less than ten minutes to do a quick sweep through her apartment, gathering up take-out containers and beer bottles.

When Finn arrived, Kay had sensed his discomfort at being back in her apartment. He'd briefed her on the four-year-old case, and sitting next to each other on the sofa, they'd gone over the investigative notes that Gunderson had copied.

His daughter had made the connection, Finn had told Kay, and she was surprised there wasn't more pride in his voice. Maeve had found the crude sketch resembling the same Morgan Hunt and Fish Club patch sewn to the crown of the cap from Micky's abduction scene.

Kay had commended Maeve for her sharp eye, and when Finn had told Kay of his daughter's plans to join the cadet program, Kay could tell he wasn't pleased.

It was almost midnight before they'd finished going over the case. At her door, Finn hesitated on her landing, and Kay couldn't help thinking there'd been something else he'd wanted to share.

"Nothing. It's late," he'd told her when she'd asked what

was on his mind. *"I'll talk to you tomorrow."* And he'd left down the stairs and into the night.

Kay had tried to sleep, but the promise of the lead and thoughts of Micky had made Kay's night restless. She'd been up at 5:30 a.m., called the Frederick County Sheriff's Office at six, and been informed that Detective Otis Reaney, the lead investigator on the four-year-old case, started shift at eight thirty.

She'd gone for a run, needing to burn off the anxious energy, her sneakers taking her over Federal Hill, around the Inner Harbor, and into the cobblestoned streets of Fells Point. Then home. She'd showered and dressed and been on the road by seven forty.

And now, as she pushed the 4Runner steadily west through the lush Maryland countryside, Kay glanced at the photo on her passenger seat.

Frances Gallo.

The city prostitute looked hollow-eyed and vacant, her face covered in bruises, her lips cracked and swollen as she stared deadpan into the camera at the Frederick Memorial Hospital after being found wandering some backcounty road. The only other photo in Gunderson's folder was of the woman's ankle. It had been chafed, the skin riddled with open and weeping sores. The result of some kind of a shackle, Kay was certain. And that certainty gave her hope.

Hope that Micky Luttrell was still alive.

As Kay hurtled west through the sprawl of flourishing crops, the concrete and filth of the city seemed a million miles away. Still, her mind was back there. Micky Luttrell and the Frances Gallo case hadn't been the only things keeping Kay awake last night.

Linus Mooney's words had haunted her as well. *"Jimmy*

Hollywood. Shot in the face. Right after she blew his dick off."

Linus's conviction that Savalas had shot a man dead seemed solid, and his challenge for Kay to look it up hadn't gone unheard. At the office last night, she'd hoped to look through old reports, but Savalas had been working late as well. So Kay had gone home and conducted her own search.

From her home computer, she'd Googled the name Jimmy Hollywood and found two old *Sun* articles online. A narcotics raid gone bad, the media had called it. Two dealers dead by their own guns.

Had Linus been there? More important, had Savalas?

Kay hadn't gotten any farther in her search before Finn's visit, and she hadn't mentioned it to him. Wouldn't until she knew if there was merit to the potentially career-ending allegation against Savalas.

As the green landscape gave way to development, Kay edged the SUV into the right lane and onto Frederick's first exit. Just off the interstate, she spotted the glass-and-red-brick structure of the Frederick County Law Enforcement Complex, the new facility housing both the County Sheriff's Office and the Maryland State Police Barrack B.

Kay parked in the VISITORS section, and as she gathered the files from the passenger seat, she hoped Otis Reaney was waiting for her.

26

"**WHERE THE HELL IS KAY?**" Savalas looked as though someone had not only pissed in her cornflakes this morning, but had followed the insult with sugar and expected her to eat it.

"She's running down a lead that came up last night," Finn said, joining the rest of the task force at the boardroom table.

"What lead?"

"Something to do with the CODIS matches," Finn lied. "Said she'll be a couple hours."

Savalas didn't look pacified. And as Finn opened his notebook, he wondered how long Teodora Savalas would last. Trying to micromanage a Homicide squad of ten detectives was only asking for early burnout.

Then again, the sergeant, in her crisp suit and starched shirt at the head of the boardroom, hadn't asked why Bobby hadn't shown yet this morning, so perhaps her micromanagement was directed only on Kay. *Or,* more likely, Finn guessed, it was that Savalas needed Kay there. As if, in spite of all her abrasiveness toward Kay, *without* her Savalas lacked confidence at the helm of her own task force.

"We'll go on without her, then." Savalas straightened her papers against the table and requested updates on the inquiries into the cold cases of missing and murdered prostitutes as well as the ever-widening inquiry into slaughterhouses and commercial pig farms across the state. Finn only half-listened, wondering how Kay was making out up in Frederick County.

If the Frances Gallo lead was valid, it could be a big one. Kay had been fired up last night when he'd brought her the case, and Finn had loved seeing Kay's energy. As much as he hated admitting it, he'd missed her from the day he walked out. But last night, being in her apartment where they'd practically lived together for almost two years, the loss had truly hit home.

Still, it was a loss he had to live with.

He knew Kay had believed he'd come from Angie's

last night, and he hadn't corrected her. Because as much as he missed Kay, the last thing he wanted was for her to think he was interested in some kind of a reunion.

It wasn't even in the cards.

And as long as Kay believed he was still with Angie, he wouldn't have to explain why he hadn't stayed with his ex-wife to work on things. Explaining to Kay, or anyone, was not something Finn was ready for. Not when he, himself, was still grappling with the truth.

"We might have something." Bobby was slightly winded when he came through the door. Crossing to the boards, he pointed to the photo of the camo cap with the Morgan Hunt and Fish Club patch. "Morgan County, West Virginia." Bobby moved to the map of Maryland and its surrounding states. He planted his finger on the most eastern area of West Virginia, tucked up where western Maryland bottlenecked between Hagerstown and Cumberland.

"MCM, the initials on the patch," he said, "stands for the Morgan County Militia."

"Christ," Finn said.

"This guy's militia?" Savalas asked.

"*Was* militia. I've been chatting with a few of my contacts at the field office. Finally connected with a Special Agent Galen Burke from the Domestic Terrorism Program. Based on his information, this Morgan County group disbanded a few years back."

"What about former members?" Finn asked, the taste of their first sure lead strong now.

Bobby nodded. "Agent Burke's putting together a list. Members. Affiliates."

"Someone in that group will know our guy," Savalas said. "We need that list today."

"Not today, Sarge. Burke says they've got undercover agents in the field. He's got to make contact with them, gather information."

"I want to talk to this Burke guy." Savalas stood from the table.

"You will. He's promised to come by tomorrow. But he won't have anything until then."

"He knows this is a missing cop we're talking about?" Savalas's voice sharpened.

"Absolutely. Any other scenario and it'd probably take a week to get us anything usable. As it is, Burke's pushing."

Savalas nodded, and as she dismissed the task force and left the boardroom, Finn suspected she'd still try calling the field agent when she got back to her office.

At the boards, Finn studied the map. With one finger he followed the distance between Morgan County and Frederick. Seventy, maybe eighty miles.

He thought of Kay at the Sheriff's Office, of Frances Gallo found wandering in the hills. Was it finally coming together?

He needed to call Kay.

And they needed to find Frances Gallo.

27

AND YOU'RE THINKING this guy who dumped Frances Gallo up in the hills four years ago is the same guy who snatched your cop?" Detective Reaney lounged back in his chair, one stitched Western boot propped against an adjoining file cabinet. Kay had spent the past fifteen minutes briefing him on Micky's case, the Jane Doe, and Stacey Blyth.

"I wouldn't be here if I didn't think it was a strong possibility," she said.

"Funny, that's what your former sergeant said when he showed up four years ago." Reaney's chair snapped back on its springs as he sat up. "Never heard from him after that so I figured he hadn't found anything to connect to his old case."

Kay liked Otis Reaney from the moment he'd stepped into the cool foyer of the Frederick County Sheriff's Office and greeted her with a solid handshake. He was a big man. Not tall as much as wide and solid. Built like a tank, she'd thought as he'd led her through the corridors of the Law Enforcement Complex to his bright office.

He had an oddly asymmetrical face, talking more out of the right side of his mouth, and one eye was significantly smaller than the other. His nose looked as if it might have been broken years ago and had mended with a slight curve in it. When Reaney smiled though, the crookedness of his features disappeared.

Kay liked Otis Reaney's smile.

But he wasn't smiling now. "So what exactly is the connection between all this and my four-year-old case?"

Kay slid the photo of the camo hat across his desk. Followed it with the copy of Gallo's sketch.

"A hat?"

Kay pointed to the crude sketch of the emblem. "Did Frances Gallo draw that?"

Reaney studied it for a moment. "Yeah, I didn't think it meant anything. She drew it a few times while she was in the hospital here, but she never told us what it was."

"You don't recognize this patch?"

"Other than from Frances's drawing, no."

"And the Morgan Hunt and Fish Club?"

"Never heard of it. So that's your connection? A hat?"

"So far."

"Do you have any idea how many Frednecks wear camo caps?" The somewhat disparaging reference to the residents of Frederick County could only be made by an outsider. Otis Reaney was a Baltimore man. Born and raised, he'd told Kay when they'd first sat down. Always wanted to be a city cop, but his wife was a country gal and he'd made the move for her. Twenty-one years in Frederick and he was still considered city folk.

"I know it's not much," Kay explained, "but it's not as though there's a lot of other physical evidence to go on from your case."

"The girl was found naked and wandering down an old quarry road up in the mountains in the middle of the night. There wasn't much on her to be considered evidence."

"What about a rape kit run?"

Reaney chewed at the corner of his lip. "Her being raped didn't come out till later."

"She was in shock," Kay said, tamping down her frustration. The staff at Frederick Memorial should have known better, should have done the kit the second the girl came through the doors.

"By the time she said anything about rape, the doctor said it'd be too late for any viable results," Reaney said. "Hell, we didn't even know who she was for those first couple of days, until we matched her to the missing person's report and called her friend from the city."

"That would be Ginny Myers?" Kay asked, referring quickly to the notes.

Reaney nodded. "She's the one who reported Frances missing. Pretty sure the Myers girl was a prostitute too."

"How long had Gallo been missing?"

"In all, six days. And doctors figured she'd been wandering the woods for at least one of those days. Dehydrated, mosquito-bitten, scratched up from sticker bushes, and completely disoriented."

"What did you make of this?" Kay slid over the closeups of Gallo's ankle.

"At first we thought she'd maybe got herself caught up in some rocks. There's a lot of crevices and ravines up in those mountains. Wasn't until the swelling went down that we figured she'd been restrained. Plus the way she reacted when they touched it—"

"How was that?"

"Screaming. Fighting. Going nutty."

"Did you question Gallo about the injury?"

"Of course I did, Detective. I questioned Frances about a lot of things while she was up here. But the girl was incoherent."

"Traumatized."

"Completely. She couldn't even string three words together until her friend Myers came up to get her. She kinda snapped out of it a bit then, but still she didn't make much sense."

Reaney stood and moved to the file cabinet. From the top drawer, he pulled out the case file. Kay noticed that he didn't even have to look for it, as if the case had a special place in the drawer, in his career, and in his heart. The personalization of the case was also evident in the way Reaney never once referred to Gallo by her last name. It simply wasn't that way in the city. Especially in Homicide, where the cynicism bred by so many drug-related crimes wore at the soul.

"You're welcome to the file. Might be stuff there your sergeant didn't think was relevant at the time and didn't copy." He handed her the three-inch case folder. "Most of the notes are pretty jumbled. When Frances *did* talk, a lot of it was fragmented. Not the kind of interview style I'm used to. Mostly she just sat on her bed, rocking, staring into space. Kinda spooky, to be honest. And every once in a while she'd blurt out a few words."

"After she went back to the city, did you ever try to reinterview her?"

Reaney nodded. "About two weeks after her friend Myers took her back, I tried to follow up. Hoped maybe Frances had come around a bit more, you know?"

"And?"

"And, she was gone."

"What do you mean 'gone'?"

"Up and left, according to Myers. Probably taken to the streets again. I called Myers a couple of times after that to see if she'd heard from Frances. Then Myers's number was disconnected. Not that I think Frances would have ever been able to really tell me much anyway. Even when she did seem to find the odd moment of clarity, a lot of it was nonsense."

"Like what?"

"Like . . . I don't know . . . she talked about pigs."

Kay felt a jolt of adrenaline. "Pigs?"

"Yeah. On and on about the pigs. The last time I saw her on that hospital bed, she was practically screaming about how the pigs were gonna get her. The pigs were gonna get her."

28

ANOTHER SWELTERING MORNING. The sun, high over the shed, beat on its steel roof, and Micky could feel the heat radiating down into the dank interior.

Still, she drew the blanket around her sweat-dampened skin. Even though she'd seen him drive off early this morning, she refused to be naked. After all, the blanket, Micky had decided, was the only thing that distinguished her from the pigs who shared the shed with her.

Of course, the other difference between her and the pigs was the gentleness with which he handled them, moving quietly around them, cooing and stroking them. It appeared that the savagery that boiled inside him was reserved solely for her.

Then again, she had herself to blame, at least in part, for his most recent savagery. His attack on her last night was her fault, prompted by her verbal assault of him earlier in the day. It had been late afternoon, the sun slipping behind the stand of trees that bordered the small clearing, when he'd come into the shed with the pigs' feed bucket.

She'd already decided that she needed to humanize herself to him. So she'd told him her name. But he'd ignored her. She'd told him she had a daughter. A husband. But he'd simply gone about his chores, emptying a tin of food for the feral cats, topping up the pigs' water. All without ever looking at her or acknowledging her rambling.

And the longer he ignored her, the angrier she became, until Micky had finally yelled at him that she was a cop.

But he hadn't flinched at the revelation. And the cold realization sank in: he already knew. *Knew* she was a cop, and didn't care.

She'd watched him take up the long-tined pitchfork and work fresh straw across the adjoining pen, the dust swirling in the thin shafts of sunshine around him. She'd wanted to cry. She'd wanted to scream.

Instead, she'd watched his slow, deliberate movements, and in time Micky took a new tack. She'd surprised herself with the steely calm in her own voice. "I'm going to kill you," she'd told him at last. "You realize that, don't you?"

He'd stopped then, his back going rigid, the fork balanced in his broad hands.

"I'm a cop. And before I get out of here, I swear to God, I'm going to kill you."

Still he didn't respond. Instead, he'd simply propped the fork in the aisle, latched the gate, and wordlessly left the shed.

"I'm going to fucking kill you!" she'd screamed after him.

And *that* was why he'd raped her again last night, in the dark. Only herself to blame.

She hadn't even heard him come into the shed. Hadn't woken until he was almost on top of her. When she'd comprehended his nakedness, she'd targeted the vulnerability of his crotch. But her reflexes were too slow, and he'd easily overpowered her.

He'd been drinking again. She'd smelled the beer on him, and although he'd had no problems getting an erection, he hadn't been able to finish. His anger had built, his frustration filling the shed as he hammered away at her. Until, finally, he pummeled her with his fists before disappearing again into the inky darkness.

Now, in the light of day, as Micky paced the length of

the pen, the shackle biting into her ankle, she fantasized about killing him.

She eyed the pitchfork again. She'd tried all morning to reach it. Had taken the twine off one of the bales of straw in her pen and fashioned it into a feeble lasso, attempting to snag the handle, to no avail. And even now, she imagined driving the long tines into his body and watching him die on the dirt floor of the pen.

Of course, she also considered that she'd still be a prisoner, fastened to the shed's foundation beam by a twenty-pound chain. Unbidden, the images of sharing the pen with his rotting corpse played over and over in her mind. She'd still be his captive, but at least the raping would stop. And she'd have had the satisfaction of killing him.

In the dingy light of the shed, Micky looked across at the key hanging from the beam in the aisle. The key that taunted her . . . close enough that she had memorized every tooth and groove in it, yet far enough away that even if she *could* get the pitchfork, she wasn't certain it would even reach.

No, she needed some other way to pick the padlock. Micky surveyed her reachable surroundings, her gaze stopping on the bales of straw. She'd used the corner behind the low straw wall to relieve herself, covering it each time with dirt and old hay, the smell hardly noticeable over the stench of the pigs.

Now Micky moved to the bales. As the pigs rutted in the outdoor pen, the sun gleaming off their black-and-pink backs, Micky hauled the top bale down. It bounced off the dirt floor and rolled.

Micky righted the blanket over her shoulders, and when she reached for the next bale, she saw the writing. It was barely discernible in the dim light, carved roughly into the soft, weathered barn board. She moved closer, her hand trembling as she traced the rough edges of each letter.

Kris.

As Micky leaned in closer, bracing herself along a crossbeam, her fingers found the nail wedged between the beam and the boards. She withdrew the small, rusted nail from its hiding place and turned it through her fingers as she read the crude block letters.

P. E. E. B. L. E. S.

The nail warmed in her palm.

Kris Peebles.

Micky felt cold and her scalp tingled.

Kris Peebles. She'd stood in this very spot, her hands gripping the same rusted nail, and carved her name into the weathered plank.

Looking around the dank barn, Micky tried to swallow the panic she felt rising inside her.

She wasn't his first.

Kris Peebles. She'd been shackled in this pen just like her.

Only Kris Peebles had given up, Micky thought. She'd left her name in the wood like a sort of epitaph because she believed she'd never get out, because she wanted someone to know that she'd been here. That she'd suffered here. Probably died here.

There was no controlling the shaking in her hands now as Micky returned the nail to its hiding spot. Kris Peebles. How long had she been here? Exactly when had she given up?

She wouldn't carve her name into the soft wood alongside Peebles's, Micky decided then. *She* wasn't going to die here.

She would get out of this place. And when she did, she'd find Kris Peebles's family . . . her mother, her sister, her brother, her husband, her children . . . whoever was out there missing Kris Peebles right now, Micky would find them. Because she was *not* going to die here in this pen, alone, with only him and his pigs as witnesses.

Micky turned to the next bale, tugging at its twine until it too rolled.

Then, Micky's gasp caught in her throat and she felt the energy drain out of her as panic rushed in.

There were others.

Initials. Names. Carved in different strokes. Different letters.

How many?

Sandra Gates. J.C. Helen P. Arndt. F.G. And more.

Micky backed away from them, shaking. In the dinginess of the shed, the splintered letters blurred in front of her.

How many women had died in this pen?

She stumbled against the dislodged bale and collapsed onto the dirt floor, feeling her own hope slip. Was that how it had been for Kris Peebles? Had she seen the names? Understood the hopelessness? Had she added her own name, then simply given up?

Micky thought of Andy. Of Emma.

She couldn't be another name on that list.

Fighting back tears of fear, Micky started to push herself up off the dirt floor, but stopped when something jabbed her palm. With her eyes still locked on the carved names, she curled her fingers around the small object, then brought it closer.

And now, as she studied her find, nestled in her palm, Micky could no longer hold back her screams.

29

"It's too bad Reaney hadn't put that bit about the pigs into his case notes," Kay said to Gunderson as she waved down their waitress for more coffee. "You might have made the connection."

Jimmy's down in Fells Point was an old-style American diner, a Baltimore landmark nestled only a grease splatter away from the water. Too late for lunch and too early for dinner, Jimmy's usual bustle of serving big-portioned breakfasts day or night had eased, and Kay and Ed Gunderson had snagged the back corner booth for privacy.

She'd called her former sergeant after leaving Frederick, needing his take on the Gallo case, and over plates of artery-clogging eggs and pork, she'd brought him up to speed on the DNA matches, the hair samples, and Stacey Blyth's rape.

"I only wish the city police had taken Gallo's ordeal more seriously," she said, pushing aside her unfinished plate, "instead of just writing her off as a prostitute, like she somehow deserved what she got."

Gunderson tossed his paper napkin onto his plate. "*I* should have taken it more seriously. By then, though, I'd started to give up on ever finding my Jane Doe's killer. When I finally got up to Frederick, it had been weeks after Gallo had been found, and Reaney was on to other things. I went through the case file, and when I called him back for some follow-up, he'd gone on vacation." Gunderson shook his head. "I should have kept on him. We might have gotten this guy already."

And Micky would be home right now with her daughter and husband, Kay thought.

"I think Micky's up there," Kay said. "In the county."

"You can't jump to that conclusion, Kay. There's no saying this mope didn't drive Gallo up there when he was done with her. Dumped her, thinking she'd get lost in the woods or die before she was ever found. In Reaney's interview notes Gallo talked about a long drive. From what I could tell of Reaney's personal notations, even *he* figured she'd been dumped up there."

Kay shook her head, waiting for the waitress to top up their coffee. "She was missing six days, Sarge. What if he had her all that time, and the long drive she remembered was the drive up to the county originally? What if everything in between that drive and her being found on that back road is nothing but scrambled memories?"

Gunderson's nod was slow coming. "It's certainly possible. Have you found Gallo yet?"

Kay shook her head and sipped the hot, black coffee, remembering Finn's disappointing call an hour ago. "Finn and Bobby are still looking for her."

"She could be your key. What about any of the other old cases?"

"The task force is going through them, looking for links, compiling updates, reinterviewing where we can. We just got a list of employees from the slaughterhouse out on Ostend. It's not a long list of names, but we'll check them out."

"And the red pickup truck?"

Kay nodded. "We've got state and county putting out descriptions at every roll call. But who's to say he hasn't ditched the truck by now? Or lives in a whole other state." She thought of the Morgan County Militia from West Virginia Finn had told her about on the phone.

"What about MVA records?"

"We're doing that. Cross-referencing red pickups with anyone in Micky's past, anyone connected to prior crimes. So far, nothing. Do you have any idea how many red trucks are out there?"

Gunderson nodded, then sat back in the booth. "And how's Kojak holding up?" In his voice Kay could tell he truly sympathized with his replacement. He wasn't looking for a show of loyalty. He had to know where he stood with Kay, that no one could fill his shoes, especially a sergeant assigned to answer departmental minority requirements instead of the need for experienced and qualified leadership.

"She's in over her head," Kay said. "And I'm not so sure about her priorities. I think she's more concerned about proving herself than actually finding Micky Luttrell."

"So, she ask you to take the sergeant's exam yet?"

Gunderson's intuitiveness shouldn't have surprised her. "Yeah."

"And did you?"

"No. And you wanna bet she'll never let that one go," Kay said, remembering Savalas's icy silence in the elevator yesterday.

"Well, I'll say this for Savalas. Taking her sergeant's exam was one of her better moves. For herself *and* for the Department."

"How's that?"

"Just the way she's always out to prove herself. That kind of attitude ain't any good on the streets, you know? It'll get in the way of an investigation every time. Could even get someone killed."

"Shot a man in cold blood, she did." Linus Mooney's words echoed in Kay's mind.

"I know it ain't easy for women on the force," Gunderson went on. "It *is* a good old boys' club. I don't care how much they talk about that equal-opportunity bullshit. But the thing is, as long as the job's getting done, us 'good old boys' don't care if you got a dick or not, you know?"

Gunderson swilled back the last of his coffee. "You know all this shit though, Kay. You got it figured out. *You . . .*" He pointed at her. "Don't *you* be leaving the streets, you hear me? Best damn murder cop I ever worked with. You'd be wasting yourself by ranking up, being a paper-pusher and a ball-licker."

"Thanks." And Kay felt that last nudge of confidence she needed to finally say no if Savalas ever pushed the exam again.

"So, what *do* you know about Savalas's history?" Kay asked, Linus's accusation whispering in her brain.

"Not much. Why?"

Kay shrugged, unwilling to offer too much until she'd had a chance to dig further. "The name Jimmy Hollywood mean anything to you?"

"Hollywood. Sure. He was a dealer out in the Western a long time ago. Pretty major player until he got himself killed. I remember the captain had the mother of all hate-ons for the guy."

"How'd he die?"

"Took a couple of bullets. You should ask your sergeant about it. I think she was one of the narcs who went undercover to get Hollywood."

Kay nodded slowly. Processing.

"Or is Savalas the reason you're asking?" Gunderson asked. "You catching wind on something?"

"I'm not sure yet." And as her cell phone went off at her hip, Kay was glad for Finn's intrusion.

"Did you find Gallo?" Kay asked him.

"Sort of," Finn said over the digital signal. There was static and then Kay heard a PA system behind him. "But you're not going to like this, Kay."

30

FRANCES GALLO WAS A NUTJOB.

Finn snapped his cell phone shut, Kay's frustration still ringing in his ear.

"Come on, Slick. Let's get out of here," he said to Bobby, then nodded to the receptionist behind the front desk of the Spring Grove Hospital Center. "We'll be back for visiting hours." He heard the sharpness in his tone as his frustration threatened to get the better of him.

It had taken all day to track down Kay's victim from Frederick County. He and Bobby had started in Gallo's old neighborhood, where she'd been arrested several times for solicitation. A handful of the local residents remembered her, but no one had seen her in years. It appeared Frances Gallo had simply vanished after her ordeal in the county.

And then someone, recognizing her photo, offered Finn and Bobby a different surname: Newalt. Turned out Gallo was her married name, from a marriage to a wife-beating bastard that had ended years before she'd taken to the streets.

Back at Headquarters, they'd run a search and discovered that Frances Gallo had reverted to her maiden name of Newalt when she'd been picked up for assault two months after returning from Frederick. A disgruntled "customer" had threatened her when she wouldn't put out, Gallo had said, claiming he'd "mistaken her as a prostitute."

Newalt-Gallo's public defender had filed an NCR plea, whereupon Gallo had been referred to court medical for an evaluation and deemed not criminally responsible and not competent to stand trial. So Gallo was sent to Spring Grove—the state-run psychiatric hospital in Catonsville—until such a time as her doctors found her to be competent.

According to staff at Spring Grove, however, Frances Gallo's competency was expected to occur sometime around the second coming of Christ, leaving Finn to wonder what they'd actually get out of the woman when they *did* interview her.

There'd been no swaying Gallo's doctor, Marie Ouellette. "I don't care if it was the mayor's daughter who was kidnapped," Ouellette had said. "I can't allow you to speak with Frances except during stipulated visiting hours."

"You don't understand," Finn had argued. "This is—"

"No, Detective, *you* don't understand. Any change, however minute, to a patient's routine, especially someone as fragile as Frances, alters their entire structure. Interrupting her schedule could set Frances back considerably, or throw her into a state where she wouldn't be of any assistance to you anyway."

"What about *your* sessions with Gallo?" he'd asked the doctor. "Has she ever talked about this attack four years ago?"

"Please, Detective, I don't need to provide a refresher course on doctor-patient confidentiality, do I?" Ouellette had said, ushering him and Bobby out of her office.

Now, as they crossed the hot asphalt of the main parking area outside the administration building, the sun's raw heat burning his skin, Finn could only hope that tomorrow's visit would provide them with something.

They were running out of time.

If they hadn't already.

Finn cranked the AC as he steered the Impala through the centuries-old, fifty-building psychiatric hospital complex, finally turning onto the aptly named Asylum Lane, which led out of the two-hundred-acre campus. He thought of Micky and remembered Andy Luttrell's parting words yesterday regarding his wife's partner. *"For Micky's sake, don't let up on the son of a bitch."*

"What's your feeling on Macklin?" Finn asked Bobby in the passenger seat.

From behind the mirrored Oakleys Bobby appeared confused by the question. "Jack Macklin? I don't know him that well. Why?"

"You know anyone who's worked with him?"

"Only Kevin Bryant. He's with the Southwestern. Him and Mack patrolled together for a while."

"Bryant ever say anything about Macklin?"

"What exactly are you getting at, Finn?"

"Just wondering if you've heard any rumors." Finn shrugged. "I don't trust the guy. He's not acting right."

"And what exactly *is* right when your partner's disappeared? The guy feels guilty. Wouldn't you?"

"Sure. But . . ." Finn steered into the northbound traffic, headed for the city.

"But what? You think Mack's somehow a part of this?" Bobby shook his head. "You got it wrong, Finnerty. We got a serial rapist's blood at the scene of Micky's abduction. Not Mack's. Besides, from everything I've heard, Mack's a good cop."

"Maybe," Finn said finally. "Maybe not."

31

DARYL LIKED WHEN HALEY'S COMET was slow. He could take the back booth for himself and watch the TV over the bar.

And he could watch Delilah.

Two nights a week Haley didn't work. She called Delilah her "apprentice," but Daryl suspected the girl was actually Haley's underpaid niece.

Delilah was slim but still boasted full breasts and wide, child-bearing hips like her aunt. He'd often considered taking Delilah for himself. But she'd be missed. Not like some whore from the city.

So Daryl kept the fantasy in check and only stared. And whenever he did, he was reminded of another. Of the whore that almost got away. She had looked a lot like Delilah.

Her name had been Nicole Fullerton. Not that he ever made it a habit of knowing their names. Names only linked them to their former lives, and they were with him now. Didn't need names.

But for the one that looked like Delilah, there'd been no escaping her name. Every time he'd walk into the shed, she'd say, *"My name is Nicole Janese Fullerton. My name is Nicole Janese Fullerton."* Over and over. It didn't matter if he was coming in to feed the pigs or to use her. *"My name is Nicole Janese Fullerton,"* her voice growing weaker with each passing day.

Maybe she'd thought he'd somehow like her more if he saw her as a name instead of what she really was: a used-up whore, no good to no one but him. Even then, Nicole Janese Fullerton hadn't come through for him. Hadn't produced.

She'd got away—sort of—before she'd ever come close to fulfilling his need.

As Daryl gestured to Delilah for another beer, he remembered the morning when he'd discovered how close Nicole Janese Fullerton had come to getting away.

He'd been doing contract work at a slaughterhouse down in Montgomery County, making sixteen bucks an hour under the table to help with the Easter slaughter. He'd stayed the three days in Gaithersburg, pulling double shifts, and hadn't worried about the girl, or the pigs. After all, he'd left scraps and water.

But he'd been in for a surprise.

He'd come home late that third night, burned out and bone-weary, and had gone straight to bed. Not till the next morning, stepping off the front porch, did he sense a change.

First, there was no sign of the pigs. And when he entered the shed to take care of the hard-on he'd sported since rolling out of bed, there was no *My name is Nicole Janese Fullerton*. In fact, Nicole Janese Fullerton was nowhere to be seen. Her scrap bucket hadn't been touched. And the shackle had been jimmied.

The pigs' scraps too hadn't been eaten, the contents of their trough spoiled and infested with flies.

And finally, Daryl had heard the boar behind the shed, his deep, wheezing grunts reminding Daryl of the times when he brought them the good stuff: sugar beets, apples, sweet mash, and jelly doughnuts. Mama too was vocal, and he heard her smacking her jowls.

Through the slats, he'd seen their large pink-and-brown backs, twitching and heaving as they rutted.

Daryl had been confused by the shift in the pigs' energy. And even when he circled the shed's perimeter to find them hunkered together at the far corner, he wasn't entirely registering.

For a long time he'd stared at the pale limb protruding from the mud and waste, the skin gray and smeared with manure. And, still, his brain was slow to grasp the reality.

Now, as Daryl polished off his beer, he could still remember the buzzing of the flies and the numb stupor that had come over him as he'd watched them gnashing their jaws. The feeling of disbelief and understanding hitting him at the same time.

He'd heard stories of farmers keeling over in their pigs' pens. Heart attacks. Strokes. Only to be found days later partly eaten. Some might think that it was the pigs' way of getting even. But Daryl knew it was simply an issue of availability.

Pigs were opportunists. Like him. Offer them fresh meat and they'd take it over the powdered slop and scraps rotting in their trough any day.

Nicole Janese Fullerton had somehow freed herself from the old shackle, but in spite of her efforts, she'd never made it past the outer pen. Judging by what had been left of her, it must have been shortly after he'd driven off for his three days of work.

Daryl hadn't for a second believed the pigs had harmed her. No. More likely she'd collapsed from exhaustion, struggling through the thick muck and probably panicking when the boar or Mama had simply come to investigate. She'd never been a healthy specimen to begin with.

Even into the next day, the boar had guarded her carcass, not allowing Daryl anywhere near it. Only once the smell had started wafting to the house had Daryl beaten the boar off with a shovel, scooped up what was left of

Nicole Janese Fullerton into the wheelbarrow, and carted it off to the old well.

Daryl had marveled at how much the pigs had devoured over those four days, and he'd concluded, that afternoon, that the pigs made a much more efficient disposal than the well.

As he tipped back the last of his beer now, Daryl thought of the one in the shed now. A cop.

He wondered if the pigs would devour her too when the time came. And Daryl smiled. He'd like to see that. *A pig for the pigs.*

Still, he'd have to be careful around that one. Screaming at him about how she was going to kill him. He'd almost wanted to kill *her* then, just to shut her up, her voice like daggers in his ears.

He was about to gesture to Delilah for another beer when Daryl spotted Eddie come in the door and felt himself involuntarily tense up. Fucking Eddie. He'd been in the Morgan County Militia too. Years ago. One of the reasons Daryl had quit.

They'd come to blows a few times when Daryl could no longer tolerate the insults. The first time had been at the last Morgan meeting Daryl had attended, and the second had been out in the parking lot of Haley's Comet.

Daryl had taken a good beating that second time, and he knew when he'd met his match. Now, as he watched Eddie cross to the pool tables, Daryl slid out of the booth.

Eddie wasn't worth the trouble.

And besides, there was more fun waiting for him at home.

32

THE BOARDROOM WAS DESERTED.

On the rest of the Homicide floor, the midnight shift was trickling in. Sitting at one of the long tables, Kay was alone. For the past two hours she'd gone over the task force logs, reread Otis Reaney's investigative notes, reviewed the cases her fellow detectives had flagged as having similarities and the results of their interviews with former witnesses on the old cases. But the connections seemed weak.

Kay looked to the boards where she'd tacked a topographical map of Frederick and the outlying counties, the Catoctin Mountains and the Blue Ridge farther west. A red pushpin marked where Reaney said Gallo had been found. The old quarry road was only a fine, dotted, red line, denoting it as little more than a rough, gravel pass.

Next to the map, Kay had taped the case photo of Gallo. She prayed that the vacant look in the prostitute's face and her disjointed statements were a result of shock, and not an indication of something more permanent. Then again, Gallo *had* been held at a state-run mental facility for the past four years; her residency there couldn't be without good reason.

Still, Frances Gallo's ordeal gave Kay hope. Gallo had been reported missing six days before she'd been found. Kay wondered how many of those days had been spent in the hands of her abductor.

It was the first real evidence that supported the possibility that Micky could still be alive. And somewhere, up in that mountain wilderness, Kay had to believe Micky was fighting for her life.

They needed more than a hunch, though, before they could assign the authorized agencies to scour those ridges and ravines, the flats and the rivers that had no name. Real backwoods country.

Frances Gallo was the key. But they had to wait for visiting hours.

Kay pushed aside the Gallo case notes and drew out the ten-year-old Homicide file. She'd pulled it from the archives only a short while ago, having waited all evening for Savalas to finally leave.

The shooting death of Jimmy Hollywood.

After her meeting with Gunderson, Kay had rushed to the State Pen. She'd pulled to the curb behind the Intake Center just in time to spot Linus Mooney limp out onto the sidewalk. Even from across the street she'd seen his twitchiness, and when he'd folded himself into the passenger seat of the Lumina, Kay could tell he was jonesing. She was glad she'd managed to intercept him, to ensure he didn't go back to the neighborhood for a fix.

As she took directions from Linus to his aunt's house in Hampden, she pushed him on the subject of Jimmy Hollywood. This time, however, Linus was not so eager to share. She blamed it on the withdrawal.

"Why should I believe you anyway, Linus?" she challenged him.

"I don't care if you do," he said. "Like you said, you ain't got nothing to offer me anyway, right?" He stared straight out the windshield as Kay steered north onto the JFX. "Not unless you can score me a little H to take care of this superflu I got going."

Kay had looked at him in the passenger seat, his knees bouncing, his face twitching, and had surprised herself when she realized how much she would have loved to accommodate the junkie, get him a hit, just to find out more about what he had on Savalas.

"Didn't think so," Linus had mumbled eventually, and slumped farther into the passenger seat, his gaze turned to east Baltimore.

"So were you there? The night Jimmy Hollywood got shot?"

"Maybe I was. But you don't believe me, so it don't matter. Besides, you might be able to protect me from Casper and the Doggos, but no way you protecting me from no cop. Hell, I don't even know if you ain't crooked too."

"I'm not."

"So? D'you even look into the case?"

"I'm trying." Until tonight, though, Kay hadn't had the opportunity to dig out the file. "But everything I'm finding says the two rounds that killed Hollywood were fired by Andre Bicks, a rival dealer," she'd said, recalling the details she'd gleaned from the *Sun* article she'd found last night.

"That's what they want you to believe."

"You're saying it's a cover-up?" Kay asked, leaving the expressway and steering into Hampden.

Linus shrugged. "All's I'm saying is it was her pointed that cannon right at his dick and pulled the trigger. I know what they said in the news. Some sorta shoot-out in that old warehouse. But you tell me, Detective, you ever seen a dealer blow another dealer's dick off?"

He said nothing after that, until Kay pulled to the curb of his aunt's house. From the cool interior of the police car, she had looked out at the late-afternoon haze hanging over Meadow Mill and TV Hill on the other side of the Jones Falls Expressway and told him she'd be in touch regarding the availability of his bed at the treatment center.

And when Linus had reached for the door handle, he'd turned to her one last time and said, "It's what they want you to believe."

Now, Kay scanned the Hollywood autopsy results, reading through Dr. Sarah Dixon's notations and medi-babble. Two gunshot wounds had been documented, just as Linus had suggested: one to the mid-forehead, and the other to Hollywood's groin area. The detailed descriptions of the wounds that usually accompanied any autopsy protocol, however, were missing.

Kay rifled through the pages in case the remainder of the ME's report had been misfiled.

But it hadn't been. Two pages of the assistant medical examiner's report were missing. And the missing documentation bothered her.

Kay reached for the phone.

She hadn't expected to find Dr. Sarah Dixon still in her office, and Kay was rehearsing the voice mail she'd leave when the assistant medical examiner picked up.

"No rest for the wicked," Dixie had joked over the phone. "In fact, you must have done some terrible, terrible things in your life too, Detective, calling me so late from the office. What's up?"

"Do you remember the Jimmy Hollywood shooting?"

"Hollywood." Dixie seemed to run the name through her head for a moment. With a dozen or more autopsies conducted every day down at 111 Penn Street, the Office of the Chief Medical Examiner for the State of Maryland, Kay didn't expect Dixie to remember every one she'd performed, especially one from ten years ago.

"Hollywood. Hollywood. The drug-dealer shoot-out?"

"That's the one. Listen, I've got some missing pages in the report. Do you have the original on file?"

"Sure. When did you want it?"

"Can I come over now?"

"I've got one foot out the door, Kay. Been here since eight this morning. I need out of this place. Tell you what," she said in her soft, Southern drawl from her hometown of Atlanta, "how about I grab the file and you buy me a drink. You know where The Wharf Rat is?"

"Yeah."

"Good. Give me ten minutes to dig out this report and I'll meet you there."

"One more thing, Dixie. Could you grab the Andre Bicks report too?"

"That was the other guy, right? No problem."

Kay gathered up the Hollywood case. At her desk, she slid the file into a plain plastic bag, unwilling to run the risk of anyone seeing her with it. If Linus was right, and there was a cover-up, Kay needed to know what she was dealing with first.

By the time she found a parking spot on Pratt and walked up to The Wharf Rat, Dixie was already there, sitting at a secluded corner table, sipping a Corona. Kay barely recognized the assistant medical examiner without the white lab coat and the tight ponytail.

"Looks like you could use one of these," Dixie said, tipping her beer toward Kay, then gesturing to the waiter.

Sarah Dixon was a fine-boned woman with fair features and a serious mouth. Even when she smiled, there was a degree of earnestness in the expression. Setting down her beer, she slid the Hollywood autopsy report across the table.

"So why the inquiry? This case was closed ten years ago."

Kay turned to the opening pages. "Something came up, and when I pulled the case file, I noticed the missing pages. I just want to be sure I'm getting all the facts."

"Well, there aren't a lot of facts to that one. Couple of dumb-ass drug dealers shooting each other dead in a warehouse. Ballistics matched the rounds to their guns, and their guns to them. Open and shut."

"Maybe."

"I remember the morning we cut those two," Dixie said. "Hollywood was one of my first on the job. Jonesy and I flipped a coin to see who got which drug dealer. They were both a mess. That's what happens when you play with .45s."

"Could you tell who'd taken the first shot?"

"Right, Kay. We're the psychic pathologists." Dixie smirked as she poked at the slice of lime lodged in the neck of her beer bottle. "I *can* tell you that it probably took Hollywood longer to die. Bicks took it square in the face, but Hollywood bled out a lot more."

"Meaning he was alive longer."

"Heart's gotta be pumping for the kind of blood loss he suffered."

"So that would have been from the groin shot?"

Dixie nodded. "It was a perforating GSW to the left groin area. Fractured the pelvis, ripped open multiple loops of small bowel, and lacerated the aorta before exiting the lower back."

"Wait," Kay said, imagining the track of the bullet through Hollywood's body. "So the shot traveled in an upward angle?"

"That's how it appeared, unless he was on the ground already, but then you'd think they'd have been able to recover the bullet."

Kay read the detailed description of the two gunshot wounds:

GSW #1: Massive craniocerebral trauma due to a penetrating gunshot wound to the mid-forehead with soot present on skin surrounding the entrance wound . . . consistent with close-range discharge of a firearm . . . a deformed, large-caliber, copper-jacketed bullet recovered from the left side of the occipital bone.

GSW #2: Perforating GSW to left groin area . . . lacerated the abdominal aorta . . . causing hemorrhage along the wound track . . . transecting the spinal cord . . .

"His spinal cord was severed," Kay said.

"Absolutely. The groin shot dropped him."

"Wait"—Kay read further—"there was soot and gunpowder residue in the wound track?"

Dixie nodded. "And on his pants. It was a contact shot."

"What about the head shot? Close-range?"

"Not as close." Dixie reached across for the file and scanned her notes. "With the head shot there were traces only of gunpowder stippling. No soot. With the stippling, I'd say you're looking at no more than twenty-four inches."

Kay visualized the scenario: the angle of the groin shot, the bleeding, the severed spinal cord, and the head shot . . . "So it's possible then," she theorized finally, "that Hollywood took the groin shot first, the gun pressed into his jeans when it was fired."

"Up close and personal."

"He went down, and then she fired the second round into his head from a standing position over him."

"She?" Dixie's beer bottle stopped in midlift as she looked across the table at Kay.

"He," Kay corrected. A quick recovery. "And what about Andre Bicks?"

Dixie opened the second report. "Bicks suffered a per-forating gunshot wound to the face. Took out the back of his skull."

"But no soot or gunpowder?"

Dixie scanned Eddie Jones's notes, then shook her head. "Doesn't look that way."

"Which means the round shot at Bicks was from a greater distance."

When Kay looked up to meet Dixie's eyes, she saw the confusion that settled there as the assistant ME also seemed to be putting the pieces together on the ten-year-old case.

"So how's that supposed to work?" Kay asked. "Andre Bicks shoves the muzzle of his .45 into Hollywood's crotch, squeezes off one round, then puts a second one into his brain while he's bleeding out on the floor. And is this before or *after* Hollywood has shot Bicks's brains out through the back of his skull?"

"I don't know." Dixie seemed flustered all of a sudden. As though the lapse in logic between the two reports had somehow been her fault. "It . . . it doesn't make sense."

"No, it doesn't," Kay said then. "Unless there was someone else there that night."

33

Thursday, August 2

FRANCES GALLO WAS LITTLE more than a memory of her former self.

She looked nothing like her photos from four years

ago. Across a table from Kay, the twenty-nine-year-old rocked at the edge of a molded-plastic chair. She was thin. Easily forty pounds lighter than what Kay had seen in the photos taken at the Frederick Memorial Hospital. Her cheeks were sunken, her complexion sallow, and dark shadows marked her haunted eyes.

Her slender hands—the skin dry and the short nails dirty—were planted firmly on the table in front of her. Fingers spread, as though she needed the solidity of the table to anchor her. And the only time she moved them was to scratch at her scalp. A nervous gesture, Kay had come to realize.

Her dull brown hair had been cropped short, no doubt for easy maintenance, and some of it lay close to her scalp, while the rest stuck up in wild tufts. Her rocking was constant, rhythmic, stopping only when she heard sounds from corridors beyond the small, private room.

Now, from the farther reaches of the centuries-old, three-story stone building, a patient screamed. A wild, curdling call. Gallo's head cocked. Birdlike. And when the screaming ceased, her head bowed once again and she resumed her swaying.

They'd gotten nothing so far from the psych patient. And aside from Gallo's nonsensical mumblings and a few fleeting, unfocused glances, there was no acknowledgment that Gallo had heard their questions or even registered that they were there.

Still, Kay had pressed on, keeping her tone soft as Marie Ouellette, Gallo's doctor, had instructed.

Do you remember four years ago, Frances?

Do you remember the drive up to the county?

Do you remember the man who took you?

Over and over, Kay asked the questions. But Gallo simply stared ahead. Mute.

Even copies of the E-FIT composites of the driver of the red pickup didn't elicit any response from Gallo.

Still, Kay pushed. Asking the same questions, over and over, until she felt as if the walls of the sterile room were closing in on her.

Finn too seemed unnerved, staring out the French doors that led to a shaded courtyard, unable even to look at Gallo. But then he'd been on edge from the moment they'd driven onto the sprawling grounds of Spring Grove in Catonsville. Parking outside the administration building, he hadn't immediately gotten out.

"I can't handle crazies," he'd told Kay then.

And when Dr. Ouellette had warned Finn that although he could sit in on the interview, he was not to speak to Gallo due to her fear of men, Finn was only too happy to oblige.

"Frances, what do you remember about the man?" Kay had asked the question a half dozen times already, only this time she reached for Gallo's hand.

Frances Gallo instantly recoiled, resuming her anchoring position only once Kay retreated.

"We need to know about the man, Frances."

She shook her head, still rocking.

"Did he hurt you?"

Nothing.

"Did he rape you?"

Gallo's right hand darted up again, scratching feverishly at her scalp. Another tuft of hair raised.

She mumbled something incoherent.

As she had several times already, Kay looked to Dr. Ouellette at the head of the table, hoping for an interpretation of Gallo's indiscernible mutters. But both Ouellette and the nurse behind her only shrugged.

Gallo's doctor was a small, round woman with otherwise calm features but a grim look in her eyes behind the black-framed glasses she wore. From the moment Kay shook Ouellette's hand she'd sensed the doctor's reluctance. "I won't have her pushed too hard," she'd told Kay. "Frances has finally begun to show some promise of recovery, and I won't stand for a setback just because you think she might be able to assist your investigation. I apologize if that sounds harsh, but my priority is my patient."

Kay leaned away from the table now. "Do you know if Frances had a history of mental illness?" she asked the doctor.

Ouellette shook her head and nudged her glasses farther up her freckled nose. "Not that we could find out. Her family wasn't extremely forthcoming. They'd written her off years ago. We talked to her friend Myers, I think it was. She seemed to have been the closest to Frances. But Ms. Myers indicated that besides a brief addiction to heroin, Frances had never shown signs of the behaviors she displays now."

The sound of her doctor's voice eased Gallo's rocking temporarily, but her hand dug at her scalp again. This time when she brought it back to the table, several short hairs were caught in one stained fingernail.

"So you're suggesting that all of this"—Kay nodded at Frances's rhythmic movements—"is because of her ordeal four years ago?"

"Well, it's not exactly that straightforward. It's quite possible that Frances *did* have some mild psychoses beforehand, and that whatever she experienced during her abduction was what finally put her over that edge. Of course, that's a very simple way of looking at it."

Simple or not, Kay's mind struggled to comprehend

the kind of hell Gallo must have suffered to have become the wavering, skeletal individual of a woman that now sat across the table from her.

"Frances?" Kay softened her voice. "Frances?"

Gallo's eyes flashed a quick glance, a piercing blue that caught Kay's for a second, and she wondered if Gallo actually saw her.

She drew her chair around the table, coming closer to Gallo.

Gallo tensed.

Kay's gaze fell to Gallo's hands on the table, and the faint scarring that marked the back of her wrist.

"He used restraints on her," Kay said to Ouellette. "The man who abducted her. Has Frances ever talked about that with you? About how long he'd kept her?"

Ouellette shook her head. "No. But I can tell you that any form of restraints will send Frances into an episode. We attempted to restrain her once. Frances went into a psychotic rage that put one of our staff in the hospital."

Kay knew better than to try to touch the woman; instead, she leaned closer to Gallo. She smelled starch, a faint odor of sweat, and unwashed hair.

"Frances, tell me what happened."

More furious scratching.

"Do you remember the man? The man who drove you out of the city?"

Her rocking intensified, and when Gallo's hand came back to the table, Kay realized that it wasn't dirt under the woman's nails. It was blood.

"Please, Frances, we need to know about the man."

More mumbling. More rocking.

"Frances, listen to me. He's taken someone else. Another woman."

Nothing.

Kay wanted to scream at Gallo for answers. She struggled to keep her voice calm. "We need your help to save her, Frances. Please. Give us anything. What about . . . what about the pigs?"

And then the rocking stopped. The muttering stopped.

Now a low whine started deep in Gallo's chest and her head started to sway.

"Tell us about the pigs, Frances."

The whine amplified into a moan, and Kay was vaguely aware of Ouellette standing, moving to the side of her patient.

"You remember, don't you, Frances? You remember the pigs."

The moan grew louder, and Gallo's hands became fists. Then: "They'll get me. The pigs. No. He says they'll get me."

"Tell us about the pigs."

"Pigs are there. They're gonna get me."

"What will the pigs do, Frances?"

Her knuckles were white now, and she'd started a slow drumming on the tabletop as her head swayed almost violently. "Pigs. No! No!"

"What will they do?"

"Don't let them get me!" she shouted, her voice shrill and echoing through the small room.

"Frances, what will they—"

"They'll eat me. They'll eat me. They'll eat me!"

Ouellette and her nurse moved in, grappling with Gallo as she started swinging, her fists pounding the table now as her screams rose.

Kay backed away, but not fast enough. One of Gallo's clenched fists swung upward, the knuckles catching Kay sharply in the cheek, just under her left eye. The pain seared, and she spun backward, almost falling over her chair.

Finn caught her. "Jesus, are you all right, Kay?"

"Dammit." She cradled the side of her face with one hand. "Yeah. I'm fine." But her legs felt shaky.

"I knew this was a bad idea," Dr. Ouellette said as she and the nurse led Frances Gallo around the table toward the door.

Gallo's screams rose as she fought her caretakers' attempts at restraint, desperate to tear herself free of them as Kay wondered what hallucinatory horrors Frances Gallo's mind was creating, what nightmares she was reliving.

But then, in the midst of the insanity and the terror, Frances Gallo went suddenly still. Inches from Kay, she drew in a deep breath. Her posture straightened and her eyes came up. And as the echoes of her screams died within the small, hollow room, Gallo's eyes widened and locked onto Kay's. Behind those glassy blue eyes was a startling lucidness.

Her voice was low, raspy, and her words were measured. "He's a monster, you know."

Kay flinched when Gallo's cold hand darted out and clamped onto her wrist. There was amazing strength in those thin arms.

"A monster," she said again. "But it's the pigs you have to save her from."

"Where, Frances? Where is he?"

Gallo's grip only tightened painfully around Kay's wrist.

"Frances, where are the pigs?"

"They'll eat her. The pigs. Oh my God, the pigs! The pigs!" And the high-pitched ranting started all over again.

"Frances, please, you have to—"

"That's enough." Ouellette wrenched Gallo's hand

from Kay's wrist and placed herself between Kay and her patient. "She can't give you any more, Detectives."

"But, Doctor—"

"No." Ouellette once again struggled to catch Gallo's flailing arms. "It's done. I'm sorry."

And as Ouellette flung open the door and dragged her patient from the meeting room, Kay could only watch as Frances Gallo kicked and screamed and threw more punches at imaginary pigs.

34

HE REFUSED TO LOOK AT HER.

Micky guessed it was because by meeting her gaze, he'd have to acknowledge her. The only time he ever really looked at her was at night, when he'd slip into the barn and she'd wake to find him staring at her through the dark. Then he'd either rape her, or sometimes, he'd just walk out as silently as he'd entered.

In the daylight, however, he'd slam his way into the shed, coaxing the pigs aside while he emptied their slop bucket. Their relentless and demanding squeals seemed to irritate him this morning, and he couldn't get the slop into the long wooden trough fast enough.

From the low straw bed, her legs drawn up beneath the musty blanket, Micky watched him work. She'd decided the other day that he preferred raping her when she least expected it, launching surprise attacks, catching her off guard. Perhaps he really did perceive her as a threat. Unlike all of his other women.

She thought of all the names etched into the boards

behind the bales. All the women. And she thought of the tooth she'd found. She was certain it was a human molar. When she'd held it in her hand yesterday, she'd been overcome by fear, her mind scrambling to come to terms with the kind of force it would have taken to bust it from someone's jaw. Or had a body decomposed right here in this pen? Either scenario was horrifying and Micky had screamed.

She'd screamed and screamed. A last-ditch effort to be heard. To be saved. But as her throat grew raw, she'd realized the futility of it. No one could hear her screams. He had to know that, otherwise he'd have made it so she couldn't.

Micky hated him on an even deeper level today.

All those names. All those women. All that torture.

And as she watched him push straw around the pigs' indoor pen with the long-tined pitchfork, she wanted to kill him more now than ever. When he leaned the fork against the divider between the pens to tend to the pigs' water, Micky eyed the fork's long, soiled handle.

Her heart notched up by a fraction.

It was within reach.

She gauged her distance from it. And his. But if she moved, the chain on her shackle would give her away, and he'd easily reach the fork before she could. Then he'd probably beat her with it.

The sound of a car's engine outside snapped her attention off the fork. Turning on the makeshift bed, she peered between the slats. Past the heaps of rusted junkers and old car parts, a subcompact nosed into the clearing. The midmorning sun glared across the windshield, masking any occupants.

Micky's heart raced.

A quick check over her shoulder assured her he hadn't yet heard the car himself.

The engine idled low, then shut off. There was only the monotonous buzz of cicadas, and him banging about in the next stall.

Micky wanted to scream. But she couldn't. Not until the driver was out of the car. She needed to be heard.

So Micky waited. Precious seconds.

Then the door cracked a little.

Wait for it.

She had one chance. Knew her scream would set him off.

Wait.

The door swung open the rest of the way, but still the driver stayed behind the wheel.

What in hell were they waiting for?

And the rest unfolded as though in slow motion. The instant she saw the woman stand from the vehicle, the head of blond hair barely clearing the top of the door's frame, Micky screamed.

But she hadn't heard him leave the pigs' pen. Hadn't heard him clear the partition. And what little scream she did get out was buried in his palm.

Micky fought him, wrenched her head from side to side, trying to free herself from his iron grip. One scream. It was all she needed.

Then she felt his lips against her ear. "You wanna die right now, cop?"

She despised the whimper that seeped from her throat.

"Do you?"

She shook her head.

Still he kept his filthy hand clamped tightly over her mouth, and together they watched the woman toss her long hair over one shoulder, then bring a hand to her eyes to block the sun as she surveyed the clearing.

"Hello?" Her call carried on the hot breeze and echoed through the first stand of trees. "Anyone here?"

"You make so much as a peep and I'll kill you on the spot," his voice rasped in her ear. "Then I'll go out there and take her. Got that, cop?"

Micky didn't care. The other woman could run. She could drive off. Get help.

All Micky needed to do was kill him.

It *had* to be now.

Craning her eyes back toward the pigs' enclosure, she saw the fork, still within reach. She needed to disable him, just long enough to grab the fork. And even as Micky imagined burying the manure-caked tines deep into his chest, she heard another car door.

"Mmmm." The pig man's response to the second occupant rattled in Micky's ear and sent a shudder of revolt through her.

The child that jumped from the car was no older than four or five; her fine blond hair danced in the breeze, and her small hands batted at the errant strands.

"Mama, why are we stopping here?"

"Camille, I told you to stay in the car." The sharpness of the woman's tone betrayed her nervousness. "Now."

The girl turned, clambered back into the rear seat. Micky watched the tiny hand reach out to grope for the door handle. The woman called out again, "Hello?"

The pig-man didn't move, no doubt not trusting Micky to keep quiet, and probably hoping the visitor would simply drive off. But the woman was determined. She took the front steps and knocked on the door. Waited. Knocked again, and finally came off the porch.

"Hello?" She started across the clearing.

"Fucking stupid cunt," he muttered, and his filthy hand tightened around Micky's face like a vise, his fingers burying into her flesh as he turned her to face him. "One move, one word, and I'll kill them both, you hear me?"

His grip on her was so fierce, she couldn't nod.

"I'll kill that bitch. Use that pitchfork over there. Do it right in front of her daughter too. And when I'm done with both of 'em, I'll hang 'em up, gut 'em, and feed 'em to the pigs if I hear even a whisper outta you, got that?"

As the horror of his intent sank in, Micky struggled to nod. She heard the girl's voice again: "Mama?"

"Camille, stay in the car." The woman was closer to the shed now.

Innocent victims.

"Or maybe," he whispered through crooked teeth, "maybe that little one, I'll have some fun with first. How 'bout that?"

The cold glee in his voice, the way he licked his lips only inches from her face, gave Micky little doubt he'd do it.

He pointed his index finger at her then. "One word, and I swear . . ."

When he slid his hand from her mouth at last, Micky hated that he hadn't even hesitated, as if he knew she wouldn't scream. *Knew* he had her.

And then he was gone. Over the divider and into the pigs' stall again. Grabbing up the fork on the way.

Micky wanted to scream. To scream for her life. And for theirs.

Innocent victims.

Could she even trust he'd let them go?

She turned again to the slats between the boards, desperate to put a visual on the woman. *How close was she?*

She could still scream a warning. The woman could run for her car, get in, and drive away.

Sure, he'd come back to the shed and kill her. But at least the woman and her child would be safe. The police would be called, and they'd come here. They'd find her body. They'd get the pig-man.

Micky spotted the woman now, weaving her way through the heaps of rusted metal and old junkers. Then him. Too close. Far too close. He'd be on the woman with his fork before she'd even registered Micky's scream and started to run for the car.

"Can I help you?" His voice was almost sweet.

He straddled the outer enclosure's railing, propped the fork, and wiped his hands on his jeans. As he dropped to the other side, he looked back at the shed. Micky could have sworn his eyes met hers through the boards. And when he did, he smiled right at her.

The breeze carried their voices away. He shortened his gait, matching the woman's stride as they walked to her car. There, Micky watched him wave a hand in the air, gesturing directions for the woman.

Micky didn't breathe until the woman swung open her car door; even then she didn't trust he'd let them go.

She felt ill when she saw him waggle his fingers at the child in the backseat, saw the sick bastard's smile even from the distance of the shed. But what stopped Micky's heart was the sound of the little car's starter cranking uselessly, refusing to turn over the engine. It sputtered twice. The woman cranked it again, the rhythmic whining producing nothing.

And again.

Start, dammit. Micky willed the engine to rumble to life. *Start!*

Then the pig-man leaned into the driver's window. The blood rushed to Micky's head, fear sent a prickling heat across her scalp. He was going to kill the woman. Right there. Sitting behind the wheel of her subcompact piece of junk. Then he'd use the girl.

There was a distinct popping sound, a metallic thud. The hood releasing.

The pig-man circled to the front of the car. He smiled again when his eyes seemed to bore through the boards and find Micky's. Only this time it was a different kind of smile. And when he licked his lips, Micky prayed silently to God that the car would start, that the psychotic son of a bitch would let them drive away.

And if he didn't . . .

Micky was helpless.

She couldn't watch.

Her face still pressed against the rough boards, she dropped her gaze to the pigs' outer pen where the big boar rutted. With deep, throaty grunts, it furrowed through the sludge with its large, disklike snout, the wet mud oozing out from between his cloven hooves.

The car starter cranked again. And again. Futile.

She couldn't watch. Kept her eyes on the boar. His grunts deepened as he nudged something deep in the muck.

"Try it again," she heard the bastard shout at the woman from under the hood of the car.

Still, the engine wouldn't turn over.

Micky kept her eyes on the boar as he pushed the unearthed treasure around with his snout. It took Micky several long seconds, staring in disbelief, to recognize what the boar had found.

The realization was even slower coming.

"I'll hang 'em up, gut 'em, and feed 'em to the pigs."

Then, finally, Micky registered the long, stained femur as human. And this time, it was Micky who muffled her screams with her hands.

35

"I NEED TO FIND HER."

Since leaving Spring Grove Hospital, Kay had been haunted by the unsettling images that Frances Gallo's condition bred in her mind. Over and over she'd grappled with the level of violence Gallo must have suffered to cause her deep descent into the insanity she and Finn had witnessed this morning.

More than ever, Kay worried about Micky Luttrell and what horrors she might be suffering while they seemed to chase frustratingly cold leads. Even Finn had clearly been disturbed, pointing out that Gallo had been missing six days before she was found wandering in Frederick County. Micky was moving into her fifth. "If this *is* the same guy," he'd added, "then Micky Luttrell's only one day shy of a basket case."

But Kay simply had to believe that Micky was stronger than that. Stronger than Frances Gallo with her history of drug abuse and prostitution.

Now, sitting in the air-conditioned comfort of Constance O'Donnell's therapy room, Kay said it again: "I need to find her." She looked to the windows. Beyond the half-louvered plantation shutters, the unforgiving afternoon sun baked the courtyard of the Towson Medical Center.

She'd almost canceled the appointment, but Finn said

he had his own errand. Now that she was here, Kay was glad she'd kept the slot in the therapist's schedule. She needed help. Help to comprehend what she'd witnessed at Spring Grove.

"Gallo's been in state care for four years," she explained to Constance. "She's had treatment. But this girl . . . besides a brief moment of clarity, she's just gone."

Constance nodded. "From everything you've described, she's PTSD."

"For four years?"

"There's no time limit on chronic post-traumatic stress disorder. Some people can take years to overcome it. Some never. Gallo might fall into the latter category. Of course, since she *is* so deeply affected, I'd be surprised if she didn't have some major issues in her past which have compounded the PTSD."

Constance set aside her notebook. There'd been no notes in today's session, no discussion of Kay's personal life. From the moment Kay sank into the too familiar leather couch, the only thing on her mind was Frances Gallo. And Micky Luttrell.

Kay stared at the blank page. For four years she'd been coming to see Constance O'Donnell, the police-appointed psychologist. Department regulation had dictated the first dozen visits after Eales's beatdown and the death of her partner. But even once O'Donnell had signed the paperwork allowing Kay off desk-duty and back on the streets, Kay had continued to see the therapist. Only now the sessions were on Kay's dime. No departmental benefits. No record. This was *her* hour, the place she came to decompress, to let her guard down and be herself. No shield, no gun, no politics. And no need to prove herself to anyone.

But today's session wasn't about her. It wasn't the first

time in her history with Constance that Kay had brought her work to the sessions. Serial murders. Sexual homicides. Her worst cases. Constance's bizarre and personal love affair with psychopathology had allowed her to offer a valuable outlook to the investigations, a psychological analysis versus a cop's gut feeling.

"It's been shown," Constance explained, "that men and women with a history of drug or alcohol abuse, victims of childhood abuse or neglect, sexual abuse and rape, are far more likely to develop PTSD. These past experiences can alter the chemical balance within the brain, skew perceptions of fear and anxiety, and, by doing so, put the patient under a greater risk of developing PTSD. You said this woman had worked as a prostitute?"

Kay nodded. "Along with some mild drug use."

"Well, even you know that childhood abuse is a significant predictor of prostitution for women. If I'm left to guess, I'd say Gallo was very likely the victim of abuse as a child, and that's what directed her to prostitution in the first place. Once there, she's regularly abused by her pimps and clients, so even *before* this abduction, the fuel for PTSD was already there, waiting for the ignition.

"The fit you witnessed when you brought up the subject of the pigs is pretty typical of post-traumatic stress disorder."

Kay clenched her jaw and felt the tenderness that had settled there and up into her cheekbone. Gallo had clocked her good.

"Violent outbursts are common in chronic PTSD sufferers," Constance went on. "As well as intrusive images. It can be something as seemingly insignificant as a sight or smell or sound—you asking about the pigs, for example—and the patient can essentially relive the traumatic experience in the form of vivid flashbacks or nightmares. In most cases the flashbacks seem highly real to the patient, and they'll experience the original emotions all over again."

"So maybe that's a good thing? I don't mean putting Gallo through those emotions again, but the flashbacks . . . if we can get her to relive the ordeal, maybe she'll remember something that could help us."

But Constance was already shaking her head. "It's doubtful. From what you've told me it's unlikely she's even capable of articulating what she's hallucinating."

"So another dead end." Kay closed her eyes and eased her head into the couch's back cushion. She wished she could rid herself of the images that lived in her brain now: the militiaman in the red truck, the raggedy face in the composite, the bonds, the brutal rape of Stacey Blyth, the vicious vehicular Jane Doe homicide, and the pigs.

"You're taking this one pretty personally, aren't you?" Constance asked suddenly.

"When have you known me not to?" Kay rubbed her eyes. "Besides, taking it personally is what's going to find Micky."

"And what if you don't find her?"

The silence that filled the therapy room then felt heavy. That same question had kept Kay from sleep for the past four nights.

"What if you don't, Kay?" Constance asked again.

"I can't even consider that right now."

"Will you blame yourself?"

"Of course I will."

"You're doing everything you can."

"And it's not enough." Suddenly Kay wanted to leave. Wanted to race back into the city, straight to the boardroom, and stare at the map again, at the photos and the notes, as if somehow an answer would jump out at her.

When Kay left the couch now, she felt the low ache that gripped her body, the exhaustion from too many sleepless nights. She started to pace.

"Aren't you concerned that by personalizing the case you'll compromise your performance within the investigation?"

"Not in this instance," Kay said, even though Constance had a point. Mistakes *could* be made when emotions run too high in a case—warrants rushed, interviews botched, evidence mishandled—and those mistakes could cost the State's Attorney's Office a conviction down the road. But here, for Kay, a clean conviction wasn't her goal. Micky Luttrell's safe return *was*.

At the window, Kay turned to Constance. "She's got a baby, you know? Micky does."

Constance's nod was barely perceptible, but it was there. Four years of seeing the therapist and Kay could almost feel the words Constance held back now.

"This is a woman with everything going for her," Kay said. "Marriage, career, a child." And Kay remembered the feel of Emma Luttrell in her arms three nights ago when she'd stopped in on Andy, the baby waking before she could get out the door, and Andy handing her over while he fumbled to prepare a bottle. Kay remembered the profound ache that had stayed with her hours later as she clutched herself in bed and cried for the deepest loss she'd ever experienced.

"That's part of this too, isn't it?" Constance asked.

"What? The baby?"

Constance nodded. "It's affecting you."

Kay buried her hands in the pockets of her slacks. "How can it not?"

Only Constance had known of Kay's pregnancy last year. Constance and Vicki. But Vicki DiGrazzio hadn't found out until it was over, until the miscarriage had put Kay in the hospital and staff had called Vicki as her listed emergency contact.

It was an afternoon Kay knew she'd regret for the rest of her life. An arrest that, in retrospect, she would gladly have let go.

But the biggest reason Kay would never forgive herself was that she shouldn't have been on the street to begin with. The BPD's policy on pregnant officers was clear: light or limited duty, with no prisoner contact as soon as the pregnancy was made known. Only, Kay hadn't made it known. Because, selfishly, the last place she'd wanted to be when she and Bobby were closing important drug murders was working behind a desk.

The sad irony of it all, however, was that it hadn't been a significant arrest. Just another drug-dealing street punk with a bench warrant for a simple failure to appear. Just another nobody.

But that afternoon, last summer, Tyrel Jerome Johnson *had* been a somebody in Kay's life. He'd been the man who, with one well-aimed kick, had brought her to her knees on a gritty sidewalk in east Baltimore when she'd tried to cuff him. The man who had taken the one most precious thing she'd felt she had going for her.

In the end though, Kay didn't blame Tyrel Johnson. She blamed herself. She should have let Bobby make the collar.

One moment of stupidity. One moment that Kay would have done anything to revisit and do right, to—for *once*—not let the job be her priority.

Bobby had offered to drive her to the hospital, but Kay thought she was all right. The bleeding and the pain didn't start until later that night, at home in her apartment. Alone. She could still remember the weight of her fear when she'd seen all the blood.

One month into her second trimester.

Still, she'd managed to drive herself to Mercy, the fear far overshadowing any physical pain that night.

The doctor had never been convinced it was the blow that had caused the miscarriage, stating that it was more likely chromosomal factors, genetic abnormalities, uterine structure, or any number of underlying issues, suggesting that the baby might already have been dead before the encounter with Tyrel Johnson. Still, Kay knew that, even when the pathology results from the examination of the remains had come back inconclusive, she would carry the guilt forever.

Staff must have contacted Vicki sometime during the D-and-C surgery. The assistant state's attorney was there when Kay had woken up, and she would never forget the accusation that shadowed her friend's concern.

"Did Finn even know?" were the first words out of Vicki's mouth.

"He doesn't need to."

"He should be here."

"No, Vicki. He shouldn't."

Vicki had stayed until Kay fell asleep. She'd never mentioned the miscarriage again.

In the morning Kay had checked herself out, driven home, and called in a few personal days. During those days, and just about every day since, Kay had gone through the gamut of emotions. Sadness. Guilt. Emptiness. Blame.

And then there were the fleeting moments of relief. The relief had caught Kay off guard the most, even though it made complete sense that she'd feel it. After all, in the four months she'd known of the pregnancy, Kay had never really settled into the notion of motherhood, hadn't convinced herself she'd be able to raise a child, be a good mother. The miscarriage had taken away all those insecurities, all the doubt.

In sessions, Constance had said all of it was natural.

In sessions, Kay had felt okay with her emotions.

But alone, in her apartment, or driving her car, or standing in the checkout line at the grocery store, Kay carried a deep guilt at even thinking that the loss might have, in some way, been for the best.

But none of that mattered now.

Micky Luttrell *had* a baby. And now—nowhere closer to finding Micky—Kay couldn't help but imagine what horrors Micky was suffering.

"You mentioned you're working with Finn again," Constance said, her voice aggravatingly calm. "Does he know yet? About the miscarriage?"

"No. Why should he when it's no longer a possibility?"

Constance offered one of her you-tell-me shrugs that never failed to piss Kay off, even though she knew it was the therapist's job.

Kay turned to the window again. Both during and after the pregnancy, Kay had often thought of Toby, Finn's son, dead at the age of seven. Finn had only ever spoken of Toby a couple of times, but it was enough. Kay knew exactly how much Finn would have wanted this child.

"What's the real reason you haven't told him, Kay?"

Kay shook her head. How many times had she imagined telling him? Telling the man she missed almost every day since letting him go that it had been *her* fault their baby had died?

"He's already lost one child," Kay said finally.

"And have you weighed the deceptiveness of not telling him against this grief you carry on your own?"

A million times.

"He's your partner now, isn't he?"

"We're working this case together. We're not partners."

"Still, you used to always tell me that there can't be secrets between partners, between you and the person who's got your back."

Kay closed her eyes again, her hand involuntarily settling on the flatness of her tummy. It had all been so simple with Finn before, when they were partners and lovers. Those last months before she'd fucked it all up, before he'd finally concluded that, ultimately, she couldn't choose him over the job . . . those last few months had been so easy. She just hadn't recognized it until he was gone.

"We all have secrets, don't we?" Kay said finally.

"You're saying Finn keeps secrets from you?"

And as the cool quiet of the therapy room settled over her, Kay thought of the man she still loved, the man who owed her nothing. "Probably."

36

THE VOLLEY OF GUNFIRE was rhythmic, the nonstop bursts filling the air with waves of aftershocks as round after round was discharged. Finn could almost taste the burned cordite in the back of his throat, smell the acrid, metallic odor of ignited gunpowder as he let loose the last three rounds in his clip.

Weapon still poised, Finn dropped the emptied clip and slid the second magazine up into the grip of the Department-issue Glock 17, cocked the slide, and squeezed out one shot after the next, embracing the kick of the semiautomatic as the brass casings ejected from the semi's slide.

With both clips empty, he lowered the nine mil to the bench. He flexed his firing hand, feeling the ache from dozens of fired rounds. When the red range-light glared, Finn removed the heavy ear protectors and started to collect his spent brass from the floor as the range officer stepped into the firing station behind him. Wordlessly, the officer reached for the overhead switch and the target clattered back along the rail.

The shooting range in the basement of the Northeastern District wasn't anything fancy. Certainly nothing like the indoor ranges they showed on TV shows. Just a long, plain room with pocked concrete walls and wooden shooting benches that were worn from years of countless rifles, handguns, and ammo dragged across them. The narrow booths at the end of the seventy-five-foot lanes were lined with white acoustic tile, shredded by years of flying brass from thousands of guns. Thousands of qualification courses.

As per the state guidelines, all officers, regardless of rank, were required to qualify once a year, under the scoring standards set by the Maryland Public Training Council. Now, as the tester unclipped the paper target for scoring, Finn didn't bother to look. He knew he'd done lousy. Just as with the night-shooting course they'd fired first.

He'd scored a 65 in that first course. Never had his shooting been so substandard. His lowest score ever had been an 85, with 70 being the MPTC's cutoff. But today the Glock seemed heavy in his hands, clumsy almost. And his nerves were twitchy.

He wanted to blame it on his mood, on his having arrived at the range late, with no time for any kind of practice round.

After dropping Kay at HQ, he'd thought again of Andy Luttrell's mistrust of his wife's partner. Bobby had mentioned Kevin Bryant, Jack Macklin's old patrol partner, and Finn had done some digging.

It wasn't the way he preferred to do things—going behind a cop's back—but Finn needed to hear what Bryant had to say about Macklin. So he'd driven to the Southwestern District offices and found Kevin Bryant in the parking lot having a smoke.

Macklin's old patrol partner had been reluctant from the moment he'd gotten into the Impala with Finn.

"I ain't got nothin' to say about Mack. You working the rat squad, Detective?"

"Just trying to find a missing cop, Kevin," Finn had said.

"Macklin's partner."

Finn nodded.

"Can't help you. I haven't talked to Mack in a couple years."

"Why's that? You were partners. Shared a car."

"Tell me, Detective, do you still talk to your old patrol partner?"

"Not often, but, yeah, I do. Then again, we were part-nered for more than six months," Finn said, and Bryant seemed unsettled knowing that Finn had done his home-work. "You transferred out early though. Anything to do with Macklin?"

"No." But something in the way Bryant looked away told Finn otherwise.

"What did Macklin do, Kevin?"

Bryant's hand had gone to the door handle and Finn knew then he wasn't getting anything from him. The blue wall of silence was impenetrable. "Why don't you bust someone else's balls, Finnerty. I ain't no snitch."

Now, as Finn dumped his brass and returned to the firing bench to reload, he wondered what Kevin Bryant was hiding.

The tester moved into the booth beside him, a fresh target in hand. "Another sixty-five," he said, his voice low. "You wanna shoot this last set? You'll need a hundred to bring you up to qualification."

"Just mount the damn thing." Finn nodded to the paper target, wishing he'd curbed the agitation in his voice. It wasn't the range officer's fault he couldn't shoot straight. It was the goddamn meds.

As he slid the last of the full-metal-jacket rounds into the second magazine, the officer pressed the release button and sent the paper target sailing down the range to the twenty-five-yard mark.

"Good luck," the officer said just before Finn snugged on the heavy ear protectors and righted his shooting goggles.

Yeah, he needed luck. And he needed to be off the damned prescription, Finn thought as he cocked the slide of the nine mil.

When the green light blazed overhead, Finn assumed the stance, his grip firm on the Glock's Pachmayr grip. He controlled his breathing, aligned the sight, and gently nudged back against the five-and-a-half-pound trigger pull.

Instantly a hole appeared in the paper target down the range. Just right of center.

Focus, Finnerty.

It had to be the goddamn injections making him edgy, and Finn made a mental note to call his doctor. He'd been warned of the possible side effects, but until today, Finn hadn't noticed them.

A second round. And a third. Closer to center now.

He *needed* to qualify.

To hell with the embarrassment; without qualification, he'd lose his gun. He'd have only one more chance after this. And if he failed both, the range officer would take his gun right then and there. He'd be manning a desk for a month, until he completed the remedial training and then tried to requalify.

Finn couldn't see where the fourth and fifth rounds placed, wondered if they'd even punched holes through the target. When he lined the site again, the red bead wavered. Finn never remembered the gun feeling so heavy in the past. And then his vision blurred. There was a shimmering in his right eye, and as the now familiar tingling started up his shooting arm, Finn knew he wasn't going to pass.

Dropping the clip from the Glock, he cleared the barrel and set the duty gun on the bench. Bracing both hands against the worn wood, he waited for the volley of the other officers' shooting to cease, each shot a muted pop through the ear protectors. The light turned to red.

Finn didn't wait for the range officer's final determination. He packed up his equipment, reloaded with hollow-point, and was holstering his duty weapon when the tester stepped into his booth. "Sorry, Detective," he said, even before the target had retracted all the way back down the lane. "You're gonna have to come back."

"I know."

"Hey, it happens. You had an off day."

But Finn didn't need to hear any placation. Collecting his spent brass, Finn felt the tremor in his hand, even in his legs now. And as he left the range, he wondered how long he'd be able to hide it.

37

"WILL YOU BLAME YOURSELF?"

Kay had replayed Constance O'Donnell's question through her head over and over during her drive from Towson. Each time her answer was yes. She *would* blame herself if they didn't find Micky in time.

Now, in the boardroom, as she briefed the task force on the Frances Gallo case, Kay wondered if any of the other detectives assigned to the team would blame themselves if Micky Luttrell was dead.

"And the connection is the Morgan Militia patch on the hat?" Savalas asked from her seat near the head of the table, trying hard to look as if she had it all under control.

Kay nodded. "It's one of the few details Detective Reaney managed to get out of Gallo before she completely shut down. And we've got the connection of the pigs."

"Gallo didn't recognize the E-FIT composites though?" Savalas asked.

"No, but then we're not dealing with someone who's got both feet planted in reality. I can't say for sure she even *saw* the composite we put right in front of her."

"Well, if Micky Luttrell's disappearance *is* related to

this four-year-old Gallo case, then we've still got time. You're saying there was evidence he kept her?"

Kay didn't like the lack of urgency in Savalas's voice. "Yes, there's the evidence of restraints, plus the fact that Gallo had been missing six days. It *could* mean he keeps his victims, but we can *not,* for one second, think we've somehow got extra time."

Her eyes went to Finn at the end of the table, hoping for backup. But he didn't look well. Worn. Deflated almost. Preoccupied. He'd been silent from the moment he'd stepped into the boardroom.

"So where are we at with this militia angle," Kay continued. "I thought Bobby had someone—"

"Special Agent Burke is on his way," Savalas said. "Bobby's meeting him downstairs."

Kay turned back to the boards. On the map she pointed to the area where Gallo was picked up. "We need to put our focus out here now. In the county."

Savalas shook her head. "We're not going to narrow this search," the sergeant said, sitting stiffly on the edge of her chair, and Kay wondered if they were the words of Lieutenant Kennedy or Captain Gorman that Savalas parroted now.

"How can we *not*?" Kay challenged. "Gallo might have been picked up in the city, but she was found here." She pointed at Frederick County on the map, then drew her finger across to where West Virginia wedged into Maryland and Pennsylvania on the far left. "And here's Morgan County. What's that? Seventy? Eighty miles from Frederick?"

"Yes, and Baltimore's only fifty from Frederick," Savalas said, straightening her jacket and resuming the head of the table. "We're not narrowing this search and possibly overlooking something closer to home."

"What about the connection of the pigs?" Kay asked.

"Have you completely ruled out the slaughterhouse avenue?"

John Nolan cleared his throat from across the table. "Ricky and I have been through that employee list Kay got from Krajishnik's."

"And?" Savalas asked.

"And nothing. We tracked each of 'em down and they're all either out of state or working other jobs. None of them matches the description and none of them has a red pickup truck registered under their name."

"What about under the table?" Savalas asked. "Maybe Krajishnik gets in help during the higher-volume times and pays them off the books? Reinterview Krajishnik. And let's start looking at other slaughterhouses."

"Any luck on the pig farms?" Kay directed the question to Ricky Corbett.

"So far, nothing. But we're talking sixty-plus farms through Maryland and that's just the commercial operations. That doesn't take into account every Ma and Pa Kettle raising a couple of pigs for their kid's 4-H project."

"We're not looking for Ma and Pa Kettle. I'm pretty sure we're looking for someone who works alone. Someone who fits with the other aspects we know about this guy so far. Besides the angle of the pigs, we've got the red pickup. *And* there's the Morgan County Militia. Any one of these angles won't get us very far. But . . . if we put all three together," Kay said, "we have the basis of a profile. We need to get lists and start eliminating based on these three criteria. If we can narrow the field, we might actually get this son of a bitch."

The sound of Bobby's laughter brought everyone's attention to the door, and when her partner stepped into the boardroom, he was followed by a suit. The long-standing wisecrack was that you could always spot a Feeb by the suit, and the man following Bobby was definitely FBI. The sleek, dark gray, double-breasted appeared tailor-made, and the perfectly knotted tie looked expensive.

But the first thing Kay registered about Galen Burke was his eyes. Even from across the boardroom there was no missing those calm, gray-green eyes as they settled on her, their paleness seeming to contradict his dark skin-tone. Special Agent Galen Burke was black, or at least partly black, his skin the color of light caramel, and his short, ebony hair had a tight wave to it under the hair product.

He was a tall, obviously fit man, with precise cheekbones and a strong jawline, and when he smiled, it looked genuine. But for Kay there was something almost too perfect about Special Agent Galen Burke. And Kay never trusted perfection.

Bobby made quick introductions, and Kay was aware of Burke's eyes on her as she briefed him on the cap found at Micky Luttrell's abduction site, Gallo's drawing of the militia patch, and the time frame they were running against, hoping that Burke, unlike Savalas, would at least recognize the need for urgency.

When Burke finally moved to the front of the room, Kay heard the hint of a soft, Southern drawl in his words that made her think Louisiana.

"As I've already discussed with Detective Curran, this Morgan County Militia is no longer active." His voice was easy and unhurried, with a resonance one might imagine hearing on a late-night jazz station. "Even though the membership was relatively benign, it *was* on the FBI's watch list for several years until the leadership fell into infighting and the group became defunct five years ago. From what we've gathered from agents in the field, a number of these former Morgan County members are now very active in other militia groups throughout West Virginia, Pennsylvania, as well as Maryland."

"Bobby said you have a list of these former members?" Savalas asked.

"We're compiling it."

Kay spoke up. "We need that list so we can start—"

"It's not quite that simple," Burke said, stopping her.

"Our suspect could be on that list, Agent Burke. We need to investigate these men, talk to them. Starting today."

He shook his head as he unbuttoned his suit jacket. "There are other issues at stake here, Detective."

"Like what?" Kay asked. "Your investigations? The FBI's protocol? Afraid you'll blow an illicit firearms bust? What's more important than the life of a cop?"

"The lives of other agents, Detective." When Burke's gaze locked onto hers, Kay shifted in her chair. "Believe me, I wish this was as simple as handing over a list of former members and you finding your perp on it. But there are agents' lives at risk if this isn't handled properly."

Burke pulled out a chair now, but he didn't sit. Propping one foot on the chair's seat, he braced his elbow on his knee and leaned in to the table. Aiming for informal, Kay thought, as if it had suddenly become some kind of a team huddle.

"You need to understand the nature of these militant groups in order to know what we're up against," he said, "to know the kind of threat they pose and the very real danger our undercover agents could be in if their affiliation is discovered."

Kay sensed the impending lecture, the carefully scripted federal rhetoric.

"The thing is, the Domestic Terrorism Program has always worked toward developing nonconfrontational dialogue between the leaders of these militia groups and local law enforcement. Some of the groups, however, are antigovernment extremists. They're not interested in any kind of proactive contact with law enforcement. Waco and Ruby Ridge, they only add fuel to the fire of their government-conspiracy beliefs.

"That's why the FBI's Critical Incident Response Group in Quantico developed the Militia Threat Assessment Typology. It's a categorization system geared toward recognizing the different threat levels each of these groups poses based on their membership, philosophies, paranoia, provocation and threatening behavior, and criminal activity," Burke went on.

"Groups are classified into four categories. The first two, like the former Morgan County Militia, are relatively benign. They do conduct paramilitary training and embrace organized, antigovernment philosophies, however their stance is generally one of a defensive nature where violent action is planned only upon a perceived government provocation. Their criminal activity is minimal, usually involving illegal weapons and minor firearms violations. But we do still watch them. And we do have dialogue with them.

"With the last two categories of groups, on the other hand, there's no talking to them. So we resort to infiltration, developing undercover relationships with their members. These groups—especially those classified as category four—at first seem harmless because they grow out of less threatening militia groups. They're usually smaller or somewhat isolated, or actually a fringe cell made up of members who want to pursue a more aggressive strategy. It's *these* groups that can often quickly evolve into something far more potent and unstable."

"So what does all this have to do with our missing cop and this Morgan County group?" Savalas asked.

"Most of the members still active from the Morgan County group now belong to groups in these last two categories, so obviously we have an investigative interest in them."

"Meaning you have agents undercover in these groups," Savalas stated.

"Precisely. So as much as I'd like to, we can't just round 'em up and interrogate them. Not without backlash."

Savalas had asked the question, but it was to Kay that Burke seemed to keep returning his attention.

"You do understand that this list you have could contain the name of our suspect?" Kay asked. "That you and your Domestic Terrorism Program could be talking to our perp and let him walk?"

"And that's *precisely* why this has to be handled by us, Detective. By agents who have experience with these kinds of people. *We* will conduct those interviews because we *can't* afford a mishandled questioning. First thing your paranoid, government-hating militia freak is going to do is kill your cop, if he hasn't already."

"So you're thinking she's already dead then?" Kay challenged.

Burke stepped back from the chair, his height looming over the table once again as he brushed back his perfect jacket and slid his hands into his pockets as if he might be posing for a fucking *GQ* ad, Kay thought. "To be honest," he said, "from what Detective Curran has told me about the case and from what I know of these kinds of people and their contempt for law enforcement, I'd say, at this point, five days in, you'll be extremely lucky to find Micky Luttrell alive."

38

IT HAD BEEN A LOOSE SPARK-PLUG wire. He'd felt it right away, leaning over the engine of the compact car and fiddling the belts and cables. But Daryl Eugene Wardell had pretended to check the rest of the woman's engine, as he'd entertained the notion of doing just what he'd threatened the cop he'd do: kill the woman and her kid. He'd toyed with the plastic-coated cables for a long time, listening through the open windows to the singsong voice of the child in the backseat asking her mama if they were leaving soon. Once, he'd even turned his gaze back at the shed where he knew his cop was watching him from behind the slats, and then he'd started contemplating another possibility: killing the *cop* and the kid, and keeping the woman.

She smelled good. Smelled fresh.

But he hardly needed more heat right now.

So Daryl had wiggled the cable, tightened the spark plug, and the engine caught.

He'd watched the car drive off down the lane, disappearing through the trees and dense undergrowth. And when he'd heard the distant whine of the little car's engine way out on the gravel road, he'd jumped into his truck, driven to the end of the long lane, and closed the gate.

The rusted steel-framed gate sagged on its hinges,

creating a deep rut in the hard-packed dirt from dragging it. Daryl had considered replacing the gate and the sun-bleached NO TRESPASSING sign, but new fixtures only drew attention, even along the rarely used side road.

With the gate secured, Daryl gunned the truck back up the steep drive, the tires hitting the ruts a little too hard. The fantasy of killing the woman and her child had been brief but vivid, and being denied the pleasure pissed him off. Only one other time in his past had he been so lucky as to have a woman come to *him*. Daryl couldn't recall exactly how many years ago. But he *did* remember her.

It was before the idea of keeping them in the shed. Before his other plan had ever been imagined.

She'd been a simple girl, in her beat-up Pontiac, lost and without a map. It had been easy to tamper with her car and promise to drive her into town later for the part it needed. He'd even fix it himself, he told her, no charge, if she'd only do him one favor first.

He'd been surprised when the little slut had actually agreed and not only sucked him off, but let him have sex with her too. When she'd changed her mind, though, partway through, telling him all of a sudden that it hurt and demanding he stop, Daryl had gotten rough with her.

Too rough.

Her face had turned blue as he'd held her bulging throat in his hands. She might actually have been dead before he came inside her. He'd never known for sure. But it had been good.

What he remembered most about the girl came later, after he'd done his chores, after he'd so calmly driven into town to run his errands, then come home and showered. The memory of sex with the Pontiac girl had given him the mother of all hard-ons, and when he'd seen her lifeless body on his bed, he'd tried to have sex with her again. He'd pretended she was still alive, just sleeping. Only, her flesh had been cooling by then, her body already stiffening. And Daryl hadn't been able to finish.

Now, as he brought the pickup to a stop in a cloud of dust by the house, Daryl jumped out and headed for the shed. His long stride quickly swallowed up the distance. He couldn't explain the anger he felt. All he knew was that the blonde in the car could have been his if not for the cop. The blonde in the car would have been easier keeping. And the blonde in the car smelled better.

Just inside the door of the shed, Daryl cranked the water's shutoff valve wide-open, and the rubber hose jumped to life like a long, black snake. The pigs, perhaps sensing his mood, fled from their pen to the outside. Only the boar stayed. Curious. Calmly eyeing Daryl as he passed, the hose unreeling behind him, the pistol-grip nozzle clenched firmly in one hand.

His cop was up on her feet before he reached her pen, the blanket tight around her.

"Take it off," he demanded.

"What?"

"Take it off."

She didn't move. Staring at him. Defiant. "Fuck you."

The blonde in the car could have been his.

Daryl tossed the end of the hose over the top rail and followed it. When he landed on the other side, he saw her eyes flit quickly to the line she'd drawn in the dirt, as if he hadn't before noticed the large semicircle marking the area within her reach.

"Take it off," he said again.

And this time when she ignored his demand, Daryl charged.

He came in low, avoiding her swing, and when his shoulder aligned with her diaphragm, he heard the wind rush out of her. Whatever plan she might have had for him was gone the instant he hit her. Her knee came up, but it was a feeble attempt, and he easily kicked her legs out from under her.

Taking up the spray gun, he snatched her hair in his other hand and dragged her, half-crawling, to the stack of straw bales. She was ready for a fight, spinning around and lashing out even as he yanked the blanket away from her.

Naked now, she squirmed to her feet. Bruises riddled her thin body, and dirt and blood were smeared across her pale skin. She was strong though. Fit. She'd certainly last longer than the sickly, drug-deadened whores he usually picked up.

If he decided to keep her.

She stood even straighter now. As though boosting herself up, full of cop bravado and cockiness, in spite of standing stark naked before him.

"What the fuck do you want from me, huh?" she asked between gulps for air. "Gonna rape me again?" She waved her fingers, taunting him. "Come on, hillbilly! Do it. Rape me!"

Daryl's hand tightened around the pistol grip of the spray gun. Wary.

"Come on, hillbilly. Rape me! I like it."

He realized then that she'd rip his balls off with her bare hands the first chance she'd get.

Daryl took a step back and squeezed the spray gun's lever. Instantly a shaft of cold water blasted from the nozzle. He'd aimed for her face but hit her in the chest instead. When she tried to scream, he aimed higher and shut her trap with the harsh stream.

He heard her sputter and cough, and the smacking sound of the high-pressure water against her flesh filled him with unexpected satisfaction. As did the almost instant redness of her skin from the force of the water.

And as he kept the pressure of the spray on full and moved in on her, Daryl wondered if it was possible to drown a person on dry land.

39

KOJAK'S OFFICE didn't seem big enough for Kay's anger.

Special Agent Galen Burke's refusal to share the list of militia members hadn't sat well with any of the detectives on the task force, least of all Kay. But what had clearly affected her most was Burke's suggestion that Micky Luttrell might already be dead. In the boardroom, Finn had watched Kay struggle to bite her tongue, silently refusing to give any merit to Agent Burke's opinion. After all, by believing Burke, they lost their one most important tool: *hope*.

"He or one of his colleagues could be interviewing Micky's abductor," Kay argued with Savalas now, "and if they don't know what to look for, it could cost Micky her life. We need to be part of those interviews. *We* know what this guy is about, *not* the Feds."

"They're the governing agency in this militia thing," Savalas told her calmly. "Besides, Burke has a point: they know these individuals better than we do. Best thing we can do right now is wait to see what Burke comes up with."

"Best for who? The FBI? Or Micky?"

"Both." Savalas nailed her a stare.

But Kay was unfazed. "This is *your* task force. You can talk to Lieutenant Kennedy. Captain Gorman. At the very least get Finn and me in on the interviews—"

"Kay."

"—as observers. We might pick up on something they miss."

When Kay looked to him, Finn knew she wanted his support, but Savalas was already shaking her head. "Burke's been briefed. He knows what we're looking for. He just needs time to coordinate with the field agents."

"Micky Luttrell doesn't *have* any goddamn time." And Kay was about to turn out of the office when Savalas stopped her.

"Kay. I need to know if you've seen Jack Macklin lately." Savalas was cool, dismissing the Burke issue and unemotionally changing tack.

Kay stopped. Shook her head. "Not since Monday. Why?"

Finn heard her suspicion.

There hadn't been time to fill Kay in. After the tight-lipped conversation with Macklin's former partner, Finn had sought out Savalas. Behind her closed office door he'd spoken openly of his suspicions of Macklin.

It had taken surprisingly little to convince Kay's sergeant to let him look into the Vice detective a little further. Convincing Kay, on the other hand, wasn't going to be half as easy. Her bond with Jack Macklin was forged in the loss of her own partner Joe Spencer four years ago. A loss for which she blamed herself, no doubt as much as she believed Macklin did for Micky's abduction.

"I'd just like to know where Macklin's at," Savalas said.

"Emotionally. Last thing we need is a vigilante off doing his own investigation."

"Then bring Mack on board," Kay said. "Make him part of the task force. He can help. *And* you can keep tabs on him."

"You know I can't do that."

"Why? Because he's too personally invested?" Kay asked. "We're *all* personally invested. Micky's one of our own. If *you're* not personally invested—"

Savalas held up a hand. "Don't go there, Detective." Then, turning to Finn: "Is Macklin's police car at the impound already?"

"It should be."

"All right. Get the Mobile Crime Lab down there. Quietly though."

Finn hated the confusion that tightened Kay's face now. Wished he'd had a chance to tell her beforehand.

"What's going on?" Kay looked to Finn. "You're searching Mack's police car? What the hell for?"

"Finn has reason to believe that Detective Macklin could be hiding something," Savalas said.

"This was *your* idea?"

Finn nodded.

"Hiding something about what? About his partner's abduction? How in hell can you even think he's involved after all the leads we've been following? Mack has nothing to do with—"

"Nobody's saying he does, Kay," Finn told her at last. "But there's something not right about the guy."

"What's not right about him is that he's just lost his partner. Put yourself in his shoes, for Christ's sake, Finn. How would *you* feel? How would *you* act? Do you even know?"

"Detective." Savalas stopped her. "You're going with Finn to the impound."

"Like hell I am." Kay threw open the door before Savalas could stop her a second time. "I am *not* going to be a part of any goddamn witch hunt."

40

MICKY LUTTRELL BELIEVED IN FATE. She believed that although there could be different paths taken at different times in one's life, ultimately they all led to one's destiny. And it was precisely because of this belief—that everything happens for a reason—that Micky had been able to get through what she had in life.

Fate had made her an orphan by her mother's suicide. And unlike some of the horror stories she'd heard, fate had put her in the hands of good people in foster care, people who had taught her that life was worth surviving the bad stuff.

Again at twelve years of age, fate had spared her when Giles Baldwin had broken into the house of Frank and Maria Anderson and killed her adoptive parents in their bed. And with that, fate had directed her to the Academy, top of her class, and a promising career in policing.

Fate had given her Andy. And, best of all, sweet Emma.

But was it fate that had her walking up Harlem Avenue five nights ago? Right into the hands of some hillbilly wackjob?

How could that be?

Was the pig-man her destiny?

No.

Dying in this shed like all the women before her could *not* be *her* destiny. To have survived so much and end up here, shackled in this foul, dank pen, in the hands of some psychopath . . .

This was *not* how her life was supposed to end.

In the corner, the straw bales were only obscure, hulking forms in the growing darkness. But Micky's memory could still see the names scratched into the old boards.

Certainly this was not what all those other women had imagined for themselves either. Mentally, Micky struggled past that thought. She'd *never* seen herself as a victim. And she wouldn't start now.

Micky Luttrell was a survivor.

So maybe fate *was* at work here. Her fate colliding with his.

Maybe this *was* her destiny. After all, unlike all the other women who had probably died in this filthy shed, *she* could do something. She was a cop. She had training.

She was a survivor.

She'd kill the son of a bitch, just as she'd promised him. Put an end to his raping and torturing and murdering.

And as she peered through the slats at the sun setting behind the slanted, weather-beaten house, the sky ablaze in amber and red, Micky swore to God that she would be the pig-man's last.

She'd stopped counting the number of times he'd raped her. It didn't matter. He could do what he wanted to her body. He couldn't rape her soul.

And besides, the more he raped her, the more opportunity she had to kill the motherfucker.

And she *would* kill him.

Shifting the old blanket off her shoulders, Micky winced at its coarseness against her skin. His brutal hosing had left her raw and bruised.

And there were more bites. He had raped her again, after his assault with the high-pressure water. It was the only time Micky hadn't struggled. She'd been too drained. He'd actually seemed more pissed off by that, finishing quickly, calling her a "fucking whore" when he came, and then storming off through the shed.

She'd waited, unmoving, naked in the water-soaked straw, until she'd heard the screen door of the house slap shut. That's when Micky had realized he'd left the hose. Still shaking, she'd taken it up, kinking it twice to lessen the pressure, and had washed herself. The icy water came slower this time, softer, and she'd worked at washing every trace of him off her.

Now, as she watched the house under the fiery sky, Micky tried to imagine him behind those dark windows. She wouldn't sleep tonight, she decided. That's when he usually crept into the barn and caught her off guard.

Not tonight though.

Tonight she'd be ready. Tonight the pig-man would never know what hit him.

41

IT WAS BOBBY who'd told her about the blood.

Kay had been leaving Headquarters, walking up the last grease-stained ramp to where she'd left the 4Runner on the roof of the police parking garage, when Bobby had stopped her. The Crime Lab had finished with Jack Macklin's police car, he'd told her.

"They didn't even have to luminol it," he'd said. "They found the blood with the lights. The CrimeScope picked up traces on the passenger-side floor and the front of the seat. Not a lot, but enough to take samples of. Course, DNA'll take weeks, unless Savalas has them rushed."

"What about typing?"

"Finn had the Lab do it on the spot."

"And?"

"Same type as Luttrell's."

"Goddamn it."

"It doesn't have to mean anything, Kay. Macklin and Micky have been riding together for a year. There's all kinds of reasons her blood could be in their car."

"And is your blood in our car, Bobby? We've been partners for a lot longer."

He'd shrugged. Clearly—like Kay—he wanted to believe the best of Jack Macklin.

"Listen," he'd offered then, "Mack even said they had a rough night. Maybe Micky got into it with a john. I'm sure Mack's got an explanation."

"Then I'm dying to hear it," Kay had said, before getting into her car.

And for the next three hours Kay had tried to find Macklin for that explanation. She'd checked his shifts with Vice, but the detective had called in a few days. She'd driven to his address on Aliceanna Street and rang his apartment several times. When she couldn't reach him on his cell either, Kay had gone down to J-Rays on Herkimer. But there'd been no sign of Mack.

With nowhere else to search, Kay had picked up some takeout and sat on the rooftop terrace of her apartment overlooking Federal Hill, watching the red glow of the DOMINO SUGAR sign grow brighter as daylight leaked from the sky.

She'd tried to reach Linus Mooney at his aunt's house, but had been told Linus wasn't in. And after Kay's pushing, the woman had finally admitted that she hadn't seen her nephew since the morning and was worried he'd gone back to the neighborhood.

Kay worried too. She needed Linus. And not just for his testimony on the Big Mo shooting last week. More important to Kay was what Linus represented in terms of Savalas. He knew more than he was saying about the ten-year-old homicide of Jimmy Hollywood. She was sure of it.

". . . pointed that cannon right at his dick and pulled the trigger," he'd said. "You ever seen a dealer blow another dealer's dick off?"

And Kay agreed with his theory. Unless it had been an absolutely badly aimed shot, the one to the crotch had all the markings of a female shooter, a woman with anger. Perhaps with a score to settle.

If Linus *had* seen Teodora Savalas tuck that .45 into Hollywood's crotch and "blow his dick off," then *that* testimony was even more important to Kay than anything on Big Mo's shooter.

After all, there was no statute of limitations on homicide.

As darkness fell around her, Kay had thought of Finn. If there was anyone she'd trust with what she'd learned, it was Finn. But she owed him an apology first. For this afternoon.

Now, as Kay started down the planks of the east pier at the Bridge Marina, she silently rehearsed what she could possibly say to excuse her performance in Savalas's office.

She hated admitting when she was wrong. And she still hoped she wasn't in regards to Macklin.

The lights along the Hanover Street bridge spanning the Patapsco shimmered off the calm water of the Middle Branch, illuminating the dark concrete vaults of the bridge's underbelly with smatterings of refracted light. She hadn't been sure she'd find Finn on the boat until she'd spotted his car in the lot, and even then she wasn't sure why she'd even thought he'd be here. A gut feeling? Or maybe hope?

The cabin lights of the forty-three-foot Slocum were ablaze, but as she neared, Kay heard voices. Finn's. And a woman's.

She stopped just short of the gangplank. Angie? No, his wife hated the boat, Finn had told Kay. Made her seasick even when it was docked. Another woman?

"Do you think Finn keeps secrets from you?" Constance had asked this afternoon, and even though Finn didn't owe her the whole truth about his life anymore, Kay had always just assumed she *did* know everything about him.

"Never assume," her father had always told her. "Only makes an *ass* out of *u* and *me*." And Kay wasn't up to feeling like an ass twice in one day.

When she turned to head back to the parking area, she heard laughter. She didn't want to look back, but couldn't help herself. And in the quick glance she caught the outline of a woman taking the companionway steps.

Kay kept moving. Until she heard her name.

"Detective Delaney?"

In the dim light the woman's features weren't discernible, but the voice sounded familiar. She couldn't place it until the woman stepped into the light of one of the pier's sodium lamps.

It wasn't Angie. And it wasn't some girlfriend.

"Maeve?"

Kay hadn't met Finn's daughter until last spring, in the hospital room of her girlfriend. Her black hair was still cut in the same haphazard, short fashion, and styling product made some sections spike out at odd angles around her pale face. She wore a plain T-shirt and shorts, and at the ends of those long, slender, tennis-fit legs she wore her expensive sneakers barefoot. Just like her father, Kay noted.

The girl possessed Finn's handsomeness. Strong, distinct features. And in spite of her attempts to defeminize herself, Maeve Finnerty had matured into an attractive young woman with an undeniable natural beauty. She seemed happier too, more settled into her own skin somehow, and not nearly as sullen and tight-lipped.

"You here to see my dad?"

"Yeah. But I . . . I heard voices. Figured he was—"

"With a girlfriend?" Maeve blurted with a smile.

"—busy," Kay corrected, as much thrown by the girl's bold delivery as she was the information.

"Well, he's not." She waved a hand at the boat. "He's all yours." And Kay wondered if she'd only imagined the suggestiveness in Maeve's voice.

"Listen," she told the girl, "I never had the chance to say it last year, but I'm really sorry about Julia."

The girl's smile struggled, then faded.

Kay wanted to say more but didn't want to reveal her knowledge that Maeve's relationship with Harris had gone much deeper than friendship. "So your dad tells me you're thinking of the Academy?" Kay asked instead.

"Yeah. He's not happy about it though."

Kay nodded. "Do you blame him?"

"I guess not."

"I think if it's what you want, you'll do great, Maeve. That was certainly a good catch you made on the county case the other night."

"You gonna get the guy then?"

"I plan on it."

"Good."

"You know, after this case . . . after things settle down a bit, if you ever wanted to do a ride-along or take a tour, even just have someone . . . a woman to talk to about what it's like, feel free to look me up," Kay suggested before she'd considered the potential awkwardness of her forging any kind of relationship with the daughter of her ex-lover.

"That'd be cool. I'll do that." Maeve nodded, her smile returning, as she righted her leather pack over one shoulder.

Kay couldn't help feeling she'd just won points with Finn's daughter—a girl who'd harbored nothing but animosity toward the "other woman" in her father's life—and Kay wasn't sure why it felt so good.

"I look forward to it," Kay said, about to head to the boat.

"By the way, Detective Delaney."

"Kay. It's Kay."

"Kay then." Maeve nodded to where *The Blue Angel* was moored in the last slip, a hulking white fiberglass shell, its sails neatly wrapped, and its mast rising into the darkness. "In case he hasn't told you, he's not with my mom anymore."

"Do you think Finn keeps secrets from you?"

Kay nodded, but suspected Maeve could tell she hadn't known.

"It was nice to see you again," Maeve said before turning.

"Likewise." And as Kay watched the girl's easy, confident stride, she tried to imagine why Maeve had told her. And why Finn hadn't.

She found Finn in the galley, putting away dishes.

"You don't have to apologize, Kay," he said, after she'd explained her unannounced visit. "I have a pretty good idea the connection you feel with Jack Macklin." He handed her a soda. "No one wants to suspect a fellow cop, including me."

"But you do suspect him," Kay challenged. "Even though there could be a perfectly good reason for Micky's blood to be in that car?"

Finn opened himself a soda. "Yeah. I do."

"Even though we've got DNA evidence linking Micky's disappearance to these past cases?"

"I'm not saying Macklin necessarily did something to Micky Luttrell, okay?"

"What then?"

"I think he's crooked. I think he's done things, and I think other people are too afraid to speak up." And Finn explained his visit with Mack's former patrol partner.

"So why didn't you tell me about Kevin Bryant?" Kay asked when he was done. "You went to Savalas first." *Went behind my back,* she wanted to add, but didn't.

"There wasn't time. Besides, I knew your instinct would be to defend Macklin."

"You would never have done that before. When we were partners."

Clearly Finn didn't know how to respond. He turned his focus to clearing the galley countertop.

She missed Finn. The feeling came stronger than it

ever had since he'd left her for Angie. Watching him now, in a white BPD T-shirt and khaki shorts, his feet sockless in the stained deck shoes, Kay felt the stir of old yearnings. She missed Finn's substance. Missed him in her bed at nights, the feel of him spooning behind her, the sense of safety she'd always felt with his arm thrown over her. Because sometimes she needed to feel safe, to feel protected, to feel that someone had her back in life.

And as she watched him, Kay found herself looking at Finn differently, now that she knew he was no longer with his ex-wife. Found herself entertaining the aspects of their relationship she missed so deeply.

"We've lost our rhythm," she said when the silence grew too long. "You and me."

"We're not partners anymore, Kay. It happens."

"Do you miss it?"

"Sometimes." He thought for a second. "But it's better this way."

"How?"

He shrugged, trying to come off as casual, but the steadiness in his voice betrayed the level of thought he'd obviously put into the issue. "We both had too much at stake in each other as partners, and you know it."

"You mean being in a relationship?"

He nodded. "I don't know how much you remember about the basement of Hagen's funeral home three years ago, but you have no idea how close I came to shooting Bernard Eales. How badly I wanted to. To hell with procedure. My career. I wanted his brains all over that room. And all because of what he'd done to you, what he'd come to represent to . . . this." He made a circle in the air between them with his index finger. "To 'us.'"

He shook his head and for a long moment stared at the can of soda in his hand. "That's not a good partnership, Kay," he said at last. "Our priority has to be the job, not each other. When we were partners . . . I worried too much."

"But not now?"

"Now? Well, now you have Bobby and I have Scooby, so it's a moot point." Then he added, "It's better we're not partners."

She wanted to ask him about Angie, why he hadn't told her. But Kay was still processing the new information, confused that Finn had made more of an effort *not* to tell her whenever she'd mentioned his ex-wife.

"I saw Maeve," she said when she didn't know what else to say. "She looks good."

Finn nodded and Kay sensed he was thinking of his daughter's future.

"I think you should be proud she wants to follow in your footsteps," she said.

"It's no life for a girl."

Kay shrugged. "I'm doing okay."

"Right, and how many times have you been shot at, beat up, and almost killed?"

"Maeve will be fine, Finn. But she'll need your support. Your approval."

"So what are you going to do about this militia angle?" Finn asked then, no doubt uncomfortable with the subject of his daughter becoming a cop.

Kay took a long swig of soda and her eyes watered from the carbonation. "I was thinking of talking to the captain."

"Go over Savalas?" Finn shook his head. "She'll only

have you standing in deeper shit. Besides, if you ask me, you don't need to go to Gorman. I think you can get whatever you want from the Feds on your own."

"What are you talking about?"

"Special Agent Galen Burke."

She wasn't sure what to make of the way Finn drew out the man's name, ennunciating every syllable crisply.

"Come on, Kay. Don't tell me you were the only one in that boardroom who didn't notice."

"Notice what?"

"Burke likes you."

"Bullshit."

Finn shrugged. "Don't believe me then. But if you really want in on those interviews, I don't think it'd take much, if you know what I mean."

Kay shifted on her stool, unsure whether Finn meant for her to be flattered or insulted.

"And I think you should," he added, before she could react, "because you wanna bet Special Agent Burke wouldn't recognize a homicide suspect if he stared one in the eye."

Kay couldn't explain the sudden urge to defend Galen Burke just then, especially when she'd said pretty much the same thing in Savalas's office earlier.

"He's just another federal suit," Finn said. "Distributing resources so his unit can gather info on everything from militia to environmental protesters, antiwar groups to activists who feed fucking vegetarian meals to the homeless." He crushed his soda can in one hand and turned to the galley. "They can label it domestic terrorism or anything else they want. Bottom line, they don't know homicide."

Kay felt unsettled by Finn's rant. True, he wasn't saying

anything about Burke that any member of the task force wasn't probably thinking as well. But it was the way he said it, the hostility in his voice.

"Burke likes you." Was it jealousy?

"It's late," she told him, not knowing what else to say. "I should go."

As she dropped from the stool, Finn tossed his crushed can to the trash and missed. When she reached the companionway steps, she heard the shatter of glass across the teak flooring.

She spun in time to see Finn catch himself on the corner of the galley bar. He was shaking his head as he swore at the smashed tumbler at his feet.

He held up a hand to stop her when Kay moved toward him.

"I got it," he said, reaching for the broom and dustpan. But when he squatted to clean up the scattered shards, he didn't look right to Kay. He seemed shaky, almost enervated, and he used the bar for support.

"Are you okay?"

"Of course I am."

And Kay wished she could believe him. "Finn, what's going on?"

"Nothing." He swept up the last of the shards. "I'm tired, is all." And when he turned at last Kay didn't trust Finn's smile. "Just need some sleep. I'll see you in the morning."

Kay nodded, knew there was no sense pushing. "Sure," she said at last. "Have a good night."

He didn't walk her out, and as Kay stepped from *The Blue Angel*'s deck onto the pier, Constance's question echoed through her mind again.

"Do you think Finn keeps secrets from you?"

42

MICKY JOLTED AWAKE.

The shed light was on. Panic seized her heart, setting it tripping in her chest.

Frantically she scanned the interior of the shed, certain the pig-man must have slipped in while she'd fallen asleep.

But he was nowhere, and Micky tried to remember if he'd left the light on earlier. Her brain felt foggy, her body shaky.

She sat up, rubbed her eyes, and looked to the pigs' pen just as the boar lumbered into the shed. She'd watched the enormous, brown boar off and on through the day, gnawing on the newly exposed femur like a dog with a bone.

Micky had wondered which girl it had been, which of the names etched into the shed's boards had belonged to the cleaned-off bone. And she wondered how much more of her was buried in the thick muck outside the shed.

Had he fed her to the pigs? Or had the pigs killed her themselves?

Separated only by the shaky barrier, the boar smacked his huge jaws, thick white foam clinging to his lips. He smelled too. Different. A heavy, musty odor. Micky watched as he sidled up to the largest sow and nudged harshly at its spotted flanks. The sow held her stance, ears flattened back along her thick neck, grunting quietly as she braced herself against his insistent prodding.

Micky wasn't prepared for the boar's next maneuver. In one fluid motion that seemed uncharacteristic of the huge animal, it mounted the sow. There was no struggle, no protest from the sow under his tremendous weight, and the boar's mass rose above the top of the partition. Micky grasped the blanket tighter around her.

Moments later the chanting started. A low, rhythmic sound that started deep in the boar's throat and seemed to keep time with his smacking jaws. The foam at his mouth thickened, bits of the stringy mucus flying off him as he champed.

And then Micky heard the pig-man. There was the slap of the screen door and the thud of his boots coming down the old, weed-choked steps of the front porch. Through the boards he was barely a shadow crossing the clearing. At the fence, in the shaft of light from the shed, he stopped, braced his forearms against the top rail, and watched the copulating swine through the open door.

For a long time he didn't move, his gaze fixed, his body rigid; only his tongue flitted out from time to time over his lips. And as the pigs' chanting grew louder, his hand went to the crotch of his work pants. He massaged himself slowly, his eyes never leaving the coitally joined pigs.

When he left the fence, Micky's heart raced. Aroused by the pigs, he was coming for her.

Fate, Micky thought.

Her hand closed around the cool water hose, the rubber slippery from the sweat beaded along it.

This *was* her destiny. She was here to kill the pig-man.

At the pen's low divider, he paused. With bleary eyes he sized her up, his gaze traveling from her to the chain on her shackle. This time, though, she'd tucked the chain in alongside her so he couldn't grab it and yank her feet out from under her.

She watched the muscles in his face contract into a tight smile, revealing crooked teeth. Micky imagined he recognized her newfound determination, and it turned him on even more.

His long legs scissored over the pen's top rail, the untied laces of his work boots swirling around his ankles. Micky wondered if the boots were steel-toed. One well-placed kick could easily end her life.

Micky started to stand, and this time when he rushed her, she was ready.

Her fate colliding with his.

In the last second before he reached her, Micky drew back her blanket and swung the hose. The heavy pistol-grip sprayer made a whirring sound as it sailed through the air in a wide arc.

It was well-aimed. And the pig-man ducked too late.

The brass nozzle caught him along the side of the head, resonating a hollow but meaty-sounding thud. And even while Micky wished it had connected with the softer depression of his temple, she saw a small trickle of blood as his hand came up. He teetered for a second, staring at the blood on his hand when he pulled it away.

But Micky couldn't wait to see if the blow would bring him down. He was within the circle. She could reach him.

And she did.

In one blind lunge, she was on him. Bringing her knee up in a quick but solid angle as she'd been taught in the self-defense classes she'd taken down on Lombard, Micky caught him square in the nuts. His startled cry came out in a stench of sour breath. And before he'd even doubled over, she kicked the same leg across and under him.

Hope rushed in as the son of a bitch went down.

Micky threw herself on top of him, knee driving into his sternum, feeling the air rush out of him. Her hatred exploded in a sea of rage. She heard her own scream as she drew back for a fuller swing and took aim, already visualizing the palm-heel strike she'd use to crush his wind pipe. At best: potentially lethal. At its worst: she'd stun him long enough to get the hose around his thick, ugly, motherfucking neck.

But he was fast. Still gasping for air, he heaved himself sideways, and Micky's blow skimmed past his shoulder. She cried out in pain as the dirt floor absorbed the power of her strike.

Then he was on her. His large hands blocking every desperate blow, his mass overpowering her. And when she heard his laughter, Micky felt her determination slip. He had her hair in one fist, and as the world spun in slow motion, Micky was powerless to stop the forward motion as he swung her head squarely into the bottom beam.

She saw stars even as she felt her blood warm her face, and she welcomed the first wavering shadows of blackness.

His hands clamped around her neck and she couldn't take in air. Her lungs sucked futilely against the pressure, and her throat burned under the constriction of his calloused fingers. When the tingling sensation started along her torso, her arms, and head, when she felt suddenly cold and floaty, Micky realized she'd gotten it all wrong: *her* fate was irrelevant in the face of his.

And as the gentle blackness swallowed Micky Luttrell and she felt her body surrender to it, she prayed to God, *Be good to Emma.*

43

Friday, August 3

KAY HAD RECEIVED the phone call just before 7:00 a.m. She'd been dreaming of pigs again.

Otis Reaney's voice had been broken and the transmission choppy as he apologized for the lack of a good signal. The Frederick County Sheriff's Office detective was using his cell, and "the reception in these goddamn mountains," he'd explained, "is for shit."

Kay had sat up in bed, pushing the nightmare images from her mind.

"I'll keep this short." Reaney's voice had sounded as if it came through a long, damp tunnel. "Got a body up here in the woods," he'd said, and Kay's chest tightened. "I don't think it's your cop. Doesn't really fit the description."

Static crackled over the line. "Figured with your interest in Frances you'll want to see this," he'd said. "Can you get up here?"

"I'm on my way."

"Sheriff's Office can give you directions . . . signal's cutting out." A final burst of static and Reaney was gone.

Kay had felt jittery as she'd jotted down the directions from the Frederick County Sheriff's Office. She'd left a voice mail for Savalas, then called Finn. And within a half hour after Reaney's call, Finn sat in the passenger seat as Kay caught I-70 off the Beltway.

Now, as she followed Sabillasville Road northwest out of Thurmont, Kay checked her watch. "We made good time," she told Finn, who studied the map. "Sheriff's Office says the crime scene's less than fifteen minutes out of town."

Ahead of them, past the fields and flats, the Catoctins were a looming mass of dark green in the haze of morning heat.

"'Bout halfway up we're looking for Indian Head Road," Finn said as the 4Runner took the first steep grade. "So tell me more about this phone call you got from Blyth."

It had been late last night. Kay had barely walked through her apartment door, her emotions still jumbled, and the phone had been ringing. For an instant she'd thought it might be Finn calling. The fantasy dissolved when she'd heard Stacey Blyth's thin voice over the line.

"I can't get him out of my head," she'd told Kay. "Funny how I spent four years trying to forget him, and now, since your visit, it's like it happened yesterday."

"I'm sorry."

"Don't be. In a way, I'm kinda glad."

"How's that?"

"Because I think my girlfriend's right. Becka says I won't be able to let go until that son of a bitch is caught. So I started thinking, maybe . . . maybe I should try to help."

Kay had heard the deep sigh over the line and felt the girl's acquiescence: resigning to remember, resigning to face her past.

"I . . . I think I might have found something for you," she'd said at last. Then Stacey Blyth spoke again of the bumps on her attacker's arms. The same wartlike lumps that had been described by the prostitute.

"They're actually tumors," she had told Kay. "Benign, connective-tissue tumors. I didn't know what they were before. Like I said, I've spent the past four years trying to forget the details. Now though . . . I want you to get this monster. So I did some research."

Kay remembered the biochemistry and genetics text-books stacked on Blyth's coffee table.

"I think the son of a bitch has neurofibromatosis," Blyth had told her. "It's the only thing that looks like what I saw on him. And trust me, I've looked through a lot of medical journals and slides. Even skin cancer doesn't look the way NF does."

And now, as the Frederick County mountain road shifted from asphalt to gravel and every sharp turn and hill offered more potholes and washboard, Kay explained to Finn what she remembered of Blyth's description of the condition she believed her attacker suffered from.

"It's an inheritable genetic disorder," Kay told him, "that affects the cells in nerve tissue. Blyth says there's no cure. The only thing doctors can treat is the symptoms."

"And what are the symptoms?"

"Individuals are affected differently. There's the tumors. Most are benign. Some can become malignant. Others are surgically removed if they become painful. It can also affect bones and the spine, causing chronic pain or even skeletal abnormalities. There's also the possibility of blindness, hearing loss, even brain tumors."

"Well, wouldn't that explain a lot?" he said derisively. "So you're thinking our perp has this NF?"

Kay gritted her teeth as her SUV's suspension struggled over another section of washboard. "I don't know what to think right now, Finn. There are so many angles coming at us with this one. I was going to ask Dixie this morning what she knew about NF, whether she could determine its presence in the samples we've got from this guy."

"And even if he *does* have this neuro-whatever, how does that help us?"

"Well, maybe he's got other noticeable symptoms. Something that makes him stand out, like these tumors of his, something people remember. We could also check with local doctors or look into NF support groups."

When Blyth had spoken of the psychological aspects of the genetic neurological disorder last night over the phone, Kay had realized that—like her—the girl was trying to grasp a truer sense of her assailant, to get inside his head. And Kay had liked the girl even more.

"Chances are there's at least a couple area NF support groups, set up to help victims deal with the disorder."

It felt wrong referring to him as a "victim" . . . the man who had abducted Micky, who had so sadistically raped the young Stacey Blyth, who had put Frances Gallo into a mental facility, probably for the remainder of her life.

"Well, we already know this fucknut's a wacko. I doubt he's gone to any group-therapy shit. There!" Finn pointed out the windshield to the T-intersection partially concealed by the next curve.

Kay skidded the big tires of the SUV and a cloud of dust billowed around them as she took the right. Indian Head was even narrower, and a crumbling concrete railway overpass angled above them. There were no shoulders along the winding mountain roads, only milkweed and Queen Anne's lace growing tight against the bordering ridge of gravel.

Countless overgrown lanes snaked off the dusty road, disappearing back into the darkness of the trees and brush. Most had gates bearing warnings: KEEP OUT, NO TRESPASSING.

Higher and higher, one curve rougher than the last, the sunlight swallowed up by the dense vegetation of the forest where only flashes of sunlight managed to speckle the road now.

It was the Frederick County Sheriff's Office's mobile "command bus" that they saw first, an enormous white hulk through the trees, and Kay wondered how long it had taken the driver to maneuver the full-size bus up the mountainside. Other vehicles filled the roadway as well: FCSO black-and-whites, a couple of Thurmont Police cruisers, one dark, unmarked Chevy that Kay guessed was Reaney's, and a Crime Scene truck. And when Kay saw two ATVs sitting idle at the head of what looked to be a footpath, she wondered exactly how far into the woods the body was.

Kay pulled her 4Runner in behind the last cruiser. After the long drive in the AC, the cloying heat of the morning felt as if it was already spiking into the high nineties, and the humidity of the surrounding forest was stifling with no trace of a breeze. Virginia creepers swallowed up whole trees, and the dense foliage overhead seemed to choke out not only light, but air as well.

Overhead, the buzz of the cicadas was nearly deafening. The only other sound was the crackle of a police radio, held by the FCSO patrol who manned the ATVs, and then the rapid-fire shutter of a camera.

Kay turned in time for the cameraman to catch several shots. She hadn't seen him when they'd pulled up, but now she could just make out the *Frederick News-Post* car parked at the end of the line of vehicles.

"Christ, even up here you just can't lose 'em," she mumbled to Finn as she crossed to the ATVs and the patrol officer. Gravel ground beneath her runners, and her T-shirt was already sticking to her skin.

The young officer in the brown Sheriff's Office uniform looked a little wan. Kay wondered if he'd already been back in the woods and seen the body.

"Be sure no one gives that guy our names, will you?" Kay said to the patrol as she showed him her shield and shoved a thumb at the media hound.

He nodded. There were sweat marks under the arms of his brown shirt. "Detective Reaney's down at the site," he told her. "Said to ride you in. Didn't know there'd be two of you though." The officer fingered the radio at his hip, clearly unsure how to take command of the situation, then turned to Finn. "You know how to drive one of these, Detective?"

But Kay answered him. "Yeah. Give me the keys."

He did so, then nodded at the thin trail disappearing into the forest. On either side of the dirt path the ground cover had been crushed by the wheels of the ATVs. "This here trail goes back a ways. About a half mile in you gotta cut right. It's marked with tape. The rest of the way in isn't trail though. Just follow where the other machines have gone in. It's rough going, so you wanna take her slow."

"Gotcha." Kay was already at the nearest ATV, a big, black, two-seater Outlander. It had been years since she'd done any off-roading, but after a quick survey of the controls, Kay felt comfortable. And anxious.

She took up the closest helmet, made some adjustments, and straddled the driver's seat. Starting up the four-stroke engine, Kay tossed Finn the other helmet. "Come on. Get on."

You wanna take her slow, " the patrol had warned her, and as Kay opened the throttle, she knew "slow" wasn't an option.

44

FINN COULD ALREADY SMELL the decay. It hung in the thick, sultry air. Putrid and unmistakable. Clinging to him like his sweat-soaked shirt.

When Kay finally stopped the ATV next to two others, Otis Reaney had just made his way up out of the ravine fifty feet away. The Sheriff's Office detective was a bull of a man. Solid and wide, and perhaps just a little out of shape. He was winded when he joined them, and he used one sleeve to wipe the perspiration beading across his brow.

Kay made the introductions. Between the vibrations of the Outlander and the white-knuckled grip he'd maintained during the ride into the site, Finn could barely feel Reaney's handshake.

"Glad you could make it," Reaney said, his attention going back to Kay. And as she shut off the ATV, he seemed impressed that she'd been the one to maneuver the four-wheeler over the unforgiving terrain.

"Even if you hadn't come seen me two days ago and put Frances fresh in my mind," Reaney told Kay, "I would've thought of her the second I saw this girl."

Reaney gestured for them to follow him through the raspberry and sticker bushes, along a single path that had been tamped down between the ATVs and the ravine. "Some buddies out on a fishing trip found her last night, but didn't want to risk four-wheeling it out in the dark. First light they rode back to their trucks and called it in. Watch that," Reaney said as he held back a branch of thorns for Kay.

"Lucky for us they had a GPS with 'em. They way-pointed the body, then went south to their trucks. With the data from their unit we were able to find a closer access point." He shoved a thumb in the direction of the road, still a ten-minute, bone-jarring ride out.

"No way someone brought her in all this way just to dump her," Reaney speculated, swatting at a mosquito as he stopped at the brink of the steep ravine. "I figure she must've wandered in on her own, lost her footing, and fell down this bank, or the other side. Can't say for sure right now, but it looks like her neck's broke."

About thirty feet down, the trees gave way only marginally, and sunlight dappled the slow-moving creek below. Through the undergrowth, Finn could just make out flashes of white skin down where the creek spilled out into a shallow, rocky pool.

He was immediately impressed with Reaney's handling of the crime scene. Where it could have been overrun with FCSO and Thurmont PD scoping for a gawk, the detective had kept the personnel on the scene limited to only those absolutely necessary: two crime-scene technicians, three uniforms who searched tediously through the ferns and forest-floor growth, and a plainclothes who Finn guessed was Reaney's partner.

"Detective!" one of the TPD uniforms called out to Reaney from the ATVs. He held up a thick, black Motorola radio. "O'Hearn's at the road. You want me to get him?"

"Meet Dave halfway. I want O'Hearn ASAP."

"Rudy O'Hearn," Reaney explained to Finn and Kay. "Armed Forces Police. Specializes in entomology. Sure, we can collect whatever's needed and send it on to O'Hearn. But I figured, given the possible connection to your missing cop and the press this thing might get, we'd better not screw around. I'd rather have O'Hearn collect his own maggots."

"Maggots? How long do you figure she's been down there?" Kay asked.

"More than a few days," Reaney said. "County ME can probably narrow it down when he gets here. Or O'Hearn can age his creepy-crawlers. I think decomposition might have been worse except she got snagged up in the creek. It's spring-fed so the water's pretty cold. She's still a mess though."

"Let's see her," Kay said, and Finn heard the restlessness in her voice.

Reaney pointed to the guideline secured between the trees and the smaller saplings along the precipitous slope. But when Kay's hand closed around the rope, Reaney stopped her.

"There's something else you should know," he said, a graveness in his expression as the detective looked toward the body in the creek.

"What is it?"

"The girl . . . she's not the only victim here."

45

DARYL HEARD THE FOUR-WHEELERS.

He'd started hearing them just after daybreak, lying in his bed, staring up at the stained ceiling. He heard them off and on while he cleaned out the shed. And he listened to them now as he rolled himself on the mechanic's trolley underneath his F-100. They sounded like four-strokes, he thought as he removed the drain cap and let the thick, black oil spill into the catch tray beside him.

Odd.

Daryl felt curiosity more than concern when he wheeled out from under the pickup and leaned back against its fender. His gaze fixing on nothing in particular, he cocked his head and tried to gauge the location of the ATVs.

Daryl wiped a rag through his grease-stained hands, as the distant throttle of another four-wheeler echoed up the mountain. Whoever it was out there blasting around, they'd be wise to steer clear of his property, Daryl thought as he remembered the last two four-wheeling yahoos who'd made the mistake of venturing too close.

Three autumns ago, if his memory served him right. They'd come in off the road, probably on the trail of an injured deer they'd already plugged one hole into. Hunters who had no aim, Daryl always thought, had no right calling themselves hunters.

Their ATVs had sounded closer than the ones this morning, rattling up and down his road until Daryl found himself almost daring them to open the gate and let themselves in.

Then he'd heard the screaming and had instantly known what had happened. He'd put on his camo jacket, even smeared on some face grease as he went out the door. The cries had grown fainter, raspy, as Daryl had crept through his personal battleground, but they were soon replaced by the higher-pitched panic of the second hunter.

He found them in the east corner of the property, only a few dozen yards from the old well. Not until later had he been grateful for that particular convenience.

He'd already known which snare had been tripped. And he'd been smiling long before he'd laid eyes on the pair. The one who'd been caught was limp by then, the tightening wires the only thing keeping him upright, suspended over a thick puddle of his own blood, while his frantic buddy worked uselessly at the razor wires.

It had been easy moving in on the guy with all his squealing and sputtering. Daryl got within ten feet of him before he ever knew he was there, and the yahoo only knew because Daryl wanted him to. After all, no thrill in shooting a guy in the back. You needed to see his eyes.

Even faced with the business end of Daryl's twelve-gauge, the dipshit was slow to realize Daryl wasn't there to help. It took a few long moments before Daryl saw the fear he was after.

He remembered laughing when the shithead fumbled for the rifle strapped over his shoulder. He was still laughing when he pumped the Mossberg once and blew the yahoo's fool head off.

Daryl never knew if it was the blast of the shotgun or his friend's brain matter splashing him in the face, but the guy strung up in the snare had come to then. Daryl had stepped over the dead hunter and stared into the dying man's eyes as the life dribbled out of him.

The exhilaration had been well worth the task of getting rid of them. He'd dragged both men to the old well, dumped them one after the other, rifles and all. He'd found their ATVs on the road just down from his drive, considered keeping one, but knew better. So Daryl had loaded them one at a time up onto the truck, covered them with a tarp, and made two trips to the old quarry. He'd considered dumping them into the gorge. Even after the hot summer, the water level was plenty deep for the four-wheelers.

But then he'd decided the smarter thing to do would be to actually park the machines as though they'd been left there. The Sheriff's Office had spent days searching that old quarry. But they never did find those two hunters.

Now, three years later, as Daryl listened to the ATVs in the distance and thought of the two hunters rotting in the bottom of his old well, he wondered if—after all this time—the snare they'd tripped and he'd repaired was still active. He wondered if he'd be able to find it again and thought he should try.

More pressing than that, however, were the four-wheelers. He fingered the keys in the pocket of his coveralls and eyed the Maverick. The truck's oil change could wait, Daryl thought as he crossed over to the old sports car. Ever faithful, she started up on the first crank. And Daryl nosed the Maverick along the drive, and down the mountain.

46

SIXTEEN YEARS ON THE JOB, half of those working murders, Kay couldn't remember if she'd ever been as deeply affected as she was by what lay at the bottom of the ravine.

Making her way down the sheer slope, the smell of decay intensifying with every step, Kay knew it wasn't good even before she'd laid eyes on the naked, bloated remains listing in the stream. In the midsummer heat the body in the creek, in spite of the eight or ten inches of cold spring water, had certainly passed the early stages of decomp.

It wasn't Micky.

The woman had fallen faceup, and Reaney's guess at a broken neck had been a no-brainer, her head wedged in a severely wrong angle between a rock and her shoulder. Across her bloated body, the skin had blistered and was peeling. Marbling was pronounced along the limbs, extending across the chest and distended abdomen, the greenish black discoloration marking the decomposition of blood within the vessels just below the skin's surface.

Her face was the worst: swollen beyond recognition, the lips mushroomed out, and the skin almost purple. There would be no visual identification of the remains, and Kay hoped she was a hooker. That her prints were on file somewhere.

The hands and feet were already gloving, the skin sloughing off, detaching in one piece like a glove. It would be work, but Kay suspected they'd get at least a couple usable prints.

She waved at several slow, metallic-colored flies. Reaney had given both her and Finn a good dose of bug repellent before they'd gone down into the ravine. It worked for the mosquitoes, more or less, but did nothing for the flies. And as they crawled across Kay's skin, she shuddered as she imagined where they'd been.

More than any other decomp case Kay had worked, this one was rife with insect activity. Rudy O'Hearn, the Armed Forces Police entomology specialist, had arrived not long after Kay and Finn had finished their preliminary survey. Now the bug guy squatted in the shallow stream, the water lapping over his boots, as he examined the insect microcosm playing out across the woman's body. He was a small, eager man with a careful and serious demeanor. He'd already snapped dozens of photos of the insects laying claim to the exposed flesh and now picked through the maggots and carrion beetles with a pair of long forceps. Some he deposited into jars of ethanol, while others were placed in live-specimen containers.

He smiled when he lifted one of the flat receptacles to the light and rattled several maggots around its bottom.

"We'll raise these little guys in the lab," he explained when he noticed Kay's stare.

"And then what?"

"Determine species. That'll give us a time frame. Different insects are drawn to carrion at different stages. Some prefer the freshly dead. Others aren't attracted until the putrefactive gases are present. And then there are others who are only interested in the molds or the other insects. But these here are likely your typical blue blowflies."

"And what does that tell you?"

"Blowflies are generally your first on the scene. They can arrive within minutes of a body hitting the ground."

"So what's your guess on how long she's been out here?" Finn asked.

"Won't know until I run all the stats. Temperature, humidity, weather data for the past few days. Then replicate the conditions in order to raise these beauts." He leaned across the body and extracted several larger maggots from the corner of the girl's nose. "These look to be second instar. Meaning, your second crop. In this heat, blowfly eggs can hatch in one or two days."

"Which means what? She's been here three, maybe four days?"

O'Hearn's balding head bobbed once. "It's a good estimate. But like I said, I'll have a more accurate time frame once I factor in the temperatures and other environmental factors."

Kay swatted at a couple of mosquitoes. She felt faint. It was the heat, she was sure. The saunalike humidity had sapped her energy. And she should have eaten before they'd left the city.

Time had ceased to have any meaning in the heat and stench of the small clearing. She had no idea how long she'd stood there at the water's edge, the toes of her runners already soaked from sliding on the slick rocks, her gaze raking over and over the dead girl, scrutinizing every aspect as though, somehow, something would speak to her, give her direction.

And always, involuntarily, Kay's eyes returned to the other victim in the ravine.

The other life that had been lost.

She wondered if the men who'd found her had recognized the double tragedy in the woman's death.

Just below the stream's surface, the tiny, perfectly formed feet and legs were barely noticeable between the woman's swollen and peeling thighs. The feeble current stirred them, making them appear almost animated. She'd heard of it happening—the bloating and putrefactive gases expelling a fetus—and Kay wondered if another day in the heat would have caused a full discharge.

"You doing okay?" Finn's voice was a whisper as he moved alongside her.

Kay nodded.

"You don't look too good."

"It's this fucking heat."

The little feet dipped and swayed in the stream.

A life ended before it had ever taken a breath. All because of a monster.

"Someone's gotta be missing this girl, Finn."

"You mean a husband?"

"Or boyfriend." She couldn't take her eyes off the fetus. "Why haven't we heard about a missing pregnant woman?"

"Not every Laci Peterson becomes a media frenzy."

Kay looked past the stream into the thick woods. "He's got to be close."

She scanned the bank, the dense underbrush, and beyond. "She can't have come far," she said, and suddenly Kay imagined Micky somewhere beyond the dark trunks of the maple and basswood, the choking creepers and kudzu. She imagined screaming Micky's name into the woods. She imagined getting an answer.

"Or she might have wandered for days," Finn argued. "If this *was* one of his victims, I doubt he would have hunted for a new victim until she was gone."

"You mean Micky."

Finn nodded. He looked as sapped of energy as she felt. His T-shirt was damp, and even his hair under the short ponytail was soaked with sweat. "Micky was snatched Saturday night." Kay knew he was thinking aloud. "If Micky *was* this girl's replacement, then she could have been out since Saturday. Maybe longer if you figure he might have spent a day or two looking for her."

"Unless he realized she was pregnant and didn't want her," Kay said. "Maybe he wanted to get rid of her. Drove her out here, dumped her in the dead of night so she wouldn't find the road. Or maybe even pushed her down into this ravine himself."

"Which means he could live in the next county. Or fucking West Virginia for all we know."

Kay's frustration was about to brim over.

"But what about the shackle then?" She pointed to the steel jaws around the woman's ankle, held together with a heavy padlock. The device looked medieval, but even though rust had started eating the surface, it wasn't that old. And forged directly to the shackle was what looked to be at least twenty pounds of chain, the heavy links snaking through the rocks along the creek's bank. "She *had* to have escaped," Kay said. "The eye screw is still attached to the chain. If he was dumping her, why wouldn't he have removed the shackle and chain?"

But Finn didn't have an answer.

"Jesus Christ, Finn. Who is this son of a bitch?"

Loose stones rained down the slope as Reaney descended again. He crossed the rocky streambed to join them. "We're not finding any kind of footprints, Detectives. Ground's too hard up on either side of the ravine. There's no telling which direction she came from."

"We need a dog out here," Kay said, and Reaney was already nodding.

"Once we get some of the personnel cleared out and lift her out of here, we'll bring in the K9 unit." He removed his cap and ran one meaty hand through his sandy-colored hair. "You two be wanting a ride back outta here soon?"

Kay shook her head. "No. I want to help carrying her out of here." It wasn't that she didn't trust the county's technicians to handle it properly. Kay just wanted to be there for the girl and the fetus. She couldn't explain why.

Reaney nodded, then moved on, giving instructions for his men to wrap up the scene.

Kay scanned the forest again, the heat and humidity washing over her. And she imagined eyes, imagined they were being watched, but she doubted that was true.

Where are you, Micky?

And as Kay considered all the copies of all the case

files collecting dust in Ed Gunderson's basement, all the missing prostitutes over the years, she wondered how many more bodies these woods must be hiding. How many girls' bodies were lost out here on this mountain-side, never to be found?

47

THEY'D STAYED UNTIL THE BODY was moved, lifted from the water, zipped into a white body bag, then securely strapped into a stokes basket supplied by the Rocky Ridge Volunteer Fire Company. They'd had to haul her up out of the ravine with ropes, before she was hand-carried back to the road where the OCME's van was wait-ing to transport her to the city.

It was late afternoon by the time Kay started up the 4Runner, leaving it to cool down at the side of the road while she wrapped up with Reaney.

"I'll call tonight," he'd told her. "Let you know how the dogs do. We'll find this son of a bitch, Detective." And when he shook her hand, he held it longer than a hand-shake. "I promise."

Back in the city Savalas had been strangely silent while Kay and Finn had briefed the task force. And as Kay had pointed to the area on the map where the girl had been found, in the heart of Frederick County, Savalas hadn't so much as acknowledged the accuracy of Kay's investigative direction so far in the case.

Then again, it wasn't acknowledgment Kay was after. It was Micky.

The sky over Baltimore was already darkening when

Kay and Finn parked on Penn Street and walked into the cool lobby of the OCME's foyer. The basement was even cooler. But not a good cool. It was laced with the faint odor of decomposition. Kay smelled it the second they stepped out of the elevator.

Autopsies for the state of Maryland were routinely conducted in the morning. However, the Frederick County girl, with her possible link to Micky, was an exception. The basement was deserted, save for a couple staff and a pathology assistant in the main autopsy suite.

"Your girl's in no-man's-land," the assistant said, referring to the isolation room: a laminar airflow room where the low-pathogen environment was more conducive to working decomposition cases.

The smell of their Jane Doe became stronger as they took the heavy double doors out into the cavernous delivery area. The OCME van that had transported her from the county was still backed up to the platform, directly across from the closed steel door of the isolation room.

Dr. Sarah Dixon had already been hard at work on the girl's body. Cutting and dissecting, weighing and documenting. She stepped back from the bloated remains on the steel table and gave Finn and Kay a nod as they entered. The intern next to her looked a little green. She wore a face mask, the strings pulled tight, as though it could block the stench. Dixie, however, was clearly immune.

"Leave it to you two to bring me the juicy ones," she joked.

"What can you tell us, Dixie?" Kay asked.

"Well, all bets are off. With this much putrefaction, making anything beyond an educated guess is a crapshoot."

"Any idea of age?"

"Based on the lack of any atherosclerosis or degenerative joint disease, and looking at the teeth and skull, I'd put her in her late twenties, early thirties."

"Time of death?"

"You're best to wait for O'Hearn. The insects will give you a much more accurate TOD. Three or four days. Maybe five."

"So give us the rundown."

Dixie waved a hand at the remains, her gloves slick with decomposition and body fluids. "She was dehydrated. Sodium and chloride levels were high. And she was definitely malnourished. No partially digested food was present in the stomach or the large or small intestines. You've also got a complete loss of muscle mass. And that kind of loss takes time."

"How much time?"

"Weeks. Months, even. And this girl had been through the wringer. When I cut down through the skin and soft tissue, she's full of bruises. Like someone used her for a punching bag. Three fractured ribs too, in the early stages of healing. But the cause of death was the broken neck."

"What about prints?" Finn asked.

Dixie nodded to where the intern was hunched over a stainless-steel table. "How are those coming?"

The intern was a small, demure girl who appeared clearly shaken by the condition of the body. In one gloved hand she gingerly held the shed skin from the victim's right hand, nails still attached. Kay watched as the intern delicately wormed her own latex-covered hand inside the shed skin, wearing it like a second glove, then worked meticulously at making clear prints on a print card.

Dixie glanced over the intern's shoulder. "These look good. If this girl's in the system, you'll have a name by tomorrow."

All four of them watched as the card filled, one print at a time, until the door swung open. Savalas looked peaked even before she stepped inside the isolation room. She kept one hand on the door, as though having already decided she wasn't staying, and Kay wondered how many autopsies the sergeant had observed in her too short homicide career.

"Just got a call from Reaney," she reported, her eyes never leaving the gooey and fetid remains of their Jane Doe. Maggots still worked at the orifices, and water and decomp fluids had dripped from the bag to a small puddle on the concrete floor. "The K9 teams came up empty. Apparently the trail was either too old or it kept looping back on itself."

Or, Kay thought, *her captor had driven her there.* But—although not entirely outside the realm of possibility—the idea of his walking his victim a mile and a half into the woods seemed a little far-fetched.

"How are you two making out here?"

Kay nodded. "Fine."

"Well, then"—Savalas looked up from the table, her mouth tight—"I'll leave you to it."

Kay listened to the fading staccato of Savalas's heels through the steel door. "What else can you tell us, Dixie?" Kay asked, turning back to the body. "What about the shackle?"

The iron ankle restraint had already been removed, the lock snapped with bolt cutters. It sat along with the length of chain and the heavy eye screw on the neighboring gurney.

"Rule of thumb for putrefaction," Dixie said, "is one week in the air equals two in the water. Based on the preservation, I'm presuming this ankle was submerged?"

Kay nodded.

Dixie indicated the horizontal striations left by the shackle. "Here you've got significant scarring with granulation tissue in the underlying soft tissue. Under the microscope I found the presence of numerous hemosiderin-laden macrophages."

"Which means?" Finn asked.

"Old hemorrhage."

"How old?"

"Like I said, given the damage from the decomp, I can't even make an educated guess, but she'd been wearing that contraption for a while."

Kay struggled with the images that were haunting her mind now.

How long had he kept her?

She didn't want to ask, but had to. "And what about the fetus?"

"Oh, now *that's* interesting." Dixie's face lit up. "Come on, let me show you. You'll want to see this."

But Kay didn't.

48

IT LAY ON THE COUNTER next to a sink in the back corner of the main autopsy suite. Fully formed but so very small. The tiny corpse was almost lost amid the sea of stainless steel surfaces and surgical tools.

Kay thought she might be sick.

"Based on organ weights and body measurements," Dixie explained, as she lead them through the room to the back, "fetus development looks to be somewhere at the beginning of the third trimester. Given the mother's state of malnourishment, I can't give you anything more precise than twenty-five to thirty weeks."

At twenty-three weeks, Kay knew from the one and only prenatal book she'd bought a year ago, the baby would have started moving. Her thoughts went to the Jane Doe in the isolation room. What had she felt when the baby had started kicking inside her?

"As you can see, the baby's in much better condition than his mother," Dixie went on. "Not as decomposed because the amniotic sac in the womb is a sterile environment, so it's actually quite well preserved."

Dixie's voice became a garble of words in Kay's ears, distant and hollow, as a low droning sound seemed to take over.

The baby's limbs were long and his body lean and covered in a fine, downy hair. Lanugo, Kay remembered from the book that was still in her nightstand.

Coming closer, Kay could see he'd been autopsied like his mother, the tiny Y-incision across his paper-thin, purplish skin making Kay nauseous. And when Dixie rolled the fetus onto its side, the ceiling felt too low and the fluorescents overhead too bright as Kay tried to make sense of the gross disfigurement she saw before her.

". . . severe scoliosis . . . personally never seen this level of skeletal malformation," Kay heard Dixie say over the ringing in her ears.

The tiny spine looked contorted, twisted. As if someone had wrung the baby. Even its arms didn't seem right, deformed at odd angles and curled as though the muscles had atrophied.

Kay felt suddenly very hot.

"Could physical injury to the mother have caused

something like that?" she asked, and the involuntary memory of Tyrel Johnson reeled through her exhausted brain: Johnson coming at her, hitting the sidewalk, and all that blood on her bathroom floor.

"No," Dixie said. "This is more likely something genetic. I'll need to look into it a bit more, talk with Jonesy, run some tests . . ."

Stacey Blyth's phone call came back to Kay. *Skeletal abnormalities . . . An inheritable genetic disorder.* And then there was the shackle. Not weeks, but months, Dixie had said regarding the scarring along the mother's ankle.

"Neurofibromatosis," Kay said finally, not wanting to believe what her mind was imagining. "It's neurofibromatosis."

Dixie looked from Kay to the fetus, her nod slow coming. "Well, that's certainly possible."

"Can you test for it?"

"Sure. But, Kay, there are a number of conditions and factors that could result in what you're seeing here."

"Just do it, Dixie. I don't care what it takes or who I have to sleep with. We need those results as soon as possible."

"I'll do my best."

And Kay trusted that the assistant chief medical examiner would.

She was aware of Finn following her out of the autopsy suite, down the wide, polished corridor to the elevator. She felt weak in the knees, and when she closed her eyes, all she saw was the disfigured fetus curled up on the stainless steel counter. An image that she knew would be with her forever.

"You all right?" Finn asked when the elevator arrived.

Kay nodded. Knew he wasn't convinced.

"You're thinking the baby was his." Finn punched the lobby button.

"We need Savalas to authorize a rush on a paternity test. The DNA will still take a couple of days. Run it against the blood we found on Micky's abduction scene. But if what we saw down there is neurofibromatosis . . ."

"Well, like Dixie said, it could be any number of things." And it was clear that the implications of Kay's theory didn't sit well with Finn either.

"Trust me," Kay said as the elevator opened, "I'm praying it's something else."

It felt strange walking out of the OCME's at night, Kay thought, seeing darkness beyond the lobby doors instead of the welcome sunshine that usually awaited them after hours spent in the basement.

The night air was heavy, with a foreboding stillness to it. The calm before the storm. Kay heard the low rumble of thunder rolling far off over the city.

"You sure you're all right?" Finn asked again as he unlocked the unmarked.

But Kay didn't get a chance to answer.

She felt the sudden displacement of air to her left before she ever registered Jack Macklin coming at Finn.

"You fucking rat, Finnerty!" Macklin was a blur as he launched himself at Finn, the collision almost taking both of them down.

Kay caught herself on the Impala and turned in time to see the collar of Finn's shirt fisted in Macklin's hand.

"Mack!" Kay yelled at him. "Mack!"

But she was nothing to the Vice detective. He spun Finn around, the element of surprise still working to his benefit. Finn let out a low grunt when Mack slammed him up against the unmarked. Hard.

"Mack, for Christ's sake." Kay was on him, grappling with his thick forearm, forcing herself between the two men.

Macklin tried to shake her off, and when he finally threw a punch, Kay's interference deflected it just enough that it barely clipped the side of Finn's cheek.

"Son of a bitch, Macklin." She heard Finn behind her even as she pushed Macklin back.

But Kay never expected Finn's retaliation.

His fist was a blur past her face. And then Macklin was reeling backward.

"Jesus! Finn!" When Kay spun on him, there was a rage in his eyes she couldn't remember having ever seen. "What the hell are you doing?"

"You fucking had my car searched." Macklin blubbered between bloodied lips. "Nothing but a goddamn rat!"

"Yeah?" Finn came at him again. "And you're a fucking crooked cop, Macklin."

It was Finn Kay had to hold back now, ready to take another round at the Vice cop. "What is *wrong* with you, Finn?"

"I'm onto you, you hear me?" Finn shouted at Mack even as Kay pushed him toward the car. He flexed his fist. Two small abrasions along his knuckles had started to bleed.

"Finn, go home," she said.

His eyes never left Macklin.

Kay grabbed his face and turned him to her. "You hear me?"

She waited for his nod.

"I'm going to talk to Mack," she told him.

As she crossed the lot to usher Macklin away, Kay knew Finn was watching. And she almost didn't trust that he wouldn't come after them.

49

THE SIP & BITE DINER on Boston Street, between Fells Point and Canton, was just down from Jack Macklin's apartment on Aliceanna. The full-plate diner served everything from breakfast to Greek cuisine, twenty-four hours a day. Tonight, all Kay wanted was coffee.

She'd been ready to take Mack's car keys back on Penn Street until she realized the Vice cop was more pissed off than he was drunk.

In fact, Macklin seemed quite sober.

His big hands wrapped around his cup, he stared out the diner windows as the first huge drops of rain pelted down and a roll of thunder rattled the plate glass.

Macklin's lip had stopped bleeding.

"That's going to swell if you don't get some ice on it," she said.

"It'll be fine." He sipped his coffee but she could tell it hurt. "Looks like you got yourself a bit of a shiner though," he said, pointing to the faint bruising Kay knew had settled under her eye from Frances Gallo's hallucinatory fit yesterday.

"It's nothing."

Another rumble of thunder. And the rain came harder. A week's worth of ninety-degree heat had brewed up the mother of all storms.

"Listen, Kay." He leaned into the table, and under the harsh diner lights he looked wasted. "I can explain the blood in the car."

"I don't want bullshit."

He shook his head. "No bullshit, even though I wish

I could say it was one of the johns that night who gave Micky a bloody nose."

The words came slowly. Carefully? Or were they simply difficult? Kay couldn't tell.

"Truth is *I* did it."

"*You* did?"

He nodded. "It was a shitty night. We had an argument. It was an accident, Kay. Still . . ." He grunted and shook his head. "Christ, the last thing I said to my partner was 'sorry' while she's wiping the bloody nose I gave her."

"What was the argument about?"

His hesitation made Kay believe him. "She wanted to end it," he said finally, and looked out the window.

"You and Micky were having an affair?" Kay was surprised. And she wasn't.

Macklin's nod was barely perceptible. "She said she didn't want to do it anymore. Wasn't ever going to leave her husband. Was through with lying, she said."

Kay thought it was shame she saw in the young detective's eyes when they flitted to hers briefly.

"It was never the same after she had the baby," he added.

"You were having an affair . . . during the pregnancy?"

"It's not like I'm proud of it."

"How long, Mack?"

He closed his eyes, the pain clear.

"How long?"

"The past year. Since just after we started riding together."

Kay could only stare. She thought of Andy Luttrell at home, caring for the colicky baby day and night.

"The baby's not mine, if that's what you're thinking."

"Why didn't you tell me sooner? Before they had to search your car?"

"Like I'm just going to admit that? It's not *my* reputation I was thinking of, Kay. Micky's the one who's married with a kid." And then, as though he'd divulged everything he was going to on the subject, he changed it. "So what about the body you found up in the county? You think it's the same son of a bitch? You think Micky's up there?"

But as much as she wanted to, Kay couldn't offer Jack Macklin much. She kept the details minimal, and when she mentioned the shackle, Macklin seemed to take comfort that it could mean Micky was still alive. "If she plays her cards right," he'd added.

"This guy," he said when Kay had finished, "he's one sick fuck, isn't he?"

"Do you know something, Mack?"

He nodded. "I've been pushing some of my regular pimps. Seeing if anyone knows this mope in the red pickup."

"And?"

"Pimp named Big D remembered the guy from a year or so back, cruising for girls over on Wilkens. When he picked himself up a tranny, apparently they all had a good laugh about that one. Until twenty minutes later the truck comes back and he dumps the tranny out onto the street. Didn't even slow down, D said. He'd beat that gender queer almost to death. Had to call an ambo. Of course, the fag never pressed charges, and I can't find the guy, girl, whatever.

"But I'll say this," Macklin added, "if I find this sick bastard first, I'm gonna kill him."

"Mack, you can't—"

"And what about this wackjob in Spring Grove? You get anything from her?"

Kay shook her head.

"Is she nuts cuz of what this moron did to her?"

"I don't know. I don't think so. I mean, not entirely. Gallo has a history."

Macklin was shaking his head, and his mouth tightened in what looked like defiance. "Not Micky."

"What do you mean, Mack?"

"Micky's strong. She'll make it through this." Emotion threatened to take over. "She will, Kay. I swear. We just gotta find this sick motherfucker."

50

OUTSIDE KAY'S APARTMENT Finn had watched the storm roll in over the city, then listened to the rain pounding the Impala's roof as the windows steamed up. He had no idea how long he'd sat there waiting to see her 4Runner turn onto Hamburg, or how long he intended to wait. He only knew he needed to see her.

He had questions.

Serious questions.

And when he did finally see the SUV's headlights pan up the dead-end street and Kay parked along the flooding curb, Finn got out. Rain soaked through his shirt and jeans, even as Kay made the mad dash to the sheltered doorway of the converted row house.

She invited him up, but he couldn't face the memories. So in the covered entranceway, his hair drenched and his T-shirt clinging to his skin, Kay told him about Macklin's affair with Micky Luttrell. Something about the explanation seemed too easy.

"He's hiding something, Kay."

She shook her head. "And how the hell is he supposed to be involved with Micky's disappearance?"

"I'm not saying he is. I'm saying he's hiding something."

"Why is it you've got such a hate-on for Macklin, anyway?"

"Let's just say I don't tolerate bad cops well."

"You don't know that he's—"

"Christ, Kay. You're actually buying his story about an affair? Come on!" He brushed back his wet hair, and his hand trembled. He tried to control it, but knew Kay had noticed.

"What's going on with you, Finn?"

"I don't know what you mean."

"Going after Macklin like that."

"He came after *me*, Kay." But Kay was right. In situations of confrontation, Finn had almost always been able to maintain his cool. Tonight though, when Jack Macklin had come at him, he'd seen red. And he couldn't explain why.

Maybe it had nothing to do with the Vice cop. Maybe it was his failed qualification yesterday. Maybe it was the fallout of too much advice from his doctor, and too few answers. Too many tests. Too many meds. Fucking spinal taps and injections.

"Finn." He pulled away when she tried to touch him. "Talk to me."

No. He wasn't going to be anyone's sympathy case. Especially Kay's.

"Listen, I . . . I know you're not with Angie anymore."

How? And how long had she known?

"Is that what this is about? Finn?"

He shook his head.

"You're not . . . Tell me you're not drinking again."

"Oh, for Christ's sake, Kay."

Thunder reverberated over the city, and a flash of lightning strobed the sky.

"You're keeping something from me," she said, her voice soft, "and whatever it is—"

"And what about you, Kay? What are you keeping from *me*?"

The lines in her face tightened. "What are you talking about?"

"I'm talking about lies. Secrets."

The suspicion had sparked after they'd visited the Luttrell house, when he'd seen Kay's reaction to the baby. And then tonight, in the chill of the autopsy suite, he'd seen the sweat that had broken out across her skin and watched the blood drain from her face as she'd stared at the fetus from the county Jane Doe.

He knew Kay too well.

She shook her head. "I don't know what—"

"Yes, you do, Kay."

"Look"—she reached for the heavy wooden door—"it's been a long day. I think—"

When he caught her arm, she winced. "Tell me, Kay."

"What? What do you want me to tell you, Finn?"

"Maybe what you should have told me from the start."

She dropped her gaze, unable to look at him. And Finn knew in that moment that he *had* guessed right.

He squeezed her arm tighter. "Tell me."

When her words came at last, he heard them but their meaning was slower to be absorbed.

Pregnancy. Miscarriage.

They washed over him and through him, cutting deep. And when the thunder crashed again, Finn didn't even flinch. He was numb.

"I wanted to tell you, Finn. But how? You were already with Angie when . . ."

Kay had carried his child. A child of *theirs*. And he'd never known.

". . . and by the time I finally had the guts to tell you, it was too late. The baby—"

"When, Kay? When did it happen?"

"Last August."

His calculations came fast. "Second trimester?"

She nodded.

"How, Kay?"

He saw the pain in her eyes, knew she was reliving the miscarriage.

"How?"

"Bobby and I, we had an arrest turn sour. I—"

"You were on the street? Department regulations . . . but you never said anything, did you?"

She wouldn't look at him.

"You never told anyone because you didn't want to go on light duty. Because the job was more important to you than our . . ." He couldn't say it. To say it made it more real, made the loss deeper.

And when Kay finally dared to look at him, it was all there. In her eyes. In the lines around her downturned mouth. The pain. The loss. The grief.

The guilt.

He wanted to hold her.

He wanted to scream at her.

Instead, Finn walked away.

51

Saturday, August 4

"HER NAME IS KRISTINE ELISE PEEBLES. Age twenty-six. With a string of solicitation charges longer than my arm," Kay reported to the members of the task force circling the main boardroom table.

The prints taken off the Jane Doe had been run through AFIS, and Kay had felt a small victory when she'd picked up the results this morning. With more answers came more direction.

Kay had come into the office early, tacking more photos to the boards and adding Kristine Peebles to the list of victims. And by eight thirty, in spite of its being the weekend, the rest of the members had filed in.

Only Finn was absent. Kay regretted last night, outside her apartment, her back literally up against the wall. It wasn't the way she'd imagined telling him. Then again, if left to choose the perfect opportunity, would she ever have told him? With the rain pouring down around them, Kay had guessed Finn was bluffing. But the secrecy had gone on too long, and Kay wasn't up to calling his bluff.

Even though she'd expected it, his anger had disturbed her. It had taken her hours to find even a semblance of sleep, in spite of the exhausting day, and what little sleep Kay did have had been filled with nightmares of Peebles's body in the creek, of marauding pigs, and, most distressing of all, giving birth to the disfigured fetus.

"The strongest connection in the Peebles case is the shackle," Kay said, pointing to the board where she'd mounted photos of the scarring along Peebles's ankle. Next to it was a five-by-seven of Frances Gallo's chafed and abraded ankle. "With the scarring on Peebles's ankle deeper than Gallo's, we're assuming he managed to keep Peebles for a longer period of time."

"And these two are related to Luttrell's abduction how, again?" Corbett asked.

Kay turned to the board where she'd documented the ties between the cases.

"Initially through the Morgan County Militia cap. And the DNA." Kay started with the scant evidence from Micky's abduction site, walking the task force through the visuals and the arrows she'd drawn across the board linking the various photos and reports.

"We've got the hairs found on Micky's scene, a match to the hairs from Sergeant Gunderson's twelve-year-old Jane Doe vehicular homicide. And there's the pig angle. The smell of pigs on the man in the truck in Micky's case, and pig manure transferred from the vehicle to the Jane Doe's body.

"Then there's the DNA from Micky's scene. CODIS matched it to two old rape cases. Although we can't locate one victim, Stacey Blyth's description of her attacker fits those from the witnesses on Saturday night," Kay said, referring to the "bumpy skin" that Blyth had textbook-diagnosed as neurofibromatosis.

"In Frances Gallo's case we have her sketch of the Morgan County Militia patch, no doubt belonging to her abductor. There, again, we have the connection of the pigs. Gallo's experience definitely involved pigs. And the link between Gallo and Peebles is the physical condition of the two women, the geographic proximity of where they were found, and the ankle shackle."

Nods rippled around the boardroom table.

"So, if we consider location"—Kay moved to the map—"Peebles was found approximately here, in a ravine." She'd learned from Reaney that the stream didn't actually have a name and appeared nowhere on the map. *"Got some back roads up in these parts don't even have names,"* he'd told her.

"And Frances Gallo was found along this old quarry road. Twelve miles apart. It's a good bet Micky was taken up to this same area." Kay made a wide circle with her fingertip.

At the corner of the boardroom table, she saw Savalas shake her head. "We can't dismiss the possibility," the sergeant said, "that our perp didn't drive Gallo out to that area himself to dump her. Peebles too. And if *that's* the case, then he might not be anywhere *near* this vicinity. And if Peebles *did* escape on her own, who knows how long she'd been out there, or how far she'd come," Savalas said.

Kay shook her head. "She can't have come far. Even if she was wandering for days and in circles, at some point she would have run into a road. She would have followed it. Just like Gallo did."

"You can't presume the victim's mental state, Detective. Especially in her physical condition." Savalas stood now, notes in hand, and Kay felt the power shift. "I spoke with Special Agent Burke. He'll be in touch later today with a status report on the militia angle. So until then, we need to focus on the cold cases." Savalas nodded to the stack of case files. "I want reinterviews of witnesses and victims, if there are any live ones. Find anything that fits the profile of our perp. The more information we have on him, the better."

Kay cleared her throat, refusing to sit down. "I disagree, Sergeant. I think we need to be up in the county.

Assisting in a canvass of the area. We need search teams and aerial. We need—"

"That's the jurisdiction of the Frederick County Sheriff's Office."

"And you're suggesting they'll turn down our help?"

"No, I'm saying that it's their job. And they're doing it. According to Reaney, he has officers searching the area, talking to the residents. And just like we're letting Burke do his job, we have to let the county do theirs. They know the area best."

Everything out of their hands, Kay thought, her frustration mounting. Maybe she *was* too personally involved to see reason.

"Our job," Savalas went on, "is to cover the bases here. There are reports to be filed, Detective. And we need as much as we can get on this guy. That means going through these cold cases."

"Right. And meanwhile, Micky's out there." Kay's finger struck the map, landing precisely on the Catoctin mountain range.

Savalas shook her head. "We have nothing to confirm that, and I'm *not* going to have us miss something by having everyone race up there to scour some mountainside. There's work to be done right here. Focus on Peebles. Find out if there were any witnesses to her abduction. And find me the boyfriend or whoever is the father of this baby."

Savalas stopped when Finn walked through the door, and Kay tried to ignore the deep pang of guilt when his eyes met hers for a mere second.

"I don't think you'll find any boyfriend," he said, crossing the boardroom to hand Savalas a printout. "Peebles was reported missing by her sister in January. Seven months ago."

52

KRISTINE PEEBLES WASN'T PREGNANT before her abduction. Kay had already guessed that last night, staring at the malformed fetus in the autopsy suite. But guessing and knowing were two different things. Not to mention that the idea of Peebles being "kept" for seven months was disturbing on a whole new level.

Now, as Kay stepped off the elevator at the OCME and followed the corridor to Dixie's office, she had a good idea what the assistant medical examiner was about to report.

Dixie had called just as the task-force meeting wrapped up. She'd sounded tired over the phone, and when Kay stepped into the ME's office, she saw the dark circles under Dixie's eyes.

"You were right on the money with the neurofibromatosis," she told Kay, after explaining her late night with a colleague from Johns Hopkins and how they'd processed the samples on the bench themselves. "Was it a lucky guess or do you have some inside info on this creep?"

"The latter. So the baby was his?"

"We'll know more once the Lab compares our results to the suspect's DNA profile you got from the blood at the abduction scene and see if it shows indications of mutation."

But Kay already knew it would.

"What can you tell me about this NF thing?" she asked Dixie.

Dixie leaned back in her chair and rubbed her eyes. "You understand I'm no expert on the disease?"

Kay nodded.

"Type one neurofibromatosis is also called von Recklinghausen NF," Dixie said. "People often mistakenly refer to it as the elephant man's disease. Of course, Joseph Merrick may have had NF, but he also had a mess of other disorders that caused his deformities.

"The thing with NF, unlike many other genetic diseases, is that it can manifest itself anywhere from mild to severe, and the age at which symptoms appear is variable. Seeing such gross deformities in a six-month-old fetus is definitely one for the textbooks. Also, the severity of the disease and symptoms is not necessarily passed on with the gene."

"Meaning?"

"Meaning, the father of that fetus downstairs might have an extremely mild form of the disease which does not tremendously impact his ability to function or have any visible symptoms at all, while the fetus, obviously, was affected to a much greater degree. Scientists still don't know why it is that the same mutation of the NF1 gene can cause such disparate symptoms. There's also no saying that there were members of his immediate family with visible signs either."

"But it is inherited, right?"

"As an autosomal dominant trait, yes, meaning that you only need to inherit one copy of the gene to get the disease. Or it can actually result from a spontaneous genetic mutation. Just because the fetus has NF doesn't necessarily mean the father does."

"Let's assume he does. What can it tell us about our perp?"

Dixie's description of the disease matched what Kay had already gotten from Blyth two nights ago: the tumors of the skin, internal organs, and nerves, sometimes even invading the brain. ". . . possible skeletal deformities, and cognitive and learning disabilities. Or," Dixie said, standing from her desk at last and rolling her shoulders, "as I said, your guy, if he *does* have NF, may demonstrate none of these symptoms."

But as the image of Micky's abductor, Blyth's rapist, and Gallo's and Peebles's captor became more solidified in her mind, Kay knew better.

53

FINN RELOADED, the full-metal-jacket rounds sliding neatly into the clip. No tremor in his hands. No shaking.

Solid.

He was almost pissed when he saw the center cluster of holes he'd punched so neatly into the paper target on his last round. An easy 80. If only he'd shot that two days ago.

Only two other shooters were at the indoor pistol range in Glen Burnie. Two punks trying out their shiny, new Smith & Wesson .50-caliber magnum. A fucking hand cannon. Hooting and hollering after each resonating boom.

Still, it was better here than in the basement range at the Northeastern District. Here, only twenty minutes south of the city, anonymity was possible. With his repeat qualification next week, Finn had come to practice. And to clear his head.

He hadn't seen much of Kay all day. She'd slipped out after the morning's task-force meeting and the delegation of assignments, while he'd teamed up with Bobby to find Kristine Peebles's sister. According to Melissa Peebles, Kristine had always been a troubled girl, growing up in an abusive home and taking to prostitution at fifteen. From Finn's standpoint, Melissa Peebles hadn't come out of the childhood much better.

"Kristine was always hooking up with the wrong guys," her sister had said between tears that seemed more show than sincerity. *"Doesn't surprise me she's dead. I've kinda been expecting it, you know?"* She'd smiled sweetly at Bobby when he'd handed her his card, and Finn wondered what excuse Melissa Peebles would use to call the young detective.

Sending a fresh target sailing down the range, Finn thought of Micky Luttrell, envisioning her young face. But it wasn't the one they'd used on Channel 11 or on the front page of the *Sun*. The face Finn imagined was from a year and a half ago, when Micky had thanked him for the letter of commendation he'd sent to her sergeant. Her smile had been so full of hope and enthusiasm. And Finn remembered thinking she looked far too young for the uniform.

Like Maeve.

A cadet in the Academy, Finn thought as he plunged the clip of rounds into the Glock's grip and cocked the slide. And she was barely eighteen.

The first round hit its mark. The paper target wafted slightly under the pressure of the missile. At seventy-five feet, though, Finn couldn't see the hole. He squeezed off a second and a third round and imagined the conversation he'd have with Angie, how they'd try to talk Maeve out of it. But Finn knew that, ultimately, his daughter would do what she wanted.

More rounds fired. Still his hands felt steady.

And Kay was right. Maeve would be good at it.

With the clip empty, Finn dropped the magazine and again reloaded.

Kay.

Above everything else preoccupying his mind today, there was Kay. Last night too thoughts of Kay had kept him awake. Watching the headlights along the Hanover Street bridge pan the teak walls through the portholes of *The Blue Angel*'s aft cabin, Finn had imagined what Kay had gone through. On her own.

Or had Vicki been there for her? The assistant state's attorney was probably Kay's closest friend. Finn hoped that Kay had told at least one person, that Vicki had been there for her.

He remembered Angie's miscarriage. It had happened after Maeve and before Toby. He remembered the months of virtual silence afterward, and when Angie finally *did* start sharing her grief, it was still more months before she'd ever suggested trying again.

Finn wondered what it had been like for Kay.

Alone.

And as Finn fired another volley of rounds at the paper target, he wished, more than anything, that he could have been there for Kay.

54

KAY HAD STAYED CLOSE to home base most of the day, spending hours in the boardroom. Waiting . . . hoping for Special Agent Galen Burke to make an appearance.

She'd sifted through the cold-case files along with

Corbett and Nolan. It was disheartening work. Case after case of missing prostitutes. Raped prostitutes. Murdered prostitutes. Women so easily preyed upon while society turned a blind eye.

And when the seemingly endless stream of files got to be too much, Kay had left under the guise of a late lunch.

She'd driven up to Hampden, hoping to talk to Linus Mooney about the Jimmy Hollywood shooting. But Linus's aunt hadn't seen him since yesterday, and when Kay learned the truth—that Linus had been given $70 for groceries before he'd left the house—she knew he'd gone back to the neighborhood for a fix.

Angry, she'd cruised the east Baltimore streets. Ashland and Bond. North of Johns Hopkins Hospital. There were two new memorials in the bloodstained neighborhood since Kay had been through last. RIPs spray-painted on walls, stuffed animals duct-taped to lampposts splashed with red-colored handprints. She'd gone to Linus's apartment, half expecting to find him there. Dead. But it appeared that he'd wisely steered clear of the place.

Then, as Kay drove by the junkies shuffling along the dark sidewalks looking for their next fix from the corner boys, she at last resolved that Linus Mooney was truly a lost cause. There was no saving him, no chance that getting him clean would keep him clean.

As the hot air washed over her through the open window of the Lumina, she'd thought of Antwon Washington and tried to take comfort in the one person she truly *had* saved from the streets. A year and a half ago the boy had been bent on avenging his brother's murder, a mission that he had chillingly accomplished. Still, Kay had managed to pluck Antwon off the drug corners and keep him off. Just the other week the boy had called, bragging about how he'd been allowed to skip a grade and was already making plans for college.

But Linus . . . The most Kay could hope for the junkie was to get him off the streets long enough to give his testimony. In the Big Mo shooting, but more important in Savalas's shooting of Jimmy Hollywood ten years ago.

Down on East Madison, she'd run into an Eastern District unit parked in the litter-strewn lot of a convenience store. Pulling alongside the cruiser, she'd learned from the uniforms that the District had upped police presence. Tensions were rising in the blocks east of the State Pen where the Ashland Boys continued to battle for territory, and there were threats of a showdown.

Kay had given the uniforms a heads-up on her witness and driven back to HQ. Now, as she parked the Lumina in the police parking garage and walked down the oil-stained ramps, Kay wondered how Finn had made out on the Peebles angle. He'd jumped at the chance to work with Bobby today, and Kay wondered how long he'd continue avoiding her. Wondered how much time he'd need, and whether he'd ever be able to forgive her.

Kay was about to open the unmarked steel door that served as the back entrance to HQ, but stopped mid-reach. Angling down the last ramp that spilled out onto Frederick, the long, effortless stride and the tailored, dark gray suit were unmistakable: Galen Burke.

"Burke!"

He'd reached the bottom of the ramp, and stepped out into the glare of late-afternoon sun.

"Burke likes you." Finn's voice echoed in her mind.

"Hey! Burke!"

"You can get whatever you want from the Feds on your own."

Burke turned. Lifting a hand to block the sun, he peered back into the cavernous parking structure, and when she caught up with him, he smiled. Kay wasn't sure why.

"Got yourself a bit of a shiner there, Detective?" He pointed at the faint bruise Frances Gallo had left on Kay's cheek and under the corner of her eye. "Hope your boyfriend didn't give you that."

"I don't have a boyfriend," she said, playing into Burke's fishing expedition. "Are you coming or going?"

"Going. I was just upstairs speaking with your sergeant," he said in that slow, easy Southern accent.

"So do you have anything for us?"

"I filled in your sergeant, Detective."

"So, fill me in too." She tried on a sweet smile, and he seemed amused. "Come on. I can walk you to your car. Where are you parked?"

He nodded past East Baltimore Street, to the public parking structure a block and a half down.

"Good. We'll walk slow," she said.

He smiled again, and Kay figured Galen Burke knew exactly how good he looked when he did.

"So where are you at with these militia members?" she asked.

"Well, we've interviewed a half dozen of the group's former members," he said, starting to walk.

"I'm impressed."

"Why? I'm just doing my job." But something in his modesty made Kay think Galen Burke *had* put in extra effort.

"And what did you get?"

"Not what you're after. But I do have some additional names. You gotta understand, these guys are a tight-lipped bunch." Burke stopped at the curb, waiting as two radio units pulled into the cordoned-off street in front of Central.

"And remember, we've got nothing to use as leverage with these guys. Nothing to hold them on," he explained. "After our interview, they walk away. And the last thing we want is them tipping off your guy."

Kay nodded. Traffic cleared, and when she stepped into the street, she was startled when Burke settled his hand along the small of her back. He must have felt her stiffen because he removed it just as quickly, sliding it nonchalantly into his pocket instead.

"So far I haven't seen any red flags in any of the men we've interviewed," he added.

"And you'd know what to look for?" Kay regretted the question the second it left her lips.

"Don't let the suit fool you, Detective."

"It's Kay."

"Kay." He stopped when they reached the other side of East Baltimore Street. "I'm not just some paper-pushing monkey for the Feebs, you know? I *do* have some half-decent credentials."

"I'm sure you do."

This time his smile made Kay wonder if he'd mistaken her tone as flirtation.

"So what about these new names you've got?" she asked. "Anything promising?"

"Possibly."

"If you really want in on those interviews, I don't think it'd take much," Finn had said. *"If you know what I mean."*

"So what would it take to be part of those interviews?"

As he stared down at her, backlit by the reflection of the sunset against the mirrored windows of Central, Kay saw Burke's amusement again.

"As I said before, Kay, you haven't dealt with these types of individuals."

"No, but I've dealt with serial murderers. And I *know* this guy, Burke. He's been living in my head for a week now."

"I'm sure he has."

"You need me on those interviews, Burke."

He didn't respond, only stared at her.

"As an observer, at least." She was only a hair away from begging, Kay realized. "I promise, I'll know this guy when I see him."

When he lifted his stare to gaze west down East Baltimore to The Block, where the tawdry, neon signs of the strip clubs and porn places flashed, Kay watched a muscle along Burke's jaw twitch a few times. His cool, gray-green eyes seemed distant. And then: "I'll see what I can do."

"Good. When are you bringing in the next guy?"

He shook his head. "It's not like that, Kay. We go to them in most cases. And I doubt we'll be able to arrange for anything until Monday."

Kay bit her tongue. It was enough that Burke was even considering including her, she wasn't about to push him for faster results.

"You know"—Burke's voice became smoother somehow, more relaxed—"we could talk about this over dinner. I mean, if you weren't busy."

"No. I mean, yes, I'm busy. I've actually got an appointment," she said, wondering why she was suddenly so flustered. Then realized it was disappointment. Disappointment on two levels: because of the case, and because she rather liked the idea of getting to know Special Agent Galen Burke a little better.

"A rain check then?" he asked.

"Sure."

"Good. I'll be in touch." With a final smile, Burke left her there.

And as she watched his easy stride down Frederick, the wind whipping back his suit jacket to reveal his strong, lean physique, Kay wondered about Galen Burke's credentials.

55

"WHAT I SEE HERE is definitely a disorganized offender." Constance O'Donnell waved at the array of photos.

Kay had made arrangements with the therapist earlier; otherwise she guessed she'd be sitting in some restaurant with Galen Burke right now. She'd driven to Constance's ranch-style home in Harford County, nestled on one acre of treed land and patrolled by two impressive German shepherds. But Kay knew the dogs. Had been here before, under similar circumstances, desperate to understand a killer's mind. She'd also promised Burke that she'd recognize Micky's abductor, so more than ever Kay needed to know the son of a bitch. Intimately.

Sitting in the therapist's cool dining room, the long, cherry table strewn with crime scene photos and case notes, Kay listened as Constance ran through the dichotomy between organized and disorganized offenders as defined by the FBI's model relating to a killer's methods.

". . . below average intelligence and a marginal student at best," she said, rattling through the long-established "traits" of a disorganized, serial offender. "Probably a high school dropout. An underachiever. He probably has a menial job, requiring little contact with people."

Kay thought about Krajishnik's slaughterhouse.

"Very likely a nocturnal individual, he generally commits his crimes in a blitz style, quickly overtaking his victim."

Kay envisioned the blood on the sidewalk. Micky's blood. It hadn't been an easy abduction, but it had clearly been quick, otherwise someone would have seen something.

"He probably lives alone, without a partner. Possibly with his parents. And he may not own his own home, but rents or could even be a squatter.

"Unlike the organized offender, who is typically nonsocial, the disorganized offender is *asocial*. The fact that you haven't received any tips in spite of the media coverage only reinforces that theory. This guy is removed from society. No friends. No social circles. And that could be, in part, due to this neurofibromatosis. It's a stigma. Depending on the evolution and severity of his physical symptoms, he could have been ostracized at school, even beyond. Singled out, ridiculed. He could reject society because it rejected him. Along with a lousy childhood, quite possibly one involving abuse, this all feeds into his anger, and into his belief that the world somehow owes him. And *that's* the earmark of a classic psychopath. He takes what he wants because he thinks it's owed to him."

"Okay, I don't disagree that he's a psychopath, but there's planning to these abductions. If we're assuming he's up in the county, then he's coming into the city for the express purpose of obtaining another victim. He's organized enough to pull that off."

"All serial murderers show some level of organization in their crimes," Constance said. "The fantasy requires at least a modicum of organization and planning. But this isn't even a perpetrator who falls into the 'mixed' category of organized and disorganized."

Constance stood now and went into the kitchen for more coffee, still speaking. "The way he raped Stacey Blyth, taking her from behind, he's depersonalizing her. He probably does that with all his victims. He can't or doesn't want to see them as people. Or he doesn't know *how*."

When Constance returned, she paused in the door, her mug cradled in her fine hands. Even dressed in jeans and a white cotton shirt, Constance O'Donnell carried a professional grace about her. "The most telling thing in Blyth's rape," she said, "is that it didn't follow any plan. It's as though he just happened upon her at that bus stop and took her, because he felt he had the right.

"Or the Jane Doe from twelve years ago. I'm sure he had other things in mind than running her down when he abducted her. But when she tried to escape, as you presume she did, he became enraged. We see that in the way he didn't run her over just once. An organized offender would be more likely to maintain his cool, learn from the experience, and continue with his plan.

"But this guy . . ." Constance stepped over one sleeping dog and resumed her position at the table. "This guy is driven by impulse, by what he feels is rightly his.

"Of course, this organized/disorganized dichotomy isn't flawless. It's too simple and far from perfect. Psychologists and behaviorists have been debunking the theory for years. It's only meant as a guideline."

Kay nodded.

"Besides which, you know all this stuff," Constance said. "We've been down this road before."

"Yes, but I've never dealt with a guy like this. I need these criteria."

"They're just generalizations. You shouldn't let them box you in."

"I know."

"And the trouble with disorganized offenders is that they're often devoid of normal logic, making them one of the hardest to catch. No one can truly follow the twisted reasoning behind why he chooses the victims he does or what satisfaction and pleasure he derives from his crimes."

Constance scanned the photos across her table, her gaze stopping on Kristine Peebles. "Maybe a better way to look at this guy is through motive," she said finally. "Holmes offers an interesting breakdown of motive into several types. Again, it's a simple typology, but it can offer another way of looking at serial killers."

"And this guy falls into some category?"

Constance nodded. "He could be visionary, but I doubt it. I don't think he's psychotic or hearing voices. He's got his own plan, and that plan has a purpose.

"If he's hedonistic, we probably would have seen more evidence of torture on this girl's body," she said, pointing to Peebles in the creek. "And based on the victims we know of, he's clearly not indulging in any form of cannibalism, which quite often plays into the hedonistic category. My best guess, based on what you've got here, is this guy is mission-oriented."

"He believes he's got a mission?"

"Exactly. In his mind, his acts are justified because he's getting rid of a certain type of person. In this case, prostitutes. Sure he could be targeting them because they're easy prey, but he could also believe he's doing society a favor. Then he uses them for his own purpose."

"And what's that? Sex?"

"Hard to say. In most cases the disorganized offender seeks erotic pleasure in keeping his victim alive and performing perverted and destructive acts on them. It's the power over the victim that excites them more than the act of sex. In fact, it's often theorized that disorganized offenders are actually incapable of completing the sex act."

Kay pointed to the photo of the fetus. "Obviously that's not the case here. I'll tell you what I think," she said, the culmination of one man's violence against women speaking to her now. "I think all he *wants* is the sex. He doesn't feel he should have to pay for it, so he takes it. Brings a hooker home, so he can rape her as often as he wants." Kay felt sick as she imagined Micky Luttrell in his hands now.

"It's like he *needs* sex," she went on. "Can't go without it. Like he's come to expect that woman at the end of the shackle as his privilege, his right. Otherwise, he wouldn't have replaced Peebles with Micky so quickly."

Constance nodded.

"What I don't get though," Kay said, "is why he didn't replace Peebles even sooner. I mean, at six months pregnant, how desirable would she have been?"

"Like I said, Kay, these guys defy logic. We can't know what his ultimate goal is, or what fantasy he's playing through his actions. Or what kind of mission he's fulfilling."

"But if he's so efficient at abducting these women, then why *not* replace Peebles sooner? Unless . . ." And then Kay's thoughts turned cold, her vision of Micky's abductor shifting, fleshing out by another degree in that moment of realization. "Unless the baby is part of his mission."

56

IT WAS RAINING for the second night in a row. Wind lashed at the house and the treetops, and sheet lightning flashed across the sky.

The rain hammered the gutterless, tin roof and poured off in a wall of water while Daryl sat on the porch. It was his best spot to think, and since last night he'd been doing a lot of that.

Hearing the ATVs yesterday, he'd taken the old Maverick down the mountainside. He'd guessed right; they'd been just off Hornets Nest Road. He'd almost turned around when he spotted all the cop cars, but couldn't help himself.

He'd slowed as a sheriff's deputy waved him on, but there'd been nothing to see. Only when he'd driven into Emmitsburg for more beer had he heard talk of their finding a body up past Buzzard Creek somewhere, and Daryl had wondered if it was her.

She'd got away over a week ago. Best he could figure, he'd left the pitchfork too close to her pen. She must have used the end of the handle as a lever to remove the heavy eye screw from the foundation beam. Must have done it in the middle of the night because by morning she'd been gone.

He'd spent two days whacking through the woods, trying to find her. Twice he'd actually spotted footprints, but never a trackable trail. And by the end of the second full day, after getting himself turned around too many times, he'd given up, figuring no one would ever find her anyway.

But they had.

She'd been one of the "easy-keepers," he called them. Never putting up much of a fight. But that wasn't the reason he'd been so pissed off she'd got away.

Her, he'd taken special care of. And with her, there'd been money at stake.

Daryl listened to the thunder roll out over the mountain. He thought of the baby. The baby was the only reason he'd tried so hard to find her. The baby was money.

When he'd discovered she was pregnant a couple of months ago, he hadn't known what to do. Then, when he'd been in Gaithersburg for three days' slaughtering, he'd heard one of the packers talking about his cousin. Made fifteen grand selling her baby to some baby broker.

Fifteen grand.

But Daryl had got nothing. Whore running off like that. Probably died out on that mountainside somewhere with a fifteen-thousand baby rotting inside her.

For that, Daryl hoped she'd suffered.

And if it *was* her the cops had found, he refused to become paranoid. The police would never trace that used-up whore back to him. Just in case, though, he'd parked the truck in the implement shed and would use the Maverick till things died down.

Now, as another sheet of lightning illuminated the clearing, Daryl looked to the shed. It was time. The cop wasn't worth the risk anyway. He could stick her down the old well and be done with the whole mess. Go on a little road trip for a while.

Or, maybe he'd take her with him. After all, she could already be knocked up.

Leaving the porch, Daryl stripped. The rain bit into his skin, invigorating him, and as he lifted his hands to the sky, the lightning made Daryl feel alive.

Yes, a road trip. His pops, God rest his miserable soul, had a sister in Garrett County. He could visit. Stay with his cousin Randy. Hell, he might even share the cop with Randy.

And as Daryl made his way, naked, through the downpour to the shed, he thought sharing might even be fun. But until then, she was all his.

57

Sunday, August 5

THE BOARDROOM WAS HOT, only adding to Kay's irritability. Another morning wasted on cold cases while Micky was in the hands of the man who'd taken up permanent residence in Kay's brain and who seemed even more real today than he had in the past week. As she sifted through the dusty case files with Bobby, her gaze returned repeatedly to the boards, to the topographical map of Frederick County and the Catoctin Mountains south of the Maryland/Pennsylvania line. A vast, rugged wilderness. He was there, with Micky. *Had* to be.

Savalas hadn't even come in yet, and that only pissed Kay off more. If she'd known Kojak hadn't intended to come in, she would have driven up to Frederick, to help with Reaney's canvass.

But Savalas wasn't the only no-show. Finn too was absent.

"We're wasting time," Kay said for at least the tenth time.

Across the table Bobby pushed away from his stack of cases. "You want lunch?"

Kay shook her head. "I need to make some phone calls."

At her desk, Kay looked again at the lab report she'd picked up this morning. The confirmation of paternity had been rushed. It was a technicality for Kay, a document that would help build their case against Micky's abductor and Peebles's killer. But Kay wasn't interested in building a case. She didn't care about the meticulous gathering and documentation of evidence.

All she wanted was Micky. Safe and alive.

Kay massaged her neck, working at the kinks that had settled there after hours of cruising east Baltimore looking for Linus last night.

She half-imagined Linus dead of an overdose in some abandoned row house, shooting too much in response to his jonesing. Either that or Deandre "Casper" Thompson had already gotten to him.

Kay reached for the phone and punched in the number of the Fugitive Unit.

She recognized the growl of the Fugitive sergeant who answered: "Cooper."

"Stan. It's Kay Delaney."

"Of course it is. And she's calling to find out why we ain't got that asshole Casper in custody yet, huh?"

"Exactly."

"Well, you tell that Homicide broad from me," he joked, "that if she brought some doughnuts once in a while to us guys down here in Fugitive, we'd be happy to haul in *all* her deadbeats."

"Stan, I'll bring you a whole fucking truckload of Krispy Kremes if you find that shithead today."

"Gotta be cream-filled." A chuckle. "Listen, we're working on it, Kay."

"Any closer?"

"Probably. Things are coming to a boil over there in East Bawlmer," he said in his Maryland accent. "Casper oughta be showing his ugly mug any day now."

Leaning back in her chair, Kay explained her situation with Linus Mooney, his testimony against Casper in her Big Mo homicide, and stressing the need for Casper's capture to ensure Linus's safety. A half-truth, really, since the testimony from Linus that Kay was most interested in was against Savalas.

As Kay thanked Stan Cooper and hung up, she drummed the end of her pen against her desk. Restless. Frustrated. Something had to break, she thought, crossing the Homicide floor back to the boardroom.

In the doorway, she stopped.

"Mack?"

At the front of the room, his back to the door, Jack Macklin stared at the boards of photos and notes.

"Mack, you shouldn't be in here," she said, joining him. But the Vice cop didn't acknowledge her. His eyes were on the photos of Peebles, the fetus, the shackle. He didn't look good.

"Is that where the son of a bitch is?" he asked, nodding at the county map.

Kay took his arm and turned him from the horror splashed across the boards. "You can't be here," she said, leading him out.

"Tell me you got something new with this dead hooker. Are they at least doing a search up there?"

Kay nodded and contemplated suggesting he contact Reaney to help up in Frederick. But she knew Jack Macklin, with his emotions on high, would only end up being a liability. "We're doing everything we can."

"Christ, Kay, you have no fucking idea what it's like just sitting around. I feel so goddamn useless. I can't work. Can't eat. Can't sleep. Just thinking about Micky out there."

"I know."

"I need to find her, Kay. I need to—" Mack stopped, his gaze locked past her shoulder down the corridor of baffles.

Kay turned as Andy Luttrell hiked his daughter's carrier more firmly into one hand, staring in return.

"I gotta go," Mack said then. "I'll talk to you later, Kay." And opting to avoid Micky's husband completely, Mack turned out the stairwell door.

Andy Luttrell looked wrecked, and as he watched Mack leave, Kay wondered if he suspected the affair. Kay felt his tension as she crossed to meet him, away from the boardroom door and the horrific photos.

"How are you holding up, Andy?" she asked, leading him to her cubicle.

"Fine." But his face remained expressionless as he settled the baby's carrier onto the corner of Kay's desk. Emma's head bobbed and drool slid down her chin as her wide blue eyes locked onto her. Kay wondered if she'd ever not feel the twinge deep inside her.

"You don't look fine, Andy."

Andy Luttrell's shirt was wrinkled and stained, and it didn't appear as though he'd shaved since Micky's disappearance. His eyes were bloodshot and hazy, and he looked as if he were sleepwalking.

He shrugged. "Emma's been keeping me up." But Kay knew it was more than Emma preventing Andy Luttrell from sleeping.

"Listen, why don't I try to find someone for you, Andy? They can give you a hand, stay with you a few hours here and there to help out."

"I don't need anyone's help, Kay. I need my wife." Andy popped the baby's pacifier back into her mouth. "I heard Macklin. He said something about the county?"

Kay nodded, debating how much to share with him. "We have reason to believe she's up in Frederick County."

"Why's that?"

"Another victim."

"Dead?"

She nodded again, slower. "But we have very good reason to believe Micky's still alive, Andy."

"I know she is." A startling conviction was in his voice.

"You know?"

"I can feel it," he said, matter-of-fact. "But you have to find her, Kay. Soon. Before it's too late."

And as she thought of Frances Gallo down at Spring Grove, rocking and chanting, and Kristine Peebles held captive for seven months, Kay worried less now about finding Micky alive and more about finding her in time. If and when they did find Micky Luttrell, would she ever be the same?

58

MAYBE THEY WEREN'T EVEN LOOKING for her any-more? How long had she been here? A week? A month? More?

Time seemed distorted somehow. Whenever she woke now, Micky never knew if it was morning or afternoon, never knew how long she'd been asleep, a half hour or a whole night?

But with growing certainty she knew they weren't coming for her.

They'd given up. Probably thought she was dead.

Shifting on her makeshift bed, her arms tingled and her legs felt shaky. Outside she could hear the pigs rut-ting, the mud sucking at their cloven hooves as they waded through the muck that had only deepened with the onslaught of rain.

And all the while, there was the faint odor of rotting meat.

The pounding in her head hadn't let up either. Micky couldn't remember the last time it hadn't hurt. She felt hot, feverish. Then chilled. Curled up and shivering, she'd tried to ignore the flies and the pigs, the stench and the pain.

When she spotted movement just inside her pen, Micky blinked several times, her blurred vision clearing. A kitten. One of the feral cats.

She'd seen this one before. The little striped tiger cat. Only this time he was closer than she'd ever seen him, prowling warily across the dirt floor of the pen, angling for her scrap bucket.

Micky sat up cautiously, not wanting to spook the

animal. When she made quiet kissing sounds between her dry lips, the kitten froze.

Reaching into the bucket of scraps, Micky found a spiral of bacon fat, the grease cold and congealed. She tore off a small piece and tossed it to the kitten, then watched as it inched toward the offering, sniffing it before taking up the fat greedily.

The kitten licked its lips and studied her in the murky light of the pen. Micky tossed him another piece. This one closer.

When she did, she winced against the pain. The last few attacks had been particularly violent. So violent that she'd taken to removing herself from them when they were happening, her mind shutting down while he raped her body. And a part of her had actually wished he'd just kill her. Get it over with.

Hell, she'd even considered doing it herself. After all, it was in her genes, wasn't it? Her birth mother had done it. Hung herself with six feet of rope. Besides, why give *him* the satisfaction of killing her?

More than a couple of times now Micky had eyed the length of chain that anchored her to the crossbeam. All she needed was something secure to hang it on, even if it meant she was kneeling. *Where there was a will . . .*

The kitten was only two feet away now. Something about the tilt of its head as it waited for another morsel of fat reminded Micky of the stuffed animal she'd had as a child, a tattered and worn, brown-striped kitten, aptly named Kitty. She'd been told that her mother had given it to her.

Micky waved the last cold segment of bacon in front of the kitten, coaxing it closer. Inch by inch, until Micky could just touch its soft fur. It hesitated, but the lure of the bacon was too great, and as it gnawed at the piece clenched between her fingers, Micky moved fast. Ignoring the kitten's needle-sharp claws, she snatched it up. It hissed once as she brought it to her chest, into the folds of the old blanket, and clutched it tightly.

Her stuffed kitten.

And Micky rocked it.

In time the kitten stopped struggling. The flies droned louder. Keeping one hand around her newly acquired pacifier, Micky passed a limp wave across the scrap bucket, but the buzzing persisted. She saw the flies on her ankle and felt them circle her head.

Micky swatted at them, the sweep of her hand stirring the air and the smell of rotting meat growing stronger.

She reached to her shoulder and ran her fingertips over the tender swelling. His bites during his attacks had become more savage. More penetrating. The wounds didn't feel good. They were weeping and swollen, and she discovered now that although they were painful, the skin around them was actually numb.

Same with her ankle. Micky saw the metallic flies along her raw and abraded skin under the shackle. They shimmered like jewels, but she couldn't feel them. She shooed them away and they dispersed in a glittering cloud.

It was then that Micky first saw them. Small. White. And moving. Her heart quickened as the realization sank in. Maggots.

She brushed at them, each swipe of her hand increasingly frantic. And this time, when she caught the odor of decaying meat, she knew exactly what it was.

Micky's scream finally spewed out, like a knife against her raw throat.

In her arms, the terrified kitten hissed and spat. But

Micky hardly felt the razor-sharp claws hooking into her skin, raking open gashes and drawing blood, as it tore free and scurried off in a blur of fluff.

Micky wheezed in a breath and screamed again. And again.

59

EVEN ACROSS THE BOARDROOM, Finn could feel Kay's agitation. He wondered if she'd gone home and come back, or if she'd been here all day. The evening meeting had been called by Savalas with word that Agent Burke had an update. As they waited, Kay filled them in on the progress she and Bobby had made with more of the cold cases: another half dozen with possible links to the "pigman," as Kay had started calling him.

Finn only half-listened. As he watched Kay, he thought about talking to her. They needed to. And until Savalas's surprise meeting, he'd hoped to do just that tonight. Now Finn eyed the pink phone message on top of Kay's notebook. He'd already read the scrawl indicating Jack Macklin's intention to stop by to see her, and Finn wondered how much of Kay's time the Vice detective would take up tonight.

"All right," Savalas said, joining Kay at the front. "I want these cases divvied up so we can start going over the evidence and reinterviewing—"

"No." Kay's voice stopped Savalas cold. "These cases aren't critical. These women are probably already dead. In fact, I think there's a good chance we'll find their bodies up in the county when we find Micky."

Tension simmered between the two women. "This task force will not narrow its focus, Detective," Savalas said, "when we have absolutely *no* proof that Peebles and Gallo weren't simply dumped in Frederick. There could be critical information in those cold cases: evidence that could shed new light, eyewitnesses who could offer a lead on this perp. We're going to reinterview—"

"The only people we should be interviewing are the residents right here." Kay traced a broad circle around the area of the Catoctin Mountains with her finger. "Anything else, and we're only"—when Kay turned, her eyes went to the boardroom door—"wasting precious time."

"Agent Burke," Savalas said, "we've been waiting."

Finn followed Kay's gaze. He didn't like Burke's smile or the way his eyes lingered on Kay as he circled the long table.

"You have something for us?" Savalas asked.

Burke nodded and took the head of the table. "As you know," he started, "we've interviewed several former Morgan County Militia members. A couple here in Maryland, others in Pennsylvania and West Virginia. Although none panned out into suspects, they did give us some viable leads on other individuals who are a little more familiar with the former Morgan Militia roster."

"And?" Kay asked.

"And I think we might have a candidate for you." Burke held out his hand. "But I don't want anyone getting excited just yet. The way these guys were talking about this individual, this could just be an old grudge. Figure they'll send some heat his way as a joke. So I don't want to get overly optimistic. I need to run some background checks."

"And does this guy have a name?"

"Not till I know more," Burke said, no doubt believing that Kay or someone else on the task force might take it upon themselves to move in sooner than the FBI might deem protocolary. "If this *is* your guy, the last thing we need is him getting spooked. It has to be handled properly."

"And what exactly is 'properly'?" Finn asked.

Burke caught his eyes briefly before turning once more to Kay. "I'm agreeing to let Detective Delaney in on the interview. As an observer."

Finn couldn't restrain his smirk then and wondered when exactly Kay had gotten to Burke. Had she called the agent herself?

"We'll head up tomorrow," Burke went on. "I can brief you on the way."

"Finn too," Kay said, nodding toward him. "Detective Finnerty knows this guy as well as I do. He'd be an asset." Then, mimicking Burke: "As an observer."

Burke seemed to consider Kay's request. "I'm not sure we'll have access to a one-way," he said finally, referring to a formal interview room equipped with an observation window, "or even how this interview will go down, but if—"

Burke never got to finish.

Leonard Valente from Stangert's squad suddenly filled the doorway. "Shit's hit the fan over in the Eastern," the detective said. "Major fireworks. And we got reports of officers down."

Kay was the first on her feet. "Jesus Christ."

The room came alive as everyone stood.

Officers down.

Finn was behind Kay as they went out the door. And then there was Burke: "I'll ride with you two."

"You?" Finn asked.

The Fed nodded as they headed to the elevators. "Sounds like you need all the manpower you can down there."

60

KAY BROUGHT THE LUMINA to a hard stop along the curb of Bond Street. The block was a tangle of emergency response vehicles and police cars, cherries and light-bars strobing through the dusk, and as she jumped out of the car, there was the sound of gunfire. Two rounds. Then a third. Muted popping from within the squat brick warehouse across the street.

The building was clearly abandoned. A realty sign had been graffitied over, and smoke billowed out of the broken windows.

"Looks like maybe one of the Ashland Boys's Molotov cocktails," Finn said, nodding to where flames licked at the north windows.

Kay circled the car to the trunk and took out her vest. Tossed Finn Bobby's. Adrenaline kicked her pulse up a notch as she slipped the Kevlar over her head and righted it around her holster for clearance.

Savalas and Bobby had been right behind them on the white-knuckled drive over. The sergeant looked wan in the harsh strobing lights, carrying an extra vest as she joined them. Without hesitation, Burke shrugged off his suit jacket and tossed it into the car as Savalas handed him a vest.

"QRT's on their way," Savalas told them, her voice tight. "And the Fire Department. Listen, I don't want any heroics."

Kay nodded to the dark building just as the staccato of another two rounds sounded off. "We can't let fire personnel in there until we've cleared it," she said, snugging up the straps of her vest. Underneath the Kevlar's compression her heart raced now, every nerve alive and ready.

Bobby was already vested as he jogged over, a police radio in hand.

"Just talked to Stan Cooper," he said. "He's around back with his team. Says they had a bead on Casper when the Ashland Boys hit. Fire seems contained in a back room at the north end of the building. Gunfire's mostly up there too." He pointed. "They've got two officers down. Not sure how serious yet. Ambo's around back, but they're under fire."

"Then we go in from this end," Kay said, and felt Savalas about to object.

"There's something else, Kay." She didn't like the graveness in Bobby's voice. "Coop's got a witness. Says this was all on account of Linus."

"Shit." Kay withdrew her nine, checking the clip and cocking the slide. "So Casper's inside?" she asked, digging out her Maglite from her gear bag.

Bobby nodded. "They think he's got Linus."

And then Kay was in motion, sprinting across Bond, Glock in her hand as the acrid odor of smoke grew stronger.

"Kay! Wait for Tactical!"

She heard Finn in the street behind her.

"Goddamn it. Kay!"

She ran for the south side of the building, the gaping door there smokeless. Tunnel vision setting in. Find Linus. Get out.

Through the sagging doorframe, Kay's eyes adjusted

to the murkiness. What little light slipped through the busted-out windows was choked by the smoke, but Kay didn't turn on the flashlight. Not unless she had to, she thought, picking her way over debris.

The warehouse was cavernous, most of it gutted. Ahead of her, far ahead, Kay could see the amber shimmer of the flames. She hoped there was little fuel within the old structure to burn.

"Don't be dead, Linus," she muttered, flexing her grip around her Glock and inching forward through the murk. "Don't you fucking be dead."

In the farther reaches of the building she heard shouting, then more gunfire. A goddamn war zone. And she wondered if the Doggos were firing at police or if the Ashland Boys had swarmed the place.

Her eyes stung and her pulse ratcheted up even more. *Don't be dead, Linus.*

More shots. Still Kay moved forward, until she felt the shock wave of a bullet pass her cheek a microsecond before she heard the crack of the gun. The slug—traveling at twice the speed of sound—splintered the old wood of the support beam beside her.

Kay dropped into a crouch. Only, it wasn't fast enough.

She barely saw the muzzle flare of the second shot through the smoke when she felt the impact of it. Like getting hit with a Louisville Slugger. Hard.

And Kay went down.

She couldn't breathe, each shallow intake painfully expanding her rib cage. Belly to the gritty floor, Kay remained motionless, assessing her situation, her exit, her ability to move.

The side ballistics panel of her vest had taken the impact, but still, she was in too deep.

Far too deep.

Somewhere to her right, through the smoke, she heard Finn's voice. Burke too. Both of them sounding impossibly far away.

And then Kay heard a long, low gurgle and a wheeze.

She'd never heard the sound before, but thought she recognized it.

Daring to switch on her Mag for an instant, she panned it across the littered floor until she saw him. Linus. Only twenty feet in front of her. His face was turned to her, the slight rise and fall of his chest coinciding with the sucking sounds.

"Jesus Christ."

Kay turned off the Mag and navigated the debris on her hands and knees, her own breathing shallow as the pain in her ribs threatened to immobilize her.

She knew it wasn't good before she ever reached Linus. Even in the limited light she could see the dark stain that bloomed across his shirt, and blood bubbled from the chest wound. Holstering her nine, Kay half rolled the junkie, inspecting for an exit wound, but could find none.

"Linus," she whispered, leaning over him. "Dammit, Linus, you stay with me." She tore open his shirt. Buttons flying. Then bunched up the excess material and desperately pressed it into the wound, staunching the flow of blood and the intake of air into his chest cavity. "I'm going to get you out of here."

But in his wide eyes Kay saw something between terror and death.

The smoke was thicker now. To her left she saw the bright beams of flashlights panning through the haze. Had the Quick Response Team arrived and already gained control of the situation? Still, Kay wasn't going to risk calling out.

It was then that she heard the distinctive metal-on-metal rasp. A gun's slide being cocked. Too close. And too late to go for her own weapon.

At first Deandre Casper Thompson was nothing but a shadow behind the semiautomatic leveled at her. As he took a step through the smoke, Kay could see past the chunky barrel of his semi, into the gang leader's face. She recognized him from his mug shot. He looked even nastier in person.

"Casper, listen to me." She kept her voice level, hiding her fear. And as her left hand maintained the pressure to Linus's sucking chest wound, she extended her right away from her holstered gun. "I'm police. You shoot me and—"

"And what? I'm gonna get me a lethal injection? I'm already dead, cop. Tonight. Right here. I know I ain't leavin' alive, so why should you, huh?" He turned the gun sideways, gangsta-style, as if somehow his aim would be better when he tried to look cool. Then again, standing only five feet from her, Casper hardly needed good aim.

"Casper—"

"Say good night, cop."

It wasn't real. Everything going slow. Casper's mouth tightening into a sneer. His eyes growing cold. She could almost see his fingertip whiten against the trigger.

This couldn't be how it all came down, Kay kept thinking. Not like this. At the hands of a shithead yo, a street punk half her age, in a smoke-filled warehouse in east Baltimore.

Not like this.

Unbidden, the image of her mother flashed in her

mind. Her father on his fishing troller. Finn, and the un-
born child she'd lost. And when the ear-shattering blast of
the close-range gunshot filled the air, Kay had a prayer in
her head.

But the round hadn't come from Casper Thompson's
gun.

He teetered before her, his shooting arm lowering and
the heavy semi slipping from his hand to the floor. Kay
was confused, until she spotted the neat, round hole in
the center of the thug's forehead. A thick line of blood
oozed from it a second before he dropped, and when he
did, Kay thought he looked like a marionette that had
suddenly had its strings cut.

She was shaking, her hand still blocking Linus's wound,
as she searched for Finn.

"Kay, we gotta get out of here." The voice came from
behind her, and she felt his arm circle her waist.

"No!" She refused to remove her blood-soaked hand
as she looked into Linus's unblinking eyes. "He's my witness. I can't—"

"Kay! He's dead. Leave him!"

This time he hauled her back, dragging her away from
Linus Mooney's body, across the debris and into his arms.
And when Kay looked up through the smoke, she saw it
wasn't Finn who had saved her life. It was Galen Burke.

61

WHEN THE SMOKE HAD CLEARED, three officers had
been injured, and a half dozen Doggos and Ashland
gang members lay dead, along with Linus Mooney. Kay

had been surprised the body count hadn't been higher considering the number of casings she knew littered the warehouse floor.

Only seconds after Burke had dragged her out, the Quick Response Team had stormed the place. In fact, the last round that had been fired in that maelstrom of bullets and bloodshed had been Burke's. Like other officers who had discharged their weapons, he'd relinquished his off-duty Sig for ballistics comparison. Kay could only imagine the long hours it would take to process the scene, to match bullets to weapons, and weapons to the dead and the living gang members who had been rounded up. But Kay's thoughts were more on Linus Mooney: her only witness to whatever had gone down ten years ago with Jimmy Hollywood and Savalas.

Bond Street was clogged with ambos and BCFD pumpers all the way down to Ashland. Burke had led Kay to one of the EMS trucks, demanding that she get looked at, and he'd stayed to be sure she did.

"Hurt like a son of a bitch, didn't it?" he asked, holding up her vest and inspecting the damage from the slug that had been pancaked by the layers of Kevlar.

She nodded, wincing against the EMS technician's prodding.

"You'll have a nice bruise," Burke told her with what sounded like firsthand experience. "I don't know what those meatheads in there were packing, but you're damn lucky you weren't hit with a higher caliber."

Kay held out her hands as the EMS technician ran saline over them to wash off Linus Mooney's blood.

"You should probably get started on antiretroviral meds," Burke said. "He was a junkie, wasn't he?"

Kay nodded and wasn't looking forward to the four-week course of prophylaxis for HIV. "I'll take care of it."

Her hands shook as she toweled them and she hoped Burke didn't notice.

"Listen," she said finally. "Back in there . . . what you did . . ."

"You mean saving your ass?" Burke's smile, so easy and genuine, made Kay wonder how many hearts the agent had broken in his life.

"Yeah. Saving my ass. Thanks."

Burke shrugged. "Don't worry about it," he said as though he saved lives on a daily basis.

"All in the line of duty, right?"

"Sure." Another engaging smile.

Then, Kay finally spotted Finn. His eyes met hers across the sea of strobing lights, but Kay couldn't read his expression before he turned away. Again, she wondered where Finn had been when the shooting went down.

Then there was Savalas. Kay tossed the towel aside and excused herself from Burke.

Unlike others on her squad, with soot on their hands and clothes, Savalas and her suit were pristine. It bothered Kay for some reason.

As she neared, she knew Kojak was about to chew her out for her dangerous, headlong rush into the building earlier, but Kay didn't give her a chance.

"I want to talk to you," she told her sergeant. "Now."

62

WHEN JACK MACKLIN stepped into the Homicide offices at nine thirty, he heard the phone bleating. Five,
six times, before someone picked up. The first row of
cubicles was strangely vacant, even for a night shift.
Macklin followed the line of empty work stations to the
boardroom. It too was deserted, and as he stood alone in
the big room at the far corner of the Homicide floor, he
wondered if Delaney had gotten his message.

His eyes went to the boards again. Photos of the
hooker they'd found up in the woods.

"Hey! Anybody from the task force in?" someone called
from the cubicle maze of the main floor. "Line three."

Macklin scanned the empty table, his eyes locking
on the phone, the third light from the bottom glaring
red.

"Anybody?" they called again.

"I got it." Macklin cleared his throat, picked up the
receiver, and punched the line. "Task force."

"Yeah . . . I'm calling 'bout that . . . missing cop." The
voice over the line sounded muffled, and Macklin wondered if the caller was attempting to disguise himself. "I
got the right number?"

"Yeah, you do."

"Good, cuz I ain't wastin' my breath more than once,
ya hear?"

"You have information?"

"Could be. I heard about that body yous found Friday
in the Catoctins."

"Uh-huh." Macklin moved to the board, drawing the
phone cord as long as it would reach, and studied the

colored pins stuck into the map of Frederick County.

"Well, I think I know someone in those parts you might wanna talk to."

63

"I KNOW YOU KILLED Jimmy Hollywood." No dancing around, no testing the waters, Kay had decided. Just hit Savalas with it and watch her squirm.

But she didn't. The sergeant looked washed-out behind the wheel of her parked Crown Vic, one arm braced against the closed window, the other in her lap. Kay saw the fist Savalas made then as she stared out the windshield.

"Linus Mooney told me."

"Mooney? Your witness in the Ashland shooting?"

Kay nodded. "He was there. Ten years ago. The night you shot Hollywood. And he told me everything."

A flash of surprise crossed Savalas's face. There and gone in an instant. "Then Linus didn't know shit."

"Oh, he knew plenty. And I've got it all on tape," Kay said, wondering if Salavas had the balls to call her bluff.

Savalas shook her head and let out a long breath. "You have no idea the can of worms you're opening, Detective."

"Enlighten me then." And when her sergeant looked unconvinced, Kay added: "Because I don't want to have to take that tape to IAD."

"You'd be making a big mistake."

"Convince me."

Savalas looked out the windshield. The Crown Vic was angled along the curb of Bond, and the sergeant seemed to monitor the activity in the street, but Kay sensed her thoughts were miles away from the gang shoot-out they'd just witnessed.

"This is beyond your scope, Delaney. Unless you've done undercover work—"

"Right, I'm just some shit-for-brains Homicide cop. The token female on the unit," she said, certain Savalas understood the snub. "I wouldn't understand. Well, maybe those geniuses in IAD will, huh?" She reached for the passenger-side door lever, but Savalas stopped her.

"Look, I know you don't like me."

"It's not about 'like.' I want a *sergeant,* not a friend."

Savalas took a breath. "I know the rumors. Me and Deputy Commissioner Powell." Another breath. "We're friends. Nothing more. And despite what you think, I don't need to blow-job my way up the ranks. Maybe one day you'll believe that."

"Maybe. But I'm not here to debate whether you belong in that corner office back at HQ."

"Fine. You want to know what really happened with Jimmy Hollywood?"

"I'm all ears."

Savalas let out a breath, and for the first time Kay thought she saw real emotion in the woman's face. "You can't know what it's like until you've gone undercover. Deep cover. That's how they set me up with Jimmy Hollywood. I hadn't done undercover work before. Not like that." The words came slowly, her voice low but steady, as the effects of the memories washed across Savalas's face. She spoke of the months needed to develop her position with Hollywood, having to snort coke occasionally to maintain cover, even having to sleep with the drug dealer at times.

"Sometimes it came to a choice between doing the coke or sleeping with him. If he was high, he didn't want sex. But if he wasn't . . . sometimes he'd just take it."

"He raped you?"

Savalas bit her lip. Nodded. "More than once. And the team listened to it all. They had Jimmy's place bugged."

"They didn't stop it?"

"If they had, it would have blown the whole operation. And every member on that team had way too much invested."

Kay struggled with what she was hearing, imagining Savalas's team members hunkered in a panel van down the street listening to her rape. Doing nothing.

"I always figured they got off on it, you know?" Savalas said, her bitterness painfully clear. "Bunch of sexually frustrated, impotent cops with their hands down their pants, listening to the whole thing."

"You went to your sergeant, right? Went higher up?"

Savalas nodded. "After the first rape, yeah. The very next day I went to Gorman. He was my sergeant back then," she said of the department's captain, the same man who'd assigned her into Homicide prematurely, perhaps hoping Savalas would make a fool of herself. "The son of a bitch refused to reassign me."

"You should have gone to your FOP rep. Someone."

"And risk my career?" She shook her head. "I come from a long line of cops, Kay."

"So what? You took the law into your own hands then?"

"It wasn't like that." Savalas's face, flooded with the lights from the emergency vehicles, looked suddenly ten years older. Kay wondered how many lines were there because of Jimmy Hollywood alone. "I don't even know

Linus Mooney," Savalas said. "I had no idea there was a witness."

"So tell me your version."

After some thought, Savalas said, "It was just another deal. Me and Jimmy meeting up with this dealer Andre Bicks. Only the deal went sour."

"How?"

"Jimmy shot Bicks. Shot him when I was making the handoff. Son of a bitch could've shot *me*. One minute Bicks was handing me the shit, and the next he's on the floor. His blood all over me. Do you have any idea what that's like? To see a man shot dead right in front of you?"

Kay shook her head. But she *did* know. It wasn't just Spencer four years ago. It was Antwon Washington and that night last year, when the twelve-year-old had un-flinchingly put a bullet through the brain of his brother's killer. Point-blank. While Kay had watched, helpless to stop it. But worse than that, she'd covered it up. And she'd dragged Finn into it. She'd taken Antwon's gun, cleaned it off, and the next time she and Finn had gone sailing, she'd dumped it off *The Blue Angel*.

"Department didn't have you wired?" Kay asked.

Savalas shook her head. "Not with Jimmy's hands all over me all the time. And I knew then, with Bicks bleed-ing out on the floor at my feet, the deal gone bad, that Gorman would keep me on even longer. I wasn't going to let Jimmy keep raping me. So I took Bicks's gun. Jimmy didn't have a clue till I shoved it into his crotch and pulled the trigger."

Savalas's description gelled with Dixie's autopsy notes. *And* with how Kay had imagined the shooting had gone down ten years ago.

She thought she saw tears in Savalas's eyes. "Sometimes

it's not about the law, Kay. Sometimes it's only about justice."

And then, as Kay felt Savalas's tightly meshed defenses come down a little, as she felt the subtle shift in her relationship with the sergeant, Kay almost wished she could admit that she too had crossed that blue line. But Kay never would. Ever. It was Finn's career on the line as well.

"Sometimes," Savalas said, "justice is the only thing that matters."

64

IT WAS 1:00 A.M. when Daryl left his booth at Haley's Comet. The fourth Natty Bo had gone down well, but he knew Haley wouldn't give him a fifth because his tab was still owing. Stupid cow. Sometimes he thought he should just kill her.

Maybe tonight. Why not? Wasn't as if he had anything better waiting at home.

As he crossed the bar's parking lot, Daryl toyed with the notion of killing Haley. He could wait in his car for her to close up. Grab the cow on her way out. Or maybe just keep things simple. Use the twelve-gauge he had in the trunk and just blow her head off right there in the lot. Just for the fun of it.

Daryl's mind vibrated with images of the bar's owner crashing down in a blubbering pool of fat and blood, her gargantuan legs collapsing under her weight. He was already feeling his hard-on when he spotted the car at the back corner of the lot. A car from the city. Had to be. The shiny Mustang wasn't from these parts.

Daryl didn't look directly at it, but watched from the

corner of his eye as he approached his dusty Maverick. From behind the Mustang's windshield, in the dark interior, a cigarette flared.

Opening the Maverick's door, Daryl smelled the trace of cigarette smoke on the warm breeze. He half-wondered if it was a cop sitting behind the wheel of the Mustang, but then scratched the idea. No cop would be showing up in a flashy car like that.

So who was the driver waiting for at 1:00 a.m.?

Daryl sank in behind the wheel of the Maverick and cranked the engine. In his rearview he kept an eye on the other car as he pulled out of Haley's lot. And when the sports car—headlights off—pulled onto the blacktop well behind him, Daryl smiled.

65

Monday, August 6

BURKE HAD BEEN RIGHT about the bruising.

In the privacy of the women's washroom down the corridor from Homicide, Kay inspected the tender welt along her ribs. The redness had transformed to a vivid purple, and it still hurt like a bitch when she drew too deep a breath. Better than being dead though.

Kay knew she would remember staring down the barrel of Casper Thompson's semi for the rest of her life. And she'd always remember that—if not for Galen Burke— she would have been at the ME's office this morning, her body adorning one of the stainless-steel slabs.

Burke had called her at home late last night, his voice

over the phone sounding different somehow. Less formal. And his concern sounded genuine. She hadn't seen him after she'd pulled Savalas aside at the scene, and over the phone Kay explained to Burke her trip to Mercy Hospital with Savalas to check on the officers who'd been shot, and, at the same time, to start her first round of AZT and lamivudine, the postexposure HIV prophylaxis.

It had been a strangely quiet drive to Mercy with her sergeant, but in the silence between them, Kay sensed a newfound and mutual respect, a sort of bond born of secrecy. There'd been no need for further discussion about Savalas's confession, as though the sergeant trusted Kay to keep her secret.

And Kay would. After all, what Teodora Savalas had done ten years ago was no different from what Kay herself had done for Antwon Washington.

Kay drew her shirt down over the bruise and checked her watch. It was almost noon, and a small part of her worried that Burke might have gone back on his word to include her in the interview.

Last night on the phone, before he'd wished Kay a goodnight, he'd told her to be ready to head up to the county in the morning. But so far, he hadn't shown, and like the rest of the detectives in Homicide and Violent Crimes, Kay's time had been swallowed up by the paperwork to be filed on last night's shooting.

When the washroom door opened, Finn called in first. "You alone?"

"Yeah." She was tucking her shirt in when Finn stepped into the washroom.

"How is it?"

"Fine."

He nodded. "And how are you?"

"Okay."

"Listen . . ." Finn shifted from one foot to the next, and Kay watched the tension in his face, guessed he was sifting through some prepared speech he'd been running over and over in his head for the past two and a half days since Kay had told him about the miscarriage.

"We need to talk," he said, and not too easily.

"I know."

But Finn didn't get a chance. Bobby swung open the washroom door. "Burke's here. Says he's ready to go. And by the way," he added as Kay and Finn followed him out, "I'm going too. I don't care what that Feeb says."

Fortunately, Burke didn't argue. Kay guessed it was because the FBI agent was already behind schedule. Even hurried, Galen Burke had a calm, easy manner about him, and Kay thought he looked different, perhaps not as uptight, in his casual wear: a fresh, white T-shirt tucked into jeans, and a loose cotton shirt hanging open to help conceal the leather hip holster.

"I did a background check on this guy," he told them as they took the elevator down to the parking-garage level. "Pretty much fits your profile. Belonged to the Morgan Militia for a few years. Currently works at a slaughterhouse. Not sure about his most recent hairstyle, mind you," he added as the elevator doors opened. "But he does drive a pickup. And he's got plenty of past run-ins with law enforcement."

"Do you know anything about his medical history?" Kay asked.

Burke looked at her as they took the first ramp in the garage. "No. Why?"

"I'll explain on the way."

66

MACKLIN HAD BEEN PROVIDED with the nickname Red.

The tipster who'd called Homicide last night said he didn't know Red's real name, but told Macklin about the bar the Fredneck frequented. Haley's Comet.

Macklin had driven straight out to the county, the long dark stretches of Route 40 leading him past Mount Airy and through Frederick, even farther west until he'd found the back-road bar. There'd been no sign of Red's truck, but the caller had mentioned an old Maverick Red sometimes drove. And sure enough, after an hour of waiting, the black Ford Maverick had rumbled into the lot.

Mack had waited outside the bar for a couple more hours, then followed Red's car up through the hills, deep into the mountains. Lagging back as far as he dared, there'd been no hiding that he was tailing, and he hoped the hillbilly was too drunk to notice.

When Red had turned onto a NO EXIT road, Macklin had cruised by. A mile or so down the mountain he stopped, locked the doors, and dozed with his Beretta in his lap. And at first light, Macklin had backtracked, this time turning onto the rough NO EXIT road. Sure enough, a half mile in, Macklin found the gated lane.

Now he waited. No way was he stepping foot onto the property of a former militia zealot until he was certain the man was away. So, sitting in the Mustang, tucked in a narrow lane hidden by brush, Mack thought of Micky.

He'd never meant for it to go as far as it did last week. Never meant to fight with her. All he'd wanted to do was explain.

He'd talked about how innocently it had all started:

fixing a few parking tickets for friends, taking free meals at restaurants on his beat, checking license plates, then background checks for certain individuals. He hadn't known those individuals were mob-related, and by the time he had, it was too late. Then there'd been more favors, not to mention the free blow jobs from hookers, and easy drug money off busts.

Through his entire explanation, Micky had been silent in the passenger seat.

She'd listened as he justified milking the pimps for money. A mutually beneficial relationship, he'd explained. After all, what cop didn't need to supplement his salary?

Micky had said nothing, but he knew she didn't approve.

"It could really help," he'd told her. "You got the house, the baby. And with Andy not working . . ."

Micky had only looked away.

"Christ, Mick, all the guys do it. In fact, if you *don't,* they start to worry. Start to wonder if you'll be there to get their back, you know? I need to know you've got my back, Mick."

Still she'd said nothing.

"Mick?"

When he'd reached across the center console for her, she'd hit him.

"Goddamn it, I trusted you, Mack."

"And who's saying you can't?"

But she'd hit him again, and he'd defended himself. The bloody nose had been an accident.

"What you're doing, Mack, goes against *everything* that makes this job important to me." And the last words she'd said to him, cupping her bleeding nose with one hand, were "I don't know if I can be your partner anymore."

Some days Macklin wondered how he'd gotten in so deep. Some days he wanted to just walk away from it all. The bribes, the payoffs, the drug money. Even the job. But most days, Macklin saw no way out.

Starting up the Mustang again for some AC, Macklin almost missed the Maverick. The old car, its black coat dulled by years in the sun, sped past in a swirl of dust.

It was him. Red.

And as the Maverick flew down the mountain, Macklin put the Mustang in gear, waited several long seconds, and finally eased onto the roadway, nosing the car back toward the NO EXIT road and Red's home.

67

THEY WAITED IN BURKE'S federal-issue Malibu in the gravel lot of Wheeler's, a small slaughterhouse operation north of Emmitsburg a mile over the state line.

"We'll wait till he comes out," Burke had told Kay. "I spoke with his employer this morning, and he said they start early and finish anywhere between two and three."

He'd instructed Finn and Bobby to park near the entrance of the lot, on the chance Burke's suspect decided to bolt. Just past the glare of the sun across the Impala's windshield, Kay could see Bobby in the passenger seat, sipping his latte while Finn watched the building's side door. He looked irritated, she thought.

It had been a long, hot drive, the AC barely keeping up with the sun beating in on them. Burke's easy banter, however, had swallowed up the time. Expecting the federal agent to be stiff and humorless, Kay had been surprised at the casual Burke. She liked him. They'd shared their backgrounds, and he'd spoken openly of growing up in New Orleans "a mulatto," he'd called himself, referring to his mixed heritage. "My father's Creole black and my mom's French."

"Are your parents still down there?" Kay had asked.

"Not anymore."

"Katrina?"

Burke had nodded. "They lost everything. Got them out in time though. That's what matters most. I moved them up here."

She'd spoken a little of her own parents, but soon the subject had come back to the case. Burke had filled Kay in on everything he knew about his suspect: a speckled criminal record ranging from firearms violations to assault, his years of militia involvement, and even the fact that he'd been a rebel in school, dropping out halfway through high school. She'd been impressed with how much the Feds had on the guy, stuff that wasn't in the system. From everything Burke had given her, he fit the profile—almost too neatly—and Kay had still wished there'd been some kind of medical history available.

Now Burke drummed the steering wheel with his long fingers. "You're prepared for the fact that this might not be your guy, right?"

Kay nodded and looked at the color photocopy of the mug shot Burke had handed her back at HQ. She studied the face again, comparing it to her memory of the E-FIT composites they'd gotten the Monday morning after Micky's abduction. Any similarities were vague at best, but with such disparity between the two composites, Kay hadn't put much weight in a true comparison.

Still, she'd studied the five-year-old mug taken by Pennsylvania State Police: the sunken cheeks, the dark eyes, the downturned mouth. Was it him? She thought she'd know when she saw him, but now Kay wasn't so certain.

"You got anyone else on that list of yours?" she asked now.

Burke shook his head, and then Kay realized how much the agent had riding on this guy being Micky's abductor.

"And what if he isn't?" she dared to ask.

"We start again. Go through the lists. Reinterview."

"That could take weeks."

"I know." His voice made it clear he understood the implications of time working against the possibility of finding Micky alive. Then Burke nodded out the windshield.

Kay followed his gaze to where several workers exited the side door of the low concrete-block building.

"There he is," Burke said. "Black ball cap."

Wearing a short-sleeved shirt tucked into faded jeans that sported a belt with an oversize buckle, he was a small, wiry man. His movements were quick and his crooked smile came easily as he joked with coworkers.

"That's not our guy." Kay's voice sounded distant to her own ears, as a buzzing in her head grew.

"He could have cut his hair," Burke suggested about the short curls visible beneath the faded cap.

Kay's chest felt heavy. She shook her head. "It's not him."

68

HE'D CONSIDERED PARKING down the road and going in on foot, but taking the car meant having the means of a getaway.

Macklin had sat in the idling Mustang for a good minute outside the weather-beaten house. Waiting, in case someone else lived in the dump. The house sagged on its frame, decayed and leaning almost impossibly to one side, and several chunks of asphalt sheeting from the sides of the house lay scattered in the small clearing.

When no one came out, Macklin shut off the engine and took the steps to the caving-in porch. He had to use his shoulder on the door, the humidity swelling the old frame.

The inside was a sty. Filth covered every surface. Junk and clutter spilling from cupboards and boxes. Gun and porn magazines. Militia memorabilia. The stench and grime of the place made Macklin's skin crawl.

His off-duty drawn, he moved through the squalor of the main floor. The kitchen appeared to be the main living area, dishes across the counter and trash overflowing. Through a short hall and to his right was a narrow bathroom, dank and foul. And across from it, a bedroom, littered as well, with a well-worn mattress, the sheets a tangle, and one stained pillow on the floor.

The stairs to the second level were practically rotted out. It didn't look as if the hick had ventured up for months. Still, Macklin called Micky's name.

Nothing.

Abandoning the house, Macklin turned to the outer buildings. A pseudo-garage of old barn board housed the red pickup, but no sign of Micky. A smaller shed that might once have contained chickens was empty save for two feet of petrified shit.

Macklin turned to the only other outbuilding. A large shed circled by an outdoor corral. Along the shaded side of the corral a half dozen huge pigs basked in the deep muck. They eyed him suspiciously, but didn't move even as he started over the fence. Just as well, Mack thought, gauging by their size, he wouldn't hesitate to shoot them.

Inside, the shed was dank, ripe with the stench of pig shit and urine. She couldn't be in here, Macklin kept thinking even as he moved through the pen to the low barrier that separated the pigs from the only other pen in the shed. Couldn't be.

At first he thought the second, smaller pen was empty, until he spotted the mound pressed up against the boards of the outer wall.

She looked dead. But then Macklin saw the slow rise and fall of the old wool blanket that covered her. And a shaft of light through the boards touched her face.

Micky.

Macklin studied her form, unable to move, caught somewhere between relief and shock.

Of course she was still alive. Micky knew what it took to survive. He'd never questioned her smarts. After all, that's exactly why he was here. He *knew* Micky would never have let it go, what she'd learned about him. She would never simply have requested reassignment.

Not self-righteous Micky.

She would have started digging. And how long would it have taken her to shake down the pimps he'd been squeezing? She'd find out about the arrangements, the threats, the payoffs. And talking to the right slimeballs she might even find out about the hooker he'd killed last year. She'd go to the brass, initiate a full-out investigation. He'd be done.

It was too bad too, because Macklin kinda liked Micky. In fact, before that last night, he kinda had a thing for her. He *would* have had an affair with her if she'd wanted. But he knew Micky well enough to know he'd only have gotten more of her holier-than-thou crap.

It was then that Macklin brought the off-duty weapon up. Hesitated.

The blanket moved, and Micky's eyes opened.

Do it, Macklin, you chickenshit. Just fucking do it.

It was either this or years in prison. And a cop in prison . . .

Do it now.

It would only be harder if she looked at him.

And in the dim light of the shed, Macklin aligned the sight of the Beretta.

69

"I AIN'T TALKING to no cops. Specially no nigger cop." Burke's witness had a mouth. And an attitude. Both of which Finn would have loved to knock out of the racist piece of shit right there in the dusty parking lot of Wheeler's slaughterhouse.

As soon as Burke had stepped out of the federal-issue Malibu into the hot sun, Finn had followed suit. Burke and Kay had reached Eddie Winchester first, and Finn heard the man's vile mouth before he even reached him.

No words were needed from Burke when Finn approached, and he had to hand it to the Fed: he was smooth. With one glance, the agent passed the interview to Finn. Now, in the full, hot sun Burke stood with Bobby at the grille of the Malibu, within earshot, but far enough away that Winchester didn't feel compelled to pull even more insults out of his prejudiced verbal arsenal.

"I ain't got nothing to do with no missing cop," Winchester said to Finn. He withdrew a pack of Marlboros from the cuff of his black NRA BRING OUT THE BIG GUNS T-shirt and lit up.

"Then you won't mind if we go to your place to take a look around, right?" Kay asked.

"Damn right I'd mind." His eyes went a little wild at the threat. "I know my rights. And unless your skinny ass has got a warrant in your back pocket, ain't none of yous gonna set foot on my property. Besides, I already told yous guys who's been snatchin' up them hookers."

"What are you talking about?" Kay asked. "Told who?"

"I don't make it a point of asking cops' names. But I told him over the phone—"

"You spoke with someone on the phone. The police?"

"Dang, are all you cops this slow? Fuck, yeah. Just last night. And I told him I wasn't gonna talk to no cops. Then he sends you all up here—"

"Who?" Finn asked. "Who'd you call?"

"Bawlmer po-leece." Winchester strung out the syllables as though imitating the switchboard operator. "Obviously the dick didn't take me serious, otherwise yous guys'd be all over Red's ass, not mine."

In the look Finn shared with Kay he knew that she

too was wondering who might have taken the call last night. With the east Baltimore showdown the office had been chaos, and Finn wondered if the message was still sitting on someone's desk right now.

"And what did you tell this 'dick'?" Finn asked.

"That he should be looking at a numbnuts named Red. Don't know his real name. We just call him Red, cuz of the red pickup he drives."

"And you know this 'Red' how?"

"Knew him from over in Morgan County. Had us a club back there," Winchester said, clearly not ready to admit his affiliation with the militia group.

"This Red guy, is he still in Morgan County?"

"Never was. His people were from way south o' there, so I heard. But I think he's over this way more. Either that or he drives a hell of a long way for a beer."

"He's got a watering hole around here?"

"Not here. Down round Harmony. Just off the 40. I see him there sometimes. Always by himself. Smelling like his goddamn pigs."

Finn could feel Kay's energy shift. "And why do you think this buddy of yours is our guy?" she asked.

"Ain't no buddy of mine. Never said that. Sumbitch tried to kill me once. Busted a beer bottle right there outside of Haley's Comet and ambushed me in the parking lot." Winchester yanked down the collar of his T-shirt. A gnarled scar snaked across his collarbone. "Took a couple dozen stitches. I wanted to kill him for that, don't get me wrong, but I ain't landin' myself into no trouble on account of that retard."

"So you calling us," Kay said, "that's not just your way of getting even with him? Have some city cops jack him up for a while, drag him in and harass him?"

"Nope. I called cuz it's just the kinda crazy-ass sicko thing I'd expect from the jackoff, is why. And cuz he's the kinda asswipe who would probably have to pay for it all his life, if you know what I mean. And if he can't pay for it, he'd just take it. Makes sense he's the one been snatching up those whores from the city."

"So why should we believe you, Eddie?" Finn asked.

The little weasel took a final drag on his cigarette before grinding it beneath the sole of one black leather sneaker. "I don't give a shit if you don't. If Red snagged hisself a cop instead of a whore, that's just fine by me. Maybe she'll even kill his stupid ass. If he hasn't already killed her, that is." And something in the way Eddie looked at Kay just then made Finn think the slimeball preferred the idea of Red's having killed Micky Luttrell.

Finn moved in closer, drawing Winchester's greedy eyes off Kay. "Look, Eddie, no one's kidding anyone here. We know you were Morgan County Militia. So let's just get real for a second, okay? Explain to me—dumb-ass cop that I am—why you would turn on a fellow militia member, even if you don't like him?"

Winchester shrugged. "Civic duty?"

"You're going to have to do better than that."

"Look, the guy's a wackjob, okay? Shouldn't've been in the Morgan club. Or any club if you ask me. Lucky for me he quit after I joined so I didn't have to deal with the dumbfuck too much. It's wackos like Red who give us a bad rap, you know? And then him going around and wearing the Morgan cap two, three years after the moron stopped going to the meetings, that was just wrong, you know? Can't tell you how many times I wanted to rip that hat off his retarded head and beat him with it.

"I say, unless someone else knows the shithead's real

name and where he lives, your best bet's to hang out at Haley's. Might be a day or two, but he'll show. Otherwise you could be searching them mountains for weeks. If that's even where the numbnuts is at."

70

SHE DREAMED OF HER ADOPTIVE PARENTS, the Andersons, of their brain matter spewed across their bedroom floor and the hot, slippery feel of blood against the bottoms of her bare feet. Then she'd dreamed of Emma, horrible dreams that left a crushing feeling around her chest long after she opened her eyes.

And then Micky saw him.

Not the pig-man.

Macklin.

She blinked several times, certain she must be hallucinating. Beneath the blanket she was soaked with sweat, yet she felt chilled. She wiped her eyes.

It *was* Macklin. *They'd come for her.*

But . . .

Micky craned her head around, peering between the slats. Macklin's Mustang was like a mirage in the middle of the clearing, the sun shimmering off its metallic blue paint job.

There was no "they." Just Macklin.

As Micky's eyes came back to him and saw the dark outline of the semiautomatic in his hand, she understood. And there was no holding back her strangled whimper.

"Macklin . . . don't . . ." She shook her head. "Please." Another cry. "I'll never . . . I promise . . ."

Through the dim light she couldn't read his face, but in that suspended moment, that split second before the gun blast, Micky prayed it was mercy she saw there.

She didn't feel the impact of the bullet. Didn't feel any pain. Only the hot splash of blood.

Then Micky saw why.

Macklin's eyes went wide and his mouth made a silent O. The semi dropped from his hand and landed silently in the muck at his feet as Micky watched the blood bloom across his T-shirt. More bubbled from his lips and leaked down his chin. And then Macklin seemed to fold at the middle. His knees buckled and he slumped forward, caught by the low railing. There was the smell of hot blood and voided bowels.

And Micky threw up.

71

"HOW CAN NO ONE know this guy?" Kay asked Otis Reaney.

The County Sheriff's detective shook his head. "There's all kinds of yahoos living up in those hills that we don't know about."

"But he's got to come into town for groceries, supplies, right?"

"We'll get the word out. Don't worry."

After their interview with Eddie Winchester, they'd driven from Pennsylvania into Thurmont, and during the drive Kay had stared out the passenger-side window at the rising, green mass that was the Catoctins to the west, thinking of Micky, praying they wouldn't be too late, and imagining a "numbnuts" named Red.

They were so close, and at the same time it felt as if they were at a standstill.

The four of them had grabbed a late lunch and met up with Otis Reaney at the Thurmont Police Department. Situated in the basement of the town hall, the cramped and airless quarters of the station smelled of burned coffee and bleach. The side briefing room had been set up as a command post of sorts, and blown-up topographical maps covered one side of the room, the mountainside divided into parcels and coded in marker. The codes corresponded with lists indicating the various sectors already searched. Reaney assured them that although progress might appear slow, they were being systematic, speaking to every resident and checking every drive.

Kay appreciated Reaney's thoroughness. Still . . .

"Someone's gotta know this Red guy." She studied the maps, her eye going to the mark along the old quarry road where Frances Gallo had been found, dazed and wandering. "Gallo was found four years ago, so we know he's been around here at least that long. And none of the locals know him?"

"You've seen that mountainside, Kay," Reaney said. "There's a lot of uncharted area. He could be a squatter, living in the woods."

"He's not the invisible fucking man. Besides, he's got pigs."

"Trust me, we're knocking on every door. But with this guy being militia, I'm not taking any chances. I'm sending out only two-man units, and we've got limited manpower."

"Well, you've got three more right here." She wasn't going to speak for Burke. "Finn, Bobby, and I aren't leaving till we find this son of a bitch. So where do you want us?"

Reaney checked his watch. "The teams are going to start coming in soon. I'll want to go over everything they got today, see if anything sends up a red flag. It might help to have you brief the teams as well."

Kay nodded, but her eyes went back to the map. Northwest of Thurmont, seven individual mountains were marked with contour intervals, each roughly circled by roads ranging from paved to gravel. On the second-farthest mountain from Thurmont, Kristine Peebles's decomposed body had been found in the creek. Kay leaned in to read the map. Friends Road circled the northern and eastern portion of the mountain, the closest road to where Peebles had been found. And intersecting it, heading north, was the old quarry road on which Frances Gallo had been found.

Comparing the marked sectors on the map to the search list, Kay could see that Reaney's canvass had focused on the sector in which Peebles had been found, and from there spread south toward Thurmont.

"What about this area up here?" Kay asked, pointing to the most northern of the mountains, just below the state line. "You're not searching north of Friends Road?"

Reaney joined her at the map. "Peebles's body was found here." He planted a thick finger near the middle of the most-searched mountain. "Gallo two miles east. Gallo didn't have the wear and tear on her that Peebles had, so we're assuming she pretty much stayed on the roads.

"Based on what little the dogs were giving us before the rain, we think Peebles came from the south, following the creek up. If she'd come from the north, from this mountain here, she'd have hit Friends Road. And you'd think she would have stayed on the road."

That had been Kay's thinking initially too. But what if Savalas was right, that they really had no way of knowing Peebles's state of mind? Delirious, dehydrated, and malnourished, she could have stumbled onto the road and simply wandered off it again, falling into one of the steep ditches and back into the woods, meandering on from there.

"Besides," Reaney went on, "this mountain here, north of Friends Road, is even rougher. The woods are denser, ravines are deeper. Some of 'em sheer drops. Look at the contours." The pale green lines were tight, indicating steep rises in elevation. "I just don't see how she could have made it through there."

But looking at Reaney's carefully laid out search plan, Kay felt unsettled at the virtually untouched area of the mountain north of Friends Road.

"I want to start up there tomorrow morning," she said, her finger on the map. "Finn and I can start. Give us a map, the sectors, whatever you've got."

Reaney nodded, clearly unwilling to argue with her.

"Unless, of course, we find Red at Haley's Comet down in Harmony tonight."

72

MICKY PULLED HER LEGS to her chest and rocked.

It was dark now. She preferred it that way. In the dark she couldn't see Macklin's blood still speckled across her hands and arms. She couldn't see it congealed along the top rail of the divider or, even worse, the dark crimson stains on the pigs' jowled cheeks.

Macklin's had been a slow, agonizing death. She'd heard gut shots were like that. No doubt the shotgun blast had shattered her partner's spine, and Micky wondered if he'd felt less pain because of it. Seeing him like that, suspended on the other side of the divider, his face contorting into a grimace, Micky hadn't been sure what to feel. Relief? Horror? Sadness?

He'd stared at her, blinking, and she wondered what he saw, what he thought, in those last miserable moments, his blood and his stomach contents sprayed across the shed. She knew Macklin had still been alive, paralyzed from the steel pellets that had blown through his body, when the pig-man hauled him off the rail to the shit-covered floor of the pigs' pen, bleeding out while the pig-man rifled through Mack's pockets. Still alive when the hillbilly held up his detective's shield.

"Well, lookee what I found me. A poh-leece man. Now why'd you figure this bad boy here was pointin' a gun at you, huh?"

It was more words than he'd spoken to her at any given time in the past, but Micky didn't feel any obligation to answer.

"Tsk tsk tsk." He made the sound between the gap in his front teeth while he waggled one index finger at Macklin in the shit. "Bad cop. No doughnut." And he spit in Macklin's face.

Micky heard the low gurgle of Macklin's breathing.

"And what do you think we should do with 'im?" the pig-man asked. "Maybe I'll string him up and gut him. What do you think?"

Eventually he'd prodded Macklin with the toe of his

work boot, and through the divider Micky had seen his limp, bloodied body list.

"Ooey, I think that boy's finally dead."

Micky hadn't watched as the pig-man dragged Macklin's body from the shed. He grunted and wheezed and crashed through the shed until she'd heard him around the side.

She had no doubt in the deliberateness in where he left Macklin's body: in the thick muck on the other side of the wall from where she spent her days on the straw bed. Only the old barn boards and five feet of space separated her from Macklin's body.

She'd tried not to look, but she had. And even now, in her mind, she could see his face half-covered in mud, his eyes seemingly locked on her. She'd thought he was dead, *had* to be, but then Macklin had blinked.

Twice.

Micky hadn't looked after that. She'd cried. And for the rest of the day, she'd kept her back to the boards, especially around midday, long after Macklin had to be dead and the pigs had finally ventured to his body, and she'd covered her ears as the pigs squealed like a pack of wolves fighting over a fresh kill.

Now, in the dark, she clutched the kitten to her chest once again. She couldn't remember when she'd caught the animal, only that she wasn't letting it go this time. And as Micky rocked it in the dark, the kitten no longer struggled.

Yes, the dark was good.

In the dark she couldn't see Macklin's partially devoured remains in the yard.

In the dark the pigs slept.

And in the dark, the pig-man couldn't stop her from finally, mercifully, ending her own life.

73

HALEY'S COMET was a typical back-road bar off Route 40, south of Harmony, with beer-ad posters tacked to the darkened wood paneling and with flickering neon signs throughout. Multicolored Christmas lights dangled from the ceiling panels over three pool tables at the back, and along the south wall sat a jukebox and three video poker machines.

Kay and Finn had spent more than two hours at the Thurmont PD station meeting with Reaney's teams. But the teams who'd canvassed throughout the day reported nothing of a man driving a red truck. Or a black Maverick, as Eddie Winchester had described to them.

Reaney's men searched the MVA records for black Mavericks, but Kay had already guessed the sports car Red used as a backup was likely unregistered.

So Haley's Comet was their best bet at the moment. While Bobby and Burke had gone to set them all up at the Super 8 in Thurmont, Kay and Finn had driven west, across the bottom of the Catoctins, in search of the bar Red reportedly patronized.

"I only know him as Red," Haley Beals told them now. The bar's owner was a large woman who frequently perched herself onto a stool behind the bar to take some of the load off her feet. "Doesn't surprise me he's in trouble."

"We just need to talk to him," Kay clarified, but could tell the woman didn't believe her.

"He's usually pretty quiet. Comes in, has a couple beers, leaves. Gotta keep on him for his tab though." She pushed a damp rag across the deeply scarred bar.

"So you don't have a phone number or an address for him?"

"I only know he'll come around sooner or later."

"When was he in last?"

"Last night. Left an hour or so before closing. It was getting a little rowdy. I don't think he likes the noise."

Stacey Blyth had mentioned auditory sensitivity when she'd described neurofibromatosis four nights ago.

"Have you ever noticed anything abnormal about Red?" Kay asked then.

"Abnormal? You mean besides the fact that he doesn't talk to anyone and he's borderline repulsive?"

Kay nodded. "Anything physical?"

Haley shook her head. "Ain't the most attractive man in the world."

"Any bumps on his arms, under his skin?"

"Not that I've noticed. But it's usually pretty dark back there in his booth." She nodded to the farthest booth in the corner. "And as far as I can remember, he always wears shirts. The sleeves buttoned down, you know?"

"So you expecting him tonight?" Finn asked.

Haley shrugged her beefy shoulders. "Can't say."

They thanked Haley and left the dim bar. Outside, the sky was already darkening, the last tinges of red fading to black. Finn had parked the Impala near the back of the lot. It was a good spot, with a view of the entire lot and Harmony Road. If Red showed up in his truck or his Maverick, they'd see him before he ever pulled in.

"This could be a long night," Kay said, getting into the Impala and rolling down the window.

"So have you thought about how you want to handle

things if this shit for brains actually shows up?" Finn asked, sliding in behind the wheel.

Kay *had* thought about it, ever since they'd left Eddie Winchester in Pennsylvania. And she'd also thought about last year, when she and Finn had attempted to follow a suspect who'd been holding a teenage girl hostage. That chase had ended badly. Very badly. They couldn't afford the same potentially fatal results this time.

"It's not like we got a warrant," Finn said. "You want to bring him in for questioning?"

"I don't think, in custody, we'll get anything out of him." Kay remembered her last brainstorm with Constance. *"They're often devoid of normal logic,"* she'd said when describing the disorganized category of offenders that Red fell into, *"making them one of the hardest to catch."*

"I doubt there's any reasoning with this guy," Kay suggested. "Put him in an interview room, and he might never tell us where Micky's at. She could be dead before we ever find her."

"If you want to follow him, I'm with you, Kay. Whatever you're thinking."

They settled into silence then, the muffled *thumpa-thump* of the bar's jukebox stretching into the night, and Kay tried to visualize how they'd follow Red down the narrow mountain roads she'd experienced the day they'd found Peebles's body. It wouldn't be easy, and—if Red didn't show tonight—Kay would ask Burke first thing tomorrow if he could get his hands on some sort of LoJack or tracking device to plant in the son of a bitch's vehicle when he *did* show up at Haley's.

When Finn spoke eventually, his voice was soft and he never broke his stare out the windshield. "Just so you know, Kay, I don't blame you. For the miscarriage."

In his profile, however, Kay recognized the tension in his jaw, and she knew that a small part of Finn would probably always blame her.

"I just wish you'd told me. That's all."

"Why, Finn? What would you have done?"

He had no answer, but she didn't doubt he'd thought of little else in the past three days.

"Look, Finn, I didn't tell you because you were giving your marriage another try. You made that decision before I ever knew. If I'd told you, what then? Would you have given up on Angie, on Maeve?"

He only stared out at the parking lot.

"I didn't want that, Finn. I didn't want you to spend the rest of your life wondering if you *could* have made your marriage work, if you *should* have been with Angie."

She waited for his nod, barely perceptible.

"I just think that . . . that there are times in life when we need answers," she went on. "When we just *have* to know for sure. And sometimes we can't find those answers unless we actually try."

When he turned to her finally, the light from the bar barely touching the side of his face, Kay thought Finn looked sad.

"Did we?" he asked.

"Did we what?"

"Ever truly give it a try?"

"I don't know." Kay thought for a moment, thought about last weeks and months of their relationship, Finn's proposal, his attempts to find them a house. "I think *you* tried."

He nodded, and when he looked away, she wished she knew what else to say. But the one feeling that overwhelmed her now, in their silence, was how much she missed him.

"I still . . . I think I need answers," she said finally.

But Finn didn't take the bait. And as the silence grew uncomfortable, it occurred to Kay—for the first time—that perhaps she was the only one interested in trying again. The twang of a new country-and-western song stretched into the growing darkness, and Kay considered the irony of how she'd always been the one pushing Finn away.

"What about you?" she dared to ask.

He shook his head. "I don't need any more answers."

"That's not what I mean. What's going on with you?"

"Nothing."

"Bullshit. I know you too well, Finn." She shook her head and looked away. Angry. "I wish you'd just fucking tell me."

He didn't.

But there, sitting in a dusty parking lot of some sleazy mountain-town bar, waiting for a killer named Red, Finn reached across the dark car and took Kay's hand into his. He gave it a squeeze, and in that small gesture Kay felt the memory of the connection they'd once shared.

74

DARYL COULD JUST MAKE OUT the subtle shift in light between the trees, defining the clearing ahead. He'd miscalculated the hour, miscalculated the time and effort it would take to complete his work, and now it was dark. He'd come in off the road and groped through the woods, wishing he'd brought a flashlight. Two minutes ago he'd actually triggered one of his own damn booby traps. At the last second he'd felt the tension in the torqued green branch he'd mounted as the trip, and he'd hit the ground before the ring trigger released the holdback peg. The whoosh of the crossbow's spring pole was audible even over the chatter of night insects, and the thick, whittled spear sank into the soft earth with a quiet thwack.

It had got his heart racing for sure, and as he finally reached the clearing, Daryl realized he was too tired, too stressed. He was sure to get himself killed if he didn't get some sleep.

Still, his eyes went to the sagging outline of the shed. It had been a disappointing kill really. He would have far preferred to see the realization in the cop's face when the blast of the twelve-gauge hit him square on. But Daryl hadn't wanted to take any chances with a cop, specially an armed one.

For the rest of the afternoon, Daryl had tried to figure out why a cop had come alone. Why he'd pulled a gun on her.

And now, as Daryl strode across the dark clearing to the shed, his twelve-gauge over one shoulder as the moonless sky above him turned black, he almost wished the cop had shot her. At least, then, he would have been spared the trouble.

75

THE SUPER 8 MOTEL on the outskirts of Thurmont was cut into a hillside of trees. It was dark, no city lights, no noise. Only the sound of crickets in the long grass.

Finn took the stairs to the second-story walkway and

Kay's room. Burke's and Bobby's rooms were around back, but their lights had been out by 2:00 a.m. when he and Kay had come back from Haley's Comet, the stake-out a bust.

For four hot hours they'd waited in the Impala, the windows down to catch whatever breeze managed to lift off the dusty parking lot. They'd watched the comings and goings of the bar patrons, most of the time sitting in silence. Finn had wanted to tell Kay. Tell her everything. But it didn't feel right, sitting in the dark parking lot of some sleazy back-road bar.

Kay's light was on.

She was on her cell when she let him in. With a towel she dabbed at her freshly washed hair and gestured to the side table where two cold, sweating bottles of Coke sat in small puddles.

He opened one and stared at the muted TV where the CNN anchor was tinted green. Finn hadn't been sure whether it was Bobby or Burke who'd hit the tourist shops and bought them fresh T-shirts. But as he looked at Kay's FREDNECK shirt, he guessed it had been Bobby's purchase.

"So you're sure it was him who took the call?" Kay looked too serious on the phone. "Okay, Smitty. Thanks . . . Yeah, we'll keep you posted."

She snapped the cell shut.

"It was Macklin," she said. "The person Eddie Winchester spoke to last night when he called into HQ."

"How's that possible?"

"We were all out in east Baltimore." She used the towel more furiously on her hair now as she paced the old brown carpeting. "Smitty said someone called about the case, the phones were going crazy, and he passed it off to the boardroom. Said he's pretty sure Mack took the call."

"What the hell was he doing in the—"

"He was in to see me. He'd left a message earlier. Smitty didn't know Mack wasn't helping out with the task force."

"Jesus. So Macklin knows about Red. Winchester gave him the same information he gave us."

Kay nodded. "Including Haley's Comet."

"The bar owner told us Red was there last night."

"Shit, Finn. What if Macklin's in trouble?"

"You can't jump to that conclusion."

But she opened her cell phone again. It didn't surprise Finn that she'd programed the Vice cop's numbers into it. She lowered herself to the floral-print comforter, listening to the rings, dialing again, then: "Mack, it's Kay. When you get this, call me. I don't care what time it is. Call." She closed the phone. "No answer at his home. And his cell went straight to voice mail."

"So he's got it turned off." But Finn could tell Kay was unsettled.

"Tomorrow morning, first thing, I'm having HQ fax Thurmont PD a photo of Mack. We need to take it around, see if anyone saw him. Gas stations. Diners. The bar. We need to know if he's been up here."

"Stupid-ass vigilante." Finn's grip tightened around his Coke. "Like we don't have enough on our hands trying to find Micky, he's gotta be a fucking idiot supercop."

Finn tried to tamp down on the anger, but his emotions weren't so easily controlled these days. Another side effect of the drugs, he figured.

He moved to the window, drew back one edge of the heavy curtain to scan the motel's lot, as though he might spot Macklin's blue Mustang. "Last thing we need is that shit for brains inadvertently tipping this Red guy off, forcing his hand."

He hadn't heard Kay cross the room, but when he turned, she was there.

"Talk to me, Finn. Something's not right with you. I can tell."

She was standing too close. And suddenly the bottle of Coke felt as if it was slipping from his grasp. He held it tighter and felt the familiar trembling.

Kay took the bottle from him, set it on the side table, then, firmly, clasped his hand.

"What *is* this?" she asked, holding his hand level between hers. The tremors came even stronger now. Stress did that, his doc had warned. "What's going on?"

He knew he should just say it. But, then, he'd not said it before. Not aloud. Not to anyone. Even to his doctor he hadn't been able to call it by name, sitting in the bright office, staring at a poster about fucking footprints in the sand as he listened to the diagnosis, the virtual death sentence in regard to his career. And his marriage.

Because the bottom line was, he wasn't about to let Angie have to take care of him. Or Kay, for that matter.

This was *his* battle.

"Finn?"

"MS." And just like that, he'd said it. But he could see on Kay's blank expression that the truth hadn't sunk in yet. "Go figure, huh?" He withdrew his hand from hers, took up his Coke again, and tipped it at her in a toast. "Life's a bitch, ain't it?"

"Wait. I don't understand—"

"Multiple sclerosis."

"I know what MS is, Finn. But how? When?"

"Who knows how? God's idea of a joke, I guess. Just can't seem to let anything be easy." He never meant to sound sorry for himself. "It's under control. Sort of."

"How long have you known?" He hated the sympathy he heard in Kay's voice.

"A few months. I'm fine, Kay."

She shook her head, as though putting together the pieces. "That's why you're not with Angie, isn't it?"

Finn shrugged, but she had her answer.

"Does she even know?"

"Not yet." Another long swig of Coke. "But it gets even better."

"What?"

"I didn't qualify."

"So you reshoot it."

"I shot a sixty-five, Kay. I'm not going to pass. And they'll take my gun."

"What about drugs?"

"Oh, I'm on all kinds of those. Injections. Pills. I can't even remember the names anymore."

Kay was still shaking her head and Finn thought she looked kind of lost. "Well, maybe you need different ones. Maybe the dosage isn't right. Maybe you need to see another doctor. Get a second opinion." Again Kay took his hand between hers, holding it tightly as though she could stop the trembling. "This could be the drugs, Finn."

"It doesn't matter." He pulled away. "I'm thinking of leaving anyway."

"Leaving the Department?"

He nodded. "What are my options? A desk job? I can't do that."

"And who's saying you'd be on a desk? Christ, Finn,

you talk to your doctor, have the meds and dosage altered, and all this might go away."

He shook his head.

"Goddamn it, Finn, all you have to do is get these shakes under control and you'll qualify—"

"No, Kay. It's not safe. *I'm* not safe."

"What the hell are you talking about?"

"I'm talking about last night, Kay." The anger rose again. "I'm talking about standing in that warehouse and seeing that piece of shit standing over you with his fucking cannon pointed at your head. I'm talking about how I couldn't take the shot, Kay. Couldn't take the goddamn shot because my hand was shaking so bad, and unless it was a kill shot, the son of a bitch would've blown your brains out. And all I could do was fucking stand there with my gun waving around in the fucking air!"

Tears welled in Kay's cool gray eyes and he prayed she kept them in check. He couldn't handle her crying.

"If it hadn't been for goddamn Burke," he said, trying to temper his voice, "you'd be dead today. Do you get that? It would have been on *my* head. I can't take the chance of that happening again."

She moved closer, this time bringing her hands up to cradle his face. "We'll find answers, Finn," she said quietly.

He smelled her freshly washed skin then, and her hair, felt her breath on his lips as she drew him down to her. It didn't matter how determined he'd been to keep his distance, to not get involved again . . . the second Kay kissed him, Finn was lost.

He'd forgotten how damn good she felt, her lips, her hands, the ache of her body. Long ago he'd stopped torturing himself with the memories of the passion they'd shared. But now, with her sweet mouth on his, her hot body pressed against him, Finn felt any semblance of restraint and resolution scatter.

It was inevitable, he thought then. Him and Kay.

Always had been.

Always would be.

And his hands were on her now, pulling her even closer as her fingers fluttered across his chest, down his rib cage, and lower. He heard her whimper, felt it in his mouth, as his own body rocked with the desire to be with Kay again.

Only when her hands reached for the waist of his jeans did Finn stop her, his forehead pressed to hers.

"What is it, Finn?" Her words were a whisper across his lips.

"I don't want . . ."

"What?"

"I don't want anyone . . . *you* . . . to have to take care of me, Kay."

He felt her smile against his mouth. "Fine. I won't."

And Finn surrendered. Kay's expert kisses guided him. Their passion—never extinguished no matter how hard either of them had tried in the past—led them to the bed now, tearing at each other's clothes and throwing back the covers. And as Finn moved over her, then inside her, as he touched Kay's face and her eyes locked on his, her tears were no longer contained.

"I've missed you, Finn," she said at last. "More than you can ever know."

76

Tuesday, August 7

THROUGH THE CRACK IN THE MOTEL curtains Kay could see daylight.

The rumble of a Harley came from the parking lot, followed by a second. They revved for a minute, then ripped out of the Super 8. After that there was only Finn's low, rhythmic breathing.

The few hours she did manage to sleep were the best she'd had in weeks, if not months. The solidness of Finn spooning behind her was a comfort she'd never dared to dream would ever be possible again.

Now he lay on his back, one arm flung over his head, his black hair spilling across the white pillow, and his face turned toward her. Kay propped herself onto one elbow and watched him. So calm in sleep, she thought. Gone was the tension she'd seen ravage his features last night as he'd told her about the MS and his inability to fire his weapon at the warehouse. Kay knew that ate at Finn the most: that Casper Thompson would have killed her if not for Galen Burke. She couldn't begin to imagine Finn's fears, about the job, about his future, about his life.

And as she studied the lines of his face, so familiar yet almost new now in light of what she'd learned, Kay felt more afraid than she had in a long time. Not since she was thirteen and was told her mother had only months to live had Kay felt such deep fear and absolute helplessness.

"*I don't want you to have to take care of me,*" Finn had said last night.

How could she not?

Kay settled a hand on his chest, felt his heart against her palm. From the moment she'd first kissed him last night, it had felt like coming home. How could she not be with him? The man she loved. The man she wanted to be with. And again, Kay regretted that it had taken losing Finn for her to fully comprehend how important he was to her. How vital.

And now this. MS.

Last night, making love, the disease could be forgotten. It had been about them, their passion, their love. As though no time had been lost. No regrets. No miscarriage. No MS.

But in the light of day . . .

Finn took a deep breath, his eyes opening as his hand found hers. With the other he touched her cheek, wiping at a tear. "What is it, babe?"

"Nothing." It was work to smile, and Kay was grateful for the knock at the motel door so she wouldn't have to explain.

She was pulling the oversized FREDNECK T-shirt over her head when the second knock came. Even more insistent. Kay rifled her fingers through her hair and opened the door.

"How'd you sleep?" Galen Burke filled the doorway with his smile. Showered, shaved, and already dressed. When he looked past her, his eyes settled on Finn. Burke's smile disintegrated, and when his gaze returned to Kay, there was a new awkwardness about the usually smooth agent.

She wasn't sure why, but Kay felt guilty all of a sudden.

"You'll want to get dressed," Burke said stiffly. "Reaney just called. They found something."

77

THEY'D DRESSED QUICKLY and met Burke and Bobby in the parking lot. Burke had handed them breakfast in a bag, and they'd followed his car out of Thurmont and up into the mountains. Behind the wheel, Finn had eaten along the way, while Kay's breakfast still sat wedged into the corner of the dash.

Kay couldn't figure out if Burke had been purposefully vague about Reaney's early-morning call because he was pissed at her, or if Reaney hadn't given Burke the specifics of what his men had found.

"Hang on to your coffee," Finn warned seconds before the Impala's tires dropped from paved surface to gravel and rattled over a section of washboard. The tail end of Burke's Malibu was swallowed by churned-up dust.

Seconds later Kay's cell phone rang.

The signal was weak, but she recognized Savalas's voice immediately. The sergeant sounded nervous, a little hesitant, perhaps still not entirely comfortable with her new relationship with Kay after her confession Sunday night.

"We just got a call from Krajishnik," her sergeant said, referring to the owner of the slaughterhouse in Pigtown. "A couple more names came up for him, and one employee in particular he remembers always wore a ponytail."

"He didn't remember this guy sooner?"

The connection crackled and Kay worried she'd lose the signal entirely. "Apparently this guy, and the couple others he remembered, were contract only. Worked shifts before the holidays, help with the higher volume. Paid them under the table. That's why they weren't on any official employee list."

"Son of a bitch. So what's the name? This guy with the hair?"

"Daryl Eugene Wardell."

Kay ran the name through her head a few times as though it should somehow feel right, as if it would suddenly fit the image she carried in her mind of Micky's abductor. But Kay felt nothing.

"Did you run it?" she asked Savalas.

"Yes, but we haven't gotten much. No priors. No—"

"What about MVA?"

"He's not listed as having registered any vehicles, but he's got an address over in Garrett County."

"That's what . . . a hundred miles from here? That doesn't make any sense."

"That's what I thought. I've got a call in to the state police though, have them check the address."

"Make sure they've got backup," Kay said as the signal wavered. "And call me the second you hear from state."

Kay snapped her cell phone shut just as Burke's taillights flared red through the dust. Ahead of the Fed's car Kay could make out the white county cars at the shoulder and a tow truck parked across the road.

Barely 8:00 a.m. and the morning was already hot. With it came a blanketing humidity that dampened Kay's skin as she crossed to where Reaney stood with several FCSO uniforms at the edge of a steep ravine. The air was thick with the high-pitched drone of cicadas, even above the diesel rumble of the tow truck.

"What have you got?" Kay asked, eyeing the broad swath of crushed vegetation that originated from the roadway. From the dense brush below she heard someone call up, "All right, she's hooked. Haul her up."

Reaney's shirt was damp with sweat. He nodded down

into the ravine as the winch of the tow truck started whining and branches snapped.

"State chopper spotted it this morning," he explained, keeping his eyes on the cable. "They were taking a sweep over this area, headed south of here to where the search teams are working, when they saw it. Radioed for us to come and check it out. If it hadn't been for the chopper we mighta not found this for weeks. I already radioed Thurmont and they ran the tags."

Through the dense brush and sticker bushes, the sun glinted off glass.

"Car belongs to one of yours," Reaney said.

But Kay could already see the rear end of the muscle car emerge from the tangle of undergrowth and the shimmer of the metallic blue paint job.

"Detective Jack Macklin."

78

"WHAT DO YOU MEAN there's no sign of him?" Kay asked.

"We're still looking but so far there's no one down there," one of the uniforms said, his face red from the climb back out of the treacherous ravine.

Finn swatted at a mosquito, squashing it along his sweat-dampened neck. "Maybe he was ejected."

Reaney shook his head. "There'd be at least some blood, but the car is clean."

The Mustang sat on the roadway now, creepers and branches hanging off its twisted frame. The front end was nothing but mangled metal, the hood crumpled, the windshield shattered and caved in, and the driver's-side door barely attached to its frame.

"Nothing on the driver's seat, the dash, or the steering wheel," Reaney pointed out.

"Looks like the driver's door might have been open. Could he have bailed before it went down?" Finn asked, peering inside the littered remains of the sports car. The bits of crumbled safety glass glittered across the leather seats like diamonds.

On the other side, Burke wrenched open the passenger-side door. He shook his head as he pointed to the ignition. "Car wasn't running when it went over. Key's in the off position. Someone pushed it."

"Where the hell is he?" Kay asked.

Pointing past Kay's shoulder to the trunk release, Finn said, "Pop the trunk."

"Oh, God," she barely whispered as she followed his instruction.

The rear of the Mustang had little damage and the lid popped immediately.

Finn got there first. "Well, well, well," he said as Kay joined him. "Guess I was right about the son of a bitch."

The false bottom of the trunk had jarred open in the crash, but instead of a dummy tire and a jack, several bundles of cash had been tucked into the molded pockets. Finn didn't doubt they'd find drugs as well in the tangle of contents.

"Only kind of person I know carries this much cash is a dirty cop," Finn said, wondering how many thousands were in those neat packets.

With gloved hands he picked through the mess, revealing for Kay a street-beaten Bersa semiautomatic. "And the only thing this is good for is as a throw-down piece," he said, referring to any kind of an untraceable weapon that could be planted on an unarmed victim after he was shot, thereby faking a gunfight. "Believe me now?"

He could see the disappointment in Kay's face, and Finn was almost sorry he had been right about the Vice cop.

"You realize Micky could be in even more danger," Finn said quietly.

"What do you mean?"

"I never bought the affair story. How much do you wanna bet Micky found out about Macklin's corruption and confronted him the night she went missing?"

He could see Kay struggling to take it all in, to believe that the man she'd so staunchly defended had been everything Finn had suggested. And possibly worse.

"For all we know, Macklin didn't come here to *save* Micky. If he's in this deep," Finn said, waving at the wads of cash, "he might just want to be sure this Red son of a bitch did the job right."

Kay was shaking her head when her cell phone rang at her hip. She paced several yards down the road until she seemed satisfied with the signal.

Less than a minute later she rejoined them. "That was Savalas," she told Finn, and Bobby and Burke. "The slaughterhouse hunch paid off." And Finn wondered if Savalas had given credit where credit was due.

"Apparently this Daryl Eugene Wardell doesn't have his own address other than a post-office box in Emmitsburg. He also doesn't own a red pickup truck. But the address on his driver's license is in Accident over in Garrett County, a house owned by his cousin, Earl Carter. Lives there with his mother. Neither have seen Wardell in a couple of years."

"And the truck?" Finn asked.

"Carter owns it. Pays the registration every year for his cousin."

"And they don't know where this dipshit lives?"

Kay shook her head. "They claim they get a call from him once in a while, but have no idea where he's living."

"Bullshit."

"Bottom line, we can't count on getting anything from the cousin. Even if he does know something, we don't have time to squeeze it out of him. If Macklin *was* onto this Wardell guy, then he's tipped off. He could be trying to get rid of Micky or is already long gone. We need to find this son of a bitch. Today."

Finn could see Kay's wheels turning as she studied the mangled Mustang and the ravine, the surrounding woods, and then the road.

"There's no blood anywhere on the road or the shoulder, right?"

"Not that we could find," Reaney said.

"What about the road?" Kay asked. "Any ruts in the gravel, drag marks, anything?"

"Nothing."

"Then the confrontation wasn't here. If he took Macklin here, there would have been force involved, a struggle, blood. Something."

Finn said, "So you're thinking if something happened to Macklin—"

"—it didn't happen here." Kay's voice was the only sound in that narrow roadway besides the cicadas in the trees. "He's done something to Macklin and he drove the car here to ditch it."

"Great," Bobby said. "So who knows how far this guy might have driven it?"

Kay shook her head and scanned the woods again. "No. He didn't drive it far. And I doubt he towed it either. I think he drove it here, and because he had to walk back, he didn't come far."

"Unless he had help," Finn suggested.

"Not this guy." And as Kay stared into the dark dampness of the forest surrounding them, a calm confidence seemed to come over her. "Reaney," she said at last. "We need a dog out here. Right away."

79

THEY HADN'T WAITED LONG for a K9 unit from Frederick. In fact, the handler had probably taken more time preparing his dog and casting for a trail. He'd directed the bloodhound in a widening circle around where Macklin's Mustang had been sent nose-first into the ravine, until finally the dog latched onto a trail that hadn't been compromised by the FCSO personnel and the recovery team.

For twenty minutes now they'd beaten their way through the brush behind the handler and the dog he called Penny. Kay, Finn, Burke, Bobby, Reaney, and two of his men had fanned out behind the K9 team, and they'd practically been running ever since.

Initially Kay had almost been sorry to see the bloodhound lumber out of the cruiser. If the trail did lead them to Red, they'd be better off with a fully trained police dog. As it was, the worst old Penny could do for them after the man-trailing was done would be to slobber their perp to death, Burke had joked.

Still, the hound was good, beating an almost headlong rush through the woods. "Hauling ass" were the words Bobby had used about a mile back between gasps for breath.

Keeping up wasn't easy over the steep and wooded terrain. What kept Kay moving, besides thoughts of Micky, was concern over the handler's safety. Getting too far in front of them, the dog and handler could encounter Red first, and with the officer's hands full of a hundred pounds of drooling, hell-bent bloodhound, drawing his weapon in time would be near impossible.

And something else niggled in the back of Kay's mind as they thrashed through the sticker bushes and brambles, the thorns snagging her clothes and tearing at her bare arms: the Morgan County Militia. Who knew how far Daryl Eugene Wardell took his militant calling?

Only thirty or forty feet ahead of her, the handler looked like a water-skier being dragged through the undergrowth. And then suddenly, he came up short. Ahead of him the lead line went slack. The hound was circling, its nose a foot off the ground, making low snuffling noises as it turned its head several times.

"What's the problem?" Kay asked.

"No problem. She's eliminating directions of travel as well as following."

The dog cut back then, returning in the direction they'd come, and Kay was about to say something when the handler cut her off. "She's probably found his actual footsteps. Up until now she's been tracking his raft scent."

"Raft?"

"Dead cells. Skin mostly. They're shed at a high rate, and since the particles are heavier than air, they settle close to the ground or on foliage. What we call a ground scent. Depending on the wind, the dog often follows along the fringe of the scent. She's cutting back because she's probably directly on the track, his scent combining with a vegetative scent, the broken grass and plants left by his physical steps. She's more or less making sure she's still got the right trail. Either that or there's more than one trail out here."

But when the hound made another tight circle and started again in the direction they'd been heading, the handler nodded. "See? She's got it now."

Kay watched the bloodhound as it passed her, a brown hulk in the bright green ferns. There was no visible trail, nothing to indicate anyone had come through here, at least not to Kay. And just as Penny started to take up the slack in the line, the dog stopped again, this time at the base of a large maple. The nose came up, then down again, sniffing at the wide trunk.

And then Kay saw the wire. "Stop her."

"What?"

"The dog. Stop her!" Kay lunged for the handler's line herself, winding it once through her fist and hauling the heavy dog backward.

"Kay, what is it?" She heard Finn behind her. Then Burke.

With the hound under the handler's control, Kay moved forward cautiously. Pointing. In one thin shaft of sunlight penetrating the leaves overhead, Kay's eyes locked onto the silver wire stretched from the base of the maple back into the brush.

She stopped within four feet of the wire, studying the tree, the surrounding shrubs, but whatever was rigged to it was masterfully camouflaged.

His actual footsteps, the K9 handler had said. The son of a bitch had walked here. Must have set the booby trap as he went. That's why the dog had gone in circles. He'd worked at rigging it up.

"He knew we might come through here after him," Kay said, then searched the ground. Several feet away she found a dead branch, but Burke took it from her before she could get near the trip wire.

"Stand back," he said, waving her and the others aside as he approached the man trap. Burke angled in from the side, protected by the maple, and inched the heavy branch toward the trip wire. Kay could see the sweat beaded along Burke's forehead and neck, the mosquitoes flying about his face. But the agent remained steady.

The wire nudged. Nothing. Burke applied more pressure, and Kay could see the wire give a little more. A little more. Until there was a faint metallic clink.

And then it sounded as if the skies were opening. A low whoosh. The branches overhead thrashed, and almost instantly a long wooden arm lashed downward in a wide, powerful arc. Four feet off the ground, secured to the end of the arm, was a two-foot-long spike, roughly fashioned out of a green sapling and whittled to a sharp tip.

"Jesus," Finn whispered behind her.

Reaney seconded it.

"Well," Burke said, inspecting the device more closely, "at least now we know the kind of individual we're dealing with."

"Yeah, a whacked-out survivalist."

"Fucking Rambo or what?" Bobby moved in on the contraption as well. "Check out the workmanship."

Kay did. The device was meant to kill. And if this *was* Daryl Eugene Wardell's trail they were tracking through the woods, he definitely wasn't interested in warnings.

"What now?" the K9 handler asked, scanning the woods nervously as though he expected to spot more trip wires.

"Now, we be careful. Can you slow her down?" Kay asked, nodding to the bloodhound.

"Can you stop a freight train?"

"You're going to have to try. And give yourself a bit more line. More clearance. Just in case."

In seconds the handler had the hound back on the scent, struggling to keep the dog at an easier pace. This time, Kay followed alongside the dog, placing herself downwind of it. If Red had set any more traps directly over his trail, and the dog was following his scent more than his footsteps, as the handler suggested, Kay figured it was a better bet that the traps would be upwind of the dog.

But they didn't travel more than five minutes over the rugged terrain, through a dry creek bed and up the other side, before the hound slowed and started circling again.

Frantically, Kay scanned the ferns and brush for any sign of a trap or trip wire.

"Did she find another one?" Burke asked, catching up.

The handler shook his head as the dog's circles stretched farther. Twice it cut back and circled again. Kay thought the animal seemed confused. Or perhaps over-stimulated.

"What is it?" she asked.

"I don't know." The handler studied his dog. "She must be picking up multiple trails."

Kay's uneasiness rose. Was there another trap? Had he laid extra trails with the expectation he could be followed?

Her hand went to her gun.

Or was he here?

Sunlight pierced the thick canopy overhead dappling the trunks and undergrowth in crazy patterns, playing tricks with her vision. The air was still and heavy, and when a small breeze did manage to stir across the forest to the small group, Kay thought she smelled manure.

"Is that pigs?" she asked.

All the men sniffed, turning where they stood.

But even as Reaney concurred, Kay smelled something worse. Something far more sinister and disturbing. A smell that was still fresh in her senses from Kristine Peebles's body found in the shallow creek four days ago. Putrefaction.

80

AS THE CONSTANT DIN of cicada from the treetops intensified around them, so did the tension among the men. Finn could feel it, as thick as the midday heat that settled over the west face of the mountain.

It was Kay who found the well.

The bloodhound seemed to have lost the scent trail, circling and snorting through the underbrush, perhaps confused at the presence of so much decay. But beyond the dog and its handler, Kay moved through the trees, working a large stick across the ground ahead of her until she reached the low stone wall. Finn saw her lift her hand to her nose even before she waved the rest of the men over.

The stench rose as he and the others neared the crumbling wellhead. There was no mistaking the odor.

Then Finn heard the flies.

Reaching Kay first, Burke pulled her back. He squatted in the leaves and used her stick to prod the edge of the wooden lid that capped the low, circular wall, testing for any kind of trigger or trip wire.

"Looks safe," the agent said in time, and Reaney moved in.

The Sheriff's Office detective gave the slatted lid a solid kick with his boot, sending it toppling aside as the smell of decay and flies swept over them. Finn batted at the swarming insects while, behind him, one of Reaney's men shuffled back, gagging.

"Give me a flashlight." Kay gestured to Reaney's other uniformed officer.

Finn didn't want to follow the Maglite's beam into the narrow pit, but he couldn't help himself.

"Jesus fucking Christ," Burke said as Finn too moved to the edge of the old well. "There's gotta be more than one body down there."

Deep into the dark hole, past the white and tan hide of what had to be a dead deer, past bits of clothing snagged by the rough stone walls, Finn recognized the shapes caught in the long beam of light as human.

Silence settled over the team.

Across the pit's opening, Kay's face had gone pale, and Finn knew she was holding back her own shock, knew that she too had to be wondering how they would ever empty the well and sort through the remains.

Tears glistened in her eyes. "How many?" she whispered finally. "How many dead women are we going to find down there?"

And then it was as though the horror of the well fueled Kay's determination. She handed off the flashlight and popped the snap on her holster.

"If this is where he's dumping them, he can't be far," she said, scanning the woods. Then, pointing: "Does that look like a clearing to you?"

Finn saw the break in the trees Kay had spotted about two hundred feet uphill.

"Come on," Burke said behind him, and they moved together.

Cautiously. They worked their way two abreast, toward the flood of sunlight, Burke and Reaney leading, probing the forest floor. It felt like forever before they reached the edge of the clearing. Sweat slid down Finn's neck and back. He wiped at his face, and his hand went to the butt of his nine as they emerged from the trees.

He felt exposed, vulnerable, out in the open. Even with the threat of booby traps throughout the forest, there'd been a sense of security there. Cover.

The narrow clearing was cluttered with wrecks. Heaps of junk and automotive relics. And beyond them, the house.

Burke gestured directions while Reaney radioed for backup. The detective's voice was low as he gave directions based on the last road they'd crossed at least a half hour ago, and Finn wondered how long it would take for anyone to arrive, and whether they'd even be able to find the place.

"You okay?" Kay touched his arm, her voice barely a whisper. He tried to ignore the concern he saw in her face.

"Yeah. I'm good." And he drew his nine. The gun fit solidly in his hand, not like in the warehouse two nights ago. Today the gun felt good, and as he stared at the shabby house on the other side of the clearing, Finn attributed it to his growing desire to sink a bullet in the hillbilly Rambo's brain.

"Come on."

They fanned out then, moving through the west side of the clearing, silently slipping through the tangle of scraps and steadily closing in on the house. But the cover of the rusted-out wrecks was meager, and Finn couldn't escape the feeling they were being watched. Every move. Every member.

They reached the weed-choked drive together, and Finn could now better assess the condition of the house. It was difficult to believe that anyone actually lived in the decaying structure with its rusted tin roof and walls of exposed and rotting lath, the asphalt siding torn away in numerous places. More than a couple of the upstairs windows were busted out, their weather-beaten frames covered with heavy plastic, and the chimney was disintegrating, bits of deteriorated brick littering the ground below.

Creeper vines had already consumed the back and east side of the house, and Finn could easily imagine the structure completely consumed and disappearing into the landscape within a few years' time.

"My men and I'll go in," Reaney said, and before Kay could argue, the county detective added, "You guys don't have vests."

And then time stretched thin. Bobby and Burke had gone around to cover the back of the house, while Kay and Finn watched the front, keeping an ear out for any approaching vehicle.

The sun beat down on them. Finn checked his watch. Five minutes now.

He could hear Reaney and his men moving through the weakened structure, no doubt painstakingly checking each room and entranceway for trip wires or false floors. There was no telling what might await them.

Six minutes.

Finn tried to take comfort in the fact that they had yet to spot the truck or the black Maverick on the property.

Seven.

Kay too seemed anxious. Ready to storm the place shed by shed until they found Micky. And Macklin. Whenever her eyes flitted over to meet his, Finn could see her restlessness. With her back pressed to the corner of the hick's house, she eyed the shed across the clearing.

Past the rail fence a half dozen pigs basked in the shade of the boarded shed.

"Frances Gallo." Kay spoke so quietly Finn wondered if she was talking to herself. "Finn," she said louder, and nodded to the shed, "Frances Gallo was terrified of the pigs."

She pushed away from the structure and started toward the shed, until Finn caught her arm.

"No, Kay. We move together."

"Micky's in there."

"Together," he said firmly. "This freak could be hiding anywhere. He could be watching us right now."

And finally Reaney came back through the front door, onto the porch, his gun lowered. "We got nothing in there," he said. "She's not inside. No sign of her. At least not on the main floor. And we can't get to the second. Stairs are rotted out. If this *is* the same guy who's got your girl, he never had her in the house," Reaney said with certainty.

"That sick son of a bitch," Kay said. And this time there was no holding her back when she started for the shed.

81

OF COURSE MICKY wouldn't be in the house, Kay thought again, beelining for the shed. To him, whatever girl he picked up in the city and kept shackled until he was finished with her, to him she no was different from a kept dog. Or his pigs. Livestock. Why *would* he keep her anywhere else?

And as Kay followed the well-beaten dirt track, she imagined the son of a bitch taking the same route. Not just for the pigs. How often had he walked this same path to rape Micky Luttrell over the past ten days?

Somewhere behind her, Reaney was radioing Thurmont again for backup. And she was aware of Finn following her as Reaney's men, Burke, and Bobby, moved through the junkers under the scorching sun.

At the rail fence, the stink of the pigs was stronger, the stench wafting out from the small shed. There was no gate to the outer pen that circled the entire structure. Kay stepped onto the bottom rail and swung one leg over the top.

The pigs tensed, letting out several low, guttural noises, but only one of them heaved itself up onto short, calloused legs. From the shade, it regarded her with tiny, black eyes, and Kay was startled at how huge the animal was, its belly distended and its pink-and-brown-spotted hide caked with dried muck.

Kay dropped over the rail, landing on the narrow, sun-hardened path. To her left, a pitchfork was propped against the rails. Reluctantly she holstered her nine and took up the fork.

Finn was behind her, his Glock still out as he came over the fence. The large pig started toward them then, its pointed hooves making sucking sounds in the mud.

Ten feet. Five.

It flattened out its head, extending its enormous snout toward them, sniffing the air as it grunted. Another step. And another. Until it was too close.

Kay gestured with the fork and the pig stopped, but did not back away. And when it approached again, Kay poked at the loose, fleshy jowl with the fork's tines.

The pig screamed. Earsplitting and nerve-jangling. It scurried back through the wet muck, its squeals rousing the others now as they all clambered to their feet.

And then, in the pig's wake, Kay saw something that made her heart stop.

The denim jeans were barely discernible, half-buried and covered in mud. A corner of a white T-shirt rose above the dark muck like a white flag stirring slightly in the hot breeze. But it was the gator-skin Western boot that Kay recognized instantly.

"Oh, Jesus. Finn."

He was right behind her, one hand on her shoulder. But even that wasn't enough to keep the world from tilting beneath her feet.

"It's Macklin."

There was no way of telling how much of him the pigs had consumed. She spotted glimpses of flesh and bone trampled into the mud and could just distinguish the dark red-brown of dried blood crusted across the pigs' meaty faces.

"Oh my God." As much as she wanted to, Kay couldn't turn away from the horror. She retched against the bile that crept up into her throat. "The pigs . . ."

"I don't think the pigs did this, Kay." Finn's voice was barely audible above the buzzing in her ears. "The son of a bitch must have . . . fed Macklin to them."

This time when one of the other pigs approached, Kay yelled at it. And when she forked it—harder than the last—her disgust and repulsion boiled over. If it had been her nine in her hands, she might have shot the thing on the spot.

She was still gagging when she turned to the doorway of the shed, a gaping maw into a reeking black hell.

She couldn't be in here.

The words turned over and over in her head as Kay stepped into the warm stench and waited for her eyes to adjust. *She couldn't be in here.*

Just inside the doorway, Kay abandoned the fork and took up her nine again. With Finn at her back, the two moved through the shed as one. Several shadows scattered as they moved through the low shed, and at first Kay wondered if they were rats, then spotted a feral cat.

Through the main pen and into an aisle of cleaner straw. More cats scurried and disappeared. Gun firm in her hand, Kay studied every shape and shadow, expecting him to step out at any second. Her eyes checking before each step, scanning for any kind of a trap.

And then Kay saw her.

Several thin shafts of sunlight slipped through the boards of the shed, dust motes swirling in each. One shaft settled on her hair and the pale gray blanket over her shoulders where she sat in the corner.

"Micky."

Kay started to rush forward, desperate to reach her, but Finn grabbed the waist of her jeans.

"Careful," he said. "We don't know that he hasn't rigged this place."

Kay scanned. But there was nothing.

Kay clambered over the divider and moved into the pen. Another shadow flew by to her left. Kay froze, swung her nine in the direction. Again, another cat.

"Micky."

She was staring right at Kay, but in the dim light Kay saw no sign of recognition. Micky's face tightened into what looked like confusion.

"Micky. It's me. Detective Delaney. We're here to take you home."

Her eyes seemed to flit, a quick flash of white, and as Kay closed the distance, Micky cringed.

"It's okay, Micky." Kay knelt next to the young detective and caught the first sour, acrid smell of infection. Holstering her weapon, she settled a hand on Micky's shoulder and felt her entire body stiffen. "We're here to help."

Past Micky, through the slats of the shed, Kay spotted Bobby on the other side of the outer pen. "Sweet Jesus," she heard him say, and knew he'd found Macklin's remains.

A sickening realization struck Kay then. From where Micky sat on the nest of straw against the boards, she would have witnessed the whole ordeal: her partner's body being ripped apart and devoured by the pigs.

"Micky. We're getting you out of here."

As she started to take one of Micky's arms, Kay realized the girl clutched something to her chest. Kay brushed back one edge of the blanket and saw the striped fur. A kitten.

Only, the kitten was cold.

"Micky, let me help you . . ." She attempted to ease Micky's arms from the dead animal, but the more she tried, the tighter Micky clutched it.

"Jesus, Finn, we've got to get her out of here." Kay's eyes fell to Micky's ankle and the heavy chain that attached the shackle to the foundation beam, each link the size of her palm. They'd never cut through it.

"Here." From the aisle Finn snatched a key off a large spike in one of the support beams. "Try this." He tossed the skeleton key across the pen.

Kay's hands were shaking, and it took several attempts before she managed to slide the key into the lock. The hasp snapped open with a satisfying click, and Kay tried to steady her hands as she wiggled the lock out of the ring.

Micky didn't even wince when Kay finally opened the steel shackle. The ankle looked infected, oozing in the dim light.

"Can you walk, Micky?"

No response.

"Micky, come on. I need you to stand." Kay guided her to her feet.

She teetered there for a moment, but refused to move forward.

"Micky, please. You—"

"Emma." The name was barely a cracked murmur in Micky's throat. "Emma," she tried again, and hope surged through Kay.

"Yes, Micky. Emma. We're going to take you to her."

Kay knew, without her support, Micky would never have made it to the side of the pen, and once there, her knees almost gave out. Finn leaned across the divider then and, with Kay's help, lifted Micky into his arms.

Still, the blankness in Micky Luttrell's eyes disturbed Kay, and she remembered Frances Gallo's vacant stares. She thought of Andy Luttrell, of their daughter, Emma. Micky Luttrell would never be the same. But when Micky uttered her daughter's name again as Finn carried her into the daylight, Kay knew Micky was stronger than Frances Gallo ever was, that she could recover, and Kay swore she'd do whatever it took to help the Luttrells out.

From the other side of the outer fence, Galen Burke took Micky from Finn. The agent lifted her easily over the top rail, and even when the pigs grunted from the trampled remains of Jack Macklin, Micky seemed unresponsive, clasping the dead kitten to her chest.

When Kay started over the fence herself, her eyes went to the farthest shed, nestled at the edge of the woods.

"Oh my God." She froze partway over the fence.

"What is it, Kay?"

She pointed for Finn.

There, tucked behind the shed's far side, she could just make out the rear bumper of a black sports car, and through the dilapidated door of the shed, barely hanging from one hinge, the tailgate of a red pickup truck.

"The son of a bitch is here."

82

SWEAT TRICKLED DOWN DARYL'S back under the long-sleeved camo shirt. Mosquitoes feasted on the exposed skin of his neck and buzzed around his ears, but he ignored them. Every breath had to be controlled. Every movement carefully executed. Because now *he* was the hunted. *He* was the prey.

He'd been rewiring one of the spear traps closer to the house when he'd heard them thrashing through the underbrush with the dog. He'd wished then that he'd had the arsenic and warfarin powder he'd heard them talk about at one of the meetings out in Morgan County. Dust it behind you when you were cutting a trail, and the dog would be dead before it ever found you, they'd said. Lace it with some cayenne pepper and you'd stop the mutt in his tracks.

Instead, the hound had led them to the well and then the clearing, and obviously around the trap he'd constructed yesterday. He wondered if he'd got at least one cop in that trap, but then Daryl figured he should at least have heard the screaming.

Still, there were other traps.

And there was food: dehydrated packets squirreled away throughout the woods. And gallon jugs of water. All strategically placed. He could survive out here for weeks. Months if he had to.

But his best bet was the old 'shiner shed down past the creek. A bit of a trek, but it was stocked. He'd have a roof over his head, along with the deer rifle he kept wrapped and stashed under the floorboards.

The twelve-gauge strapped to his back was useless right now. The Mossberg meant business but only at closer range. Twenty feet up, squatting in the blind he'd built in the tall maple at the edge of the clearing, the shotgun would only get him killed. He was outnumbered. They'd locate him and be firing before he'd ever get the six rounds off and start to reload.

So Daryl waited.

And watched. With the camos and greasepaint he could sit up here all day if he had to and not be seen. His scent was too heavy through the clearing and around its perimeter. He doubted the bloodhound would ever locate him.

Through the leaves and down where the midday sun glared off the parts cars, he watched them carry his girl away. His eyes fixed on the woman cop though. The cop who'd stabbed Mama in the face with the pitchfork in the outside pen. It was the woman cop he wanted dead. Yes, he'd put the first round in her if he had a choice in the matter.

And just then, as she cleared the fence, he saw her point to the implement shed. To the truck. He was sure of it.

With the wind batting at the leaves around him, Daryl couldn't make out what she was saying, but when she scanned the clearing, his body stiffened. His muscles cramping, the bugs biting, the sweat stinging his eyes.

She was a hunter. Just like him.

Could she sense him?

Smell him?

When she turned in the direction of the tree and scanned the edge of the woods, her eyes seemed to stop on him.

His heart raced in his chest. How was it possible? The blind was camouflaged. Yet her eyes bored across the distance, through the leaves, and directly into his.

How?

Could she feel his fear?

He had to move.

Whether it was the dropping rope she spotted or the

motion of his clipping on and rappelling rapidly to the forest floor, he heard her shout to the others.

And then Daryl was running.

83

HE WAS FAST. And with the camo clothing, he all but disappeared into the sun-dappled underbrush.

Still, Kay was on him, following by sound almost more than sight. She was aware of Burke to her right, his long legs easily keeping pace, but the lower branches slowing him down. Finn and Bobby weren't far behind.

When they'd raced across the clearing after Wardell, Reaney and one of his officers had already taken Micky into the shade, and the Frederick County detective was on the radio again. But Kay wasn't waiting for any backup.

Branches whipping at her face, and sticker bushes and thorns tearing at her clothing and bloodying her skin, Kay pushed herself across the unpredictable terrain. Her eyes never left the blur of camo ahead of her. She needed only to think of the dark, dank pen from which they'd carried Micky for Kay to push even harder.

Past the old well now, and the stench of decomposition, then down the treacherous grade of the first ravine. To her left, Bobby had caught up, the three of them almost neck and neck now: Bobby, Kay, and Burke.

After witnessing Macklin's remains, Bobby seemed to have a new fire in him. In her peripheral Kay saw him clear mossy logs, beating the brush out of his path as he negotiated the slope with skill and speed.

But his advance was short-lived. One second Bobby

was steadily gaining on Wardell, and the next he was down, swallowed up by the underbrush and ferns. Along with his startled cry, Kay thought she heard the springing of another trap.

"Bobby!"

Nothing.

"Goddamn it, Bobby! Where are you?" Kay beat through the ferns until she spotted him, hauling himself up with the aid of a sapling.

"I'm fine," he said, his face tight with pain. "Fucking slipped. Keep going." He waved her and Burke on even as Finn caught up.

And they were running again. Wardell had gained some distance but they hadn't lost him. Not by a long shot, Kay thought as her arms pumped and the muscles in her legs started to burn. In the humid midday heat her lungs heaved for air. But she wasn't giving up.

Thirty yards.

Twenty.

Across a dry creek bed and a slight clearing, then into the brush again.

Over the pounding of her own heart, this time Kay was certain of the sound she heard. The snap. Then the violent rustle of leaves. A booby trap triggered.

There was the blur of a spiked arm arcing down, and Kay saw Wardell tuck and roll. He'd set off one of his own. They had him panicked now, rushing headlong through the woods, forgetting where he'd set his own goddamn traps.

Coming back onto his feet, he whipped a backward glance over his shoulder. The whites of his eyes glared out from the green and brown greasepaint that covered his face.

You better run, you sick bastard. And Kay pushed even harder.

She thought she could almost hear him breathing, smell his sweat, as he snaked through the underbrush, his footing sure and deliberate. His woods. His terrain.

Still, Kay felt his panic. She was certain of it. And if he was panicked, he'd make a mistake. She'd have her chance, and when she did, she'd take him down. For Stacey Blyth, for Frances Gallo and Kristine Peebles, for the countless unnamed victims, but mostly for Micky. Her hand was like a vise on her Glock's grip, anticipating the shot that would finally drop Daryl Eugene Wardell.

This time, she barely heard the click of the trap going off. But she felt the subtle pressure of the trip wire across her shin, and her heart stopped.

"Kay!"

She wasn't sure whether the whoosh she heard was the arm of another spear trap or if it was Burke. She'd frozen, bracing herself for whatever nightmare she'd triggered, then Burke was on top of her, their combined weight crashing into the ferns and soft earth.

She heard his curse as he rolled off her, and when Kay came up, she was surprised to find Wardell still in sight. But at her feet, Burke clutched his leg.

"Goddamn it," he swore again through clenched teeth, and Kay saw the small flood of crimson already staining his jeans.

"Burke!" The notion that Galen Burke had just saved her life—a second time—had barely registered when he was yelling at her.

"Go, Kay. Just go!" The stain spread, and Kay guessed the bottom of the trap's arm must have caught him as they'd gone down. "Don't lose that son of a bitch," he yelled.

Ahead she saw Wardell plunge into a ravine, out of sight.

"Go!"

And she was running again, leaving Burke writhing among the ferns. In a dozen strides she reached the top of the steep ravine. Below, she heard him hit the water. A splash, then nothing. Branches raked her skin as she half ran, half slid down the muddy slope.

The creek was shallow and silt stirred in its sluggish current where his footfall had disturbed the bottom. With the cool water leaking into her runners, Kay stopped at the edge, her duty weapon raised as she scanned the bushes on the opposite bank. She couldn't have lost him. Couldn't have . . .

Then there was the steely slide of the pump-action shotgun. She heard it a split second before the blast, but Kay was already down, diving onto the pebbled bank and rolling. Her breath caught when a rock drove into her ribs, but she came out of the roll with her nine up and steady, the sight lined to the dense mountain laurel on the other bank.

There was a rustle, and to the left of the bushes she saw the foliage break. But when she finally had him in the sight line of her Glock, he was only a zigzagging blur through the trees. No clear shot. And no telling where Finn and Bobby and Reaney's men had got to.

Kay was on her feet. Her legs shaky, her heart hammering, she plunged through the creek after Wardell.

84

THE SHOTGUN BLAST HAD come from the ravine he'd seen Kay disappear into only seconds ago, the discharge resounding through the thick forest air.

Finn had skidded to a halt when he heard it, his runners sliding in the soft earth. He'd held his breath as he waited—desperately—for the retort of Kay's nine. Prayed for it.

But there was only silence.

Now, as Finn crashed through the tangled undergrowth toward the brink of the ravine, he felt sick. Feared the worst.

"Kay!"

Nothing.

She had to be all right. But what if the sick son of a bitch had used his lead to ambush her? What if she'd run right into his waiting line of fire at the bottom of the ravine?

"Kay!"

He was gulping for air now, the soupy humidity making it difficult to breathe as he charged down the slope.

Shoot me instead, you twisted motherfucker. Sick and diseased, hardly able to aim his weapon anyway . . . why the hell not? Finn thought.

Not Kay.

And then Finn spotted the glare of her white T-shirt through the dense weave of foliage, her arms pumping as she leaped over logs and beat her way through the underbrush. Relief flooded through him.

Splashing through the cold creek, Finn scrambled up

the embankment in the direction he'd seen Kay. He could hear them ahead, but there was no spotting Wardell in his camos. Only snatches of Kay's white T-shirt far ahead.

Too far ahead.

They were on their own now. Just Kay and him on Wardell. Reaney's men were way behind. Unless Wardell suddenly doubled back, they'd never be of any use. And Bobby was out. Limping himself, Finn had left him to help Burke. One quick glance had been all Finn needed to know the agent's leg was broken, shattered by the force of the trap's heavy wooden arm as it had slammed down, the whittled spike probably just missing the agent. And Kay.

Finn pushed himself even harder, barging through the saplings and shrubs. He needed to catch up. Kay was a sitting duck so far ahead on her own, and if anything happened to her—

Finn's heart stopped the instant he heard the distant but sharp thwack. Then the world went still. No more sounds of running, no thrashing through the brush.

Just silence.

"Kay!"

It had sounded different from the others, but Finn knew it was one of the bastard's booby traps that had been triggered.

"Kay! Dammit, answer me!"

But the woods only breathed a hush and the cicadas started up again.

"Kay!"

And as Finn dove headlong in the direction he'd last seen her, his heart in his throat, the blast of Wardell's shotgun reverberated through the trees.

85

FINN'S VOICE CAME TO HER over the buzz of insects crackling across the forest, over the calls of birds in the branches, and over the rustle of the wind in the highest leaves of the canopy. She heard his call in spite of the pounding of her heart, its rhythm gradually slowing inside her chest, as her name came clearly over the last rolling echoes of Wardell's Mossberg shotgun.

And then there was only the low, sputtering gurgle of Daryl Eugene Wardell's blood. It pumped out with a faint hiss as fine bubbles gathered around the ragged opening of his throat. Kay watched some of the bubbles grow, larger and larger, until they popped, splashing small crimson dots up across Wardell's face.

Kay took a step closer. Another bubble burst under his chin, and she felt the heat of his blood fleck her skin. Something about it felt strangely good.

The wires had cut deep. And every movement, every thin gasp for air, drew them tighter across his throat and chest, his arms and legs.

She couldn't make sense of the trap Wardell had devised and then accidentally tripped. The razor wire had seemed to come out of nowhere. There'd been a snap, a sharp whipping sound, and then, ahead of her, she'd seen Wardell's body jolt, as though he'd been hit with electricity. He'd appeared suspended for a brief second, before he'd been spun around, the wires wrapping around him in an instant.

He'd made no sound except a quick gasp.

Initially he'd twitched and jerked, his hands still on his shotgun. But the wires cinched tighter, the razor edges slicing through the camo clothing and into his flesh. He'd tried to move his head, his eyes rolling in their sockets as he attempted to see his weapon.

The barrel of the pump-action had wavered in her direction when he'd drawn back on the trigger, but Kay wasn't certain if the discharge had been deliberate or if it had simply been a reflex to the pain. Now, however, the wires cut too deeply into his right wrist for him to even consider pumping the gun to chamber another round. And with his eyes locked on her, the camo-colored Mossberg dropped from his hands and hit the forest floor with a muted thud.

His pale blue eyes looked cold, Kay thought. Void of emotion. And as she stared into them, she half believed she'd find answers there. But there were none. The color washed from his face as his blood drained out around him, the muted splats of the drops hitting the dried leaves beneath him creating a sort of symphony of rhythms. Chaotic. Mad. And bizarrely lovely.

Every detail was so vivid, so clear. And Kay knew—as time slowed around her and Wardell's eyes held hers—that her brain was recording this moment, logging every minutia of Wardell's last breaths. A snapshot to carry in her mind, whether she wanted it or not. With her forever. She had no choice

Just as she had no choice in the visual memory of Jack Macklin's remains half-devoured by the pigs, sticking up out of the muck and shit. Just as she had no choice in the responsibility she felt for Micky Luttrell's mental collapse, forever second-guessing her handling of the investigation, forever wondering if she could have saved the young cop sooner.

Daryl Eugene Wardell had left his mark on Kay's soul,

just as surely as he'd left his mark on Stacey Blyth—raped, beaten, sodomized, and utterly violated at seventeen years of age. Just as surely as he'd stripped Frances Gallo of her sanity, rocking in her own psychotic delirium in a padded room at Spring Grove. And now Micky . . .

Lives ruined.

Lives ended.

There was no telling how many women Daryl Eugene Wardell had preyed upon over the years, how many women's remains they'd find in the old well or in the muck surrounding the shed.

As Kay stared into those pale, inhuman eyes, the hatred welled within her. It was black and it was cold, and her hand tightened around the grip of her Glock.

Whether he sensed it or whether Daryl Eugene Wardell had other thoughts rolling around in his evil brain, he blinked several times, and his watery eyes slithered over her. As if he was sizing her up, Kay thought. As if maybe, even in his final breaths, his depraved mind was creating one final sick fantasy.

Kay took another step toward him. Close enough now that she could smell his sweat, and the heavy, visceral scent of his blood.

"You sick . . . twisted . . . miserable fuck."

He didn't flinch at her words.

Kay wondered what he wanted to say but couldn't because of the length of razor wire embedded in his throat. When he drew a breath, the air wheezed in through his partially severed larynx and more bubbles formed.

Then Daryl Eugene Wardell did something Kay hadn't expected.

He smiled. And with a bloody tongue he licked his smugly grinning lips.

Involuntarily, Kay's nine came up. The hatred welled up as she lined his sick face in the sight of her duty weapon and felt the promise of the trigger against her finger. Less than three feet of air separated the muzzle from his smirk.

And there, in the middle of the woods, with his blood at her feet, Kay itched to bury a bullet in Daryl Eugene Wardell's demented brain. For Micky. For Stacey and Frances. For Kristine and all the other, nameless victims. For every evil thing he'd done in his miserable life.

But that's what *he* wanted, Kay realized suddenly. A bullet in his brain was exactly what Wardell was hoping for. To end his suffering, to stop the pain of the razor wires and the slow, agonizing death.

In all the world, there wasn't enough mercy for her to do it. Kay brought her gun down.

Daryl Eugene Wardell wasn't worth the bullet.

"You can go to hell without any help from me," she told Wardell, her voice soft but steady.

It was her turn to smile. Her eyes locked onto his even as she heard Finn farther back in the woods.

She had no concept of time then, standing there, waiting for Daryl Eugene Wardell to die. Somewhere behind her, Finn was still calling, trying to locate her. But Kay could only watch as Wardell's life bled slowly out. Eventually his strength waned. His head dipped sideways a couple of times, and each time he snapped it back up from the pressure of the wire around his throat, until finally he couldn't anymore. Even then, his eyes never left Kay's. His skin was white now, almost translucent under the shimmer of perspiration, and his pupils dilated as his ragged breathing finally ceased.

"Kay! Goddamn it!"

"I'm here," she called out at last, her voice broken as Finn beat through the sticker bushes.

Finn's eyes went from her to Wardell and back again. The fear and panic was still visible in Finn's eyes, in every line of his face, until the relief swept in.

"Jesus Christ, Kay. I thought . . ."

Finn didn't finish. He simply took her into his arms.

Others were calling for them now. Reaney and his men. And beyond them she thought she heard cars out on a road somewhere.

When Finn held her tighter, Kay wondered if he was crying.

Behind her she could still hear the quiet dripping of Wardell's blood. She knew there'd be nightmares. She knew the pig-man would haunt her.

But there *was* solace, there *was* comfort, even in the shadow of Wardell's strung-up corpse. It was in Finn's embrace, the only place she'd ever truly felt safe. He was her shelter, her sanctuary.

Kay held on to him and swore she'd never let him go again.

Not sure what to read next?

Visit Pocket Books online at
www.simonsays.com

Reading suggestions for
you and your reading group
New release news
Author appearances
Online chats with your favorite writers
Special offers
Order books online
And much, much more!